T0301186

KAVITHRI

KAVITHRI

Aman J. Bedi

For Nisha

First published in Great Britain in 2024 by Gollancz
an imprint of The Orion Publishing Group Ltd
Carmelite House, 50 Victoria Embankment
London EC4Y 0DZ

An Hachette UK Company

1 3 5 7 9 10 8 6 4 2

A CIP catalogue record for this book
is available from the British Library.

ISBN (Hardback) 978 1 399 60985 2
ISBN (Export Trade Paperback) 978 1 399 60986 9
ISBN (eBook) 978 1 399 60988 3

Typeset by Deltatype Ltd, Birkenhead, Merseyside

Printed in Great Britain by Clays Ltd, Elcograf S.p.A

www.gollancz.co.uk

Contents

Part One

Chapter 1

The last train of the day was late.

Kavi's railway porter uniform, a worn, red linen shirt, clung to her torso, and she popped the collar to blow air down her chest.

She sat huddled with the other porters in the shade among the hanging beards of an ancient banyan tree. The collective stench of the group – a lethal combination of sweat, tamakhu, unwashed hair, and rancid breath – ensured that everyone gave them a wide berth.

And a good thing, too. Kavi wrinkled her nose. The mood matched the stink. They were exhausted, short-tempered, and to make matters worse, Stationmaster Muthu had waddled up during the tea break, hand extended, and flicked his fingers. *Hand it over.*

She'd grumbled. She'd gnashed her teeth. And she'd paid him his monthly platform tax. All her earnings, every single rayal she'd made that day, were in that bulging shirt pocket of his.

She glared at the stationmaster, who now stood on a raised podium on the other side of the tracks. White lungi folded over his knees and tucked into his waistband, telescope jammed into one eye, thick line of ash smeared across his forehead to signify that he was in mourning – a speeding steam-rickshaw had run his cat over.

Off to the side, well clear of the porters, passengers waited, sweaty and impatient, under a corrugated iron awning. Hawkers and vendors chatted and laughed, impervious to the heat, as they counted the day's profits. Beggars lay on their backs, one eye on Stationmaster Muthu, as they fanned themselves with torn newspamphlets.

The platform itself was the site of a massacre. Splattered and stained red with chewed up and spat out betel nut that had somehow missed all the strategically placed copper spittoons.

It was the same every year. Bochan was the only city with an administrative branch of the mage academy in the south, and on testing day, all the villagers and townspeople who'd either just turned sixteen, or had never taken the tests, came streaming into the city with dreams of a better life; to test if they could be a mage, to learn if they were that one in ten-thousand who had the favour of a Jinn. Every single train would be late. Every single compartment would be packed to overflowing. And every single year Kavi would limp home from the station with swollen limbs and torn muscles; wash, eat, and head back into the city to join the long, winding queue outside the administrative branch of the Vagola (that everyone in the city simply called the Branch) for her annual attempt at taking the tests.

She shuffled on her haunches and glanced at the Gashani tribesman squatting beside her. Fresh from the mountains with a single fang tattooed down the right side of his mouth. A sign that he'd failed his rites of passage. The tribespeople were only a rung above the Taemu, who were of course, rock-bottom, and she couldn't help but feel sorry for him. Stationmaster Muthu had rostered the poor man on cleaning duty.

The tribesman, sallow-cheeked and hollow-eyed, stared at Muthu in a daze.

Kavi nodded to herself. The man was clearly traumatised by the railway station toilets. Her first month had been much the same. Actually – she swatted a fly away from her face – it was worse. They'd barely acknowledged her. And when they had, they'd cursed her, shoved her around, and beaten her with a broom if she did something wrong. It'd been weeks before she could actually porter.

Stationmaster Muthu stiffened. Snapped the telescope shut. Tucked it under one arm, dipped his knees, adjusted his crotch, and in one smooth movement slapped the clapper of a bronze bell that hung over his head.

The *ding!* pealed through the station, and the platform exploded in a flurry of movement.

Kavi's hands flew as she unwrapped the cloth around her waist and, like the other porters, tied it around her head into the shape of a turban. She tightened it. Slapped it to test the cushioning. But stayed on her haunches while the other porters stood. A condition for her continued employment at the station: the Taemu would always go last.

She smelled the train before she heard it.

Acrid smoke followed by syncopated chugging that crescendoed into a teeth-jarring rumble as the engine – a long cylinder that rotated and shimmered with orange maayin – burst past, followed by row after row of magenta compartments that stalked the shadows they left on the platform.

The locomotive had barely stopped, was still hissing, when its passengers came spilling out.

The porters surged ahead. The hawkers followed. The beggars staggered with skeletal arms extended, hands and fingers in eating-food and empty-stomach gestures.

The disembarking passengers ignored them. Their porters, weighed down with luggage, shooed them away and jostled defensively with pretend concern for their patrons.

Kavi waited. Fidgeted with her collar. It was almost her turn.

A woman in a bright-green sari hopped out of a first-class compartment and, with hands on her hips, searched the platform for a porter.

Kavi licked her lips. That there was the ideal customer. A lone, wealthy passenger who travelled light but was too spoiled to carry their own bags. The future flashed before her eyes: she'd drop the woman off at a rickshaw, pocket her hard-earned money, march back to the slums where her friend Haibo would be waiting to help with her disguise, then a brief but necessary stop at Murthy's Super Special Dosas, and then on to the Branch.

Her heart fluttered with nervous energy.

Except …

Except …

She tsked and turned to the tribesman who was still squatting next to her. 'Dai,' she said, 'why are you still waiting?'

He started. Glanced at her and quickly looked away. 'They told me to go last.'

Kavi's brows shot up. She'd risen in the railway station hierarchy.

'Look.' She tapped him on the shoulder and pointed to the woman in the green sari, who was still searching the platform for a porter. 'Go. Easy fare.'

He swallowed. Shuffled uncomfortably. 'They said—'

'It's okay,' Kavi said, and pushed him forward. 'Go.'

The tribesman stood and wiped his hands on his trousers. He glanced at her again, paused, and bobbed his head in thanks.

Kavi nodded and returned to her inspection of the first-class compartments. A politico had disembarked and was being swarmed by his followers – they buried him up to his eyebrows in jasmine garlands, slapped him on the back, and ushered him through the throng. She frowned at his glistening, bald pate as it slithered out of the station.

She'd seen these chootia in the bazaars. Seen them talk at rallies before the elections. Raaya had gone from a collection of city states to kings and queens to being a colony of the Kraelish Empire for almost six centuries, and then a hundred and fifty years ago, independence, and now the country was in the hands of these crooked—

There.

Standing at the entrance of the same first-class compartment was a tall man with gold-rimmed spectacles. No doubt a sahib from his bearing and the way he dressed – exquisite shirt and tie in the Kraelish fashion, tight-fitting trousers, immaculately groomed and oiled hair.

Kavi checked to ensure none of the other porters were approaching him, and got to her feet. She threaded her way through the crowd, never taking her eyes off the man, until she stood in front of him.

'Sahib! Porter?' She slapped the back of her hand against her forehead in a salute.

The man stared at her. Searched the platform, presumably for another porter, then scrunched up his nose and lifted a handkerchief to his face.

She smothered a flinch. 'Sahib?'

He sighed. 'Cabin 12A.'

'Thank you, sahib!'

Inside, waiting for her in 12A, were three large suitcases.

She groaned and nudged one of them with her foot. Just her fucking luck. What the Hel did he need three – *three* suitcases for? She scowled at the floor. At the suitcases. The seats. The table. The glass windows, outside of which families clustered together, chatted, yelled at their children to not wander off. Couples shared tired smiles, leaned over to whisper in each other's ears; shoulders touched, hands brushed, fingers, ever so briefly, intertwined. Kavi's gaze softened. Further down, a girl helped her grandmother navigate the platform. A man laughed at his irate wife. Friends joked and jostled for the idli vendor's attention.

She pressed her lips together, lowered her eyes, and took a heavy, shuddering breath. *It's fine. I'm fine.*

The noise dulled to a hum and the rustle of dry leaves drifted into her ears with the sound of her father's warm chuckle, the sobs of her brother Khagan, wrapped up in a bedsheet and tied to her chest, and Kamith, barely five, skipping around her, *Akka? Akka, are you listening?*

Her hands trembled as she hefted each suitcase to check its weight.

Always, Kamith.

She would find them. They were still out there, somewhere, and she would find them. She would take the tests, and once she was a mage, she would use the Venator to find them.

Kavi puffed out her cheeks. Carried the suitcases out of the compartment, one at a time, while the sahib watched with his nose and mouth covered. Once they were all secure on the platform, she stretched her back till it cracked, then bent, balanced one on her head, lifted another in her left hand, and carried the lightest one in her right, which she used to support the suitcase on her head.

She gritted her teeth as her shoulders ached, as her legs burned, and her neck, stiff from the day's work, turned raw and pinched. Behind her, the sahib walked, oblivious, ignoring the beggars, turning away the hawkers, though a particularly daring one came right up to his face screaming, 'Taste it, sahib! Free sample, take it!'

You've never offered me a free sample, you bleddy bastard. Kavi grunted and adjusted the suitcase on her head as she glowered at the samosa hawker.

Step by excruciating step, she led the sahib across a platform buzzing with excitement and anticipation. All she could hear were tests this and tests that, the enormous stipend, the land rights, the power, the prestige, the doors it would open. *If I could choose a mage class, I'd be a warlock*, a rotund teen announced to his mother, who patted him on the head. *If I get chosen by the Jinn,* said another obnoxious-sounding girl with pigtails, *after my training, I'll teach at the Vagola.*

Kavi had made five attempts since she'd turned sixteen.

The first time, they'd stopped her at the entrance and asked her what she was trying to do. *Test, sir-ji*, she'd said. The hawaldars had nodded, exchanged a glance, and beaten her black and blue.

The second time she'd waited till sundown and scaled the wall. Only to find that they'd covered the top with colourful shards of glass. She'd fallen with a loud and pathetic, *Aiiyoooo!*

The third time she'd run into hawaldar Bhagu, freshly transferred to Bochan from Azraaya, and things got exponentially worse after that.

There was no law that prevented her from taking the tests. Raaya called itself secular, a republic, all its citizens had rights. But some rules were so deeply ingrained, passed down from parent to child for generations, that they needn't be written. Everyone knew them: the Taemu cannot be allowed the privilege of testing. Not after what they've cost us.

Kavi growled and nudged her way past a gaggle of schoolboys and under an arch with a large yellow sign that said:

Welcome to Bochan
Culture #1
Beaches #1
Dosas #1

And underneath, an enterprising vandal had recently painted, *Your mother is also #1*

Traffic outside the station was in full swing: steam-rickshaws, cycle-rickshaws, horse-drawn carriages, and bullock carts all jostled for space on a road where drivers honked like Raeth himself would drag them to Hel if they stopped.

Fumes from the steam-rickshaws mingled with the pungent scent of tar melting in the hot sun and the air stung Kavi's throat as she opened her mouth to speak. 'Sahib, rickshaw? Carriage?'

The sahib gestured to a steam-rickshaw.

The driver, who sat in the backseat of the hedgehog-shaped vehicle with a newspamphlet in his lap, spotted Kavi lumbering in his direction and grudgingly vacated the rickshaw.

Once the sahib's luggage was stashed, she turned to him, and saluted again. 'Sahib.'

He looked her over. Frowned.

'Sahib.' She held out her hand.

'Ah,' he said, and reaching into his pockets, dropped a single rayal into her waiting palm.

Kavi blinked at the coin. 'Sahib? Only one rayal?'

He paused. 'You want more?'

'Sahib …' The fare for the work she'd just done was at least six rayals. 'Please.'

His face hardened. 'It's either this, or nothing,' he said, and reached for the coin.

Kavi's fingers snapped into a fist around the money. She stared at the man's face, at his eyes. So cold. So flat. So … dead.

The pressure in her core, the fever that had lived there for as long as she could remember, built and built, travelled from her chest to her limbs, to her throat, her jaw, her temples, and into her ears where a voice whispered, *It would be so easy. Reach out, grab his throat, and squeeze. Feel your fingers dig into his flesh. Feel his muscles contract. His bones crack. Hear his—*

Kavi sucked in a breath. Averted her eyes and bowed to the sahib while she choked and drowned the voice of the berserker that lived inside her.

'This – thank you, sahib,' she said with a dry mouth, and slowly backed away. Her vision blurred, but she dabbed and wiped her eyes with the back of her hand until it cleared again. Should she go back to the platform? Look for a straggler who still needed a porter?

She clenched her fist around the coin until it dug, painfully, into her palm.

No, there was no time. Haibo was waiting. And she needed to prepare.

Chapter 2

'Zofan-ji, have you seen Haibo?'

The old man, the unofficial mayor of the Bochan slums, sat on his porch with the mouthpiece of his hookah in his lap, watching the sun set over the sprawl of thatched huts and beige tents. He took a long drag and peered at Kavi's face.

Men, women, and children trudged past Zofan's hut – hungry, exhausted, but still they bobbed their heads and smiled at the old man, who acknowledged their greetings with a nod.

Kavi squeezed her eyes and scratched her head. Her recently donned wig was itchy and uncomfortable. Her eyes burned from the kohl she'd rubbed around them and the lashes she'd stuck to her eyelids. But Haibo said it would work, and she trusted him.

'Kavithri? Is that you?'

Even Zofan couldn't recognise her. It would work.

'Yes,' she said. 'Have you seen Haibo?' He was supposed to meet her at the hut, look her over and make sure her disguise was perfect.

Zofan sighed. 'Sit down.'

She blinked. 'Zofan-ji, I need to—'

'You will want to sit,' he said, voice strained.

Kavi obeyed. Carefully arranged her new salwar-kameez and sat cross-legged to face him. Zofan had lived in Bochan and the slums all his life. He mediated all disputes, allocated dwellings to new arrivals, helped people find work, and pretty much ran the place. Without him, she'd still be a cleaner at Aunty-ji's seaside brothel and Haibo would be knee-deep in sewage. He was the only person in the slums who didn't treat them like Taemu.

'You know I've done the best I can for you both,' Zofan said.

Kavi nodded, unease slowly winding its way into her gut.

'Haibo,' he said after a long pause, 'is not coming back today.'

Kavi cocked her head. 'What?'

Zofan ran thick, calloused fingers through his long, grey beard. 'The Dolmondas.'

'The gangsters?'

He nodded. 'Haibo was on his way home, but he took the shortcut – he took the route back through the Niketan colony.'

Kavi's blood went cold. That was Dolmonda turf. 'He wouldn't. He knows not to—'

'I don't know. Maybe he was in a hurry.'

'But he wouldn't—' An ache in her throat cut her off. The Dolmondas had made it clear that Taemu were not allowed on their turf. She always avoided the area, even if it took her another hour to arrive back at the slums. Haibo knew that. *He knew.*

Zofan's shoulders slumped. 'The Municipal hospital. They've kept him there.'

Kavi swallowed. 'How badly did they hurt him?'

The old man shook his head. 'It's not good.'

Her heart sank. 'I'm going, Zofan-ji,' she said, voice trembling, as she stood.

He nodded without meeting her eyes. 'I'm sorry.'

She sprinted through the winding, weather-beaten streets of Bochan. And when she ran out of breath, she jogged. The hospital was in the eastern quadrant of the city, an area where the artificers set up shop. There were still customers lined up outside Theramalli and sons: musicians with sitars and tablas whose sound needed to be amplified, zobhanatyam dancers who wanted the weight of their anklets and bangles altered, priests carrying boxes filled with chimes and bells – Kavi bowled through, ignored their protests and curses, and bundled her way into the only hospital in the city that catered to people who couldn't afford a healer.

'Where is the Taemu?' Kavi said to a woman in a blue sari who sat behind a desk.

The woman, without looking up from the paper she was scribbling on, said, 'First floor. Surgery.'

She found his body in the corridor. Blood dripping down the sides of the gurney they'd strapped him to.

'Haibo?'

Time seemed to slow. Her chest heaved with the force of the breaths she took. She leaned against the wall as her knees lost their strength and she crumpled.

'Haibo?'

'Ah, you know him?' A man with a bloody apron emerged from a room. 'Compound fractures.' He pointed to Haibo's legs, severed below the knee. 'Infected with urine. We tried to amputate, but it was too late.'

You tried to? Kavi's lips trembled as she stared at what was once her friend. His torso was covered with bruises and lacerations. His face was frozen in a rictus of horror. His eyes, the dull red irises that marked him as a Taemu, now empty and bloodshot, bulged out of their sockets. Did they even drug him before the amputation?

'Why?' she whispered.

'Ah, you see, the infection—'

'Why?' she said, louder.

'Miss?'

Haibo was the kindest person she knew. Always smiling. Always happy to help. They were the same age, but he'd looked up to her. Called her Akka, big sister. *You promise you'll come back for me, Akka? When you're a mage?* he'd said, eyes wide with sincerity, and when she chuckled and nodded, *If you end up as a warlock* – he waved around an imaginary sword – *I could be your Blade. I'd protect you.*

She reached out and pushed his eyelids shut.

'Miss? Please do not touch the body.'

Why don't you try taking the tests too? she'd ask, nudging him in the side.

He'd shake his head. *I've seen what they do to you, Akka, /don't want it.* Then his eyes would glaze over, and a faraway look would drag his face down. *But if I could choose a class, I would be an artificer. I don't think I could cope with the healer's countervail, and being a warlock just seems so . . . violent. An artificer would be perfect; the only price I'd pay would be my own memories. I have so many I'd gladly give up.*

'I'm sorry,' she whispered, sniffling and fighting to keep the tears at bay.

'That's fine,' the surgeon said. 'But you need to leave now. The body is scheduled for cremation.'

Kavi brushed her fingers against Haibo's hair, stiff with dried blood. 'Can I stay? Until then?'

The surgeon sighed and tsked. 'Fine. Just – don't touch the body.'

She nodded, waited till the man was out of sight, and intertwined her fingers with Haibo's. 'It must've really hurt, no? Haibo?' she said. 'You must've been so scared. So alone.'

She squeezed his swollen, stiff fingers. 'Did you' – her lips quivered – 'take the shortcut because of me? Haibo? *Why?* I'm not—' The tears came then and wouldn't stop. Great coughing sobs shook her entire body as she clung to Haibo's cold, lifeless hand.

And while she waited, while she watched them wheel his mutilated corpse away, and afterwards, while she stood with her eyes on her feet, breathing in the omnipresent smell of antiseptic, letting the moans and groans of the patients slither in and out of her ears, she found that her resolve, her determination to escape from *this*, had hardened.

It was dark by the time she arrived at the Branch. The line outside the building snaked around the corner and continued past the intersection. Gas lamps burned and lit the streets and footpath in corrupted yellow; shadows stretched and twisted, seeming to claw at the candidates waiting for their turn to take the tests.

Kavi joined the queue. Kept her eyes averted and avoided conversation. Seconds turned into minutes, the man in front of her stepped forward, she closed the gap. He moved again. She followed. Hawaldars walked down the line and eyed the candidates. Hawkers passed by, screamed at the candidates to try some jalebis and ladoos. Sugar-cane juice was offered at hiked-up prices. No one paid her any attention. She was just another candidate waiting for her turn. It was working.

Kavi's pulse raced as she took another step.

It's working, Haibo. All those midnight hours spent yanking-pulling-ripping the hair off the dead, trimming the scalp away, smuggling the hair to the wigmaker, cajoling the cantankerous wretch to make her a wig within her means, and then the Picchadi style back-and-forth haggling matches where they'd somehow squeezed out a third-hand salwar-kameez and a pair of rubber chappals…

She sniffed and blinked heavy eyelids. The hag had taken all her savings. *But you were right, it was all worth it.*

There was no guarantee that the Vagola flunkies inside the Branch wouldn't turn her away, but she had to try, she had to know. *Worry about that once you're inside*, Haibo had told her. She nodded, took another step. The large iron gate that marked the entrance to the Branch came into sight. She was almost there.

Once she was inside, she would only get one opportunity to pass the tests. A rejection by the Jinn was binding. There would be no second chances. Kavi dabbed at the sweat beading on her forehead as the line snaked closer to the gate.

She'd prepared for the tests. Knew exactly what each entailed. She would first be tested for endurance, to see if she could withstand the weight and power of a Jinn. If she passed, she would then be exposed to an artifice dating back to the era of the First Mages, which, in exchange for a selection of her memories, would somehow force her into the presence of the Jinn. If one of them liked what they saw, and chose, she would take the third and final test: she would demonstrate that a Jinn had gifted her with the ability to channel its maayin.

Spirit, Bridge, and Instrument, the three tests were called, and she was ready for them. Had been for the last five years. All she needed was a way into the Gods-damned building. And now she had it.

'Bhai, no, please!'

Kavi craned her neck around the heads of the other candidates to look for the source of the cry.

Outside the gate, a group of teenagers were heckling a boy carrying a basket of coconuts. They'd snatched a coconut and were now tossing it between themselves while the boy chased them.

'Please, bhai, I have to sell—'

One of the teens shoved the boy, and he fell flat on his face. His coconuts spilled out of the basket, bounced and rolled away down the street. He got to his feet with a strangled yelp and tried to chase after them.

They grabbed him by the arms. Mussed his hair and poked him in the ribs. Pinched his jaw until his mouth opened and shoved a fistful of mud into it.

Tears came streaming out of the boy's eyes as he gagged and spat.

The teens laughed and called for more mud.

Kavi stared at the crying boy. At the dirt stuck in the groves between his teeth. At the apathy on the faces of the other candidates watching.

Why was no one doing anything?

Help him.

The boy wasn't even a Taemu. *He's one of you. Help him.*

No one moved. They just watched the humiliation continue.

Was this what it was like for Haibo? Did people just stand and watch the gangsters toy with him? Beat him? Break his legs? Urinate on him?

What if it was your brother this was being done to? Would you still stand and watch? What if it was one of her brothers? If it was Khagan or Kamith being bullied. Would she act?

Would she?

A weight lifted off her chest as she stepped out of the line. She flicked the braid of her wig behind her shoulder, walked up to the bully she decided was the boss-teenager, and cuffed him. Cuffed him hard enough to hear him squeal. His goons surrounded her. She slipped a rubber chappal off one foot and smacked the closest teen on the side of the face. They froze. Cursed. And scattered.

She turned to coconut-boy and extended a hand to help him up.

He took it. Stood, dusted himself off, and spat the mud out of his mouth. 'Thank yo—' His eyes went wide. He took a step closer. Peered into her eyes.

Kavi started. Took a step back. Ran a hand over her face. Her lashes, they'd come unstuck.

'Taemu?' the boy whispered. His face twisted, his lips pursed and the veins on his throat stood as he gathered up a mouthful of mud-laced saliva.

Ack-thoo!

The thick gob of spit hit Kavi square in the face with a wet *splat.*

'Chootia Taemu!' The boy yelled and hurried away to collect his coconuts.

A hand, heavy and powerful, clamped down on her shoulder.

Kavi winced, twisted and turned to gaze up into the eyes of the last person she wanted to see. Hawaldar Bhagu.

The constable's waxed moustache twitched as he snatched the wig off her head, hair clips and all. 'You,' he snarled. 'I warned you.'

'Saab-ji—'

He grabbed her by the throat. Dragged her into the middle of the street. And flung her to the ground.

Steam-rickshaws honked and screeched to a halt. Drivers spat and yelled at her. But one look at the hawaldar and they lapsed into silence.

'Stand,' he said.

She obeyed. Did her best to ignore the eyes of the candidates watching her.

'Put up your fists,' Bhagu said.

'Saab-ji?' Kavi said, fumbling with her salwar while she searched for a way out.

Bhagu took a step closer. 'The Taemu are supposed to be fighters, right? Come. Raise your fists.'

Kavi clenched her jaw. Shook her head.

'Don't make this harder than it needs to be,' Bhagu said, and raised two enormous fists to hover under his eyes. 'Like this. Come.'

Kavi hesitated, but with a tightness in her stomach, and a cold, nameless dread seeping into her skin, she raised two trembling fists.

'Good,' Bhagu nodded and lowered his hands. 'Good, now say it.'

'Saab-ji?'

'Say the battle cry.'

Kavi's eyes bulged. She licked her lips. Tasted the sweat on them. 'I can't, saab-ji.' It was forbidden. If the Kraelish still ruled Raaya, she'd be stripped naked, strung up by her wrists in the bazaar, and whipped till she passed out. Now? There was no law against it, but she didn't want to find out what would happen.

'Say it,' Bhagu said again and reached for his lathi, which hung in a holster on his hip.

'Please, saab-ji, I—'

'Say it,' he growled.

Kavi squeezed her elbows into her sides. Took a sharp, shaky breath, and said, 'Aadhier Taemu.'

'Louder.'

There was a tremor in her voice, but again, she obeyed. 'Aadhier Taemu!'

'Yes!' Bhagu said and turned to face the candidates. 'Everyone heard, right? You heard right?'

There was a mumbled chorus of assent.

'She's left me with no choice,' he said to no one in particular, and rolled his shoulders as he squared up to Kavi.

She still had her fists up when he threw the first punch. A wide hook that crashed into her forearms and sent her stumbling. She hissed. Found her footing.

He threw the same punch again.

Her body, as if reacting to the first blow, twisted to receive the hook on her biceps. Her teeth rattled from the impact and a deep keening spread through the bones in her left arm.

Again and again, Bhagu hit her in the arms until, numb and heavy, they fell, leaving her head exposed.

But like eyes grown accustomed to the dark, she found, as her heart thundered and her blood pounded in her ears, that she could *see* the next punch coming. Its trajectory, its painful descent and eventual destination. His movements, so sharp and oozing with violence a moment ago, had turned sluggish.

She could get out of the way. Dodge. It would be so easy.

Or, she could reach out and slap his fist aside. Throw him off balance. Leave him open for her to strike back.

Adrenaline coursed through her veins. The candidates disappeared and her vision tunnelled on Bhagu and the incoming fist. The rage in her core screamed and howled for blood. The berserker reached up, wrapped its fingers around her throat, and took contro—

No.

A hammer blow connected with her temple. Lights expanded and exploded. Her ears popped. Needles buried themselves in the right half of her skull, and the impact knocked her off her feet and into a pothole filled with stagnant rainwater.

Bhagu slipped his lathi out of its holster. Raised the heavy, iron-bound bamboo stick over his shoulder.

Kavi twisted. Wrapped her hands around the back of her head, clamped her jaw shut to protect her tongue, and dug her knees into her chest.

The blows arrived – blunt and heavy when they found flesh. Sharp and searing when they landed on bone.

Kavi gritted her teeth.

'Who the fuck do you think you are?' Bhagu spat. '*Taemu* fucking scavenger filth—'

Kavi made herself even smaller.

I am nothing.

Forget me.

Please. I am no one.

The blows stopped.

She peeked through her fingers and caught a glimpse of hawaldar Bhagu's face: contorted with revulsion and hate, twisted veins on his neck, muscles bunched. He took a step back and his armoured boot crashed into her midriff. She gasped. Fought to keep her last meal down and failed.

'If I see you here again,' he said, grabbing her by the hair, 'I don't care if it's next year or the year after – if you ever try to test again, I will do to you what I heard the Dolomondas did to that Taemu today. Do you know who I'm talking about?'

Kavi's blood went cold, and she lost control of her bladder and bowels. She nodded without meeting his eyes.

He shoved her head away with a snarl.

She stayed where she was and waited. Waited till Bhagu's footsteps receded into the honks of steam-rickshaws and the shouts of the drivers.

She slowly unwound herself, groaned as fresh jolts of pain shot through her joints and lower back. Bubbles of bloody snot popped as she wheezed and pushed herself to her feet.

Kavi refused to look at the candidates. Refused to let them

see her cry. She fought the tears, strangled and suffocated them, gathered up the bile and blood and bitterness in her mouth, and spat it all out.

Chapter 3

If only she'd kept her eyes on her feet and acted the part. If only.

No one ever stood up for her, so who was she to stand up for someone else? Kavi clenched her jaw. She was powerless, a Taemu at the bottom of the dung heap, and yet …

She sighed and waited for a steam-rickshaw to rattle past before limping across the street.

Artificed lamps, a sign that she'd passed into a wealthier area, lit up the footpath and the row of woodblock prints plastered on the adjacent wall. The city used the same ones every year. An image of a moustachioed warlock who stood arms akimbo while a ball of emerald-green maayin hovered over his head. Underneath, text read:

Only one in ten thousand are blessed with the ability! Will it be you? Pass the tests and glory awaits!

The stench of ammonia wafted off the urine-soaked walls and Kavi spat.

What a waste. Everything that Haibo had done for her, had helped her with, it was all for nothing.

No, Akka, she could hear him say, *there is always next year.*

'Next year,' Kavi muttered. The tests were her only option. Her route to a better life and a path to finding her father and brothers. She could spend an entire lifetime searching and still not find a trace of them. Raaya was too big. But if she became a mage and joined the Vagola, she would gain access to the Venator, and she could find them.

No one really knew how the artifact worked or what exactly it was — after the Kraelish left, it had been decommissioned and given into the care of the Vagola — but one thing everyone agreed on was that the Venator could once locate anyone you wanted, as long as they were on the subcontinent, within minutes. 'Next year.' Yes, but she had more important things to worry about now.

Despite how well she'd stashed her rations, once the moon was three-quarters of the way across the sky, once the clock handle in the bazaar dinged at the number fifteen, they were no longer safe. The neighbourhood urchins were an industrious and motivated lot, and they'd been casing her hut for the better half of the year.

She swallowed and sped up. This would be their chance.

Only when her rations were secure, and the pint-sized thieves thwarted, only then would she start planning again. There *had* to be a better way to disguise her appearance and mask her accent. Had to. But then again, all her study and analysis of upper-class Raayan inflection and intonation, and all the wigs from all the Gods-cursed wigmakers in Raaya wouldn't matter if, like today, the hawaldars looked into her eyes.

She tsked and came to a stop. First, she had to make a quick detour.

Towering over her, with its spires and black marble bas-reliefs of clawed tentacles and tormented faces, was the temple of Raeth.

The municipal hospital would turn her away because her injuries were not life-threatening, and she couldn't afford a healer, so the temple was her only option. Bruises and wounds could prove lethal in the Bochan slums, and she couldn't afford to leave them untended.

She searched her pockets, pulled out the single rayal ensconced in them, and waddled up the steps, wincing and cursing her way to the entrance where a lone priest on night penance was laying supine and chanting into the ether.

'Swami-ji,' she said, in what she hoped was her most pious voice, and held out the coin.

The chanting stopped. The priest slowly roused himself with a series of grunts and groans. He turned to her with the most sorrowful expression on his face, and said in an equally dolorous tone, 'Yes?'

'Help.' She gestured to her face and head and the rest of her bruised and battered body.

The priest blinked, wrinkled his nose, and lifted the collar of his kurta up over his nose.

Kavi frowned. Yes, there was regurgitated fish congee on her shirt, and yes, she may have soiled herself during her beating, but the Watcher of the Dead, the Caretaker of Souls, the almighty Raeth did not discriminate on the basis of olfactory propriety, so why must his priests? She stepped closer, and said again, more firmly, 'Swami-ji, help.'

He sighed and gestured for her to drop the coin in the donation box off to the side. 'Come, child,' he said, suddenly sanctimonious, 'the Tentacled One has sent me another trial, and I must overcome.'

She left her chappals at the entrance and followed the priest into the circular courtyard that ringed the conical black temple.

'You must wash,' the priest said. He pointed to a water pump and a solitary bucket sitting next to it, then gestured to a bathroom at the base of the spire. 'I will bring you clothes. Leave the old ones here.'

Kavi bowed and obeyed.

She pumped the lever until the faucet spluttered and spat brackish water into the bucket. After a quick glance around to ensure she wasn't being watched, she peeled off the soiled salwar-kameez and left it in a heap by the pump.

The weight of the bucket made the muscles in her back twinge as she carried it into the temple's sanctified bathroom. Inside, on a stone floor that was still damp from its last use, she sat on her haunches, reached for a steel mug next to a bar of soap, and scooped the cool water over her head. She winced as it burned its way into and out of her wounds.

In the dark, in the silence, the bruises on the inside, that the priests of Raeth would not be able to heal, throbbed with renewed agony.

Haibo had loved visiting the city's temples. He found them peaceful. Even dragged her along with him on his excursions. She had been happy to tag along, sit with him while he put his hands together and mumbled his prayers, but there was one temple – a shrine, he'd called it, that she'd refused to accompany him to, and it would always upset him.

It's ours, Akka, he'd said, trying to convince her to visit the hidden Taemu shrine. *A place just for us.*

But she wouldn't budge.

She was curious, however, and had asked him to tell her the name of this forbidden Taemu Goddess to whom the shrine belonged.

No, he said, *you have to see for yourself.*

Fine. Then I guess I will never know.

He'd make a face. He'd tsk, groan, and ask, *Why, Akka? Why won't you come?*

Because I don't need to visit the shrine of a Goddess who has abandoned us.

Kavi tightened her lips, viciously dumped another mug of water over her head and reached for the bar of soap. *See where all your piety got you, Haibo? Fuck this Goddess and her shrine.*

When she was done washing herself, she peeked out of the bathroom and found a neatly folded kurta-dhoti waiting for her by the door. Outside, by the water pump, where she'd left her soiled clothes, the priest stood with a matchbox in one hand and a matchstick in the other. He looked her dead in the eye, struck the matchstick till it caught fire, and dropped it on her hard-earned, and now useless, salwar-kameez. Kavi winced as it turned into a hissing, spitting ball of fire.

The next hour was a blur. The priest summoned more holy men and together they ministered to her wounds with their famous salve – half coconut oil, half turmeric, half cow piss, and half secret ingredient to which only the disciples were privy.

Coarse hands dispassionately squeezed and twisted, raspy voices commanded her to hold up her kurta or lower her dhoti, lift this leg or bend that arm. Her stomach growled, her head throbbed, and the pungent tang of the salve made her head spin.

But she bore it, impatiently, as her eyes tracked the moon's inexorable journey across the cloudless sky. She bit her lip. *It's fine.* There was still time.

'Finished,' the night-shift priest finally said.

Kavi patted the kurta-dhoti down and studied her injuries. The mysterious yellow balm covered almost half her body, and when she moved – she gingerly stood on her toes, rolled her shoulders, stretched her back – the pain dulled into background noise. 'Thank you, swami-ji.'

'Yes-yes, ensure that you do not exert yourself, or the effects of the salve will diminish. Now, before you leave,' he said, bobbling his head, 'you must pray at Raeth's altar, and accept his blessings.'

Oh nonono, she knew what that meant. 'My thanks, swami-ji, I'm grateful for the uhm, for what you have done for me, but I must return to my uhm, what're you doing?'

The remaining priests, who'd assisted with the salve ministration, surrounded her, and slowly ushered her in the spire's direction.

It would have been so easy to make a break for it. The emaciated-looking priests were no match for her. She could have bowled them over with a sneeze. But she needed their goodwill if things went wrong next year, or the year after, so there was nothing to do but grit her teeth and play along.

They escorted her through hallowed corridors infused with jasmine incense and the dull, yellow light of dia lamps. A right here, a left there, a staircase up one level, and she was standing in front of the altar. A single protruding eyeball was sculpted into the ceiling and hung menacingly over the head priest, who waited with a tub of freshly harvested tentacles. Kavi shuddered. They were still moving, writhing on top of each other in a single mass of viscous pink.

The head priest, a heavyset man with eyebrows that trailed down past his eyes, waited for her to kneel. Which she did, reluctantly, due to more than just her bruised knees.

'The almighty Raeth will absolve your soul,' the head priest announced when she had settled. 'Unlike the other Gods, he accepts even the foul and the wretched in his sanctum' – cries of *Praise Raeth! Hel awaits!* erupted from the priests at Kavi's back while she silently seethed – 'and purifies their soul so they may serve him better, when they return in the next life.'

He launched into a prayer citing Raeth's inevitable embrace

and his supervising of souls till they were ready for an incarnation and his blah, blah, blah. She tuned the priest out. Beads of sweat seeped through the skin on her forehead as her mind cartwheeled back to her hut.

The urchins were rummaging through it. Ransacking it. Flinging her books around and ripping the pages apart. Poking holes in the thatched roof. Unearthing the stash of rice and salt and lentils and—

'Child,' the head priest boomed, bringing her back to reality, 'you will now be blessed by Raeth.'

Kavi resigned herself to her fate and bowed her head.

The head priest reached into the tub at his feet, shuffled around, extracted an exceptionally fresh tentacle, and smacked it on her head. The tentacle, somehow sensing how the rest of her day had gone, promptly attached itself to Kavi's forehead.

'You have been blessed by Raeth,' the head priest announced again, to grunts of approval and impromptu chanting.

Kavi remained on her knees, swallowed thoughts of violence, and waited for the man to notice her predicament.

Why did this always happen to her? Sometimes it felt like she was an out-of-place joke in those tragedies the actor-wallahs performed in the bazaar. The ones with the *nice women* and pure-hearted royals. She was a gag line in a dour and depressing tale, a comedian coming out of nowhere and leaving the punters with so much whiplash that it broke their necks. Gods, she hated those plays.

The priest finally spotted the holy appendage dangling from her head. He chuckled, set one foot on her shoulder, and yanked the fucker off her.

She ran her fingers over the marks left by the extricated suction cups on her forehead and thanked the head priest through a clenched jaw.

'Go forth,' he said with an outstretched arm, 'and live, till it is your time to return to Hel.'

The priests cleared a path for her, and Kavi bolted.

Chapter 4

Kavi's rations were gone. Her railway porter uniform, her sleeping mat, her cooking utensils, her trusty bucket, even her collection of rags. All gone.

Her stack of books, however, which she herself had accumulated via theft and miscellaneous skulduggery, remained unmolested. She sat in the corner, shoulders slumped, as she had for the last several hours since her return, and ran her eyes over the bound and weathered spines.

The Raayan Word: stolen from a distracted schoolgirl's bag ten years ago. *Numbers and Basic Arithmetic:* same schoolgirl, a month later. Once Kavi had worn those out, she'd snuck into the school disguised as a cleaner and acquired the rest. *Modern Raayan History, Flora and Fauna of the Subcontinent, Social Studies for Beginners*, and right at the top of the stack, with its frayed and yellowed pages: *Mages, Maayin, and the Jinn.*

She'd not read anything new in months. Not since the library peon who borrowed books on Zofan's behalf had retired.

Maybe she could sell the books. They were worth what? Maybe half a rayal? Not even that. They were outdated, torn, and most of their text was smudged and illegible. Probably why they'd been left behind.

Kavi sighed. She didn't really want to part with them anyway.

They gave her an odd sense of comfort. Her silent, stoic friends, who waited patiently for her to return every evening.

Why so sentimental, ah? she could hear her father say. *The pages can't feed you, the words on them will not save you, so why?*

Shut up, Appa.

A wave of exhaustion, which she'd kept at bay with sheer force of will, crashed down on her. Her eyelids drooped, head sagged, and it all just seemed so pointless. Life was just an endless cycle of failure, despair, picking herself back up, starting over, and failing once again.

Kavi rubbed her palms against her eyes and groaned. But it could be worse. So much worse. She only needed to look around. Her neighbour, a woman from the Gashani tribes, had haemorrhaged while giving birth to a healthy baby boy and was now permanently catatonic, stuck in a nightmare from which she would never wake. Further down, an agoma addict had made his fifth attempt at setting himself and his family on fire and finally succeeded. In the other direction, a drain cleaner had come home drunk and boxed his four-year-old son in the head, killing him on the spot.

And Haibo …

Her problems? Compared to theirs? She scoffed. Trivial.

So, what now?

She needed money to fill the pothole that was her stomach, but she couldn't go to the platform today. Stationmaster Muthu would take one look at her and send her packing. There was only one other way to make some quick coin in the Bochan slums. Well, only one way she was willing to consider. She'd been a beggar and wouldn't do that again. She'd been a thief, and those days were over. She refused to go to the gangs, and she would not sell her body. Not that anyone would want it, anyway; the Aunty-ji at the seaside brothel where she'd briefly worked as a cleaner had made that abundantly clear. So that left her with the sahibs and their artists.

There was no shame in what she was about to do. Her father would have beaten her black and blue if he ever found out, but she wasn't like him. Appa was proud of who he was and what their people once were. Kavi, on the other hand, not so much.

She slipped her feet into her chappals and crawled to the entrance of her hut. A shove, and the plank of wood that served as a door fell to the ground.

Row upon row of blocky thatched huts and beige tents stretched into the distance. The scent of freshly boiled rice mingled with the stench of the morning's sewage filled her nostrils, and like an audience applauding a well-acted play, her stomach responded with a sorrowful, low-pitched growl.

Kavi staggered from her hut and swayed as a fresh wave of hunger-induced nausea slammed into her. She allowed herself a moment to recover, then hobbled through the slums' winding gullies and hills of stagnant refuse. With each step, like leaves from a diseased tree, she let her emotions wither and fall. Pride, hard-earned but fragile, was the easiest to let go. Shame, worthless and unnecessary, sloughed off outside the neighbourhood water pump. Self-pity, dumped at the entrance to the dhobi ghats. One by one, she cast them off, until the only things left were what they expected from her, and what she would need to survive. Submissiveness. And obedience.

There was, however, one thing she could not cast aside: the balled-up inferno of fury buried deep within her chest, spitting, gathering new fuel, waiting to consume her. This, she could not discard. This, *berserker's rage*, they called it, was what damn near obliterated her people long before she was born, and the best she could do with it was to keep it chained, and hidden.

When she arrived at the street that separated the slums from the city, she found the beggars already lined up and practising their poses by the roadside: lying down with face-in-puddle, tearfully pointing to the holes in their dhotis, slapping the base of their palms against their foreheads and howling at the fate the Gods had bestowed on them.

Kavi squatted next to a particularly bedraggled and evil-smelling man and gave him a nod when he glanced her way. 'Looking good, boss.'

He snorted and picked his nose.

Steam-rickshaws hissed, honked, and zoomed in both directions. A herd of buffaloes lounged while their herders sat under a cloud of grey smoke and puffed away on their beedis. Kavi nursed her wounds, poked at newly discovered bruises, day-dreamed about shade and iced beverages and samosas until the sahibs and their entourage finally emerged through the heavy mirage that hung over the road.

Uniformed attendants cleared a space on Kavi's side of the thoroughfare and scurried to erect shamianas to protect their masters from the sun. The artists waited in a huddle, easels and canvases clutched to their chests.

With excessive bowing and scraping, the beggars entrenched themselves in the filthiest spots, and put on their most miserable faces. Attendants made their way down the line, pointing, choosing, and sending the dejected away with a flick of the wrist.

Kavi stood, stretched her back, and made her way up the line.

A man grabbed her wrist as she strolled past. 'Get back in line, bitch,' he said through a cloud of halitosis.

Kavi studied the hand on her wrist and turned to him with heavy eyelids.

'Hah? You have some important uncle or what? Bleddy ...' He blinked, registered the colour of her eyes, and dropped her wrist with a hiss.

She ignored the glares from the rest of the regulars and continued on with a quiet confidence. Here, they would let her through.

Only a handful of Taemu still walked the Raayan subcontinent, and for better or worse (mostly worse), she was one of them. She also knew, from the countless knockoffs floating around the black market, that art in Raaya was in high demand, especially art that captured pain, misery, and – of particular significance to her – the faces of the fallen.

The Taemu were special that way. They'd fallen not once, but twice. First, almost eight centuries ago, when they were colonised, uprooted, and forced into the vanguard of the Kraelish expeditionary force. And then again, after decades of violence, when they were allowed to settle on an arid piece of land in north-east Raaya, where they regained their pride, grew, and eventually made the bone-headed decision to join the Raayans in a revolt that ended with the siege at Ethuran and the near annihilation of the entire Taemu people.

An attendant took one look at Kavi, at her dark-brown skin and coarse hair, her small forehead and wide nose, her deep-set eyes and blood-red irises that screamed, *I am Taemu,* and – with raised eyebrows and an open mouth – waved her in the shamiana's direction. She gave him a half-salute and ambled through.

The Kraelish left, eventually. Internal strife, over-extension, and successful rebellions in the Hamakan Isles and Nathria forced their hand. The Raayan elite stepped in to fill the void, the Council was created, and the free, independent Republic of Raaya was born.

Free? She stopped. Spat. And waited to be noticed.

The artists were already directing their sweat-soaked models for the morning: getting a beggar to look this way or lie that way; while the sahibs at their back, in their Kraelish shirts and trousers, were deep in discussion.

'The contrast, yaar, look,' a tall sahib with mutton chop side-burns said. 'The reddish-brown hues of the mud and dirt on their faces juxtaposed with the hope in their eyes, too much, yaar.'

A bald sahib, older than the others, frowned and pointed with his sandalwood cane. 'That group there, with the armless man, if they were to be captured together, as they were, it could be a masterpiece, one to rival Dreyhas . . .' He trailed off as he spotted Kavi watching them with her hands tucked into her pockets.

'There is something different about these slums, yaar,' Mutton chops continued, 'the ones in Azraaya are just vile, filled with degenerates, hopeless, but here—'

'Wah! These poses, outstanding!' A rotund sahib tipped his hat to the beggars.

The bald sahib pointed at Kavi, and all conversation stopped. They stared at her with a mixture of disgust and curiosity, like she was a cluster of pustules they desperately wanted to pop. Excited conversation erupted among the artists before devolving into an argument about who would get to sketch the Taemu. In the end, not one, but three artists turned their easels her way.

'Sit,' they said.

She sat. Cross-legged, with her elbows on her knees.

'Move your hair away from your eyes,' they said.

She obeyed.

'Roll up your sleeves. Tear some holes in the kurta.'

Kavi hesitated. She had no other clothes.

'Do it, or we'll find someone else.'

Her trembling fingers couldn't find any purchase, so she used her teeth.

'Good, another one.'

She blinked the tears away and tore another flap open over her collarbone.

'More, and rub some dirt into the kurta, it looks too clean for you.'

When the commands ceased, the artists launched into an argument on composition and angles while the attendants served the sahibs – Kavi licked her torn, chapped lips – iced lassi in crystal goblets. Once the artistic differences were finally resolved, they set to work.

The minutes dragged on. Kavi kept her eyes on the haphazard movements of the malicious charcoal pencils and off the demands of her belly. She noticed one sahib in particular seemed unusually enchanted by her presence. The others had returned to their gibberish talk on art and colour and whatnot, but not this man. She tracked him out of the corner of an eye as he stood bent over his cane, staring at her like she was Raeth himself incarnated. Or, maybe, that was just the way his face was. She glanced at him.

He looked away and started up a conversation with the mutton chops sahib at his shoulder. The attendants now offered the sahibs skewers of grilled meat, neatly arranged on silver trays. Bowler-hat grabbed two, used his front teeth to drag a chunk of meat off the thin metal rod, and chewed it while he carried on with his conversation.

Kavi's mouth watered. She could hear him munching, could taste the spices and juices on her tongue. She swallowed the collection of saliva in her mouth, and for once, allowed a seed of hate to embed itself in the fertile soil that was her soul.

She was nothing to them.

A novelty.

A distorted emblem of an era they wished they were born

in. A reminder of a time when the Kraelish still ruled the subcontinent and steamrolled civilisation into Raaya; when their shirts and ties had lifted them above the rabble and their sons were shipped off to Kraelin to be educated and returned as the new Raayan elite.

But now?

Now they were aristocrats without power. The last generation of hereditary zamindars who could not bequeath their land to their children because it would all be claimed by the elected Council that now ruled Raaya. She scoffed. And just like the Empire they worshipped, they would all wither away and die.

An hour into the session, the butta hawker arrived.

Kavi eyed the man as he set up shop across the road; absentmindedly picking at a scab on her shin while the artists tsked at her and told her to stop moving.

The hawker carefully arranged a wire rack over a pile of smouldering charcoal, and one by one, lined a row of peeled corn upon it. A fan made of palm leaves magically appeared in one hand, while the other flipped the roasting pieces of corn. And then – Kavi bit her lower lip to stop it from trembling – and then he used a slice of lime to rub a mixture of salt and chilli powder into the corn. She flared her nostrils and shuffled closer to the edge of the footpath.

An artist hurled his pencil at the ground and stormed over.

'Dai!' The man spat at her feet. 'If you cannot sit properly, then go. Go!' He pointed a finger in the general direction of her hut.

Kavi ducked her head and kept her eyes on his feet. 'Sorry, mistake saab-ji, I will sit.'

The man spat and yelled at her some more while she raised placating arms in apology. He walked back to his canvas muttering about red eyes and filth and how he would use three – no, *four* buckets of water to wash when he returned home.

Kavi crossed her arms and tucked her hands into her armpits with a sad grumble.

The rest of the afternoon passed without incident, and when they were finally done, one of the sahib's attendants walked over to Kavi and dropped a handful of coins in her waiting palms.

Four rayals. The shroud of numb indifference she'd been fighting to hold together disintegrated, and she burst into tears.

I can eat.

She saluted the sahibs, slapped the back of her hand against her brow and left it there while the other beggars glared at her.

Once the sahibs turned their backs on her, she levered herself up with a sigh. Knees cracked and muscles groaned as the pain in her back spread.

Kavi counted the coins again, just to be safe, and set three aside to replenish her stores of salt and rice. She wiped the drool off her chin, checked the road for rickshaws, and crossed over to the butta hawker.

She brandished the silver coin stamped with the profile of Sree Golmadi, the long-dead leader of the Raayan push for independence and the most mythologised man in Raaya, and said, 'How many can I get?'

The butta hawker studied the coin while his hands continued their fanning and corn-flipping acrobatics. 'Two. One if you want extra chilli.'

'Give me two,' she said, 'one of them with extra chilli. Please.'

The butta hawker rolled his eyes but gave her a grudging nod.

If the food didn't make you sweat, the cook was skimping on the spices, or so the saying went. This butta hawker was most definitely not skimping on the chilli. Kavi's lips burned, and rivulets of sweat ran down the sides of her face as she devoured the first piece of corn.

She took her time with the second one. Enjoyed the tang, the savoury-sweet crunch of the kernels and the heat of the chilli that kept sending her back for another bite.

On the other side of the street, the attendants were busy packing up the shamiana. The artists, their work, and their patron sahibs had long since departed – Kavi froze with the piece of corn halfway to her mouth.

Not all of them, apparently. The cane-wielding sahib was still there, staring at her from across the road, studying her with the same quiet intensity as earlier.

She met his eyes, swallowed what was in her mouth, and took another bite.

The sahib, for whatever reason, took that as a sign. His face paled, the shrivelled hand on his cane trembled, and its tip stuttered on the asphalt as he stepped out into the street.

Kavi frowned with a fresh mouthful of corn. Had they met? Maybe a passenger at the station? Maybe she'd carried his luggage?

He took another hesitant step. The cane wedged itself into a narrow pothole, barely a gash on the road, and Kavi gawked in horrified fascination as the sahib was thrown off balance.

The gilded stick went flying. The sahib hopped, skipped, and fell flat on his face with a loud *oomph!*

At the other end of the road, a rickshaw sputtered and picked up speed. The driver – Kavi squinted – was wrestling with a horde of schoolboys, all piled into the backseat, one of whom was actively attempting to nose-dive out of the vehicle. The distracted driver had not seen the sahib fall, was completely oblivious to the flailing old man soon to be acquainted with all three of his tyres plus the weight of half a dozen squirming brats.

Kavi took another absent-minded bite, fully absorbed and mesmerised. Cane-sahib was about to become roadkill-sahib, and a bitter corner of her soul cackled with glee. For someone with such fancy clothes and polished shoes, the man sure looked miserable. In fact, the closer she got to him, the more morose his face seemed to get. The closer— What The Fuck Was She Doing?

Her traitorous feet had carried her halfway to the sahib.

The disoriented old man was dabbing at the blood leaking out his broken nose while the steam-rickshaw hissed and sputtered and maintained its course.

Tentacles of icy dread wrapped themselves around Kavi's head and held it in place. *Choose.* They squeezed. *Now.*

Her pupils dilated.

Her breath caught in her throat.

If she let this happen, if she backtracked to safety and left the man to his fate, then just like that pothole in the road, just like the seed of hate taking root in her, a fissure would run through her soul and rupture. On one side, the old Kavi, irretrievably lost, who, despite everything, believed in kindness and good and hope; and on the other side, the new bitter, hateful wretch she was turning into.

She tucked the half-eaten piece of corn into her pocket for later. If this got her killed, she'd find this bhaenchod in the next life and run him over with a bleddy bullock cart herself.

Kavi lunged and closed the gap. Grabbed the man by the arm. And gasped as her foot slipped into the same pothole that had trapped the sahib's cane. An audible crack, a flare of agony, a spike of adrenaline. The ankle went numb.

The sahib looked up at her in astonishment.

She growled, dropped his arm, and latched onto his collar.

Using the wedged foot as a fulcrum, she swivelled, and with a guttural roar, hurled the old man off the street.

The steam-rickshaw shrieked as it bore down on her. The driver saw her, twisted his wrist and jammed the brakes. An unsecured schoolboy flew out of the backseat and collided with the back of the driver's head, propelling the front of his face straight into the horn in the middle of the steering bar.

Kavi yanked her foot out of the pothole and stumbled. Her eyes bulged and her mouth hung open as the vehicle swayed, veered clear, and its side-view mirror came hurtling into—

Chapter 5

—chirping crickets. The scent of rain. A clothes line that hung low with heavy washing.

Fingers combing through her hair, picking, prodding.

'Turn around.'

She turned, gazed up into irises paler than hers but with enough red in them to decide the trajectory of her father's life. She shuffled impatiently. There was so much to explore in this new place.

'Stand still.' Her father dipped a thumb into a lacquered box and smeared a thin line of vermillion all the way from the root of her nose to the base of her hairline. He smiled, and the side of his face, all the way from his cheekbone to his lower jaw, collapsed with a wet *smack*, as if some invisible fist had collided with it.

'Appa?'

He kept smiling. Like nothing had happened.

'Appa?' She took a step back.

Through the frozen smile, her father's features morphed and twisted. His stubble evaporated, his nose shrunk, his brows flattened, and the lashes underneath them grew. A heartbeat, and Kavi was staring into a woman's face with eyes that were a perfect reflection of her own. Tears streamed down the sides of the woman's face as her lips trembled, parted, and whispered, 'Run.'

The top of the woman's head caved in.

Kavi screamed.

The woman's chin exploded. Pelted Kavi with debris. The woman's eyes, so luminous and warm, burst out of their eye sockets. Again and again, an invisible but terrifyingly tangible force clobbered the woman's face until there was nothing left above her neck.

But still she stood, stumbled up to Kavi and, like an elegant zobhanatyam dancer, gestured with her fingers and sent Kavi hurtling into—

—the tunnel. So thirsty. She was so thirsty. But there was blood in the water. Can't drink that. Appa said not to. The blisters on her feet had flattened and stained the rocks red. They hurt so much. But still she walked. No tears. She'd left them all in Ethuran. With her toys and her friends, and her … She frowned. Something was not right. The rocks in the tunnel were too soft. The light; where was the light coming from? It had no source, but it was everywhere.

She stopped.

The walls of the tunnel groaned and tightened around her.

She burst into a sprint.

The light dimmed, spiralled into a single point in the distance. The tunnel shrank and narrowed and forced her to crawl on her hands and knees. She sped up.

Must get out. Must get to the light.

The walls closed in, pushed her flat on her stomach. She gibbered and begged and dragged herself into—

—yellow light that punched through the dark and lit up a clean, white ceiling. A bald man smacked another man with his gilded cane.

'Chootia healer! What the Hel am I paying you for?'

'But sahib, it won't work on her— Ack!'

'What do you mean you won't? Hah?' the cane-wielder said.

'Sahib, please, it's only a concussion. She will recover.' The man backed into a large red bucket and knocked it over. Dead rats spilled out.

The bald old man shouted again. 'Are you a healer, or are you not?'

'Yes, sahib—'

'Shut up!'

'But you—'

The old man flung his cane at the healer, hitting him in the face.

'Sahib, please! Listen, I will explain,' the healer said, nursing his forehead.

'Speak.' The sahib growled and bent to pick up his cane.

'Thank you, sahib.' The healer sighed and checked his head for blood. 'It's not that I won't heal her, please understand. What is happening here, is that I cannot heal her – wait!' He raised an outstretched arm toward the approaching sahib. 'I have tried, believe me. But this woman, she … she …' His neck spasmed, his shoulders tightened, and a chill ran down Kavi's spine as he turned, slowly, to face her.

The rats at his feet twitched, convulsed, and flipped onto their feet. He picked one up, and without taking his eyes off Kavi, poked it with a finger. The bruise on his forehead vanished. The rat in his hand stopped moving. He dropped the animal, and the other rats swarmed it before it hit the ground.

'What do you think you're doing?' he said, wheezing as he stepped closer to Kavi.

She scrambled into a corner. 'M-me?'

'Yes, you.' He sat on his haunches. 'You think you can make choices?'

She glanced at the sahib, who was frozen in place with cane in hand and a scowl fixed on his face. This couldn't be real. She swallowed through a lump in her throat. It couldn't.

'Don't look at him. What? You think he can help you?' The healer shuffled closer and she flinched. 'Understand this, Taemu. You inhabit a body that has made your choices for you. That has a history you cannot change. You are trapped in it. You will live and die in it. And you will be forgotten, like the rest of your people.'

'No,' she whispered.

He backhanded her.

Kavi's ears rang. She flexed her jaw. *Why?* Why was he doing this? Why did he hate her so much? She didn't even know him.

He grabbed her by the hair and slammed her face into the clean, white wall.

'See, you're trying to make a choice again.' He held her up by her hair while her world somersaulted and her eyes rolled up into her skull. 'I'll ask you again. Do—'

He rammed her head into the wall.

'You—'

Again.

'Understand?'

And again.

Each successive hit turned into a painful, steady throbbing behind her eyes, and she tore them open with a gasp.

Chapter 6

Orange sunlight filtered through a fluttering curtain. Kavi was lying on her back, head propped up on something soft. She tried moving, *too heavy*, gave up, and stared, bleary-eyed, at the large window and the ripples running through the flimsy material that covered it.

So quiet.

No yelling, or fighting, or sobbing. Just the sound of her breath and the gentle breeze harassing the curtain. So different from her dreams, which, thankfully, were already fading. But – her ribs tightened – there was *something*, something in them that still gnawed at her; like a flicker in her periphery, a cluster of dark spots that moved every time she tried to look at them.

She flared her nostrils. And what was that smell? So familiar and so alien at the same time.

'Bad dreams?'

She froze. Her mouth went dry, and she forced herself upright.

A bald man – *the* bald man from her nightmares, was ensconced in a large chair in the room's corner. He rested his hands on his cane and glared at her over calloused knuckles.

She stared at his shiny head and protruding brow, at his

high cheekbones and the long patrician nose … a nose that was broken and bloody the last time she'd seen it.

Kavi tore her eyes off him and searched the room. It was empty, except for the bed, the chair, the man in it, and a dirty kurta hanging on the wall. But out the window, she caught glimpses of a large building with the unmistakable image of the Goddess Meshira on it: the three heads, the massive tits, the bulbous cock and saggy balls that hung over ridiculously muscular thighs. This particular rendition was nude and painted completely blue. She'd seen it—

Antiseptic. That's what the smell was, and this is, *so this is …*

The pieces of the jigsaw twitched and spun and snapped into place. The rickshaw, the sahib, the tasty piece of corn, the choice, the bleddy side-view mirror. She was in the Royal Hospital. This was the man who owed her his life. And she still had so many questions.

'Water,' the sahib said, and pointed to the side of her bed.

Kavi gulped it down. Straight from the jug. And wiped her mouth with the back of her hand. She set the jug back down on the side table with a satisfied sigh and tried to force a semblance of order into the roiling chaos in her head.

Her kurta-dhoti combo was here, hanging on the peg nailed to the wall. The holes in it were still there, the dirt she'd smeared into it was still there (plus some extra), but conspicuous in its absence was her half-eaten corn. Where …?

And her money? Was it still in her pockets?

No. Not now. Focus.

The rickshaw had knocked her out. The sahib, filled with guilt and impressed by the unconscious woman's courage, had clearly transported her to this upscale hospital, where they:

Stripped her naked and tended to the wounds from her

walloping at the hands of hawaldar Bhagu, evidenced by the latticework of gauze strips on her body.

Strapped her ankle with a bandage – it hurt, but she could move it, so not a fracture as she'd initially feared.

Dressed her in some sort of nightshirt that went past her knees, which, she decided, was now hers to keep.

And her head – she hissed as spikes of pain repelled her probing fingers.

'You have had a concussion,' the sahib said with a grunt. 'You will recover, in time.'

A wave of disorientation whistled through one ear and hissed out the other. She swayed, squeezed her temples; she was in two places, here, and in another, darker room, with blood-stained walls and the rot of decomposition seeping out of them.

'How long . . .?' she whispered.

'The physicians, they say you might feel the effects for up to six months.' He shrugged his bony shoulders. 'Or one week.'

Kavi glanced at the man. He watched her with stony eyes and pursed lips, but, she noted with a petulant pout of her own, there were beads of sweat on his brow and he was fidgeting with his cane. If she was a gambling woman – which she was, occasionally – she would bet that she was making the man nervous.

'No,' she said, 'how long have I been out?' *And how long have you been sitting there watching me? Some sort of pervert or what?*

'Not long,' the sahib said with a thoughtful tilt of his head. 'A day at most. You were unconscious for an hour, and asleep for the rest.'

Kavi narrowed her eyes. 'How do you know I was sleeping?'

He snorted. 'The snoring.'

Oh. But still, she couldn't shake the feeling the man had more nefarious motives for being here. Maybe he just wanted to thank her . . . by watching her sleep?

Fuck off. No, he wanted something.

Money? *Don't have, and he's rich. Don't be a fool.*

Her organs? Perhaps, but she didn't get that vibe from him.

Her body? Oh, please, no one—

'*Enough*. Now, tell me.' The sahib clutched his cane to his chest and said with an intensity that belied his age, 'Why? Why did you help me?'

Ah, yes. Why did she help him? *How to even explain?* Would he believe her? Taemu were supposed to be scum. Bottom-feeders who only lived for themselves, who left nothing but pain and suffering in their wake.

She carefully arranged the nightshirt over her legs and sat up. 'Sahib, why were you watching me on the road?'

The sahib started. 'I—you … you reminded me of someone.' He sighed and faced the window. 'A Taemu. I wondered if you were …'

'Related?' Kavi said.

The sahib nodded without meeting her eyes.

'We're not all related, sahib, even with' – she gestured to her face – 'all this.'

He shuffled uncomfortably. 'I did not mean any offence.'

Was he actually apologising? How strange. 'None taken.'

'You ' – he searched the room for words – 'speak surprisingly well, I mean, given your … background.'

'Thank you, sahib.' She said, with a wary smile.

'And you have a thick head—' His eyes went wide. 'No, you see, the side view on the rickshaw, it's completely gone. You, on the other hand, are in tip-top condition …' He sighed and returned to his contemplation of the window and its translucent curtain.

What a peculiar man. He looked so alone, sitting there with his hunched shoulders and leaky nose, lost, waiting for someone or something to – no. Not allowed. He was not allowed to make her feel bad for him.

The sahib sneezed, pulled out a white embroidered handkerchief from his shirt pocket, and dabbed at his nose.

Could she use that? Maybe she could say, *Sahib, I helped you because I felt bad for you.*

No.

Then what? Should she tell him the truth? About how it was so deeply embedded in her to do the right thing that her body reacted without her permission. That it had nothing to do with him. That it was her way of staying afloat, head above water, keeping herself intact in a storm that threatened to obliterate the pathetic shield she hugged around the piece of herself that was still authentic and truly her.

Bhaenchod, nah. 'No one else was doing anything,' she said.

'What?'

She gestured to his cane. 'On the road, when you fell.'

The sahib studied her with hooded eyes, as if to say, *Really? That was your reason?* But he nodded and reclined in his chair. He folded the handkerchief and tucked it back into its pocket.

'In any case, there are a couple of things I wish to discuss with you,' he said, regaining some of his composure. 'But first, an introduction. My name is Jarayas Bithun. I was the Chair of the Bochan city council for almost two decades. Before that, in my youth, I was a lawyer and a consultant.'

Consultant? Good for you, bhai.

The sahib raised an eyebrow.

'Oh, sorry.' She scratched the back of her head. 'My name is Kavi, Kavithri Taemu. I was – I am, a railway porter. Almost five years now. Before that, in my youth, I was an underboss with the Chutti-Mohan beggar gang in Dyarabad.'

Underboss, Sahib Bithun mouthed in bemusement, but

nodded. 'Thank you for your honesty. It's a rare thing to find these days, and I hope you will continue to remain so … forthcoming. Now, regardless of your reasons, you put yourself in harm's way to come to my aid. I owe you a debt.'

'Feed me, let me rest here for a few days, and we'll call it quits.' Kavi glanced at her kurta. 'And a new kurta-dhoti, please.' Some coin would also have been nice, but her pride, well and truly back after its temporary displacement, wouldn't allow her to say it.

'I was thinking of something a bit more … substantial,' he said with what she assumed was a smile, but looked more like a painful grimace. 'Tell me, Kavithri, you can read and write Raayan?'

She paused, afraid her answer would trigger a cavalcade of hawaldars to burst through the door and beat her senseless for having the audacity to be literate, before giving him a hesitant nod.

The sahib leaned forward and rested his weight on his cane. 'Forgive me for asking, but how did you – where did you learn?'

Kavi opened her mouth to spit out a well-rehearsed tale of hardship and scrounged erudition, but his earnest eyes and the honest curiosity on his face robbed her of her words.

In all her dealings with people above her, there was always, what she called, a barrier. Empathy and their belief in justice safely on one side, her plight and isolation on the other. But the sahib … His barrier was still there, but it was weaker. Weak enough for a fragment of his humanity to slip through and connect with hers. The unfamiliar intimacy blindsided her, threw her off balance, and for once, left her with only the truth. 'Chutti-Mohan – the beggar boss, he gave me numbers and letters to keep the others in line.'

Sahib Bithun nodded by reflex, caught himself, and shook his head instead. 'I don't understand.'

'I was different,' Kavi said with a sigh. 'The other children, they hated me, but what the boss found out was they also feared me. He used that. Taught me to count money, read maps, ensure they made quota.' She did what she had to do to survive. They used her. She used them. No shame in that.

'When I … resigned my post—' *escaped the gang in a whirlwind night of deceit and backstabbery* '—and moved to Bochan—' *stowed away on a goods train, walked for three days and nights, and snuck onto the back of a bullock cart* '—I found books, borrowed some from the city library. Mathematics, Raayan literature, Jinn theory. I am, what-you-call-it, an autodidact.'

The sahib inclined his head in an unfamiliar gesture of respect and shuffled closer to the edge of his chair. 'There is an opening, a post, available in one of my spice godowns, pepper-cumin-cardamom and all that. Would you be interested in it?'

Kavi pursed her lips. Carrying sacks of spices did sound tempting, but, 'I already have a job, sahib.'

'Yes, the railway station, you said, but you can read-write, and I have been looking for a godown clerk …'

Her heart missed a beat. 'What – sorry?'

'A clerk, you know.' He mimicked a pen scrawling in a ledger. 'To keep track of inventory and whatnot, like in your underboss role.'

'Yes, sahib –' *pages twenty-four to twenty-six of the social studies textbook* '– I know what a clerk is.' Rows of colourful drawings: a physician tending to a patient in pain, a lawyer arguing a case in front of a jowly judge, a khaki-uniformed hawaldar watching over a festival, a railway conductor, a merchant, a sitar player, a zobhanatyam dancer, an accountant, a shipping clerk …

She'd imagined, as she read and reread the yellowed pages in dying candlelight, what it would be like to be all those people, to do all those jobs, and here she was, being offered the opportunity to *be* someone from the book.

Another wave of upside-down disorientation surged through her skull, and she squeezed her eyes shut. This wasn't a dream, right? Sure, it was a little *unreal* to be having a casual conversation with a sahib, but – she frowned. Her dreams had been niggling at her. There was something she was forgetting.

Sahib Bithun thumped the floor with his cane. 'So, what do you say?'

'Yes, but—' *But? But what?* 'I don't have—'

'You can stay at one of my properties. Accommodation is not an issue.'

'No. I mean, thank you, but I don't' – she stifled a sudden crescendo of shame –'have any clothes, or …'

He straightened. 'I will give you an advance. You can purchase everything you need with it.'

'The other clerks, will they …' Mock, belittle, deride – What? When had that stopped her before? Why was she nitpicking?

'Let me worry about them,' he said, more forcefully. 'They will obey or face the consequences. Any other questions?'

Kavi stared at the man. Questions? Her deranged compulsion to *know* decided that this was an opportune time, and poked her in the head with its oily fingers. *Ask him, ask him, don't you want to know?* Poke-poke-poke. *Come on, ask him, ask him what happened to your piece of corn.*

The what? No. I don't need to – Shut up. 'What was the other thing you wanted to discuss, sahib?' she said, distracted. 'You mentioned earlier, you had a couple of things …'

'Oh, yes.' Sahib Bithun nodded. 'Almost forgot, there was a healer I hired, for …' He gestured to his face and then to hers. 'My nose, as you can see, is just fine, but—'

'Rats,' Kavi whispered.

The sahib frowned. 'Who?'

'The healer.' The nightmare-healer. She frantically checked the walls for blood. Nothing, all clean, no sign of her assault. 'The healer, did he use rats as his counter?' His countervail. The price a mage paid for using their Jinn's maayin.

The thick brows rose as one. 'You remember? I assumed you were out cold. Then this shouldn't be hard to ...'

He rambled on about something or the other, but Kavi wasn't listening. Her mind was in free fall.

It was real, some of it was real. Which meant ... what else? The tunnel? No, she didn't remember being in one, ever. And the woman? Such a proud face, such sad, symmetrical features; gone, smashed to a bloody pulp. Hundred per cent not real. Her father? Yes, real. That place they were in: Ethuran? She knew where it was, *what it was*, every single Taemu did, but she'd never set foot in it.

Wait, wait, wait. What if it was a memory from another life? She'd heard stories, people remembering strange things that they'd never experienced. She'd never bought into it, but she was ready to convert if it helped her make sense of things.

'... so, you see,' the sahib said, 'you don't need to be concerned. As long as you don't test, the Jinn will not find you, and this contamination will never affect you.'

WHAT?

Chapter 7

'You want me to start at the beginning?' Bithun said with a cocked eyebrow.

'Sorry, sahib. I was, uh, distracted.' She flared her nostrils. *Now talk.* What was this about testing? And Jinn. And contamination. She'd missed everything else, but her cartwheeling mind had latched onto those three words and would not let go.

'No, it can wait.' He got to his feet and slipped a thick piece of paper out of a pocket. 'You're much too fog-headed to have this conversation right now – a concussion can do that. Rest, recover, and come find me in a week. I will give you a tour of the godowns, explain your training, and fill you in on what the healer told me.'

No, no, no. She wanted to pull her hair out, drag her fingernails down the sides of her face, but she composed herself and muffled the needy, debilitated shriek in her head. 'Sahib, I'm fine. I can pay atten—'

'My address.' He pressed the piece of paper into the base of her bed.

She fought the impulse to reach out, grab the man's shoulders and shake him till he saw sense. 'Sahib, wait—'

'Rest, Kavithri.' He turned on his heel and strode to the door. 'I will see you in a week's time, and not a moment before that.

As your new employer, this is my first assignment to you.'

New employer. That's right, she was a godown clerk now. She swallowed the lump in her throat. No more noisy trains and obnoxious passengers, no more screaming knees and burning shoulders. She would never have to hold her breath to clean another sewage tank or walk home with torn muscles in her back. It was over. It really was.

But an entire week of not knowing why he'd used those three words? She opened her mouth, prepared a more persuasive argument, and gasped as a bubble of rapidly accumulating pain exploded behind her right eyebrow and spread across the rest of her head.

Through a haze of throat-clogging, nose-blocking nausea, she saw the sahib nod. 'One week,' he said, and allowed the draught to slam the door shut behind him.

One week? She snatched at the empty jug on the side table and retched into it. She gagged and spat until her head finally cleared, and she sighed in relief.

There was nothing to do but accept it. She would find out in a week's time. *Until then* . . . until then she would wait and enjoy this soft bed, this bouncy pillow, this silky nightshirt, this clean room and – she wiped her mouth with the back of her hand. What about food? With the sahib gone, would the hospital peons and factotums be willing to feed her?

The answer, she found, after wandering into the corridor with the vomit-laden jug, was a resounding, *Yes*. Three meals a day plus a limited, but reasonable, amount of snacks. All paid for by the friendly sahib Bithun, may Raeth – *praise-praise, Hel awaits* – keep his sticky tentacles off the man for a little while longer.

She spent the first day gorging herself on hospital canteen food and pondering the mysterious testing-Jinn-contamination trifecta that had stumbled out of Bithun's mouth and bashed its way into her ears.

She knew what the words meant. Well, no one really knew what the Jinn were. Just that they were once five, and now only three.

There was Harith, the warlocks' Jinn, whose countervail – the price the Jinn exacted when its maayin was used – was a form of paralysis. They said that for the duration of a warlock's cast, a sliver of Harith was in the mage's body, and the weight of the entity in the material world prevented the warlock from moving. Which was why they were the only class of mage who needed bodyguards – Blades. Then there was Nilasi, the healers' Jinn, whose countervail was non-human life force. And Kolacin, the artificers' Jinn, who took its mage's memories as payment. The other two Jinn – Zubhra, the illusionists' Jinn, and Raktha, the Biomancers' Jinn – had not chosen in centuries, and were considered either dormant, or dead.

And the testing? It had to be the three tests: *Spirit, Bridge,* and *Instrument.* Had to be.

The contamination? Something impure, maybe poisoned. But what did it have to do with the other two words? Was there something poisonous about the tests? The Jinn? Try as she might, she just could not recollect the rest of the sahib's speech or make any logical connections between the words. So, she sighed and resigned herself to a life of indolence and indulgence.

She spent the next two days lying on her back, stuffing her face, washing herself with two *(two!)* bucket*s* of water and a jasmine-scented bar of soap. She daydreamed of the fresh, clean clothes she would wear every day in her new job, the cushioned chair she would sit in, the scent of the old dusty ledgers she'd surround herself with, the feel of a pen in her fingers as she scrawled in them, the satisfaction of writing a word, of taking a thought and coaxing it into an image imbued with meaning and memory. It was bliss. Until, on day four—

'Really? A Taemu?' A bandaged head poked its way into her room.

'Yes, it is,' a nurse at the man's back said as she peered in and made disapproving noises at the sight of Kavi munching on murukus on her bed.

The man scratched the thick layer of gauze covering both his eyes. 'Why is there a Taemu in the room next to mine?'

Kavi tsked and rolled over onto her side. Popped another muruku into her mouth. So much money and the arseholes couldn't even add locks to their doors.

'Sorry, saab-ji,' the nurse said, 'is already paid for. But don't worry, she's not as smelly as they say.' She ushered the man away, but that was it for Kavi's peace and quiet.

'My name is Banerjee, your name? Don't-care-don't-want-to-know,' he said after appearing uninvited later that evening and magically locating the only chair in the room. She tried to reason with him, explain how he had his own room, own chair, but no. The bastard decided to spend half of each day in her company, whether she liked it or not.

Banerjee, it turned out, was as eccentric as they came. He vacillated between wild bigotry (*Is that Taemu bitch still in there?*) to coddling her for no apparent reason (*How's your leg today, chweetoo? Oh so-sad, so-sad).* He'd lost both his eyes and one of his arms in a factory accident, and she suspected that half his brain was gone too.

Between his raucous nightmares, ritual thumping on the wall, and tangential ranting, she woke on day seven with bloodshot eyes and a renewed sense of purpose. It was time to get the Hel out of here and start her new life.

She made one last check. *Nightshirt.* Folded and secured. On top of it, *soap:* two bars. Then *snacks:* a box of murukus. She gave it a loving pat. And snug next to the murukus and soap, Sree Tsubumani's hard-boiled novel: *The Eyes of Hel*, which she'd borrowed from the hospital library. Satisfied, she tied the cord around the satchel and dressed herself in the beige salwar-kameez a nurse had dropped off with the satchel, compliments of sahib Bithun. She flattened her hair, rolled up her sleeves, and slipped her feet into a pair of chappals. It was time.

Kavi stopped. Might as well say goodbye to Banerjee. They had, after all, spent an inordinate amount of time together. Some may even have called them friends.

His door was open, as usual, and he was lying on his back with his remaining arm behind his head; completely at peace, no mention of the spicy biryani from last night he specifically requested be made extra spicy, and which had resulted in a sleepless night – for him and for her – of explosive diarrhoea. Maybe he'd rebounded into one of his good moods.

'Banerjee, bhai, I'm off,' she said.

'Go die.'

Maybe not. She gave him a half-salute. He was a miserable little shit, but she didn't hate him for it. 'Good luck,' she muttered under her breath, and made her way down the stairs.

Bithun's estate was an hour's walk east, through the Mekuli bazaar and into the swankier districts where the wealthy curated their pockets of luxury and comfort. The slums were in the opposite direction, a two, maybe three-hour walk, depending on the heat and the foot traffic. Without Haibo, there was nothing left for her there. Someone else would have claimed her hut by now, and her books would have been used for kindling. But she had questions, and Zofan would have answers.

*

She found the old man outside his hut, squatting over a news-pamphlet while he picked his teeth with a piece of bark.

'Zofan-ji,' she said.

He finished what he was reading, looked up, and narrowed his eyes at her. 'Sit.' And while she sat, 'Heard you were clearing out the Royal Hospital's canteen.'

Kavi snorted. 'As if they'd let me.'

He waited till she had settled in, then said, 'Your hut is gone.'

'I know.'

'Haibo's things all gone, too.'

'Wouldn't expect any less,' Kavi said. 'I came here to speak to you. What news?'

She let him talk. Listened to his plans for new arrivals, his complaints about the drains in the south-east section, and nodded as he cursed the country's corrupt politicos.

'Speaking of politicos ...' she said.

'Hmm?'

'What do you know about the man who paid for my stay at the hospital?'

'Jarayas Bithun?' Zofan said.

Kavi nodded. Of course Zofan already knew.

'A powerful man,' Zofan said, combing his fingers through his beard. 'Ran Bochan for almost twenty years. Well connected, even in Azraaya.'

'And?'

'Lost his wife and daughter several years ago, then retired from office. Mostly keeps to himself now.'

All that was useful information, but, 'Zofan-ji,' she said, 'what do you *think of him?*'

'Ah.' Zofan chuckled. 'You want to know if you can trust him.'

'Can I?'

He stopped combing his beard and studied her in silence.

'I've never met the man,' he finally said. 'But during his time in charge, he sank thousands of rayals into plumbing for the slums, he arranged for water pumps to be installed, for material to be sent over for our huts – he seemed to genuinely care. But, like I said, he withdrew after the deaths in his family and the only thing I've heard since is that he is kind to his staff and is no longer involved with city politics.' Zofan paused. Narrowed his eyes at her. 'I wouldn't let my guard down, but yes, for now, you have nothing to lose in trusting him.'

Kavi breathed a sigh of relief and bobbed her head in thanks.

He waved it off. 'Now go, I have reading to do.'

'I will come visit, when I get a chance,' she said.

Zofan shooed her away, eyes already back on his news-pamphlet.

Kavi stood. Slung the satchel over one shoulder, squinted into the morning sun, and set out to meet her new boss.

She walked through the dust and the tumultuous honking of steam-rickshaws. Ignored the calls of hawkers and street-food vendors. Crossed the Dowhar Bridge and stepped into the shade of the old Kraelish quarters and their dour grey bricks and ominous arches and towers; now repurposed as a museum, a collection of administrative offices, and an arranged marriage broker.

Soon the posters on the walls that screamed *Do Not Urinate Here!* disappeared, the dosa stands and sugar-cane juice vendors were replaced with tea shops and Kraelish bakeries, and the buildings were occasionally interrupted by manicured gardens where well-dressed men and women casually strolled.

Kavi enjoyed her infrequent visits to this part of the city. It was a healthy reminder – she eyed a stray dog licking the cover of an empty ladoo box and perked her ears up as the sounds of a domestic dispute drifted out of a window – that these people were not so different from those on the other side of the bridge. They might dress themselves up, douse themselves in perfume, but underneath, they were all slowly rotting. Just like everyone else. *Just like me.*

Once, she'd imagined naively that there was a brighter side to this city, clean and beautiful, where people laughed and lived and fucked without a care in the world. The reminder that things weren't all that different on this side was oddly comforting.

And then there were the buildings themselves – said to have been built with material shipped over from Kraelin. She reached out and touched a wall. So much history beneath her fingertips.

The Kraelish were the first to discover the Jinn, the ones who became the First Mages, the first real Blades, and they'd used that knowledge to bring the continent to its knees. And then, at the height of their power, they collapsed. No one knew what happened. The history books she'd read contained one-page chapters that simply said, *The Retreat. 1250 to 1660 AK approx. No recorded history.*

So much knowledge was said to have been lost during the Retreat.

But then, more or less a thousand years ago, from the ruins of the First Empire rose the Second. Their mages were no longer as powerful, their Blades had lost the ability to bond to their warlocks, but they made up for those things with sheer ruthlessness and cunning. The Kraelish ruled Raaya for close to six centuries, irrevocably altered the structure of its society, bent its culture to suit their needs, and now here she was, walking through its debris. Another victim of its ambitions.

Number 52, Moon's Blessings Road. This was it. She stopped and rapped her knuckles on the window of a guardhouse that flanked a pair of massive iron gates.

The window slid open and a man peered at her through the grille behind it. He narrowed his eyes, licked his fingers, curled the tips of a luscious moustache. 'Wan' something?'

Kavi flashed the sahib's business card at him.

He cocked his head. Ran his eyes over her body, from the chappals on her feet to the crow's nest on her head. He paled, swallowed, and slammed the window shut. A few seconds later, he was opening the gate for her.

'Thanks, bhai,' Kavi said, bemused by the man's over-the-top reaction. She glanced over her shoulder as she walked past. He was still staring at her with a downturned mouth, his grip white-knuckled on the rails of the gate. She shrugged it off and strolled down the gravel path, but then the gardeners stopped working and gawked, and the maids scurrying about on errands slowed to exchange hushed whispers behind their hands.

Nothing new. Not the first time people had reacted to her appearance this way. They'd get used to it. This was nothing new – fuck that, bhaenchod, *this* was new. She'd never set foot in a place like this before. What was that supposed to be? A fountain? *Art, my Gods,* she'd never understand it.

A tall, straight-backed man wrinkled his nose when she arrived at the entrance to the colonial-style bungalow. 'You must be Kavithri. Footwear at the door.'

Kavi obeyed.

'Follow, kindly,' he said, and led her inside.

Silk carpets covered the floor and elaborate tapestries hung on both sides of a corridor. Large, gilded windows were thrown open with chick-blinds rolled up and tied with string. Portraits of two women – the wife and daughter, Kavi guessed – filled the spaces between them.

'The sahib will see you in the courtyard,' her guide said, and left her outside a wooden partition without another word.

Kavi puffed out her cheeks, patted her satchel, and stepped around the screen.

The courtyard, an open-air space smack-bang in the middle of the building, was bereft of any adornment or ornamentation. No plants, trees, furniture, or shrines. It was a simple square of flattened and raked sand.

Bithun, minus his cane, perambulated the enclosure with one arm behind his back and a steaming mug in the other.

'Kavithri.' He glanced at her satchel and his jaw tightened. 'Tanool didn't offer you a drink?'

She shook her head. 'No, sahib.'

He set his mug down on the sand and clapped his hands.

Her tall guide reappeared at one of the other doors to the courtyard, and stood just out of reach of the sandpit.

'Tanool,' Bithun said, gesturing to Kavi, 'offer our guest some refreshments.'

Tanool turned to her, studied the space above her head, and said in the same deadpan voice he'd used earlier. 'Tea, coffee?'

Bithun sighed.

Kavi raised both eyebrows. Stationmaster Muthu would have fired her on the spot for this level of disinterest. The sahib, it appeared, was a more lenient employer.

'Tea,' she said, and emboldened, 'extra sweet, extra milk …' she wanted to say *extra everything* but changed her mind.

Tanool glanced at the sahib, nodded to no one in particular, and left.

'Join me,' Bithun said and bent to retrieve his mug.

The sand, she discovered as she fell into step, was incredibly fine and luxuriant; almost silklike in texture.

Bithun noticed her flexing her toes in it. 'From Kraelin.'

She glanced at him. 'Really?'

He nodded.

Why? What's wrong with the sand on the Chatpaari beach?

'From the rings in Balthour,' he said with a wistful smile.

'You were a ring-fighter, sahib?'

He blew over the rim of his mug. 'In another life.'

So, this was some sort of mausoleum to his boxing career, to his youth. The things one could get up to when they had money and free time. Lucky bastard.

'What's it like over there, sahib? In Kraelin?' she asked, suddenly curious. 'I've heard stories that—'

Bithun snorted. 'Let me guess – the Kraelish are weak, are an empire in decline, a people trapped in their own past?'

She opened her mouth to say, *Yes, that's exactly what everyone says.*

'They still think of us as *theirs,* you know,' Bithun continued with a meaningful glance. 'No one speaks of Raaya as an independent nation. In fact, many of them believe the subcontinent will eventually be reclaimed.' He cleared his throat at the surprise on her face. 'Anyway, did you make good use of your week?'

Multiple naps a day, multiple meals a day; laying on her bed and getting lost in *The Eyes of Hel* and police-inspector Jurabo's labyrinthine search for a Necromancer who'd fled his scheduled lobotomisation; in between, glaring at Banerjee while he waffled on about the prodigious girth of his susu and the number of children it had spawned. 'Yes.'

'Likewise.' Bithun nodded. 'I was able to use the time to verify what the healer told me about your condition.'

Condition? Now she had a condition?

Bithun squinted at the doorway through which Tanool had disappeared. 'Would you like to see the godowns first or—'

'Sahib, please, what did the healer say?' No more waiting. She'd salted it and left it on the shelf for long enough.

It was time for a taste. Time to find out what this Jinn-testing-contamination really meant.

Bithun nodded. 'I've been thinking about the best way to explain this, and I may have gone about it the wrong way the first time. Perhaps you need more … context.'

'Context, sahib?'

'Yes, I'll start at the beginning, and, Kavithri …'

She swallowed. 'Yes?'

'Please, pay attention.'

Chapter 8

'I usually avoid healers,' Bithun said. 'I find their countervail repulsive. Distasteful. But just this once, I made an exception.'

'The man arrived twenty minutes late with his pouch of rats. Ordered a nurse to do this, a physician to get the Hel out of the way, even told *me* to sit quietly in the chair.' Bithun sipped his tea. 'He healed my nose. Then he turned to you, fast asleep and snoring.'

Kavi ducked her head. 'Sorry.'

'He took one look at you and said, *Need more rats.* He left. He returned with a bucketful of the vermin and finally got started. Two seconds later, he turns to me, *Are you sure she isn't dead?*' The sahib made a face. 'Dead? I was ready to kill that chootia right there. Anyway, you were not dead.'

'Obviously,' Kavi muttered.

'What's that?'

'Nothing, sahib. Carry on, please.'

'Right. So, he tries again. Squeezes a rat till it bursts. And another one.' Bithun mimicked the rat-squeezing with his free hand. 'And another one. Until he kills every rat in that bucket and says, *It won't touch her.* What won't touch her? *My maayin, it won't touch her.* He whines and moans and says he can't heal you.'

Kavi's mouth went dry. The only time a healer failed to work their maayin on someone was if another Jinn had claimed them. She'd never taken the tests, had never been exposed to the Jinn, and as much as she might want to be, she was *not* a mage. So what the Hel what going on?

Bithun took another sip of his tea. 'What do you know of the Azirs?'

Kavi blinked. 'The hybrids?'

Bithun nodded.

'Just the usual – Necromancers are bad news; Chiromancers leave calamity and destruction in their wake.' Necros and Chiros, due to their notoriety, were the most famous of the lot, but there were plenty of other hybrids. Riosophists, Mylothurgists, Aoramancers – freak combinations of the five primary classes where a mage was claimed by multiple Jinn. Azirs had a reputation for being, like Haibo would say, slightly cracked in the head. Most of them had a tendency to either disappear or wind up dead in some far-off country. 'They're rare though. Very rare.'

Bithun patted down a scuffed-up area of the sandpit. He seemed uncomfortable and hesitated before he spoke. 'Azirs, once chosen by their Jinn, don't live for very long.'

Kavi cocked her head. 'Sahib?'

'It's the exposure to maayin from more than one Jinn,' Bithun said. 'It gives Azirs their unique power, but over time, it warps their immune system, fools it into mistaking its own body for a foreign invader, and kills them from the inside out.'

Kavi frowned. There was nothing about this in any of her books. 'The maayin from which Jinn?'

'From all of them.'

Her brows shot up. 'All? How?'

'There is something … wrong with maayin. It's a little-known fact. *Toxic,* was the word our friend the healer used, and my source in Azraaya has confirmed this. They think accessing the maayin from a single Jinn does not allow enough of this wrongness through, so *most* mages can use it safely. But when a mage is chosen by more than one Jinn …'

Kavi pursed her lips. Scratched the back of her neck. She understood what Bithun was implying, but, 'Are you sure about this?'

'I was dubious too,' Bithun said, 'when the healer first told me. But the more I listened, the more it made sense.' He smoothed out one of his thick eyebrows. 'Then I did some digging. It was the Kraelish. They made the discovery a century after they arrived on our shores, when one of their expeditions returned from the Deadlands.'

She'd read about the place: a vast stretch of land on the northern border, covered in grey ash, where nothing lived or grew; whose only visitors were deranged scavenger crews who risked death – often by some inexplicable disease – to explore the area in search of relics from the Retreat, or, according to some scholars, artifacts that pre-dated human civilisation.

'The Kraelish sent out expeditions the moment they secured a foothold on the subcontinent. Thousands of auxiliaries and homegrown soldiers, half of whom died in the waste, or later, from its effects. Cold-hearted bastards.' He shook his head. 'Imagine trying to get our people to do that? There'd be a riot.'

'No,' Kavi said, 'Raayans are way too lazy.'

'You might be right,' Bithun conceded. 'Anyway, the Kraelish found nothing. But they were, and *are*, meticulous record keepers. Everything is jotted down and filed away somewhere. You sneeze in a meeting? The chootia will write it down. Not even joking. Anyway, every member of these expeditions who received any form of healing was recorded. And that's where they found the anomaly.

'Among the few who survived the Deadlands were a handful of non-mages, soldiers who'd never taken the tests, but whose injuries couldn't be healed with Nilasian maayin. It didn't make sense. Only mages are immune to a healer.' Bithun cocked his head and glanced at Kavi. 'Right?'

'Right,' she said with a thoughtful nod. It was exactly as she already knew – a healer's maayin would not work on those chosen by a Jinn. But if these soldiers had not taken the tests and had never been exposed to the Jinn, then how?

'The Kraelish noted it in their ledgers, sent it back to Balthour, and carried on with their conquering and subjugation of the subcontinent.' He paused and switched mug hands. 'Years later, some of these non-mages who could not be healed returned to Kraelin and went on to take the tests. And guess what?'

'What?' Kavi said, eyes wide.

'Every single one that passed, passed as Azirs.'

Bleddy Hel. '*All* of them?'

'All. The Kraelish, they checked their ledgers, found a pattern, and kept tabs on these newly minted hybrids, but otherwise let them carry on. And then, seven years later …' He took a loud sip from his mug.

'What?' Kavi shuffled closer to the sahib. 'What happened?'

Bithun snapped his fingers. 'Dead. In the space of a few months. All of them.'

She swallowed. 'No …'

The sahib nodded. 'That's when the Sinkall, the Kraelish secret police, claimed jurisdiction and took over. They rounded up the other unhealables from the expeditions, split them into two groups – half they gave jobs to and kept under observation, the rest were forced to test. The ones who *didn't* test lived full lives, but the poor fools who tested, who all passed as Azirs, were imprisoned. The Sinkall ran experiments on these men and women and discovered the contamination in their maayin.'

Bithun swirled the remaining tea around in his mug. 'Once they knew what to look for, they found the contamination in a third of all their mages, mostly past the age of forty, and most of them with some form of cancer in their bodies. The correlation became truth, and the truth flew in the face of everything they knew about the Jinn and maayin, so they buried it.'

'Buried it? Why?' If something so dangerous was discovered, why not warn people? Try to save some of them from this contamination.

'Imagine, Kavithri ...' The sahib stopped and gazed into her eyes, 'what kind of sane person would want to test if they knew they could be cutting their life short?'

Someone who had nothing to lose. But most people did, so. 'Not many,' she said.

'Not many, which is what the college in Kraelin believed at the time. They needed more mages, you see, for their campaigns, for their industry, their expansions ...' He sighed. 'I'm not sure what their approach is now, but our Vagola treats the contamination as an open secret that stays within the mage community. They've adopted the Raayan oh-what-to-do-yaar, it-is-what-it-is attitude toward the whole thing.'

Kavi mulled it over, and frowned, suddenly sceptical. 'But if the truth about maayin is meant to stay within the mage community, why did the healer even tell you all this?'

'He told me,' Bithun said, with a sharp glance at the doorway Tanool was last seen at, 'because I knew enough to ask the right questions – he was, after all, confirming something I already suspected. And besides, I paid for his new verandah and threatened to invalidate his licence to practise in Bochan.'

Kavi cocked her head. 'You can do that?'

The sahib looked her dead in the eye and said, without blinking, 'I know people.'

Kavi blinked, and Bithun resumed his circuitous stroll with a quiet grunt. 'So, when did you visit the Deadlands?'

'Never been,' Kavi said, without missing a beat.

Bithun gave her a dubious glance. 'Kavithri, do you understand why I have told you all this?'

Why? Yes, why? She'd been so intrigued by this hidden-basement history that she'd forgotten the point of the whole thing. But like the gears of a rusted rickshaw, her mind creaked and groaned and, with the weight of an entire lifetime, the answer fell into place with a teeth-shattering thud.

Her tongue sealed itself to the roof of her dry mouth. The ground at her feet, so soft and malleable, was now quicksand. She sank, frozen in place, as fine grains of sand streamed into her mouth and down her throat and clogged her windpipe. 'I am—' She sucked in air through flared nostrils. 'You think …'

He nodded. 'The healer thinks it's in your blood, dormant, waiting for a catalyst.'

'The tests,' she whispered.

'The second one, specifically,' the sahib said. 'But as long as you don't test, you have nothing to worry about.'

'Don't test? But what if he's wrong?'

Sahib Bithun frowned. 'The healer?'

She gave him a bug-eyed nod while she wrestled with the ramifications. What if she'd made it in five years ago and passed? Would she even be alive today?

He shrugged. 'Even if he is, it would be safer *not* to test, don't you think?'

But *why her*? Was it something she'd done? Something she'd eaten? Was this penance for her sins in one of her previous lives? 'But … how?'

'How could this happen?' Bithun scratched at the stubble on his chin. 'Either you've spent a prolonged amount of time in the Deadlands, or, he said, just bad luck.'

Bad luck.

Bad luck.

Bad luck was her walking in on Stationmaster Muthu taking a shit with a beedi in his mouth while he rifled through a stack of pornographic playing cards. This? This was something much bigger, more focused; the latest in a long line of well-executed attacks against her very being. How could she have not seen it coming?

The sahib stepped off the sand and gestured to a different, closed door. 'Now come, let me introduce you to the other clerks.'

'Other clerks,' Kavi repeated in a daze.

'Yes,' he said. 'So we can get you trained up, start your new life.'

A new life.

Take it, Kavi; take it and go.

They'd stacked the deck against her before she was even born; chained her in place and dealt her losing hand after losing hand and she'd played them all with a hopeful, smouldering rage in her stomach. But they'd finally fucked up and dealt her a winning hand. A chance to start a new life. So why did it feel so … *heavy?*

Why?

Because she could already see it. With each passing year, her heart would break just a little bit more, and all the books and ink and luxury on the subcontinent would mean nothing, because the knowledge of what she could have been would gnaw at her putrefying soul until the only thing left of her was an empty, brittle husk that lived to die.

She couldn't do it. Couldn't live the rest of her life watching other people do what she wanted to do, be what she wanted to be.

'Sahib,' she said.

The man stopped with a hand on a doorknob.

'Sahib, can you get me into the Branch?'

His fingers slipped off the handle. 'The what?'

'The Branch.' Her voice found its resolve. 'On Golmadi Road. Can you use your connections, to help me get in?'

He blinked. A flicker of surprise in his eyes. 'Why would you want to get in?'

Kavi stared at Bithun's face, at the assessing and measuring eyes. Just like Haibo's. She could hear him burp, see him wipe the rum off his chin and, suddenly serious, give her that same look and say, *Akka, if you had a chance, if you could start over, knowing what you do now, what kind of Taemu would you be?* He'd take another swig. *Would you still bend to survive? Or would you be one of those bastards who would rather break than be moulded – you know, the kind they mock and beat, who don't live very long, but who, when it's all over, die as a Taemu. Not like …* He'd gesture to himself, to her, and lapse into silence.

'I want to test.' This was it.

'Maybe …' The sahib made his way back to the sand. 'Maybe I need to explain again.'

'No, sahib. I understand.' This was her folding a winning hand, crawling up to the dealer, and spitting in his face.

The sahib set his tea mug aside and wrung his hands. 'Why? Why would you throw your life away? There's no guarantee that— What if you pass the first two, and fail the third test? Then what? You'd sacrifice your life for nothing.'

'But it would be by my choice.' This was her cackling while the dealer's goons got to their feet, cracked their knuckles, and closed in.

'Your choice?' the sahib said, flabbergasted. 'Why? What do you hope—'

'I want to be *more*, sahib. And … I want to find my family.' This was her choosing to die on her own terms.

'Your family?' he repeated, dumbstruck.

'My father, my younger brothers …' She nodded to herself. 'I will use the Venator to find them.'

'The Venator?' He blinked. '*The Venato*r? Child, haven't you been listening? Who knows what else they've kept from us? What if it doesn't work anymore? Is it even …'

She studied the agitated stranger spitting out scenario after worst-case scenario; so concerned for her well-being, it was almost as if *he* wanted or needed something from her, not the other way around. 'I have no one, sahib.'

He stopped. Let his gesticulating hands fall.

'My family is lost to me. And my people – there are barely any Taemu this far south, but I can tell our numbers are dwindling.' She took a slow, steady breath. 'If I succeed, if I can show that we are better than what you say we are, if I can find my family, if I can spend at least a few years surrounded by people who see me as an equal, and if I can give them something in return … then I owe it to all of them to try.'

Bithun's shoulders slumped, and he hung his head.

Kavi paused, weighed the words she wanted to say. They were selfish, but they were the truth. 'I have dreamed of being a mage for a very long time. I have tried, again and again, to test, only to be beaten and humiliated and sent back to the slums every single year. If you can help me get in, consider your debt to me paid in full.'

Sahib Bithun's jaw tightened. He reached into his pockets and pulled out a gold watch; flipped it open, narrowed his eyes at it. 'This is what you really want?'

'It is, sahib.'

Bithun sighed. 'Do you think you can handle a rickshaw ride?'

Kavi's hands instinctively went to the bruise on her forehead. 'Steam-rickshaw?'

'Yes. Steam-rickshaw,' the sahib said, with his eyes still on the watch.

'I – I suppose?' Kavi fumbled with the hem of her kameez. 'What—'

He slipped the watch back into its pocket and strode to the wooden partition. He stopped and turned to Kavi. 'Well? Did you want to wait for next year or what?'

She blinked. 'Sahib, the testing was last week.'

'For the rest of the city, it was,' he said. 'The testing today is for those with *exceptional talent.*'

Kavi blinked. Exceptional?

The sahib tsked. 'You know, for people who can afford a bribe, who don't want to mingle with the masses.'

Oh.

OH.

Her heart raced like it was being played by an enraptured tabla-maestro. 'You want me to … I can … Now?'

'If that's what you want.'

Tanool smoothly stepped out of a doorway, tray in hand and cup on tray. He sauntered up to a stunned Kavi. 'Your tea,' he said, sardonic and imperious, with his eyes on the space above her head.

She muffled her thundering heartbeat, fought the trembling in her hands, and reached for the cup. 'Extra sweet?'

Tanool nodded to the air.

'Extra milk?'

He inclined his head.

'I'm taking it with me.'

He started. 'What—'

Kavi snatched the half-full, lukewarm teacup off the tray and turned to the sahib. *Can you handle a rickshaw ride?* She'd ride on the bleddy roof if she had to. 'Let's go.'

Chapter 9

Back across the Dowhar Bridge and through the bazaar with its bangle stalls and sari merchants, its chat-wallahs, spice traders, samosa stands, tandoori ovens, and seafood vendor-grillers shrieking about how fresh their fish and prawn and squid were.

Kavi gulped down the tea, flicked the dregs out onto the road, and stuffed the cup into her satchel. The sahib wouldn't miss a measly teacup. Besides, they'd offered it to her on a silver tray. Free cup. It was hers now.

The rickshaw exited the bazaar, swerved around a bullock cart, and narrowly missed a wobbly cycle-rickshaw before it squealed through the intersection. Bithun swore at the driver and the driver cursed the slow-moving traffic.

Kavi tightened her grip on the handrail and squeezed her eyes shut. A rickshaw had brought her this far, and if her death was to be at the hands of another one, then so be it. The rickshaw giveth, and the rickshaw taketh away. She said a quiet prayer to Raeth and resolved herself to her fate.

They arrived whole, healthy, and slightly frazzled. Bithun slapped a fifty rayal banknote into the driver's waiting palm. 'Wait here.'

He glanced at Kavi, who'd disembarked after him. 'You too.'

'Sahib?'

Bithun checked the road for traffic with overly cautious eyes. 'Stay here till I return.'

A lone jalebi vendor stood outside the Branch, fanning bright orange circles of jaggery in case an errant mosquito landed on them. The gates themselves were manned by a single drowsy hawaldar seated on a three-legged stool, artificed musket propped on one shoulder and tiffin-box hanging on the butt.

Bithun exchanged muffled words with the hawaldar and the man scampered to unlock and open the gates. The sahib turned, nodded at Kavi, and disappeared into the Branch without her.

Kavi gazed up at the great building. It was all still there. Just like she'd left it. The walls she'd once tried to scale, the colourful shards of glass at the top on which she'd nearly sliced all her fingers off, the salt-caked facade behind it at whose feet she'd begged and pleaded, been beaten and humiliated.

Back so soon? Its blacked-out windows seemed to say to her.

What to do? Kavi waggled her eyebrows. *Just can't get enough of you.*

Chi! Go find another building, you pervert.

But I only want you.

Dai! No shame or what? The sun gleamed off the windows, and made it seem like the building averted its bashful eyes. *Okay, but quickly, I don't want anyone to see.*

Kavi chuckled. She'd worn it down through sheer persistence, and now — out of the corner of an eye she spotted the driver staring at her in open-mouthed befuddlement.

She tsked at herself. Turned her back on him and paced the footpath. *Get a grip.* What she needed now was a distraction.

She pulled her book out of the satchel and flipped through the pages, read the same paragraph five times, once with her finger tracking the words, before she gave up with a cry of frustration and shoved the novel back into the bag. There was nothing to do but wait. Wait and ignore the bedlam in her head.

An occasional rickshaw zoomed past, a herd of cows waddled through, the jalebi vendor partook of his own goods, and Kavi paced. Back and forth. Up and down. Small steps. Big strides. Baby steps. But still no sahib.

Can't read, so hot, need something to drink, feel sick, can't think – don't want to think. Is this a mistake? No, stop. Stop.

She stretched her hands out, steadied her breath and studied her trembling fingers. It was as if her nerves had been put through a pencil sharpener. A quick slice along the back of her hand and she could pull one out and use it as a weapon.

The gates clanked and squealed, and she pressed her hands to her stomach and sighed in relief.

Bithun acknowledged the hawaldar's salute with a rolled-up wad of banknotes. He checked both sides of the road and crossed over to the rickshaw and Kavi.

'Five minutes,' he said to the driver, who had started pumping the lever that would kick-start the machine. He jerked his head at Kavi and walked into the shade of a paan-shop that had its shutters down.

'It's been arranged,' Bithun said when she joined him.

Kavi swallowed. 'Thank you, sahib. So do I just …' She gestured to the gates and the hawaldar counting his money.

Bithun studied her with a frown. 'Are you sure you want to do this?'

'I am,' she said with a conviction that was slowly being besieged by new doubts.

'Very well,' Bithun said, and scratched the two-day stubble on his chin. 'It will all hinge on the third round, you know.'

'Round?'

Bithun frowned. 'I meant test. It will all hinge on the third test.' He clasped his hands behind his back. 'You can prove your

Spirit, you can *Bridge* the gap between the Jinn and our reality, but if you cannot be an *Instrument* for maayin …'

She wiped the sweat off her forehead and nodded. She wasn't worried about the first test. Whatever they were going to put her through, she could handle it. And if the healer was right, she had the second test in the bag. The Jinn had already marked her. She could Bridge. It would all hinge on the third test. *Instrument.* A candidate could be chosen by all five Jinn, but if they couldn't channel their maayin, they were not a mage, just an unlucky chootia who got within touching distance of a dream before it was snatched away in front of their faces.

'If the second test decides your fate …' Bithun's features sagged and his eyes glazed over with a faraway look that Kavi sometimes saw on the old-timers in the slums.

She opened her mouth to prompt him to finish the sentence when—

'… the third *will* seal it.'

Her lips tightened into a thin, straight line. *No need to say it like that, bhai. Why so dramatic?*

'I tested, you know, some forty odd years ago,' Bithun continued, either oblivious to her anxiety or opting not to appreciate it. 'My heart wasn't in it, but my mother … she insisted that I try. For her sake. It was her dream, you see, not mine.'

Kavi nodded. Yes, she knew all about dreams.

'I passed the first test – it wasn't as bad as people said, I'd experienced much worse in the ring. The second test, I tell you, I will never forget.' His eyes glassed over again, and he stared at a spot on the wall, or maybe through it, into memories from another life.

'You passed?' Kavi said.

'Hmm? I failed. Left for Kraelin and the rings the next day, but' – he lifted a fist up to his face, rotated it and studied the scars on the knuckles – 'but for a brief moment, during the second test, while I was in the presence of the Jinn, I hoped … I thought to Hel with it, and hoped that they would choose me.'

A bullock cart, rickety and filled with sacks of rice, rolled past, and the sahib lapsed into silence.

'This world is old, Kavithri,' Bithun said when it disappeared around the corner. 'And the Jinn – I once believed they were Gods, but they're something more. Gods die. The Jinn? Time is meaningless to them. They exist outside our cycles of life and death. They demand nothing, desire nothing. No worship. No respect. No prayers … utterly terrifying, and obscenely magnificent. If we ever thought that existence revolved around us, that we were the most important creature in the universe, then the Jinn are a reminder that we are nothing. Insignificant. Irrelevant.'

The hawaldar on the other side of the road finally pocketed the money and flashed the sahib a sitting salute.

'You can never return, you know,' Bithun said, ignoring the hawaldar. 'You can take the second test a thousand times, but pass or fail, you will never go to the place with the Jinn again.'

She nodded with a clenched jaw.

'Pass or fail, you will come and see me,' Bithun said under his breath.

Kavi glanced at him. It wasn't a question. She nodded.

He gestured to the rickshaw driver to start up the machine, and as he walked past her, stopped and extended a hand.

Kavi stared at the gnarled, bony fingers.

'You're supposed to shake it,' Bithun said.

Yes, I know. Give me a moment. She puffed out her cheeks, wiped her hand on her salwar, and shook the sahib's hand, wincing as he gave hers a powerful squeeze.

'Good luck.' He nodded, and before she could reply, turned on his heel and hopped into the rickshaw. It hissed, sputtered, and shrieked away down the road.

Thank you, she mouthed and turned to face the gates.

Chapter 10

She fidgeted with the strap of her satchel, adjusted her salwar-kameez, and checked the road for traffic. Warm, salt-tinged breeze ruffled her hair, the hawaldar on the other side hawked and spat, a crow cawed on some faraway rooftop.

With a shuddering breath, she stepped off the footpath, and froze.

Seven years.

That was a long time.

A long time if you had the rest of your life to live.

It had been so easy to talk big in the sahib's sandpit, but now, up close and with it hovering over her neck like an executioner's tulwar …

She could still turn back. The sahib would surely give her the clerk job. She could work, save up, maybe travel somewhere where her eyes and appearance would be meaningless. Maybe meet someone who didn't mind her sense of humour and shared her love for food. They could settle down, get a dog, or two … she could forget her father, her brothers, the loneliness and the isolation, forget her people and all the hate and violence. Forget all those nights spent in an empty hut with a candle and a bunch of worn-out books and a dream.

Could she face that girl? Could she look her in the eye and

tell her that one day, she would walk away from it all because she was scared? Scared of cutting her life short. Afraid of living with a ticking clock on her shoulder. Terrified that it would all be for nothing. That it would be meaningless. What would little Kavi say to her?

Fucking coward.

You had a chance to be more. You had a chance to find Appa, and Kamith and little Khagan. And you choose to live as a clerk. To die as a coward. Selfish chootia, fuck you, you—

Seven years.

Better make them count. She cracked her neck and crossed the road. The hawaldar bobbed his head and gestured to the gates, which had been left unlocked and slightly ajar. She shimmied her way through, careful not to get her kameez caught on the latches, and just like that, she was in.

Candidates had formed a line under a long shamiana that ran adjacent to the building. Some of them sat in collapsible chairs with a newspamphlet in their hands and a platterful of snacks in their laps. Others stood, straight-backed and cross-armed, while exhausted attendants fanned them with peacock-feathered punkahs. Off to the side, under another smaller canopy, was a table laden with refreshments: iced lassi and spiced lime juice, samosas cut into delicate bite-sized pieces and a tower of silver-leaf milk cakes.

Maybe on the way out.

She clutched the satchel to her chest and tiptoed to the back of the line. Bribes had clearly been made, but she wouldn't put it past the administrators to say *Fuck the bribe, we hate Taemu more than we love money,* and beat her halfway to Hel. She kept her eyes on the heels of the man in front of her and prayed that no one had noticed her stealthy ingress.

Seconds turned into minutes. Rivulets of sweat ran down her

back and her neck and glued her kameez to her chest. Barely anyone spoke. An attendant drifted away from his master to fetch a beverage from the table, a punkah-wallah was commanded to fan faster. The man rolled his eyes and gave Kavi a tired glance. But no one else paid her any attention.

She relaxed. Popped her collar and blew cool air down the front of her kameez. Such a short line. On a normal testing day, it started at the gates, curled down the footpath, snaked around the intersection, and continued all the way down Golmadi Road until it merged with the line outside Siluchan's idli-dosa stand where fisticuffs would ensue over who (*Me? Bitch, it's you, one tight slap I'll give you if you don't—*) was cutting whose line (*Oh, little man has a big mouth, come-come, let's see if this chappal will fit*).

From somewhere at the head of the line, a man's voice boomed, 'Next!'

The candidate in front of her took a step forward, and she followed suit.

At regular intervals, ten to fifteen minutes apart, another *Next!* was yelled out, and the line crawled inexorably toward a gaping archway that waited to swallow up the candidates.

An hour in, while she was in the midst of a particularly intense session of fidgeting and nail-gnawing, the candidates ahead of her burst into a chorus of murmurs.

'Dai! Can't go through the backside or what?' the voice shouting the *Nexts* said.

'Backside?' A deeper, rougher voice answered. 'Bhai, see this man? You think he will fit?'

Silence. Then, 'Oh, ah, okay—'

'Okay what, bhaenchod?' The rough voice again. 'You think you can handle this? See this size. See!'

Oh, Gods, what? Did she really want to know? Kavi leaned out and peered down the line.

A large, muscle-bound man, soaked in sweat and unconscious, was being carried out on a stretcher. The two stretcher-bearers swayed from side to side, knees bent into a crouch as they struggled with his weight.

'Backside, it seems,' said the stretcher-bearer with the gruff voice, shaking his head. 'I tell you, Chamchu, if they don't hire one more guy, we strike.'

'Can, boss,' Chamchu said between gritted teeth.

'Bleddy buffalo,' the boss stretcher-bearer said under his breath as they waddled past Kavi. 'What do they feed these chootia on the other side of the bridge?'

'Chicken biryani,' Chamchu spat. 'Every day.'

'Every day? Fuck off.'

'Gods' promise, boss,' Chamchu said with a groan. 'My Jaya aunty is an ayah for a sahib, she told me.'

'Jaya? That cow is your aunty?'

They cursed and complained and carried the unconscious man away. But the first test, the one Bithun said *wasn't as bad*, the one she had been quietly confident she could handle, transmogrified into the shape of a heavyweight ring-fighter – handlebar moustache, missing front teeth, cauliflower ears – steam wafting off its bald head as it thumped its fists together and loomed over her shoulder with a bloodthirsty grin. She swallowed.

'Next!'

The line took another lethargic step and Kavi finally glimpsed the source of the announcements.

Fresh beads of sweat burst out on her already sweaty forehead. A violent urge to charge the man and tackle him to the ground slipped its hook into her gut and yanked. Another, more visceral compulsion wrapped its chains around her ankles and dragged her in the other direction. *Hide,* it pleaded, *find a corner, a crevice, a hole, anything, and bury yourself in it. Hide!*

The conflicting impulses warred and clashed and rooted her in place.

At the entrance, with his waxed moustache and oiled hair, his broad shoulders and powerful arms, was the respectable hawaldar Bhagu. The man was smoking a beedi and eyeing the fidgeting candidates with barely concealed disdain.

He showed no sign of having recognised her. But she knew, from the subtle shift in his posture – chin haughtily raised, chest puffed out, the hint of a smirk on his tamakhu-stained lips – that he'd seen her.

Each *Next!* sent another candidate down the corridor he blockaded, and each heavy step brought her closer and closer, until it was just her and him. She held her breath and entered the noxious cloud of tamakhu and body odour he lived in.

Bhagu flicked the ash off his beedi, took another drag. He allowed the grey smoke to infest his lungs, held it in for heartbeat after heartbeat, then blew it right into her face.

She flinched, waved her hand to disperse the smoke.

'Next,' came a muffled call from inside the archway.

Kavi instinctively took a step forward.

Bhagu raised a hand.

Her stomach sank. She tightened her grip on the satchel. Memories of her last encounter with the man rammed their way into her head. The chunky thud of his lathi connecting with her back, the metallic snot clogging her nostrils, the venom in his eyes and the toxin in his words; her bladder emptying itself from the sheer terror, the animal fear that he was going to kill her.

Bhagu flicked his fingers. 'Go on.'

She stifled a sigh of relief and shuffled around him with her head lowered.

But just when she thought she was through, he stopped her with a hand on her shoulder. He leaned in so close his mouth was inches from her ear. 'I warned you what would happen if I saw you here again.'

Kavi jerked her head away. 'The sahib—'

'What did you do? Suck his cock? Let him fuck you?' He pulled her closer. 'Is that his kink? Does he like to fuck filth? Or something else ... maybe he watched. He can't do it himself, so he likes to watch, right?'

'No—'

Bhagu dug his fingers into her shoulder, and she hissed.

'There are places in this city, places where degenerates like your sahib pay good money for' – Bhagu licked his lips – 'real good money to a man who can make the arrangements.'

Her blood went cold, and she tried to wriggle away, but he stepped on her foot and leaned in further. She gasped. 'Please—'

'Shut the fuck up, Taemu.' He spat in her face. 'When you fail, and you *will*, I'll be waiting.' His fingers slipped down to her shoulder blade, and he shoved her into the corridor.

Her toes jammed themselves into a hidden threshold. She stumbled, fell to her knees, tore her palms on the coarse floor. The satchel went flying – book, soaps, nightshirt, teacup, and snacks burst out. The teacup shattered into pieces. The box of snacks hit a wall, the lid popped open, and her murukus splattered across the corridor.

Bhagu snorted while she scrambled to gather her things.

'What's the hold up?' A cry from further down the corridor. 'I said next!'

The nail on her big toe was broken, split right down the middle, black-blue with blood filling the grooves around it. The skin on the lower half of her palms was gone, scrubbed away, exposing raw pink flesh covered with spots of red that burned with an itchy persistence. She left the muruku box and the broken teacup on the floor and used her fingers to shovel the rest into the satchel. *No time.* She could pick the dirt out of the murukus later. Her salwar was torn too, ripped open over bloody knees. *No time.* Bhagu might not be done with her.

Kavi got to her feet, wiped his spittle off her face with her sleeve, and limped down the corridor with the bag held tight to her chest. *Don't look, don't turn around.* He'd be watching. She couldn't let him see the shame on her face, the fear in her eyes, the impotent rage that made her lips tremble.

The ball of fury, the berserker that lived chained at her core, hissed and spat. *We could kill him. We could go back there and return the pain tenfold. We could drag his face across the floor. Laugh at his screams and his pleas. Rip the skin off his palms. Bludgeon him with his own glorified stick.*

She stopped outside a door with the number 1 and the word *Spirit* painted on it. Yellow light filtered through its frame, along with the metallic groans of machinery and the hissing of steam.

'Was that the last candidate?' a voice said from behind the door. 'Fucking useless hawaldar. Go check, Manium.'

Kavi silenced her rage, swallowed her vengeance, and nudged the door open with her elbow.

Chapter 11

Kavi stepped into a domed, windowless room. Gas lamps, yellow and iridescent, hung around a single large vent in the ceiling. Half the space was dedicated to a stack of hissing metal, stained black by use and criss-crossed with tubes and pistons that smouldered and steamed. The other half contained a desk with a ledger on it, a large rectangular steel box, another door, and what Kavi assumed was the testing device. She waited while a tall man, an engineer from the looks of it, berated his apprentice over a mishandled piston.

The run-in with Bhagu had rattled her. It clung to her psyche like an unsalted leech. She replayed it over and over again: his fingers on her shoulders, on her back, his breath in her ear, his saliva dripping down her face. Her hands shook. She gritted her teeth and forced emotion and reason apart.

If she failed, if she found him waiting for her outside, like he promised …

She'd have to fight, then she'd have to leave the city. There was no other choice. The penalty for assaulting a hawaldar was a public whipping and six months in jail. For her? They'd strip her naked and whip her till she was dead.

He was bigger. She was faster. He was arrogant, would not see it coming after years of walking all over her. She would strike first. Two long strides, wind-up, and full force. No hesitation. In the balls. Then run. Goods train no.48 left after sundown and had plenty of room for a stowaway.

The engineer noticed her standing in the doorway and jerked his thumb at the table.

'Name?' He said as he walked over and picked up the pen tied to the ledger.

'Kavithri.'

'No family name or what?'

'Taemu.'

He wrote it, unflinching and expressionless, while his frog-like apprentice stared at her with goggle-eyed disgust.

'Bag.' The engineer tapped the table.

She nodded. Limped over to the table and carefully arranged the satchel away from its edge.

'Any food in your pockets? Tamakhu?' The engineer glanced at her torn salwar. 'In your clothes?'

'No.'

He cocked his head at the apprentice. 'Check her.'

The younger man walked up, presumably to frisk her for anything organic that wasn't part of her body, but took one look at her eyes and changed his mind.

'I can't, sir-ji,' he said, wringing his hands.

'Manium,' the engineer said with a long, tired sigh, 'I don't care who your father is. If you don't do your job, I will terminate this apprenticeship. Check her.'

Manium inched closer and went to his knees. 'Checking,' he said, and grabbed her ankles. He ran his hands up her legs and gagged like he was being forced to gut a rotten fish.

His posture, the look on his face, the pungent musk of his sweat; it rankled. This man genuinely, wholeheartedly, believed he was better than her.

Bit by bit, as Manium squeezed and poked, Kavi's shame metamorphosed into flat-out disdain. Disdain for this man, his behaviour, his life, his upbringing, his beliefs. Everything. He repulsed her. And she let it show on her face.

Manium mechanically groped around her crotch, worked his way up her torso, and cupped her breasts with rough fingers. He glanced at her when she didn't react, and the expression he found on her face slapped away his lecherous disgust and replaced it with stunned outrage.

She could read him like a page from a Tsubumani novel. *How dare a Taemu look at me like that? Bitch. Whore. Red-eyed, subhuman cunt.*

'This test will gauge your ability to withstand the weight of the Jinn and the potency of their maayin,' the engineer said when Manium stepped away from her with bulging eyes. 'If you leave this building as a mage, you will understand it, and you will develop the ability, like a muscle, to bear the weight and the effects. But in the beginning, this is how it will feel, and if you cannot even remain conscious, there is no way you will ever learn.'

Kavi nodded.

The engineer strolled over to the testing device: a glass chamber with what appeared to be a free-standing torture rack. Twin cables – one gold, one black – and leather hand straps, worn and stretched by use, hung from a metal slab that jutted out over the chamber. The engineer sized her up and pulled a lever on the wall.

The slab groaned and dropped a few centimetres. 'You let go, fail. You pass out, fail. Disobey instructions? Fail. Hold on and stay conscious for the duration?' He gave her a mock salute. 'Congratulations. Pass. Next.'

Kavi wiped a layer of blood off her palms and grimaced at

the abrasive pain. It chafed both her hands *and* her temper that her only salwar-kameez – so clean and fresh that morning – was now torn and smeared with blood. She took off her chappals and walked into the device without looking at the men.

There were five pairs of footprints on the floor, painted black with subtle depressions that she could sink her feet into. She tested a couple and settled for the third set from the outside.

The straps overhead were soggy from the last candidate's sweat, the grooves she slipped her feet into were still warm, and everything stank like burned milk – a sign that artificed machinery had recently been used. She wrapped her fingers around the straps and clenched her fists, hissing as they dug into her palms.

The engineer gave her an approving nod and glanced at Manium. 'You can do this one, I want to keep an eye on the crystals.'

Manium pointed to himself. 'Sir-ji?'

'Take it through the levels.' The engineer pointed at the steel box facing the testing device. 'One minute at each. Dial it down to zero after she completes the minute at level three, or if she yields.'

He stepped into the device with Kavi and attached the two cables – gold to the base of her skull, black over her heart. The tiny metal disc at the end of each cable latched onto her skin with a soft *hiss*.

'Manium,' the engineer said when he was done.

'Sir-ji?'

'Don't fuck this up.'

Manium looked away and scowled. 'Yes, sir-ji.'

'Wait for me to set the timer,' the engineer said, slipping into the stack of machinery.

Kavi stared at the steel box, at its lone embedded dial, painted green with red numbers along its curvature. One minute at each amplifier. Three minutes and she could move on to the second test. She was finally—

Unseen chunks of metal slammed together. The engineer's voice, loud and commanding, pierced through the clamour. 'Timer ready!'

The dial filled her vision. Stubby fingers caressed it, squeezed it, and in a sharp motion, spun it all the way to three.

Her jaws clamped shut and her body locked itself in place. Pressure bloomed in her chest and spread outward, turning flesh into stone, bones into iron, making it hard to breathe, to move. Fire, white-hot and searing, entered through the base of her skull and screamed through her blood.

The muscles on her neck, her jaw, stretched as she fought to stay conscious. Her limbs convulsed, her heart pounded against her ribcage and threatened to bludgeon its way out of her chest. Blood vessels in her ear canal contracted. Something warm and wet trickled out of her ears and down the sides of her face.

A gong, loud and clear, pealed through the pain as the first wave of vertigo hit.

The room spun. Alien machinery flew, the rotund man with his fingers on the dial caterwauled. She squeezed her eyes shut. Locked her knees. *Not real.*

I'm not failing.

I am not failing.

She gritted her teeth and let spittle fly with each lung-shredding breath.

Aadhier Taemu. Aadhier-Taemu. AadhierTaemu. Over and over, like a mantra, she repeated the forbidden Taemu battle cry in her head until the words merged and morphed and lost their meaning. She swallowed her screams. Let the tears stream from her eyes.

Whispers from another life, harsh and nostalgic, hung in her consciousness like a crumbling ledge, and she latched on to them. *We were fearless, Kavi. We were warriors.*

Fearless. We were … A sorrow, so deep and timeless, stroked her heart with its frail fingers, and her chest shuddered as a sob twisted up and out of her throat.

Another gong, deeper than the first, ripped her awareness to shreds.

There was nothing beyond the pain and the pressure. The future disintegrated into specks and spots of red. The past detonated into dust. There was only one heartbeat, and then the next.

What was she doing? Why this stubborn desire to not give in? Why couldn't she just let go and accept the release. So easy. Just … let go.

But her eyes would not close, her knees would not give in, and her fingers would not release their grip on the straps.

Through the pressure and the fire, a face, nauseatingly soft, with large, gleeful eyes and a broad, pock-marked nose, smirked at her.

I know you.

Yes, you.

You think you can break me?

She forced her mouth – teeth already bared from the pain – into the shape of a sneer.

The apprentice blanched and reached for the dial.

Her rictus grin faltered. *Could it go up another level?* The edges of her vision were already going black; any more and she would pass out and fail the test.

The third gong boomed through the chamber, and the engineer emerged through the steam of a hissing valve. He froze.

'What—' His head swivelled between Kavi and the apprentice with his fingers on the dial. He dropped his spanner, leaped over a cylinder, and was at the steel box in two long strides. He slapped the apprentice on the side of the head – the man stumbled away with a yelp – and jammed the dial down.

Kavi collapsed, trembling uncontrollably and gasping for air. The stench of burnt milk filled her nostrils, and she gagged. Her legs gave way, but her wrists, which she must have somehow twisted around the straps, held her up.

'Get out,' the engineer said, towering over his apprentice.

'Sir-ji, but she—'

'Get. Out.' He flared his nostrils and jabbed a finger in the direction of the door.

Manium looked up with wounded eyes as he nursed his ear. 'My father—'

'Do you understand what would happen,' the engineer growled, 'if we allowed a candidate to die? If word got out that the first test killed someone?'

'But she—'

'Disbarment from the guild. Charges in court. If we're even alive to see the day.'

Manium's head swivelled between a sweat-soaked, barely conscious Kavi, and the furious engineer. 'She's not—'

'It does not matter.' The engineer dropped his voice to a whisper. 'When they let her set foot in here, none of that mattered anymore. The Jinn are blind, Manium. They don't see her like we do. They don't see a Taemu, or a woman.' He clenched his jaw. 'Imagine this, imagine she passes all three tests, goes to Azraaya, and reports what an apprentice engineer did—'

'My father—'

'Your father has influence in the Vagola?'

'He …' Manium clamped his mouth shut, glared at Kavi as his eyes teared up and his cheeks quivered.

It's all your fault, his eyes said, and in a way, he was right, all she'd done was deepen his hatred for her people. And one day, ten years or ten months down the line, someone else like her would pay for it. Kavi sighed and worked her wrists free, wincing as her numb fingers unclenched from the straps and her bloody palms came unstuck. Still, Manium could get fucked.

The door slammed shut as he left muttering under his breath about his father and some uncle in Azraaya.

The engineer turned to Kavi with a scowl. He studied her blood-smeared palms and wrists, watched her tear a strip off the bottom of her kameez, rip it in half, and tie it around her hands. With a weary sigh, he walked over to the table.

'Pass,' he said, and scrawled in the ledger. He jerked his chin at the exit. 'That way to the second test.'

Kavi walked over to the table with trembling legs and slung the satchel over her shoulder. 'Done?'

The engineer snorted. 'Want some more?'

'No.' She raised a bloody hand. 'Thanks.'

The engineer grunted.

She gave the chamber one last look, and stepped through the door onto another corridor, wider and longer than the first. A hawaldar squatted by the door, picking his nose with a relish that could only arise from a long stretch of sustained boredom.

'Stop,' he said, and narrowed his eyes.

Kavi blinked. 'Stop what?'

'That one.' He pointed the offending finger at a door midway down the corridor. 'Suman madam for you.'

She nodded and hobbled away, past rows of locked doors flanked by flowerpots, with blackboards hanging from their faces. One door – she cocked an eyebrow – even had a string of limes and chillis hanging over its frame to ward off evil spirits.

Too late, boss, I'm already in.

Names in white chalk identified the room's occupants: *Prof.*

Rettanmurthy, Fld Capt. Jomu, Sen Lec. Bunush, Archmage Sree Sree Manshi – one Sree before a name was a big deal, but *two?* This Manshi must shit gold. She walked past with a sigh, grateful that the honourable-most-esteemed Manshi would not test her, and stopped outside a door with a chalkboard that read: *Assoc Prof. Suman.*

Kavi reached for the door handle and hesitated. A heavy, nauseous unease settled in her gut. This was her last chance to turn back. If she twisted that door handle and stepped into that room, if the healer was right about her …

So what?

So what if she only lived another seven years?

When she was dead and her body was burned to ash, the sun would still rise, the trains would still depart, the beggars would still sit on the roadside with upturned palms and empty stomachs, the gangs would still bully and kill, the rich would still enforce their laws and kill. Time would continue. *So, stop thinking and move.*

Instead, her hand fell from the door handle. Thoughts of death and desperation, of failure and fear, all swirled and coalesced into a memory of her father's weather-beaten face as he looked down at her. There was a hint of disappointment in his eyes as he launched into his spiel about their ancestors – how they'd been uprooted en masse and forced into the spearhead of the Kraelish campaign to subjugate the subcontinent, and how centuries later, when the Taemu joined the Raayans and fought the Empire to a standstill in the Methun Revolt—

They paid for each drop of our blood with a litre of their own. A litre I tell you – sit still, dai! What is this, daughter? Are you done? Now listen. It was us, not the Nathrians, or the bleddy Raayans, us. All surrendered. But not us.

We fought artificed weapons with nothing but raw steel and fury.

We made them bleed for taking our home from us.

We were berserkers, Kavi. Fearless.

It didn't matter to her father that, for their role in the Methun Revolt, the Kraelish pushed her people to the brink of extinction.

Our swordmasters were executed, our women were sterilised, our men were indentured, our elders and our children were clubbed to death. He said this as if he were listing a bunch of achievements. *And when the Kraelish were done with Ethuran, they created new laws to deal with the Taemu scattered across the rest of Raaya. Gatherings of more than three? Not allowed. Our language? Cannot. Our religion? Our Gods? Forbidden. They started their blood banks. They cut out our tongues if we— Where're you going? I'm not done, girl.*

Sit.

Listen, we were the perfect scapegoats. Outsiders. Once the enemy's spear-tip, now a thorn lodged deep in their overextended buttocks. We made them look weak, showed the other colonies that the Empire was vulnerable. So, to teach us a lesson, to rub chilli powder into a gaping wound—

The Kraelish disseminated the notion that the Taemu were responsible for instigating the revolt, that the fault for the famine that followed, during which millions died from empty rotting stomachs, as well as all the suffering and punishment meted out to the rest of the subcontinent, lay solely on their shoulders.

The Raayans swallowed it up. *Thu-thu, chi-chi, evil bastards, of course it's all their fault, beat them, throw them out of our cities, take-break their swords and all that, but* – Kavi remembered Appa flashing her his crooked grin – *we're still here, eh?*

Yes, they were still here, three centuries later, still buried all the way at the bottom of the dogpile.

We were fearless.

Swordmasters.

Berserkers.

The words shuttled and warbled between her ears and Kavi swayed on unsteady feet.

Be proud.

We were warriors.

Her ears popped. She doubled over and vomited into the empty flowerpot by the door.

When she was done, and left with nothing but dry heaves and the thunder of death's lightning footsteps in her ears, she wiped her sweaty hands on her salwar and stood. Another memory, one far more recent, rose from the muck and sank its claws into her heart.

They sat in a circle, the four of them. Kamith on her left, Appa on her right, and little Khagan a warm bundle in her lap.

'Wait your turn, Kamith,' Appa said, and gently nudged her brother away.

He broke off a piece of roti, dipped and swirled it in the pale, diluted dal, and offered it to her.

She leaned over and he gently pushed it into her mouth.

The roti was stale and stiff, but the dal made it easier to chew. There were even a few soft lentils that burst in her mouth with unexpected flavour.

Appa fed Khagan next, a smaller piece, softened in the dal so he could chew. Then Kamith. And Kavi again.

'Appa, your turn,' she said, turning away from the piece of roti he held out to her.

He tsked. 'I'm fine. Eat.'

He skipped his turn, every single time, and fed them until there wasn't a single morsel left.

Kavi set her jaw, mastered the fluttering in her chest, and twisted the door handle.

You're wrong, Appa, we never stopped being warriors.

Chapter 12

Two sets of stony eyes looked up at her.

The first belonged to a large woman seated by a window at the back of the room. Cropped hair, tattooed chin, scarified arms with muscles that stretched her military uniform tight; she rested her hands on the hilt of a scabbarded sword lodged between her legs and studied Kavi with mute curiosity.

The second – a pair of kohl-lined eyes – examined Kavi through round, gold-rimmed spectacles that sat on a sharp nose attached to a face accoutred with the traditional Raayan piercings: twin studs in each ear and a ring through the right nostril.

Surprise flickered through the woman's smoky eyes. She gestured to the empty chair facing her desk. 'Sit.'

A single stick of jasmine incense simmered on a steel plate in the corner of the room, and its scent infused the air with an incongruous sense of calm. Kavi breathed deep as she arranged herself on the chair.

'My name is Suman Baelar,' the woman behind the desk said. 'Associate Professor for artificing at the Vagola, and this is' – she flicked a thumb at the woman by the window – 'Field-Blade Greema, who is present here today for … protection.'

Field-Blade Greema cleared her throat and spoke with a voice like gravel. 'Retired.'

'What?' Suman twisted in her chair to peer at the woman.

'Retired from the active service,' Greema said without expression. 'I will be training cadets this year.'

'Right, yes.' Suman waved a hand dismissively and turned back around to Kavi. 'And you are?'

'Kavithri Taemu, railway porter. Also retired.'

Suman tilted her head, studied the dishevelled hair and the blood-red irises, the bandaged hands wrapped around the satchel, the sweat-soaked, torn salwar-kameez, and pursed her lips.

'So, Kavithri, Tae-mu,' she said, lingering on the last name. 'Here's what will happen: when instructed, you will bind with the Cremoll.' She tapped the device that sat in the middle of the desk. 'Then, we will cycle through Garicelli's List. You will engage with a memory that evokes the emotion I read out. If it is accepted, the Cremoll will drain the memory. When it finds one that resonates with the Jinn, you will experience a mild concussion, and you will *see them.*

'If you are chosen, I will then administer the final test. If you are not, if at the end of the list you are still sitting here without a Jinn, you will lose the memories the Cremoll has taken and fail the tests.' Suman's lips curved, and her voice lilted with the familiar sound of mockery. 'And return to – what was it – railway portering?'

'No.' If she failed the test, she would have to first deal with Bhagu, then plan what to do with the next – the last – seven years of her life.

Suman's manicured eyebrows twitched. She adjusted her bindi with a delicate, hennaed finger, and opened the book in front of her.

Seconds passed. The artificer flipped a page. The Blade at her back studied her fingernails. Kavi opened her mouth to—

Suman raised a finger. 'Wait,' she said, and continued perusing the book.

Kavi reclined, cracked her neck, and rolled her sore shoulders. This was the closest she'd ever been to an artificer. To any mage – her unconscious encounter with the healer at the hospital didn't count, she barely remembered the bastard.

There was a quiet confidence in Suman's every action. Every movement was purposeful. The woman's fingers were always touching *something:* the pages of the book, her sari, the red bindi between her eyebrows, the varnished wood of the desk … was she seeing its fabric? Its *code,* as the artificers called it, the arrangement of particles that made the desk, *the desk.* The book, *the book.* Did the pattern pop out at her in bright-orange maayin? Was she channelling now? Altering the pages of the book, changing the shape of the dried ink?

No, she wouldn't for something so frivolous. The price, the artificer's countervail, memory, was too precious. Kavi had read that the vast majority of an artificer's training was spent on their counter. Learning which memories to use, what to leave untouched to preserve their identity and intellect, how to create and compartmentalise new, disposable memories.

Without taking her eyes off the book, Suman reached out and pushed the Cremoll to Kavi. 'Familiarise yourself with the device,' she said, and flipped another page.

This was an older Cremoll, sculpted to resemble a tiger's head; a facsimile of the device invented by the First Artificer, Kraelin, eponymous founder of the Kraelish Empire and all-round sadist who wanted the rest of the world to experience an artificer's countervail. The black marble had long, jagged indentations to mimic where the animal's stripes would normally be, and it was smoother than she'd imagined, soft, even.

A shudder ran through the device, and a bump, a new distension in the marble, gradually rose and swelled on the tiger's head. Kavi snatched her hand away and gaped as the protuberance travelled down the Cremoll, past the ears, through the space between the eyes, and down into its jaws, where it throbbed before slowly shrinking into nothing. A shudder ran through the head and the jaws hissed open. A curtain of velvety black hung from the roof of its marble mouth to the base of its lower incisors.

Kavi reached out, tentatively ran a finger down the length of the darkness. *Nothing.* It looked tangible but had no substance. She pushed at it and her fingers slipped through without resistance.

'The entire hand,' Suman said. The artificer had shut her book and was watching Kavi over her spectacles.

Kavi nodded. Edged the rest of her hand into the Cremoll, all the way to her wrist.

She'd dreamed of this moment, played out all the scenarios, from the worst (the Cremoll's jaws clamp shut and it bites her hand off) to the best—

'Awe.'

Kavi blinked.

'Awe,' Suman said, and scratched something off on a piece of paper. 'I will repeat myself one more time, then move on to the next memory.'

Kavi had prepared them, chosen carefully. Some memories were important, some she was happy to be rid of. But she'd assumed she'd be given time to—

'Awe.'

The Picchadi matches. Kavi had stood, tucked away in the nosebleeds, and added her voice to the roar of the crowd as the invading athletes dived under outstretched arms, weaved between bodies, and lunged to return to their half of the field. The speed, the skill, the power in their legs. *Awe.*

The eyes on the Cremoll flashed. Suman's eyes turned chalk-white.

Kavi blinked. She felt a heartbeat of disorientation, followed by an absence. Something was missing. She didn't know what, but whatever it was, was lost forever.

Suman nodded as her eyes unclouded. 'Amusement.'

The pig. Slum-crusher Pedda-pandi. It was the size of a six-month-old ox calf. Its matted black fur was covered with slime and it left dung and destruction in its wake as it rampaged through the slums. She sat outside her hut and watched challenger after challenger attempt to wrestle the beast into submission and fail. Kavi smiled.

A flash. A sense of emptiness. Suman spoke. 'Confusion.'

The rust-laced air of an abandoned factory. Kavi had opened bleary eyes to find two strange men where her father and brothers should have been. They dragged her by the collar and threw her into the back of a cart where a huddle of terrified children sat sobbing.

Why? Who are these people? What do they want with me? She would soon find out, but for now, she was—

'Confusion,' Suman said.

Kavi hesitated. Glanced at the Cremoll. The eyes remained black. Why wasn't it working? She tried again. Relived the morning the beggar cart stole her from her family. She didn't want this memory. It could go. It could—

'Confusion,' Suman said again, and scribbled on the paper.

What? Why was it rejecting the memory? 'Wait—'

'Disgust.'

She stowed away the confusion about Confusion. Moved on. Disgust . . .

The latrines at the railway station. *No.* The clean up after the Raethsera festival at the seaside brothel. All the gunk and dried-up ejaculate and other ambiguous still-warm fluids that coated every inch of every—

The eyes flashed. Kavi lost what she assumed was a semi-precious memory. Suman made a face and tsked. 'Surprise.'

Garicelli's List was not a comprehensive catalogue of every emotion a human could experience. It was a collection, curated by trial and error, for what had previously worked and bridged the gap between man and Jinn. Suman skipped around, went from Disgust to Surprise to Joy, then circled back to Anxiety, Boredom, and Fear. The eyes on the Cremoll flashed when it detected the emotion the artificer had calibrated it to receive and a layer of white would fall over Suman's eyes as she experienced the memory via the device.

The Cremoll siphoned them all away, left Kavi with seconds of disorientation, but failed to activate the Bridge. None of them worked.

No mild concussion. No perceptual shift to another plane of existence. No Jinn clamouring over who would have the honour of choosing her as their mage. But with each new utterance, with each memory sacrificed, Suman's ire grew, and her impatience manifested itself in clipped words and sucked-in cheeks.

Halfway through the list, Suman drummed her fingers on the table, and said, 'Craving.'

Chapter 13

Kavi had prepared two very different memories for this one. If the first failed, the second would surely work.

When she was new to the railway porter game, when she was still learning how to approach passengers with an acceptable mixture of subservience and wretchedness, she'd often return home empty-handed and hollow-bellied. On one such evening, she'd stopped outside a samosa stand, enchanted by the scents wafting over, and watched the vendor deep-fry his samosas in a gigantic kadai. She'd ogled as he scooped them out and aired them on the counter, as he squeezed a dollop of spicy-sour tamarind sauce onto a folded newspamphlet and added a samosa to the makeshift plate. Drooled as a customer bit into the crunchy pastry, chewed on the delicate filling and licked his lips. Kavi swallowed.

The Cremoll was still.

'Craving,' Suman said with a frown.

I was right. The Cremoll wanted a different sort of Craving. More base. She sighed. There was no way to engage with this memory without triggering all the others attached to it, but to be honest, they could all go. Kavi puffed out her cheeks and remembered Sila.

Bumping into her at the water pump for the first time.

Shock-surprise. The woman had acknowledged her with a smile and a nod instead of keeping her distance, giving her the side-eye, or swearing at her. As a result, something new, something warm and tingly, took root inside Kavi. And the next time, another smile. An exchange of words.

Where are you from? Kavi asked.

Jedanpur.

How come you left?

Ran away, escaped an arranged marriage to a licentious second cousin.

And now?

Ayah for a family across the bridge, saving to open a bangle shop in the bazaar.

The woman had a quiet voice, and it forced Kavi to inch closer. She revelled in the proximity. Breathed in the pang of the woman's sweat, the scent of the coconut oil in her hair and the cheap talcum powder she used on her armpits. The woman was not interested in Kavi's name but was kind enough to share her own. Silavati. Sila.

Kavi started timing her trips to the water pump, loitering with an empty bucket until she saw the woman. At the dhobi ghat, out of the corner of her eye, she'd watch Sila wash her clothes and bash them against the smooth flogging stone as her damp sari clung to her body. She would stop, occasionally, to tuck a stray strand of hair behind an ear, and Kavi would stare, mesmerised by the sheen of sweat on her dark skin, the long braid slung over a shoulder or nestled between her breasts.

That afternoon, Kavi had waited for over an hour on the periphery of the water pump. But Sila never showed. Worried, concerned, and more than a little curious, she'd rushed over to the woman's hut.

The monsoon was on its way, and a quiet, earthy breeze

drifted up from the sea, carrying with it a sound that would haunt Kavi for months to come. She followed the moans, the hushed whispers, and the rustling of clothes to the window of the hut. She flipped her empty bucket and stood on it.

And there she was, sari discarded in a heap and blouse bunched around her waist. Sila straddled a man, gently thrust her hips into his pelvis with her eyes rolled up into her head. Kavi gripped the windowsill, and stared, bug-eyed, as the man traced the scar under Sila's navel with hairy fingers. She followed his grubby hands as he squeezed and touched. As he forced a thumb into Sila's mouth and she bit down on it. He tugged it away, slapped her breast, pinched and twisted a nipple.

Sila gasped, swatted the hand away and leaned over. She held the man's hands over his head, whispered in his ear before kissing him on the lips. The man moaned into her mouth, his back arched as she ground her—

Kavi ducked her head and lowered herself onto the bucket-stool. She sat with the thunder of her heartbeat in her ears, and a hollow ache in her chest. *Why?* Why did it hurt? She was no one to Sila. This was no betrayal. But still, it hurt, and mixed in with that hurt, twisting and tinting it, was a layer of long-neglected desire.

That night, as Kavi lay on her mat among the snores and flatulence of the exhausted workers in the common hut, she closed her eyes, and yearned for that intimacy, that contact. She dreamed of Sila's parted lips on hers, Sila's hands intertwined in hers, Sila's whispers for her and her alone. Her fingers traced Sila's scar, her hands circled Sila's breasts and brushed against the ring of fine hair that surrounded Sila's puffy nipples; but she wouldn't slap or pinch, no, she'd use her tongue.

Kavi woke with a dry mouth and a body soaked in sweat. With a ragged breath, and a glance around to make sure no one was looking, she flipped onto her stomach and allowed her hands to slither down—

The Cremoll flashed.

Kavi started at the sudden, inexplicable warmth in her crotch. *What the Hel?*

Suman's mouth twisted as her eyes cleared. 'You—'

A tingle ran up Kavi's arm and a full-body hammer blow slammed her back into her seat. The roar of a cyclone filled her ears. Her vision brightened until all she could see was the cruel outline of the woman behind the desk. She squeezed her eyes shut.

When she opened them, there was nothing.

No sound. No room. No chair. No woman talking down to her.

No limbs. Or body.

She didn't exist outside of an inconsequential flicker of awareness that floated in a vast black nothingness.

Then there was rage. Blood-red and furious, it called her name.

KAVI.

KAVITHRI.

In a sepulchral whisper, it spoke the forbidden Taemu battle cry in her ear. *Aadhier Taemu.*

Kavi hissed. *Shut up shut up, they'll hear you, they'll—*

The darkness pulsed.

Once.

Twice.

Where there was nothing was now the contour of a red circle that embraced a piece of the darkness. It sang of violence, of death, of vengeance. Kavi blinked lidless eyes and there was another. Then another.

Five perfect circles punctuated the infinite emptiness. So

large that she was barely a speck before them. Red. Green. White. Orange. And blue.

The red circle summoned her. And she obeyed. She drifted through the dark, reached out to the Jinn, and fed it her pain. Her sorrow. Her anger.

It answered.

Kavi threw back her head and screamed. She howled and thrashed as the weight of centuries of suffering crashed into her, and in that vast emptiness the loneliness, the fear, it finally crept up on her. She was going to die.

I don't want to die.

I-don't-want-to-die.

Idon'twanttodie.

The flat of a hand pressed itself into her back. And pushed.

Please. Help me.

Another hand joined the first. And another. And another. Inch by inch, they pushed her flagging body upright.

Kavi twisted her head, expected to find a set of disembodied arms attached to her back, but there were none. Instead, thick blue cables, like the ones from the bridge that connected the slums to the city, coiled away from her to join with the edge of the blue circle. A peace unlike anything she'd ever experienced pulsed through the cables and into her body.

She drifted away from the red circle, latched onto the blue cables, and dragged herself to their source. Her feet found purchase. She stepped through the blue, and into—

—the rust-laced air of an abandoned factory. Cruel eyes stripped her bare, a rough hand shoved her tiny, emaciated chest.

'Appa?'

Coin changed hands. The tall man with blood in his eyes turned his back on her.

'Appa?'

New hands dragged her away.

'Appa?'

The man bent, picked up a mewling baby and propped him on his hip. On his other flank, another boy wiped the tears and snot off his face and reached for her.

'Akka,' he whispered.

The man grabbed the boy's outstretched hand and yanked him away. With baby in one arm and boy in the other hand, he walked away from her.

'Ap—'

'*—pa?*' She opened her eyes to a warm grey ceiling.

'—overacting,' Suman was saying. 'Get her up.'

Large hands gripped her wrists and hauled her to her feet. Kavi stumbled. She was still in the nothingness with the Jinn, in a dream about her father, in a memory that couldn't be real. Her lips trembled as she searched the artificer's office. *Can't be real.*

'Appa?' she whispered and looked up at Greema, the Field-Blade.

Suman snorted.

Greema squeezed Kavi's shoulder and said in a soft rumble, 'Your father is not here.'

She righted the fallen chair and guided Kavi into it.

Suman flipped the hourglass on the table, the fine grains of white sand gushed through the narrow aperture. 'Were you chosen?'

Kavi gave her an absent-minded nod. *It never happened.*

Suman cocked an eyebrow. 'Your lies won't help you here, Taemu.'

That was not what happened. Appa would never – he would never … *would he?* A chill ran up her spine and goosebumps rippled across her skin.

She saw her father's face suspended in that nothingness. The lines and wrinkles, the dry lips and thick hair surrounding them, the red irises. Slender fingers reached around and dug into the skin on his face. Deeper and deeper until they were submerged to the knuckles. They twitched, then pulled. Dragged their way across an expressionless face, ripped it to shreds, and underneath, instead of pallid bone and gory flesh, was another face.

The woman from her nightmare in the hospital, the one who'd sent her into the tunnels. This was another false memory caused by her concussions. It had to be. The woman had the same proud chin, the same sad, tearful eyes – a word, a label drenched in meaning and love and absence wormed its way into Kavi's head and attached itself to the face.

Amma?

Walls, heavy and unyielding, slammed down and crushed the face to a bloody mush.

Kavi blinked, swayed in her chair. What was she just thinking about? She stared at the Cremoll, at the tiger-head, dark as night, and with eyes of shimmering blue.

Blue?

Kavi started. The eyes on the Cremoll had turned blue.

Nilasi had chosen.

She was a healer.

Chapter 14

She would live.

The sahib was wrong, his so-called sources, the quack-healer ... all wrong. She was not an Azir. She was a healer, and she would live!

Live to see her thirties and her forties, navigate an existential crisis, endure the slow decline of her faculties, withstand the withering of her body, eat and drink and belch and fart and settle into the comfortable senility of old age. Warmth radiated through her chest and her hands tingled. She would live.

The eyes on the Cremoll flickered, wavered, and turned red.

Kavi's heart sank.

Suman sat up in her chair.

Greema, who was still on her feet, frowned and leaned in for a closer look.

A ripple ran through the Cremoll. The eyes went dark. They flashed. First one eye, then the next.

Left eye: Red. Right eye: Blue.

They swapped. Again. And again. Faster, then slower, then faster.

Kavi held her breath, dug her fingers in the strap of her satchel as the vacillations slowed, sputtered and settled into a deep red in one eye, and cerulean blue in the other. The curtain of black in the Cremoll's mouth fizzled out. Its jaws hissed shut. They were right, Bithun and his healer. She was a hybrid. An Azir.

Suman snapped her fingers. Gestured at Greema. 'Nilasi for the third test.'

The Blade nodded and left the room.

Kavi barely noticed. A scream formed and gathered strength at the base of her throat. She fought it down. Clasped her hands in her lap and stared through the artificer and out the window at the branches and gently swaying hanging beards of a banyan tree.

One thing at a time. She would come to terms with this, like everything else, in time.

Time.

Her lips trembled.

Remember why you're here. The third test. Suman would explain what she was supposed to do. *Get through this. Think later.*

But the colours, blue and red, meant Nilasi and Raktha. She had no idea what this combination meant. Those Jinn were direct opposites. One was used to heal, the other to destroy. How did her maayin even work? Could she heal? Could she use Raktha like the Biomancers from the stories did to modify and enhance parts of her body? What was she now? Suman would tell her. Right? *Right?* She glanced at the artificer, and the malicious glee in Suman's eyes rammed a barbed bolt of alarm through her chest.

'Shall we begin?' Suman said, fighting to keep a straight face.

Kavi glanced at the birdcages Greema set down on the desk. At the mynahs trapped within. At their yellow beaks and feet, their brown wings, and the small, stocky chests beneath. She blinked at the muscular Blade looming over them with a slim dagger in one hand.

'You are familiar with the healer's countervail?' Suman asked. 'With Nilasi's price?'

'Life force,' Kavi said, staring at the birds. 'Non-human life force.'

'Excellent.' Suman pointed at one of the birds. 'This one's your counter. Proceed.'

Greema unlatched a birdcage.

'Wait,' Kavi said. 'Aren't you going to tell me—'

'What?' Suman said with a cocked eyebrow.

'How to—'

'I don't know.'

'What?'

Suman sucked her lips in. 'I don't know.'

'If the tester does not have the knowledge,' Kavi said, reciting words from an old textbook, 'they are required to summon a mage who does. The candidate must be given every opportunity to demonstrate that they can be an instrument for the Jinn.'

Suman motioned to the Blade, and the warrior sheathed her dagger and locked the cage.

'Don't you see?' Suman shuffled to the edge of her seat and rested her chin on the base of a palm. 'There is no one.'

'No one?' Kavi repeated with a dry mouth.

'Yes, no one.' Suman nodded. 'No one in this building, no one in Raaya, or the subcontinent, or the civilised world. Kavithri Tae-mu, no one has ever understood how the Raktha-Nilasi hybrid works.'

'There must be books, or records—'

'Have a seat, Field-Blade Greema,' Suman said with a dismissive wave. 'Allow me to educate the candidate.'

She turned back to Kavi. 'You're familiar with records, are you? Read much at the railway station?'

'I—'

'I will allow you a little knowledge,' Suman said. 'It will not change the outcome, today, but you've made it this far, and it would be … unfair to send you back empty-handed.'

Empty-handed?

'The Jinn are forces of nature that coexist, but do not mix well,' Suman said. 'When a mage is chosen by two Jinn, the secondary Jinn – the Jinn who chose the mage second – modifies the maayin from the primary Jinn. And the primary Jinn – the Jinn who chose the mage first – corrupts the maayin from the secondary. When Nilasi corrupts Zubhra, you have necromancy. When Zubhra modifies Kolacin,' she snapped her fingers, 'mylothurgy. Some hybrids have one ability that breaks all the rules, others have two that bend them. Your people were the only ones to have Rakthan hybrids …'

Kavi sat up straight.

Suman's eyes widened ever so slightly. 'You don't know? You don't know.' She chuckled, a low, menacing hiccup that made Kavi want to lunge at her. 'Raktha almost only ever chooses Taemu. Why do you think there are no more Biomancers?'

'I read—'

'The Kraelish exterminated the entire lot after the Methun Revolt. The slaughter jolted Raktha into silence – shocked it away from our world and made it bleed.' Suman fingered the gold bangle on her wrist. 'Just like its mages.'

Kavi stared at the desk in stunned silence. All this while she'd thought of herself as an autodidact – she gritted her teeth. *How fucking arrogant.* There were layers under layers of knowledge the intelligentsia kept buried under their institutions and labels and education. What else were they hiding?

'And now, when it chooses again, after all this time …' Suman ran her eyes down Kavi's body and back up to her face. 'It is silenced by Nilasi. Fitting. Your own people would've called you an abomination and locked you up. Isolated you and never allowed you to be within a metre of another human ever again.'

'But—'

'Enough!' Suman slapped the desk and startled the caged mynahs into a series of squawks. 'Since there is no process to test for your hybrid, and since Nilasi was one of the Jinn that chose you, we will run its version of the third test.'

She twisted in her chair. 'Does that seem fair to you, Field-Blade Greema?'

The Blade's eye twitched, but she nodded.

Suman inclined her head. 'You may proceed.'

Greema got to her feet. Undid the latch of a cage and extracted a writhing, screeching bird. She held it flat against the desk, and with her other hand, she slipped her dagger out of its sheath, and rammed it into the mynah's chest.

Chapter 15

Blood pooled under the mynah's body and stained its feathers. It convulsed. Flapped its wings and splattered Suman and Kavi with its blood.

Suman flinched, shuddered, and reached for her handkerchief.

Kavi's hands shook as she used a sleeve to wipe the blood off her face.

'First one today,' Suman said with a grimace.

Kavi blinked. 'What?'

'The Nilasian version of the third test.' Suman gestured to the dying bird. 'So messy—' She twisted her neck to glare at the Blade. 'Nothing to put under it?'

Greema shrugged.

'A towel? A piece of cloth?'

Greema grunted.

'Anything?'

'No.'

Suman sighed. She put away her handkerchief and rapped her knuckles on the roof of the birdcage with the shrieking mynah. 'All right, let's get on with it. Summon Nilasi's maayin and command it to heal. Then leverage the countervail, sit back, relax, and pass the test.'

Kavi frowned. Nilasi had chosen second. She was sure of it, which meant, 'You said it was corrupt.'

Suman scoffed. 'I did, didn't I?'

'So how—'

'Don't know. I would show you if I could.' Suman bit her lip to keep her smirk from spreading. 'As you so wisely pointed out, the maayin from Nilasi is corrupt, so ...'

The bird in the cage, the countervail, shrieked and flapped its wings, spun on its tiny claws and screamed some more; almost as if it knew what Suman was asking Kavi to do.

'I have given you the instructions to pass Nilasi's third test,' Suman said over the racket, and glanced at Greema out of the corner of her eye. 'Isn't that right, Field-Blade?'

Greema narrowed her eyes at the back of the artificer's head. 'Those are the instructions for Nilasi's third test.'

Suman raised her hands. 'There you go. I've done my part.'

Kavi stared at the elaborate patterns of henna on the artificer's palms. The vines that wound around her fingers and joined the intricate reddish-brown tapestry on her palms; the flowers and leaves and intricate dot work. Someone must have spent hours on that. Maybe her daughter? Her sister? A friend? Kavi studied her own hands, wrapped in torn cloth, and soaked in dark blood.

There had to be something. Something that could help her. Guide her. A reference. A memory. Something she'd read.

Acid scorches through my veins, and the weight of a dead God's soul settles on my shoulders.

Kavi blinked. *The Diary of an Unknown Mage.*

I am tired, reader. Tired of the endless commentary by men who will never fight. Tired of how they talk and argue and ignore the bottomless poverty of our people. There is only one language the Empire speaks, and it begins and ends with violence.

The Jinn senses my intention, reacts to it because it is parallel to their truth. Harith's maayin oozes out of my pores and I sculpt it into a dozen knives.

That was it. *Intention.*

What did she want to do with maayin?

Heal the bird. Save its life.

'I don't have all day,' Suman said, interlacing her fingers under her chin. 'There are other … matters to attend to.'

Kavi blocked the artificer out. She had to save the mynah. *Wanted* to save its life. It was her. Kept in a cage. Wings clipped. Dreaming of flight. But dragged out, stabbed in the chest, and left to bleed out on a table under hostile and indifferent eyes.

She threw every ounce of her will at the bird. *Live.*

The mynah's wings fluttered. Its heartbeat slowed.

Live. Please.

She imagined the blue strands of Nilasian maayin, which should be visible only to its healer, flowing from her skin to the dying bird; from the dying bird to the countervail; from the countervail back to her. A price. A wound for a wound. A life for a life.

Her thoughts took a sharp left, angled into the plight of the bird acting as the countervail, but Kavi tightened her lips, and forced them back on track. She was the catalyst. She was supposed to be the healer. She clenched her fists and tried again.

Nothing. No weight on her shoulders. No fire in her veins.

Was her intention not pure enough? Was her desire to succeed clouding her intention?

That wasn't it. It was like the artificer said, her maayin was different, corrupt, it bent and broke the rules, so whatever she was trying, it was wrong. She was doomed to fail long before Greema had stabbed the poor bird. It was all for nothing. A little spark of life extinguished just to make a point.

A spasm ran through the bird's tiny chest. Blood dribbled down the sides of its twitching beak, and with one final anticlimactic shudder, it went still. The countervail, the mynah left alive, went silent. It hopped closer to the bars of its cage, bobbed its head as it searched the room, stopped, and pecked the wood under its claws.

'The candidate has failed the third test,' Suman announced and pounded a rubber stamp into a piece of paper. She turned to Kavi with a friendly smile. 'You will remain a dormant Azir, free to carry on with your business.'

Why was the woman so happy?

Why the fuck is she so happy?

The tears welled up and leaked out as Kavi let her anger plunge into a pit of impotent helplessness. Maybe they were right after all. Maybe she *was* different. If this was the humanity she was striving for, this perverted, repugnant version of humanity that had trickled down from the Kraelish; this ease with which they labelled and classified and promoted and demoted; the glee with which they tore each other down and watched each other fail; if this was what it meant to be human then she would gladly be called subhuman.

'Please, escort her out,' Suman said, studying the dead bird with dispassionate eyes. 'There are valuable items in the building, so see her to the gate.'

Kavi stood and turned her back on the pair. Her face scrunched up as she fought and failed to keep the tears in her eyes and the snot in her nostrils. The broken nail on her big toe hurt like Hel, but she favoured the foot, leaned into it and welcomed the pain as she walked out of the room.

She shut the door and stood shaking in the empty corridor. All her plans, her dreams, her resolve, it all came crumbling down like a shattered gas lamp. Splinters stuck in her skin, reminded her that she could've walked away, had a new life as a clerk, but she chose ... *She chose.*

Kavi viciously wiped her face with the back of her shaking hands. She had no right to weep and whimper. She'd walked in here, on her own two feet, of her own volition. If she'd listened to Bithun, she could've— She clenched her jaw. *Not now, not going down the gully.* She would mourn, then she would find the sahib. See what he had to say, then search for a meaning and a purpose in the last seven years of her life. She adjusted the satchel to sit on her hip just as the Blade stepped out and shut the door behind her.

'Follow,' Greema said, and set out down the corridor.

Kavi fell into step.

She stared at Greema's huge shoulders; at the fluid muscle bunched under the uniform, the scarred forearms that swung menacingly at the woman's sides. Strange that she was here in Bochan, working for an artificer. Blades were trained almost exclusively for warlocks as a foil for their countervail. Most considered them a relic, an echo of a time when warlocks knew how to link with a non-mage and enhance both their abilities. True Blades, the ones before the Retreat, could somehow bond with a warlock and share their countervail, which, under normal circumstances, would paralyse the warlock. But bonded with a Blade, warlocks could move, and it made them doubly lethal. The bond went the other way, too, it gave the Blade strength, speed, and a heightened awareness of maayin. A cadre of bonded Blades and warlocks could once take down entire cities on their own.

Greema glanced at Kavi over her shoulder and Kavi looked away.

The chin tattoo – the sharp lines angling down from the corners of her mouth to resemble fangs – was a rite of passage for warriors of the Gashani hill-tribes, the original inhabitants of the subcontinent who the Republic refused to acknowledge as indigenous. And the latticework of scars on Greema's arms would mean that the Blade had seen action in the Nathrian skirmishes … or she'd tripped and rolled around in a pile of broken glass.

She kept her eyes on Greema's back and focused on catching her breath. The sudden awareness of her own limited existence was starting to suffocate her. It usually sat at the back of her head, ignored and unobtrusive, so she could carry on like everyone else and pretend it wasn't ever going to happen. But now, every breath she took was another step closer. Just like the widows in the northern districts, forced to walk – drugged out of their minds – into the pyres of their dead husbands. She was them. Only her walk would last seven years.

'Wait,' Greema said, and came to a stop.

Kavi stumbled to avoid barrelling into the woman's back.

'Stay here until I return,' Greema said, brows furrowed. 'I won't be long.' And without waiting for Kavi to respond, she strode back to Suman's office.

Kavi took the last couple of steps out of the corridor, and into the courtyard, where she shut her eyes and took a long, deep breath. And when she opened them, he was there. Bhagu. Waiting in the corner with a beedi in his mouth.

Kavi blinked.

His outline blurred and shimmered under the rays of the setting sun. It grew, transformed into a grey-black shadow with claws and wings and feathers and beaks. She squeezed her eyes shut. Opened them. It was just Bhagu. Just another man brainwashed into hating her. Not a monster. Just a man.

Bhagu dropped his beedi, crushed and muted the hiss underfoot, and stepped out of the shadow of the building.

'I told you I'd be waiting,' he said, a cruel smile widening on his lips. 'Did you really think you would pass? That you would be a mage?'

She stared at him. Numb. Exhausted. Disconnected.

He strolled up to her, spat at her feet, and reached for her collar.

Kavi let go, and her body moved. It leaned away and let his hand clutch at the empty space where she'd stood a heartbeat ago.

Bhagu's eyes gleamed as he lunged at her again.

She sidestepped. Let him stumble past. And scoffed.

He froze. The veins on his forehead stood and his mouth twisted before settling back into a grin. He cracked his neck and watched her with cold, hard eyes.

Kavi matched his gaze. 'I'm already dead, you fuck,' she said in a voice she barely recognised. 'Come, do your worst.'

He closed the gap with a snarl. Arms outstretched, poise forgotten, face contorted with a hate so pure she could never reason with it.

But he was slow. Too slow. She could see the whites of his bulging eyes. The stains on his burned lips. The spittle flying from them.

She waited till he was almost upon her. Then ducked under his arms and shoved him aside. She wanted to infuriate him. Humiliate him. Give him a taste of what it felt like, for just a moment, to be her.

He spun on his heel. Roared and launched himself at her.

She had nothing to lose. Nothing to live for. No reason to continue fighting the berserker. She clenched a fist and opened herself to the rage—

'You must promise, Kavi,' Appa said, 'to never give in to your anger.'

'I promise,' she said, holding a pouch of uncooked rice in her tiny hands.

'Bad things happen when Taemu allow their anger to take over,' he said in an oddly high-pitched voice that she found both unsettling and eerily familiar. He brushed a strand of hair away from her forehead and tucked it behind her ear. 'When you start to feel angry, count the grains in your pouch. Feel each grain, press it into your fingertips, and move on to the next.'

She squeezed the pouch and nodded.

'Promise me, Kavi.'

'I promise, Amma.'

Kavi started. *Amma?* She didn't remember – why couldn't she remember? And the pouch of rice … that never happened. What was wrong with her?

She hesitated. And Bhagu's eyes flashed with triumph.

There was a blur, the *smack!* of a fist meeting flesh, and Kavi stared at Greema's large back and massive shoulders.

'Hawaldar,' Greema said, one hand clamped around Bhagu's fist, which was halfway to her throat, 'why have you left your post?'

Bhagu blinked. Studied Greema's military uniform, and wilted. He lowered his fists, bobbed his head, muttered an insincere apology, and subsided with a limp salute. He glared at Kavi as he ambled away, and she acknowledged the promise in his eyes. *This isn't over*, it said. Bully and bullied were barrelling into a reckoning, and whether or not she liked it, she would have to prepare.

'Taemu,' Greema said without looking at Kavi, 'it is time for you to leave.'

They arrived at the gate to find it locked and unmanned. The sleepy hawaldar from earlier had left his post to chat with the jalebi vendor who was in the process of packing up.

Greema rattled the gate. The hawaldar tsked and peered at her. His eyes went wide, and he snapped her a salute before rushing over. Greema growled at him while he fumbled with the lock and stammered something about his tea break.

Kavi gripped the strap of her satchel until her skinned palms burned. This was it. She'd made it in. And failed. All her plans were in the gutter.

The gate groaned as the hawaldar dragged it open. 'Sorry, memsaab.' He snapped another salute at Greema. 'Fully open now.'

Greema spared him a glance and peered at Kavi from under furrowed brows. She crossed her arms. 'Taemu, where did you learn to move like that?'

'Eh?' Kavi blinked and loosened her grip on her satchel strap. She scratched her chin and peered at the Blade. 'Uhm, I don't know ... why?'

Greema gestured for Kavi to follow her out the gate. 'What are your plans now?'

Plans? Kavi snorted. 'No plans, memsaab.'

They stopped, just out of earshot of the curious hawaldar, and Greema stretched with a sigh. 'Can you use a weapon?'

'No.' Could chappals be considered weapons? 'Well—'

'Any experience in hand-to-hand combat?'

Kavi scratched her chin. 'I've been in a few scuffles.'

'You understand the warlock's countervail?' Greema asked. 'Their Jinn?'

'Harith?' Kavi nodded. 'Yes, I've read—'

'Do you think the sahib who bought you your way into the Branch would lend you five thousand rayals?'

'What? Memsaab?'

'Five thousand rayals.' Greema twisted her hips until there was an audible crack. 'You think he'll give it to you?'

'I— What?' Kavi shook her head. 'I don't—'

'With some training, I think you can be a Blade.'

Kavi went completely still. A knot in her stomach slowly wound itself tight. 'Memsaab?'

Chapter 16

'Candidates for the Blade programme at the Vagola are recruited from military academies and active duty,' Greema said. 'Everyone else with a death wish can pay the fee and enter the Siphon – a three-month crash course, a winnowing, an opportunity for twenty-five candidates without military experience to earn a place at the Vagola.' She cocked an eyebrow at Kavi. 'If you have no plans, and if you can get the money for the fee …'

She'd heard about the Siphon. About how the city of Azraaya came to a standstill once a year for the event. How most of the entrants died gruesome deaths while spectators watched and cheered and gambled.

She swallowed. Could she?

Maybe.

It had never occurred to her before, and it was a long shot. But it was another path into the Vagola. An unlikely one, for her, and one that would require a lot more guts and sweat and blood, but it was a way in. It could still give her access to its archives and libraries, to knowledge of the Venator, to its location, and – she'd figure the rest out.

She peered up at Greema. *Any place where you won't get wet is also where you will never have sunlight,* the Unknown Mage wrote in one of their parables. It was true. And if Greema could do it, if a woman from the Gashani tribes, only a rung above her on the ladder, could do it, then so could she.

Hope, intoxicating and miasmic, took control of Kavi's tongue, and she heard herself say, 'When does it start?'

'Hmm?'

'The Siphon,' Kavi said, 'When does it start?'

Greema's lips curled, ever so slightly, into a smile. 'In four months.'

Four months to prepare.

Kavi saluted, knuckles to forehead, palm facing the salutee, just like she'd learned at the railway station. 'Thank you, memsaab.'

Greema waved it off. 'I will see you at the Vagola, if you survive.'

Kavi stayed in the salute until the Blade disappeared back into the gate.

She let her arm fall with a sigh. Puffed out her cheeks, adjusted the satchel over her shoulder, and started out in the direction of the Dowhar Bridge.

'Taemu!'

Kavi froze. Ducked her head and turned around.

Greema was standing outside the gate with an arm raised. 'Good luck!'

Kavi blinked, and slowly mimicked the Blade's gesture. 'You, too.'

Greema nodded, let her arm drop, and walked back into the Branch.

You too? Kavi made a face. She should have thanked the woman again. You, too. As if they were friends or battle-worn companions leaving on missions. Hopefully she'd be more eloquent when she told Bithun how she'd fucked everything up and *oh, also, sahib, please may I borrow five thousand rayals so I can go get murdered in Azraaya? Only five thousand thankyouverymuch.*

She adjusted the satchel-strap again and set out. Limped and weaved through foot traffic like a wraith. Crossed the intersection and weathered the assault on her senses as she slipped into the bazaar. The kilometre-long stretch of gastronomic temptation was packed and she kept her eyes averted out of habit.

The subsequent section of market, where merchants sold a more material sort of enticement, was equally rambunctious: Raayan linen fluttered in the breeze, gilded saris were unfurled and displayed, pots and pans and spatulas clanged and clattered.

This was the only place where all the social classes in Bochan collided. You had the households of the sahibs, the politicos, the descendants of old aristocracy, and the wealthier merchants who made up the upper classes. Then there was the middle class with its multitude of subclasses, all the way from lawyers and surgeons to factory owners, priests, military officers, steam-rickshaw mechanics, newspamphlet publishers, academics, and clerks. The lower classes, who would ordinarily be serving or working for—

Kavi froze. Blinked. Stared at a raucous group haggling down a frazzled bangle vendor.

It was them. The crew from Aunty-ji's seaside brothel.

She took a step back and out of the foot traffic. There was lanky Dharavi who was always chewing on her fingernails; Komal with her shifty eyes that never really looked at you; boisterous Latta who seemed to be in charge of all the haggling; dignified Tachaini who watched the others without expression; and in the middle of them all, with each slender arm linked through one of the others, was Dremanth. Head and face clean-shaven, long lashes curled, the scar on the side of his mouth turning his smile lopsided; she could still hear his soft, musical voice from that one time he'd spoken to her. When he'd caught her staring at him, and smiled, made her heart flutter, and walked over to where she was swabbing the floor.

Looking at my scar? he'd said.

Kavi swallowed. She had been *ogling*, yes, but not at a mark on his face, at everything: the shape of his mouth and the dimples in his cheeks, the brittle curiosity in his eyes, the way his heels never really touched the floor when he walked, the vulnerability in his posture when he was alone – the man was painfully beautiful, and she'd long ago decided that she was never going to speak to him.

She nodded, and he chuckled. Reached into his pocket and pulled out a piece of fried bread, which he broke in half and offered to her.

Kavi accepted it with a mumbled, *Thank you.*

He squatted beside her, and they ate in silence. When he was done, he stood, dusted his hands on his trousers, and tapped the scar on his face. *My mother did this.*

Everyone at that brothel was the same. If it wasn't a stranger who'd deceived and broken and taken, it was a stepfather, an uncle, an aunt, a cousin, a friend who manipulated and twisted and inflicted damage so deep that even years and decades later the wounds still oozed with pus.

'Psst.'

They would never find justice, so Dremanth and the girls searched for a way to heal from within, while the rest of the world squeezed their eyes shut, dug their fingers in their ears, and yelled gibberish as they lived and died in their sanitised bubbles.

'Psst, hey, boss.'

Kavi glared at the urchin poking her in the thigh.

'You want high-grade tamakhu, boss? Hah? Okay, you want

arrack? Best quality, number one price. No? Okay, you want'– he checked over his shoulder – 'agoma? Ah-go-mah?'

She snarled and brandished a fist in his face. He called her a chootia Taemu and scurried away.

Kavi cracked her neck, gave the group one final glance, and wished them all the happiness on the subcontinent. If anyone deserved it, it was them.

The artificed rods that lined the bridge flickered and came to life as she trudged past, bathing the walkway in garish blue light. On the other side, shadows played on the grey stone of the Kraelish quarters as men and women laughed and bantered on their way to a theatre or a restaurant or whatever it was they did with their free time and money.

To her, it was just another reminder – it was in their smiles, in their gait, in their tone of voice – of the difference between her people and theirs. They were still human, still men and women, but the Taemu? The very essence of her people had been erased.

She was suddenly hollow, keenly aware of an absence that should have been filled with an identity, a place, a people, an idea.

She would never have a home. Or a family. It was all a fantasy.

Her shield, her trusty shield of irony and bleak humour, crumbled and fell to pieces. The chatty pedestrians were no longer enjoying themselves. They were having strained, forced conversations with fists clenched behind their backs. The baby in the pram, surrounded by women who cooed and pinched its cheeks, had dark circles and hollowed eyes, stiff limbs and a lolling head. Could no one else see that it was dead? The bustling street-sweepers were not *bustling*. They were twitchy, constantly scratching a spot behind their necks where the last disc of agoma had been emptied. Addicts. All of them.

She arrived at Bithun's bungalow in the midst of a fresh bout of withering cynicism. What was she thinking? A Blade? Her? She had no training. No experience. She didn't stand a chance. And the entry fee? Five thousand rayals in all likelihood was not a big deal to Bithun, but you didn't get rich by throwing money at desperate Taemu.

The guard took one look at her face and let her in. Bithun was out on his lawn, watching a gardener trim and prune a rebellious hedge.

Kavi stopped and raised an arm in greeting.

The sahib studied her, twisted his cane in his fingers. 'Hungry?'

'I—' She blinked. 'Yes.' Gods, yes.

Bithun gestured for her to follow. He walked her back out the gate and down to a nearby restaurant that he claimed had the best kathi-rolls in the city.

'Order first,' Bithun said when they found a table. 'You can fill me in while we wait.'

So she told him about the tests: about the pain of the first, the emptiness of the second, and how everything fell apart in the third. He listened in silence, tsking at this and shaking his head at that. She had just finished describing her despondent walk back to the gates of the Branch when the food arrived, and Bithun insisted they eat before discussing anything further.

Kavi wolfed down a week's worth of kathi-rolls.

Why was she being so morose earlier? Look at this chunk of meat, the caramelisation on the edges, the dark-red searing from the spice rub, the layered roti wrapped around it to cushion the heat and – she took a bite – the tang of the fresh onions drenched in lime juice. Bliss. A reason to find a silver lining. A reason to don a positive outlook and – another bite, while she was still swallowing the first one – a reason to live.

'You eat like this every day?' she asked the sahib, who was still working his way through his only kathi-roll.

'No. Cook's on leave for his son's wedding.' He swallowed the morsel in his mouth. 'I've been eating here since I was a boy. Tastes exactly the same.'

Kavi stifled a burp and glanced at the pack of Joyful Sailor beedis a patron had left behind.

When was the last time she smoked? In Dyarabad? Yes, early mornings spent scrounging through the rubbish with the other beggars, looking for stubs to burn. When she escaped to Bochan, she'd promised herself that it would stop. Appa had abhorred smoking and smokers by extension. But the beedis wouldn't have enough time to kill her anyway, so to Hel with it.

The table conveniently had a bronze ashtray and a complimentary set of matches. She set a beedi between her lips, squeezed it tight, and struck a match.

Pungent clove-flavoured fumes gushed into her mouth as the tip caught fire. She held the smoke over her tongue for half a second, and sucked it in. By the time she exhaled, it had already done the job. Her nerves faded into the background as the tamakhu sent tendrils of calm through her body.

She took another drag and used her thumbnail to flick ash into the tray. A wave of light-headedness washed over her. It had been too long. She should've taken smaller drags. She squeezed her eyes shut to stop the restaurant from spinning.

'Bad habit,' Bithun said.

Kavi cocked an eyebrow.

He raised both hands. 'Fair enough,' he said. 'So, what do you want to do now? My job offer is still on the table.'

'Will you—' She coughed and reached for the mug of water. 'I have a favour to ask, sahib.'

'Go on,' Bithun said as he watched her drink.

Kavi wiped her mouth with the back of her hand. 'Would you be willing to lend me some money?'

'For?'

'The Siphon.'

Bithun narrowed his eyes. 'You want to be a Blade.'

It wasn't a question, but, 'Yes.'

'Are you sure? I've heard that at least half the applicants end up dead. Besides, do you *really* want to protect someone who thinks you're less than them? That treats you like ...' He motioned at her.

'A Taemu.' She hadn't thought of that.

'Yes, would you place yourself at risk for someone like that?'

Would she? The petulant response was *No, fuck them. I'm not taking an arrow in the appendix for some stuck-up arsehole.* But if she kept her eyes on the goal, and her ego in check, 'Yes. I think I can.'

'Okay,' he said with a shrug. 'How much do you need?'

'Five thousand—' Kavi started. Just like that? 'Really? Sahib? You're serious? You'd give me five thousand rayals?'

He waved it off. 'Think of it as an investment. If it pays off, I will have another contact in Azraaya.'

If it pays off. Kavi swallowed. And if it doesn't? The dead Taemu decomposing in the gutter would just be another number in the red column.

Bithun scratched the stubble on his chin. 'You will need a trainer.'

She shook her head. 'I don't know anyone who—'

'Leave that with me. Also, I may be able to get you information on the Venator.'

Her eyes went wide. 'How?'

'I know an artificer in Azraaya.'

'An artificer?'

'The source I mentioned earlier,' he said, and gestured at a waiter.

The man sauntered over and launched into the menu: 'Tea, kapi, plain dosa, masala dosa, idli, vada—'

'Two teas. One extra sweet with extra milk,' Bithun said, and turned back to Kavi. 'If the device really is in Azraaya, and capable of doing what we believe it can, they will know. I have sent word. In a few weeks, we will have details – its mechanism, its location, level of access ...'

'Thank you, sahib.' Kavi bobbed her head. Hesitated. Was it rude if she asked? Maybe. But it would eat away at her if she didn't. She sat up straight. 'Sahib, not that I am ungrateful, but please, why are you still helping me?'

'You asked me—'

'The truth, sahib. Why?'

'I told you—'

'Please.'

Fatigue seeped into Bithun's features. He slouched over the table and stared at the smoking beedi.

'Sahib?' Kavi said.

'My daughter.' He sighed. 'She would have wanted me to do this.'

'I guess I should be thanking her, then.'

'She's dead.'

Kavi grimaced. How could she forget? 'I'm sorry, I didn't—'

'Two teas.' The waiter said, walking over with a steel cup in each hand. 'Egg-es-tra sweet for who?'

Kavi nodded, and he thumped the cup down in front of her.

'Thank you, bhai,' she said as the man left the other cup facing the sahib. The waiter was obviously unhappy with her presence in the restaurant but was too afraid to offend the sahib. She blew over the rim of her cup. Hopefully, he hadn't spat in her tea. 'How did she – um, what happened?'

'Ask me again, in a year's time,' Bithun reached for his tea, 'after you've made it through the Siphon and your first year in the Vagola. Ask me then, and I'll tell you everything.'

Kavi nodded. Took a tentative sip. Hot. There was no point in forcing the man to dredge up painful memories just to satisfy her curiosity, so they sat in silence, each sipping-slurping their teas, until:

'Did I tell you I was a lawyer?' Bithun said with a wistful smile.

'You mentioned,' she said, 'when we first met.'

'I could have become a judge if I wasn't so attached to my balls.'

'Your balls?' *Eh?*

'*Judges*, in our *republic*' – he twisted the word in his mouth, like it hurt him to say it – 'are castrated. A Kraelish law we decided to keep. They believe it negates certain … temptations.'

Kavi grimaced. 'That, uh, sounds painful.'

The sahib snorted. 'You have a place to stay?'

'Yes – No, I don't.' Her hut was long gone.

'You can use one of the guest rooms in the bungalow, if you wish.'

'In the bungalow?' Kavi said.

'Mhmm.'

Silk sheets, a personal punkah-wallah, and an oh-so-soft bed? *Don't be an idiot.* 'That's very generous, sahib, but um, do you have a servant's quarters?'

'Yes, but—'

'I will stay there, sahib, please.' As much as she loved the idea of living in a bungalow for three months, her gut told her that it was a bad idea, and she trusted it.

'As you wish,' Bithun said with a grim nod. 'So, tomorrow, I will find you a trainer to teach you a weapon and prepare you for the Siphon. Meanwhile, my home, and my library, are open to you.'

Interlude – I

Drisana

Half-breed, they called me.

You will never earn Raktha's favour, they told me.

And when I was left as one of the last surviving Taemu mages, one of the last mages in all five worlds with the power to pilot a makra – *you must fight for us,* they said. *It is your duty.*

I was tired, sister. Tired of the war, of those who thrived on it, the ruin it brought to our people. But most of all, the lives it extinguished. Among them, my husband, Gayan, and an unborn son who will never be blessed with a name.

So when they came to me, that last time, and told me about their plan; about how they intended to break the Chain and begged me to lead our makra to the Gate, even if it meant that we would almost certainly die, I said yes.

The skies on Kolacin's world were on fire that morning. Its moons broken and dying as they slipped between the realms of the living and the dead.

We stood, each of us, at the feet of our makra. Twelve in total.

In the funereal air of the bunker, the priests anointed us in holy oils, stripped us, and dropped to their knees.

'Begin,' I said, and we called to our Jinn, to Raktha.

I'd heard that he sometimes spoke to his favoured mages. He

had never uttered a word to me, but I'd felt his regard all my life. His presence always under my skin like the vectors implanted in me – black discs that protruded from above each elbow, under each knee, over my sternum, and between my eyebrows.

Rakthan maayin, pure, clean, and coruscating, burned through my veins, into the vectors, and lifted me off the ground. Only maayin tempered in the blood of a Taemu mage could interact with a vector. And vectors were the only known material in the five worlds that could power a makra. That made us one of the most precious commodities in all five worlds.

On my makra, *Gayathri,* the sister implants burned a fiery red, and the behemoth's jaws, forged into the shape of a wolf's, hissed and screeched open.

I floated into its maw, sank down its throat, and drifted into the pod ensconced deep inside its chest. There, in the pilot's pod, I hovered in the darkness as needles extended from *Gayathri's* core and pierced the vectors on my body.

My back arched as I screamed. The agony was overwhelming at first, but then I sought out the bells – imagined the sound of anklets jangling as I kicked my heels into the floor, as I twisted and whirled – and I could feel my heartbeat slow, my breath even out, and when I opened my eyes, I looked out through those of a leviathan, whose irises I knew would be a reflection of mine: blood-red in the right; pitch-black in the left.

Suspended inside my pod, I flexed my arms, stretched, and the makra mimicked my movements with instantaneous precision. Perfectly in sync.

This was what the enemy would never have, regardless of how many Taemu they captured and tortured, how many they brought back from the dead as mindless vessels; their makra would always fight with a lag.

Through the maayin linking us, through our Jinn, I sent my command to the other mages. 'Fly, Pilots.'

In another million years the twin suns of Kolacin would gain enough density to render this world uninhabitable. But still the Harithians fought to claim it. They'd ruined their world, allowed Raeth's touch to corrupt Harith's maayin, and when the others – the four remaining worlds in the Chain – declined their requests for living space, they resorted to violence. Three centuries of it.

We broke through the skies in formation, with *Gayathri* as the spearhead, and into the sparkling darkness above. The surface of the closest moon was a crumbling whirlpool, tentacles the size of continents twisting around the edges as they swallowed the dying orb.

And then we fell, tore through the clouds as we dived at the Gate below.

'Release,' I said. And as one, we severed our connection with our Jinn. The maayin surrounding the Gate, where the Harithians had breached and were forcing their way through, would be corrupt, and we couldn't risk exposing ourselves to it.

Gayathri shuddered as I drew from the storage cylinders on its back and allowed a burst of maayin to adjust its trajectory.

'Gate sighted,' said a voice I knew belonged to Aira.

The Gate, one of two on Kolacin that linked it with two other worlds, and via transit to two beyond, sat inside the colossal yawning mouth of a dark marble serpent. Its surface was a mirror and it glimmered and flashed as it reflected the millions swarming over the grey ash that covered the area.

'Harithian makra, eastern edge of the Gate,' Aria said, disgust and anger accompanying the announcement.

'Prepare weapons,' I said, and detached the swords from *Gayathri*'s back.

The Harithian makra spotted us. Raised their shields while ground units turned weapons upward and sent stuttered streams of dark-green maayin whizzing up at us.

These were just men and women fighting to give their children a chance at a better life. Fighting for the mistakes made by another generation. But I was angry. Angry at what they took from me. At all the suffering they had caused. And beneath it all I was a soldier, and I had my instructions: *Hold them at the Gate. Give us the time we need to break the Chain. To end this war.*

I remember *Gayathri* shuddering as she shredded through the atmosphere. I remember the burst of maayin I sent from my palms and the soles of my feet and the force with which I landed. I remember the weight of the swords in my hands and the fear I sensed in the enemy.

They were slow. Sluggish. The result of a delay between the movements of the pilot and their makra. We aimed for the protuberance on their bulbous heads where they kept the undead Taemu mage who powered their makra. When that failed, we went straight for the heart, where, like us, their pilot would be suspended.

We ripped them limb from limb. Tore entire units of makra to shreds.

The minutes turned into hours.

And still they came.

For every makra we destroyed, two more appeared.

They were desperate. They knew what we were doing. Knew what was at stake. If we succeeded, if our engineers broke the Chain, the Harithians would be trapped on their dying world for all eternity.

We fought, and one by one, we fell. Surrounded and dragged down, ripped out of our pods, bloody and limbless, decapitated, burned alive, crushed, until, once again, I was alone.

I fought with a sword held in the jaws of my makra and the other in a battered and failing arm. My maayin was almost depleted. *Gayathri* had lost an arm. And the vector on a leg was damaged. It was only a matter of time before I joined the others.

They flung themselves at me. Clung to my arm and legs. To my waist. My head. I tried to force them off, but they kept coming. Their weight brought me to my knees. Made it hard to breathe. I was being crushed. I was dying.

And, in a strange way, I found it comforting. I would never find peace while I was alive, but now, in the silence at the bottom of a mountain of twisted, broken metal, I could finally sense it.

It was close.

But into this silence, a voice I had waited all my life to hear, spoke.

Drisana.

Then louder. Angrier. With a plea in it.

Daughter.

'Raktha.'

I have waited for you, daughter. Watched and waited since the day you were born.

'I know,' I whispered.

And now, I have my champion.

My heart thundered. My blood was a storm in my ears. I tried to shake my head, but it wouldn't move. 'I have nothing left to give.'

I have chosen, daughter. Now draw my maayin and stand.

The makra shuddered, and I moaned through gritted teeth. 'But the corruption ...'

It will kill you. But not before you have done what is needed.

There was a loud groan followed by a crack, and a splinter of metal speared into the pilot's pod and plunged into my abdomen. I gasped.

You will have the power to bring a God to his knees. Draw.

My vision blurred, and the pain in my gut radiated out into my chest as I wept.

One last time. One last fight. After this, I could finally rest.

I reached for my connection to Raktha and drew.

Convulsions wracked my body as toxic maayin gushed through my bloodstream, altering and damaging as it saw fit. What had started as a stream, for the first time in my life, turned into a river, and I kept drawing.

More.

More.

Now stand, daughter.

I released the power I'd built up, and an ear-shredding detonation, with *Gayathri* in the eye, ripped through the ranks of Harithians, incinerating everything and everyone in an immense radius.

I stood.

And drew again. More maayin than any human had a right to wield, and sank it into my makra. I gave it speed. I gave it strength. And when I moved, I was death to everything I touched.

Part Two

Chapter 17

Stitches in her side. Fire in her lungs and muscles. Nausea – overwhelming, insistent, demanding.

Kavi dropped to her knees and gasped for air. She was not going to throw up. Not again. Not in front of him. A mouthful of semi-digested breakfast forced its way up her throat, but she swallowed it back down with a shudder.

'Hurk!' *No, dammit, keep it down.* 'Blurg!' She clamped a hand over her mouth and – *breathe, breathe* – used the crisp early morning air to force a placid ceasefire between her stomach and the food it was trying to expel.

Mojan, her terrifyingly hairy-faced trainer, watched her with a disapproving scowl from his vantage point under a pair of coconut trees. She could just about make out the network of scars that dominated the left side of his body.

It's the side that fighters traditionally tend to present to the enemy, Bithun said when she'd queried the distribution of her trainer's disfigurements. It didn't make sense to her, but not much about Mojan did.

The man was a retired Blade with over twenty years of experience, or so he claimed. If it wasn't for the scars, and his speech on twenty-three different ways to kill a man ('also womans,' he'd said), she would have seriously doubted the man's legitimacy.

His potbelly and never-empty flask of arrack – currently resting on said protuberance – did not inspire much confidence in her when they'd first met.

Kavi gave Mojan a friendly wave, which he ignored, and jogged over to him.

Foam-flecked waves lapped at her bare feet and she relished the bite of the cool water. Her ticket to Azraaya was booked. In three months, she would be on the *Chimabali Express*, and two days after that, in Azraaya. The thought sent a shiver of nervous excitement up her spine. For the first time in her life, it felt like she *meant* something. She was confident. She was making progress. And she would be ready.

Mojan twisted the cap back onto his flask and shoved it into a shirt pocket. He uprooted the practice sword jammed into the sand at his feet and motioned for Kavi to collect the one left standing.

Kavi's practice sword was shaped to mimic a single-edged blade that curved at the tip. A cloth, stiff from all the dried sweat, was wrapped around what served as the hilt, and she slipped her fingers into the familiar indentations with a satisfied sigh. The chafing on her fingers was addictive. The weight of the sword was comforting. She had learned to love this piece of wood.

She knew all the drills, had memorised and practised all the strikes, thrusts, parries, blocks, and combinations until the calluses on her fingers had grown a new layer and the blisters on the middle of her thumbs had burst. She'd read up on the basics, understood the importance of footwork, and identified the muscles she needed to strengthen. But today would be the first time they'd actually sparred with the weapon. Sure, it wasn't a real sword, but it *was* a weapon in its own right. She'd dropped it on her feet during one of the early practice sessions and – she clenched her toes – they were still swollen.

'Take your stance,' Mojan said, slicing the air with his practice sword. He held it in a single-handed grip and chose a side-on stance with his left foot pointed at her.

No need to worry about shields and artificed weapons and all that, he'd said when she asked about them, *you will learn about them in the Siphon. As for sword schools, he shook his head at her bemused expression, no, it's too early for you.*

But what about padding or some protection? she'd asked.

He'd scoffed and told her to be serious.

Kavi held her sword with both hands, like he'd taught her, and stood with knees bent and the tip of the wooden blade hovering between her eyes. Three weeks of drills, of muscle-building exercises and running and stretching and more running, and she could finally use what she'd learned. She took a deep breath, and held it.

'Fight.' Mojan stamped the ground and closed the gap.

Kavi had a moment to register that his practice sword was hurtling into her face before the world creaked, groaned, and slowed to a crawl.

He was fast. Too fast. She had to parry. Deflect. Duck under his sword and rotate into a strike of her own. His midriff was open. He was overextended.

The heavy, rounded tip of Mojan's sword filled her vision. *Parry parry whatthefuck parry!* Her limbs resisted, her body rebelled, and before she knew what she was doing, she'd hopped, skipped, and dodged out of range.

Mojan followed. A nimble shuffle and he was on her again.

He was testing her. She knew the answers. But her reflexes, honed by years of dodging spittle and repositioning for lathi blows and beatings, kicked into gear. She spun around the thrust and staggered away from Mojan.

Mojan paused, a flicker of surprise in his eyes, and his scowl deepened. 'At ease.'

Kavi let the sword fall and gaped at the trembling hands holding it. What was going on?

'Warlocks,' Mojan said, and reached for his flask, 'are not like other mages. Something changes when Harith picks them.' He took a swig. 'Something changes *inside.* They kill without hesitation – allies-enemies, women-children, human-animal, it makes no difference, we are nothing to them.'

Sounded familiar.

'And the Siphon?' Mojan continued, uncharacteristically garrulous. 'It's not like military training. No barracks, no real teams or squads; you are alone. You attend training, you leave at the end of the day if you're alive.' He squinted at her. 'Did you know only half made it out alive last year?'

Kavi swallowed.

'Novice warlocks are fucking brutal,' Mojan spat. 'Why are you doing this?'

She blinked. 'I—'

'Even if you succeed, if you manage to survive the Siphon and then the three years at the Vagola. Then what?'

'Then—'

'Then you will spend the rest of your life serving the Republic' – Mojan saluted the coconut trees – 'and protecting a warlock who can't even piss straight.' He took another swig from his flask and grimaced. 'I'll be honest, you've worked hard, but the truth? The fact is that it doesn't matter how much the sahib pays me, we just don't have enough time. Four months is nothing.'

Four months is a lifetime. She raised her practice sword.

Mojan sighed and tucked away the flask. 'Try not to run this time.'

Kavi tightened her grip on her practice sword. A steady

stream of sweat trickled down her chin and drip-dripped onto the sand at her feet.

He's just a man. That was just a piece of wood. She wasn't afraid of pain. But – she licked her dry lips – Taemu did not fight, not anymore; they lowered their eyes, schooled their bodies into subservience, and hid in the cracks so they could scrape by without being noticed. She was willing – Raeth's ethereal balls, she was willing – but her body was not. It wasn't ready to infringe upon the unspoken laws that governed her people.

She fought the tremble in her chin. If Greema hadn't intervened at the Branch, Bhagu would've killed her.

Mojan took his stance, and studied her with choleric eyes, waiting.

Kavi swallowed the droplet of saliva her dry mouth managed to produce and squeezed her thumbs into the sweat-soaked grip of her sword. He wanted her to make the first move.

Go. Left foot first, stamp it down, and follow with an overhead strike. She dug her toes into the sand and hesitated.

But he'd dodge. The man was faster than he looked. A two-handed overhead strike was too risky. She'd be committed. He'd simply sidestep and – *and what? So what if it doesn't work?* This was her first spar. She was supposed to lose and learn. *Move.* She gritted her teeth and inched closer.

Mojan tsked and lashed out.

Kavi bobbed under the slash. Stepped into the opening. Aimed her sword at the retired Blade's ribs and kicked up a tuft of sand as she skipped out of range.

Mojan hissed and rammed his sword, point first, into the sand. 'You're fast,' he growled, 'faster than a lot of men I've fought. But you're scared.' He reached for his flask but changed his mind. 'You cannot defend your warlock if all you do is run. Maybe if you were younger … it takes years to erase – to modify an instinct. Even harder when that instinct is so *deeply* ingrained. What was your first thought when I attacked?'

Run. Kavi lowered her gaze. Fissures ripped through her confidence and dread oozed into the jagged gaps.

'No.' Mojan spat and wiped his mouth with the back of a sleeve. 'You cannot be a Blade.'

Kavi clenched her jaw. 'Sorry, sir-ji,' she said, 'so sorry.'

Mojan sighed and pulled his sword out of the sand. 'The sahib is paying me well, but I do not have the patience to teach someone who won't fight.'

She just needed time to adjust. To get used to the idea that it was okay for her to hurt this man. That if she connected or knocked him out, a quartet of lathi-wielding hawaldars wouldn't burst out of the waves, bullrush her, and beat her halfway to Hel. 'Please, one more time.'

Mojan shrugged and shifted to a two-handed grip.

Kavi puffed out her cheeks and wrangled the stiff, rebellious muscles in her legs into submission. She locked her knees and planted her feet. It was the opposite of what she was supposed to do, but it was the only way.

Mojan took a slow, deliberate step in her direction.

Her knees twitched. Beads of sweat blossomed on her forehead. What was she doing? He was going to murder her. She had to get away. Look at the size of those shoulders, the veins popping on his forearms, the bloodlust in his eyes.

She caught herself leaning back on her heels. *No no no no no. No. Stand your ground. Think of the endgame.*

What bleddy endgame? She wouldn't live to see it. *Fine, think of a more immediate goal.*

She wanted him to respect her, and if she participated in the spar – the way he wanted her to – maybe she would earn that.

And afterwards, she'd lick her wounds/give herself a pat on the back, depending on the outcome, and return to the bungalow to enjoy the biryani that Bithun's cook had worked so hard to prepare. She'd walked past the kitchen this morning and leered at him as he pounded the spices into paste and meticulously massaged it into the meat. Kavi swallowed, grateful for the sudden efflux of saliva. She could already taste—

Mojan lunged, dropped his shoulders, and swung his sword like he was throwing an uppercut.

Kavi froze. The beach, the trees, the curious onlookers scratching their heads, all evaporated into a beige blur. There was only the weapon streaking through the air, and its destination. Her jaw. He was aiming for her jaw. But she could block. Brace her elbows and lower her wrists so the swords collided. *Then what?* It would turn into a shoving match that could only have one winner. Maybe she could parry? No, not at that angle. It was impossible to deflect. The only way out was to step back. It was the right choice. It was not cowardice. *But* – but if she did that again …

Kavi gritted her teeth and moved her sword into the path of—

Mojan shifted his weight, bent a knee, and his sword changed its trajectory.

Kavi's eyes widened. It was too late to reposition. She'd taken too long to react. He'd caught her flat-footed and floundering.

She caught a whiff of stale alcohol, blinked at the mynahs perched on the coconut tree, and Mojan's sword crashed into her.

A thousand needles of fire pierced her arm. The world *bu-bumped,* like she was in a rickshaw that had just driven through a pothole, and everything went numb.

Chapter 18

There was something strange about her forearm. Wait. Was that *her arm*? No. It couldn't be. The heat was making her delirious. She was seeing things. Everything beneath the wrist and above the elbow was bent and crumpled. Her flesh was swollen and the skin was turning blue. Her fingers were unresponsive. But yet – she ran her eyes over the rest of the limb – it was attached to her body.

A wail, insistent and ululating, cut through the ringing in her ears.

It came from a distance, from across the beach, from the other side of the city. It got louder, and closer, and louder, and closer, and then she was in a room with it. A room with adobe walls and woven mats, with a concealed cubbyhole the size of a child. She stood paralysed in the dark with her hands clasped over her mouth while the shrieks outside intensified.

It was in her head.

It was in her chest.

It sucked the air out of her lungs and tore its way out of her throat.

Something slapped her across the face. The screaming stopped.

'You're fine,' a bearded face said. 'A fracture.' He paused. 'Maybe a couple. That's all. Bloodless. A bonesetter can fix it.'

Mojan. He did this. When did he get so tall? No, he wasn't tall. She was on her knees. She should stand. She should show him she could take a hit and keep going.

Or, the berserker that lived inside her hissed, *we could punch him in the crotch and bring him down to us, headbutt him, gouge his eyes out, use our teeth to rip his nose off and spit it back in his face.*

No. Shut up. Kavi doubled over, cradled the arm in her lap, and whimpered. Please, shut up.

Mojan yanked her up and slapped her again. 'Get a grip,' he growled. 'It will heal. Four-five months and you'll be fine.'

Four … she was not going to be ready. 'The Siphon—'

'Enough.' Mojan took a step back. 'What don't you understand? You still think you'd have walked into Azraaya and come out a Blade?' He spat. 'Open your eyes. You don't have what it takes.'

Kavi wiped the snot off her face and staggered to her feet, still cradling her ruined forearm. 'Fuck you,' she said under her breath.

Mojan snorted. 'You will thank me one day, for saving your life.' He gestured to the coconut trees. 'Stay here. I will send a bonesetter. Consider your training suspended, indefinitely.'

He turned his back on her, gathered the discarded practice swords, and strode down to the road adjacent to the beach where he hailed a rickshaw.

Kavi's vision blurred and her knees wobbled as she picked her way into the shade of the closest tree. She sank into a squat and glanced at her broken arm. She felt no pain, just an occasional tingle that resembled pins and needles, but it was heavy. So heavy. Maybe nerve damage? She grimaced. Not a good sign.

It'd happened so fast. But just like that, all gone. Her chance. Her time. He took it all away from her like it was nothing. Like how they took everything from the Taemu at Ethuran.

Kavi stared at the pockmarked sand, at the dark outline that marked the sea's rhythmic infractions and the blue expanse that was its territory.

Somewhere far to the north, on the edge of the Deadlands, the ruins of Ethuran slowly crumbled into dust. Hundreds of thousands of broken swords jutted out of the barren plains that surrounded it. A marker of the Taemu hecatomb the Kraelish left behind.

At least, that's what she'd read.

Everything she knew about Ethuran came from Raayan books and Kraelish historians. She'd had no stories or legends or names of heroes passed down to her. Like the generation before hers, and the one before theirs, all she'd inherited was her people's desolation and their back-breaking despair.

She started at a sudden soggy warmth on her good hand.

A stray dog, a light-brown mongrel typical of Bochan's canine population, albeit slightly chubbier, skipped away at her sudden movement. It hesitated, but with its tail wagging, returned to her side.

'Don't have food, sorry.' She clicked her tongue and tried to shoo it away.

It ignored her, nudged her hand with its damp nose and sniffed at the pockets of her trousers.

Oh. She reached into them and pulled out a handful of crushed murukus. 'Forgot about these.'

She held them out to the dog.

'Good, aren't they? I've got a whole box of—' A wave of disorientation slammed into her. She was here, on the beach, trapped in a body with a malfunctioning arm, yet she was outside it too.

She was the sea, the sand, the trees, and the sky. She was everyone and no one. Her fears and anxiety faded. Her plans and hopes were a trivial distraction. Her body lay limp on the sand, the stray dog slobbering over her face. But her mind had left its prison. Her Jinn – she knew it was them from the oppressive, paralysing pressure on her consciousness – urged her to … to … what? *What do you want from me?*

They pulsed at her, twin black orbs in a shared abyss, one ringed with threads of azure, the other with streams of crimson.

You spoke to me once, please, how do I—

The Jinn contracted, dilated, and throbbed an alien compulsion into her being.

Kavi floundered. *Cross the line? Take the leap?* There were no words in her vocabulary to express their desire. Her desire. Their desire for her.

The pieces of the puzzle, the fragments of an idea that they'd forced into mind, slowly lurched into place.

She shrank away in horror. It was wrong. It should be impossible. What they were suggesting … She didn't fully understand how to do it, but she intuitively knew that if she did, there would be no turning back. Her decision here would send ripples through everything.

Blue slivers of maayin unwound themselves from Nilasi and slithered down into her awareness. They probed and caressed and forced their way through – into her body, where they writhed and crawled under her skin.

The dog's ears perked up, its tail stopped wagging, and it sniffed the air over Kavi's head.

This *thing* the Jinn were offering her, it violated everything she understood about maayin and Jinn and the rules of nature. Suman claimed her ancestors quarantined Raktha-Nilasi hybrids till they died. It made sense now.

A hush fell over the beach. The dog stepped away from her

body and unobscured her crumpled forearm, which had now ballooned to twice its size.

She looked so … pathetic. So worn out. She should be angry at Mojan, or at the perverse circumstances that had brought her here, but all she could find was pity. Pity for this unconscious woman who was trying so hard, who was so earnest and hopeful even when she knew she would never succeed, that they would never let her succeed.

So why did she care so much? Why did she hesitate to use what the Jinn had showed her?

No, she didn't owe this world anything. Let it burn.

Kavi's eyes snapped open, and in the same heartbeat, her hand shot out and grabbed the stray dog by its neck.

Nilasi's maayin – *her* maayin – was corrupt. It would not work the way it was supposed to. It would not heal other people or animals. *Some hybrids have one ability that breaks all the rules, others have two that bend them.* But it would do the one thing it should never be able to do.

'I'm sorry,' she whispered to the mewling animal.

Nilasi sensed her intention, agreed with it, and with what felt like an otherworldly sigh, locked her in place with its invisible manacles. Its maayin reached through her, into her, and tore its way into existence. Kavi stifled a scream as tendrils of blue fire wriggled their way out of the skin on her arms, her legs, her torso. They tasted the air, fluttered in pleasure at the panicked animal, and stretched out to it.

No.

They stopped.

Take only what is needed.

The threads of Nilasian maayin wavered, as if they were considering a request, and continued to unfurl in the dog's direction.

NO.

They froze and went ramrod straight.

Kavi clenched her toes in the warm sand. *Take.* Her jaw went slack from concentration. *Only.* A solitary trail of saliva dribbled down one corner of her mouth. *What is needed.*

The fibres of maayin spasmed, and one by one, receded until they only covered the area over her broken arm. The pressure holding her body captive subsided to a dull weight on her shoulders. The fire on her skin contained itself to her forearm.

Now – she gazed into the animal's wide, frightened eyes and smothered the surge of horror at what she was about to do – *heal me.*

Chapter 19

Her maayin wrapped itself around the whimpering animal. Tighter and tighter, until the dog howled as its forelegs shattered and it collapsed, unconscious.

Kavi gasped as feeling returned to her arm. Daggers of agony shoved their way into it with excruciating—

Stop.

The maayin recoiled from the dog. The pain in her arm eased. The blue strands hovered over the comatose animal, quivering and straining against an invisible tether. Kavi could sense their need. Their hunger. She sagged against the tree.

Gods, how could she have been so foolish? It was *healing* her, not reversing time to return her arm to its pre-injury state. The bones needed to be set. If it healed now, in its haphazard arrangement, she would never be able to use the arm again.

Mojan said he was sending a bonesetter … She licked her lips. Like Hel he was, the man was probably at a rum den topping up his flask.

She'd watched bonesetters work before. The bones had to be forced as close as possible to their natural positions for it to heal correctly. Which meant more pain, self-inflicted this time. Kavi sifted through the coconut husks gathered at the base of the tree and separated out the older, softer ones from the rest. First, bonesetters would apply sesame oil and turmeric to the affected area, then mutter some gibberish chant that had nothing to do with anything, and then they'd use their bamboo sticks and bottomless claypots.

She cushioned her arm with a row of soft coconut husks and held another firmer shell over it. No turmeric or bamboo here, so she'd have to improvise. *Breathe. Breathe. Be brave. It's just a little pain.* She checked on the dog – it was still passed out, chest heaving with each laboured breath – and stifled a twinge of shame. Quick and deliberate. No hesitation. Three spots where the bones needed to be adjusted. She tucked her tongue in and gritted her teeth. *Go on three.*

One, two – pop, pop, crunch. She hissed and blinked watery eyes. That last spot, a piece of bone had pierced the skin and blood was seeping out of the puncture. Kavi swallowed, hard, and gently pushed the bone back in with an unsteady finger, wincing at a fresh spurt of red.

The threads of maayin fluttered, somehow sensing that she was ready to use them again.

Kavi puffed out her cheeks. If she'd set the bones wrong, she'd have to break them and do this all over again. *Raeth, I know you're not my God (so sorry, bhai, mine's forbidden), but please, let this work.*

She glanced at the dog that lay flopped over on its side, chest shuddering with each thumping heartbeat …

I can't. This is wrong.

It was innocent. Harmless. She could never – Kavi snarled, overrode her guilt and reluctance, and gave her maayin the command. The threads quivered, and like an army of snakes, pounced on the dog.

More threads ripped their way out of her skin. Kavi flared her nostrils and bit down on a scream as they writhed and fused and knotted themselves down the length of her forearm. A sharp tug. A series of wet cracks. And things snapped back into place.

She gasped. *Stop.*

The azure threads shimmered and obeyed. The pain faded to a dull throb. Her fingers responded. She ran them over her calluses and tentatively raised her arm. There was a scar where the bone fragment had punched through. Pale, like it was someone else's skin. Kavi squeezed her eyes shut, took a measured breath, and when she opened them, it too was gone.

Her eyes widened. *Enough. Go … go back to Nilasi.*

The weight on her mind and body eased. Her maayin went limp and, with what she seemed like regret, slithered back under her skin.

A chuckle worked its way out of Kavi's throat. She'd done it. She'd – the dog mewled and its soft, high-pitched cry cut her cackle short.

Its legs were wrecked, but it tucked its tail under its body and tried to push itself upright.

Her vision blurred and her chin trembled. 'I'm sorry,' she whispered.

Put it out of its misery, her father's voice whispered in her ear.

No, shut up.

It stopped whimpering and went still.

Kavi's shoulders slumped. Her chest heaved with a great, coughing sob, and despite how hard she fought it, or how stubbornly she stood her ground, a hammer, forged in guilt and quenched with self-loathing, bludgeoned and pummelled her until her perspective warped and shifted and she found herself looking at the world through another set of eyes.

She'd become them. She was to the dog what everyone else was to her. She was its exploiter, its oppressor, its murderer.

The breeze had already covered its twisted, inert body with a thin layer of sand.

Never again. No more dogs. This was too cruel. She'd have to find a different countervail.

It would be so easy if she could just use trees or plants; but for a countervail to work, it needed to be anatomically similar to a human. The closer it was, the more effective. Insects, reptiles, and fish would all fail. Humans too, of course, couldn't be used as countervails. It contradicted the logic behind the magic, but had been proven impossible. No one understood why. But with the knowledge her Jinn had infused her with, she *knew;* she understood when nobody else did.

The intention was wrong. Humans *were* a countervail, but not for healing. There was something else, something much worse she could use them for. She shuddered at her forbidden knowledge. No, it was beyond her. It was something out of a Tsubumani novel. A grisly, macabre fever dream. It had to be the reason her people once locked up Raktha-Nilasi hybrids. No matter what, no matter how bad things got, she would *never* use – would never even consider this aspect of Nilasi's maayin. The other half of her ability would remain unused, and the knowledge would die with her.

Rats, on the other hand …

Kavi got to her feet, dusted the sand off her clothes, and wiped the tears off her face. Rats, she could use with a clear conscience. They ruled Bochan with a septic claw; were ruthless pillagers, infestors, disease-diffusers, and outnumbered the humans on the surface three to one. Surely they wouldn't mind? Surely.

She found a suitable spot between the trees, got down on her knees, and started digging. The grains stuck to her sweaty palms as she scooped out the sand and deposited it in a neat pile next to the nascent grave. Someday, down the line, it would be her turn, and she could only hope that her killer would be kind enough to bury her in an unmarked grave. No signs that said *Herein lies a Taemu whose hubris landed her buttocks on the sharp end of a sword;* the more nondescript the better.

Barely a minute had passed before a rickshaw screeched to a halt on the road.

Kavi looked up while her hands continued to scoop up sand.

A woman hopped out of the sputtering vehicle and slung a burlap sack over her shoulder. She scanned the beach until she spotted Kavi, gestured for the driver to wait, and hurried over.

'Are you . . .' She scratched the back of her neck as she took in the scene, muttered something about a cursed profession, and cleared her throat. 'Are you the Taemu with the broken' – she cast a puzzled glance at Kavi's fully functional arms – 'bones?'

'Hah? Whaddayouwan?' Kavi said and continued her grave-digging.

'I'm the bonesetter that Mojan-saab sent to . . .'

The dead dog farted. A prolonged, malodorous *brraaaap* that startled the bonesetter into a muffled yelp. Kavi shot upright and, breathing through her mouth, circled around to peer at the animal.

It bared its teeth and growled at her.

What the Hel? She stumbled away from it.

The dog whined.

She shuffled in for a closer look.

It growled again.

She stepped away.

It whimpered.

She moved her head to where it could see her.

It growled.

Clearly, it didn't like her very much, but thank Raeth,

Meshira, and all the other Gods, it was alive. She spun on the bemused bonesetter. 'Can you set its bones?'

'Are you mad?'

'What? A little. Maybe. Probably.' Kavi dabbed at the tears of relief that had welled up in her eyes. 'Look, can you help this dog or what?'

The bonesetter scoffed and gave her a meaningful glare. 'I don't work with animals.'

Kavi curled her lips and tsked. 'You have money?'

The bonesetter clutched her sack tighter, and a note of panic slipped into her voice. 'Why?'

Kavi slipped her arms under the paralysed dog and groaned as she lifted it. 'Pay for the rickshaw to Number 52, Moon's Blessings Road. Sahib Bithun will repay you handsomely. This dog is most dear to him.' She tried to shush the growling animal. 'A favourite pet.'

'But that's ... a stray,' the bonesetter said, daring to lean in for a closer look.

'Look, memsaab,' Kavi said with her most ingratiating smile, 'have you ever seen a stray this fat?' She rocked the dog from side to side for emphasis.

The bonesetter scratched her chin. Her gaze switched between Kavi, still smiling, and the dog, still growling.

'The sahibs do have peculiar interests,' she finally said. 'Okay, come.'

The bonesetter squished herself into the other end of the rickshaw, as far from Kavi and the dog as she could get.

It wasn't enough.

The dog in Kavi's lap farted again. The bonesetter stuck out her tongue and pretended to gag.

Kavi gave her a disapproving glare. *Have some respect, wretch. Is this how you treat patients?* But Gods, he was heavy – she shuffled uncomfortably, and it was a *he*, no doubt, given the size of those things. He was currently deep in the throes of a sorrowful whine.

'There, there.' She patted him on the head. Strange how labelling the dog *it* had removed her resistance to violence and allowed her to inflict pain on *it*. Maybe she should have done that with Mojan. She stroked the dog's ears. There were some revealing parallels here, but she was too tired to explore them.

The rickshaw rattled through a pothole, and the dog instantly switched to a growl. Kavi snatched her hand away. *Sorry, boss, almost there.*

Bithun was deep in conversation with the gatekeeper, Sebapetti, when they arrived. Kavi gently arranged the dog on the seat, hopped out, and yelled over the racket of the hissing rickshaw, 'Petti-saab, gate!'

Sebapetti glanced at Bithun, who nodded, and the man dragged the gate open.

'Kavithri?' Bithun said as he stepped out with his eyes narrowed. 'I heard from Mojan that your arm—'

'I'll explain later, sahib, please.' She motioned to the rickshaw. 'Can you get this dog to a healer?'

'Dog?' He peered into the rickshaw. 'What the Hel happened to it?'

'Uhm.' She glanced at the rickshaw driver who was lighting up a beedi. 'Run over by a rickshaw. Very sad. Please, sahib.'

'Bleddy rickshaws,' Bithun muttered and glared at the baffled driver. 'Was it this one?'

'No sahib,' Kavi said, 'not this one—'

'And who is this?' Bithun jabbed a finger at the bonesetter.

'Mojan's bonesetter. She also' – Kavi glanced at the fidgeting woman – 'requires payment.'

Bithun gave the driver, the bonesetter, and Kavi a dubious once-over.

'Sahib, please,' Kavi said, her panic rising to match the doubt in Bithun's eyes. 'I will explain everything. The dog—'

'Send Tanool.' Bithun gestured to the bungalow. 'I will handle this.'

Kavi breathed a sigh of relief. 'Thank—'

'Kavithri,' he said, studying her with pensive eyes.

'Sahib?'

'Wait in the study.'

Tanool was dispatched to the gate. A jug of water was commandeered from the kitchen. Kavi's thirst was quenched, her face was washed, and – after exchanging the empty jug for a mug of tea – she strolled down the long corridor to the study, sipped the warm, sweet beverage as the tension seeped out of her muscles, and inspected the paintings that hung on the walls. There was Bithun's wife in a big chair, his daughter in the same chair, his wife and daughter in the garden, his daughter on each of her birthdays, a charcoal print of the fighting rings in Balthour, the capital of Kraelin . . .

She stopped and slurped her tea.

Three months, that was how long it took to travel to Kraelin by sea. It once took even longer – six months, apparently – before the Hizath Canal was created. And over land? She clicked her tongue. Almost impossible. The only way into and out of Raaya was through the vast stretch of unnatural desert that connected the subcontinent to the main landmass. The toxicity of the Deadlands had diminished over time, enough to allow travel along the borders, but crossing it was another matter. One needed artificed equipment, manpower, mages, and a certain amount of madness; like the scavenger crews who ventured in there.

Also, if an intrepid Raayan explorer somehow made it to the other side of the Deadlands, what waited for them was far from a warm welcome and sweet cup of tea. The northern border was ringed by dozens of constantly warring xenophobic monarchies who killed foreigners on sight.

So, the only safe option was the sea. Three months to Kraelin, the same to return. Half a year of your life. Bithun must have really enjoyed getting punched in the face.

Speaking of being punched in the face, where was the one of her? There were at least three artists yelling instructions at her that morning outside the slums. Maybe Bithun had acquired one of their sketches.

She sipped her tea and checked the remaining paintings for signs of a bedraggled Taemu squatting beside a pile of rubbish. Maybe Bithun had hidden it because he thought it might offend her. She wouldn't put it past him.

The doors to the study were left ajar and Kavi shimmied her way through, careful not to spill any tea. Its walls were lined with book-filled shelves that Bithun had collected over his lifetime. A whole section dedicated to the biology of the human body and its musculature. Another to Raayan law. More books on history, geology, religion, music, philosophy, mathematics, and steam-science. His novel collection, however, only contained two hard-boiled Tsubumani page-turners and a pandering romance about Raayan princesses and Kraelish ambassadors.

She strolled to the large window at the end of the room and gazed into the perfectly manicured garden. If she closed her eyes and listened hard enough, she could still hear an echo of the screams from the beach. Her own, combined with someone else's. Someone in a room with the beige walls and sleeping mats. She didn't recognise it. Had never seen the place before. Another effect of her concussions? Another memory from another life? Or was this her Jinn trying to tell her something?

Aadhier Taemu, a voice had said to her during the second test. It had even called her by name. Today it had … *had what?* Unclogged a drainpipe in her head to allow this unconscious knowledge to flow into her awareness? That shouldn't have been possible. She cocked her head. *Should it?*

'Dog's been sent to a healer,' Bithun said, shutting the doors behind him.

'Thank you, sahib.' Kavi turned and bobbed her head. 'Is it the same healer that tried to heal me?'

'No.' He settled into an armchair with a loud sigh. 'There's a woman who operates out of the Kraelish quarters, slightly more expensive, but she works with a team of physicians and has her own setter, so your dog will be fine.'

Good. She didn't trust the hack from the hospital.

'Your bonesetter's been paid – Mojan mentioned he'd sent her to you, to fix your arm.' Bithun glanced at the limb in question. 'Said since you were injured during a training activity, and because you wouldn't heal in time for the Siphon, that the contract was void. Asked me to give you his *best regards* and persuade you to pursue a different career.'

Kavi sighed. Despite the man's prickly disposition and constant state of inebriation, Mojan had treated her fairly. Not once had he mentioned her race or made any reference to her people. In his own twisted way, he'd believed he was doing the right thing.

'Now.' Bithun cleared his throat and motioned to an empty chair. 'Explain.'

Chapter 20

Bithun poked her in the arm with his cane. 'This one?'

'Yes, this one.'

He gnashed his teeth and stared at it in disbelief. She could tell how hard it was for him to reconcile years of learning with this outlandish truth she'd just dropped on him. It was the perfect recipe to create a monster. So easy even she could break it down.

To start, you take: one Taemu woman.

Add: her supposed propensity for violence and criminal acts and complete lack of morals.

Stir.

Simmer.

Then: add a sinister ability that undermines your conception of the basic structure of reality. Turn up the heat.

Watch the line between human and animal blur. Wait until you can smell the threat.

Serve and enjoy your monster with a helping of coconut chutney.

'So you can *only* heal yourself?' Bithun asked.

'Correct.'

'If this is true' – Bithun pursed his lips – 'no one can know.'

Kavi nodded. He understood.

'They'll kill you if they find out. Worse, if the Kraelish ever got their hands on you …'

'The Kraelish?'

'They'd lock you up in one of their laboratories for the rest of your life.' He pressed his lips together. 'No, no one must know.'

She scratched her head. 'The Kraelish?' Besides the embassy in Azraaya, they had no presence on the subcontinent. 'But they're gone.'

'They never really left.' Bithun pointed to her cup of tea. 'Where do you think most of our tea goes? Our salt, our coal, our ore, our grain? Where do you think our engines and steam-tech *comes* from? All our linen and paper and leather? Hmm? Our economies are inextricably linked. Have been for centuries.'

He coughed into a fist. 'They *were*, anyway, until the Council signed this trade agreement with the Hamakans and the Fumeshis. Which is why it took so long to hear back from Azraaya – the mail routes were clogged with news of the Kraelish response to our new trade partners. The Empire, it seems, has doubled their military presence in the northern annexures.'

'I see,' Kavi said with a grave nod.

He gave her a dubious glance. 'Don't you want to know?'

'About what?'

'The Venator, Kavithri. I heard from my contact this morning.'

She went completely still.

'It is in Azraaya, as you'd hoped.' Bithun got to his feet and shuffled over to the window. 'My contact can get you access and help you use it, if certain conditions are met.'

The muscles in Kavi's face had gone slack. She wet her lips, and said, 'What conditions?'

'First, I must tell you a few things about this device.' He cleared his throat. 'This, Venator, is used – *was used* to keep tabs on your people.'

Kavi was halfway through a nod before it registered. 'Keep tabs? On us?' *The Kraelish were spying on us?*

He gestured to a bookshelf. 'You will not find this in the history books, but after the Methun Revolt and the fall of Ethuran, the Taemu continued to fight for at least a decade.'

She raised her eyebrows. *Here's something you didn't know about, Appa.*

'Countless skirmishes, fast-moving ambushes, raids, attacks on supply lines, sabotage. The Kraelish response was twofold. First, they deployed their propaganda machine.'

Murderers, rapists, parasites sucking the blood of the good Raayan people; creatures that appear human, but on the inside are something hideous, something evil. Fear them. Hunt them. Exterminate them. Yes, she was familiar with their propaganda. Most of it was embedded so deep into Raayan consciousness that it had become a way of life.

'Then, they created specialised units whose sole purpose was to locate and hunt down the renegade Taemu still holding out. These teams used an artifact that could pinpoint the location of a human being – from horizon to horizon – using a sample of the target's blood, or the blood of someone from their line. It was effective, but the short range made the work tedious, time-consuming, and bloody.

'So their artificers adapted it. They built a version of the artifact that could cover the length and breadth of Raaya; but because of opposition, both internally and locally, and because it fit the narrative they were selling, it was modified to *only* track Taemu.'

'The blood banks,' Kavi whispered. After Ethuran, the Kraelish had forced the survivors to *donate* massive amounts of blood. Blood that they then stored and preserved in artificed vessels.

'Yes.' Bithun nodded. 'This was what they were for.'

She'd assumed that the Kraelish were just being their usual sadistic selves when her father had told her about the blood banks, but it made sense now. They had planned for this.

'During the last months of the Second Revolt, the Empire shipped the blood banks back to Kraelin,' Bithun said, 'but they left the Venator behind, because – to quote my contact – *the bleddy thing is built into Raaya.*'

So, the Venator was still here. In Azraaya. And if what they said was true, she could use it and find Appa, Khagan, and Kamith. How old would the boys be now? Fourteen and eighteen? Would they even recognise her? Of course they would.

'The conditions,' she said, biting back a spasm of hope. 'What are they?'

Bithun strolled back to his chair and collapsed into it. 'It would've been so much easier if you'd passed as a mage.'

'I *am* a mage.'

'Yes' – he raised a placating arm – 'but telling them what you are – what you can do – will not make you a student at the Vagola.'

Ah.

Bithun nodded at the flicker of understanding in her eyes. 'Only registered mages, their Blades, and students at the Vagola are allowed into the facility that holds the device.' He shuffled closer to her. 'Did I mention that my contact is an artificer?'

Kavi wiped her clammy hands on her trousers. 'You did, yes.'

'Did you know that as part of their training at the Vagola, Blade candidates often serve as bodyguards to mages in the city? Not just to warlocks, but to any registered, fully fledged mage. A type of apprenticeship, if you will.'

She stared at him in silence. Until it clicked. And her eyes went wide.

He lowered his voice. 'Survive the Siphon.'

Her heart skipped a beat.

'Join the Vagola.'

The hair on her arms, her legs, the nape of her neck, stood on end.

'Do that, and they can help you use it.'

Chapter 21

'I'll let Mojan know that we still require his services.' Bithun reached into his pocket and pulled out a handkerchief. 'Now that you're able to' – he blew his nose into it – 'heal *yourself*, it changes everything.'

'No, sahib,' Kavi said with her eyes averted. 'I don't want to work with him.'

'Don't *want?*' He gave her an incredulous glance and tucked away his handkerchief. 'Kavithri, there is no one else in Bochan who can train you.'

He was probably right, there *was* no one else in Bochan willing to train a Taemu. Mojan was a lucky outlier. But she didn't need a trainer. She understood the sword. All his drills couldn't change the fact that she knew, instinctively, that there was a more efficient way for her to wield the weapon. It would come. All she had to do was practice, fight, and allow her body to acclimatise to the extra appendage.

And therein lay the problem. She first needed to overcome her fear of combat.

'Kavithri?' Bithun said.

She sighed and studied the marble tiles beneath her feet, the hand-knotted rug between their chairs, the grey cotton of Bithun's Kraelish trousers, the pale, hardened skin on his knuckles and the curve of bone underneath. Kavi wasn't one for fate or destiny, but for her world to make sense, there had to be reason.

Her reason for being here today could be traced all the way back, eight centuries, to the day a Kraelish vessel ran aground outside a fishing village on the Taellian coast. She could justify, explain, somersault and wriggle through any and all logic to blame everything on when the Empire found or, in their words, *discovered* her people, and eventually made them fight their war for them.

But Bithun? What had brought him to this point? It didn't make sense.

It could have been anyone on that road, frozen in front of an out-of-control rickshaw. Hel, any other sahib would have considered it a fair exchange: her body for his well-being, and left her to rot. There was no explanation for why it *had* to be him. Blaming it on coincidence was too convenient. Too neat. There had to be a reason. And Kavi thought she knew what it was.

Bithun snapped his fingers and startled her into meeting his eyes. 'Kavith—'

'Teach me,' she said.

'Teach you what?'

She gestured to his hands. 'To fight.'

He scoffed. 'You can't be serious.'

'I am, sahib.'

He furrowed his brows and said with cold, hard eyes. 'This is not something you learn in three months.'

'What if we had more time?'

'I – didn't Mojan teach you any hand-to-hand combat?'

'No,' she said, 'he was leaving it for later. He told me I would rarely be in a fight without a weapon or a mage.'

'Why, then?'

'I know what to do,' she said. 'Where to move – I'm fast, sahib, I am. But my body, it only wants to move *away.*'

Bithun's frown deepened.

She clenched her jaw and forced the words out. 'I'm scared to fight back.'

'And you think' – he scratched at the stubble on his cheek – 'learning how to box, to ringfight, will help you overcome this?'

'I think …' *That a man who left his home and family behind, travelled to a country that once ruled his own, and fought strangers twice his size in front of thousands who would've wanted him to fail, is* fearless. *Show me how.* 'I think you can help me overcome this.'

'You …' Bithun faltered. He wrung his hands and searched the study for an answer. 'You – are you sure?'

She bobbed her head.

Bithun stared.

It was imperceptible, initially, but with each booming heartbeat, the change in the man became obvious. His eyes cleared. His shoulders straightened. The tension in his jaw receded and purpose seeped into his posture.

'I will need you to trust me,' he said, without taking his eyes off her, 'completely.'

Kavi exhaled, slowly, deliberately. 'Thank you, sahib, I trust—'

'The bond between a fighter and his – *her* – teacher is sacred, Kavithri. No lies, no secrets. If you lose faith in me, start to doubt what I teach you, it will all be for nought. You understand?'

She swallowed.

'The first truth we must face is that three months is not enough' – he raised his voice when she opened her mouth to interject – 'time to build the strength and flexibility your body will need to survive in the ring.'

'The second,' he said, 'is that you will still need to dedicate a portion of this time to your sword-work. Boxing by itself will not help you make it through the Siphon.'

She nodded.

'Which means we will have to improvise – take shortcuts. So, I will only teach you what I believe is essential for you to last five rounds against an experienced fighter.'

'Five rounds?' Her chest tightened. 'Against *who?*'

'I will find you an opponent.'

'Where?'

'At the end of the three months,' Bithun said, 'I will take you to the local ring, and you will fight in an official match.'

She jammed her hands into her armpits. 'An actual …'

'Yes.'

'Where they gamble on …'

'Yes.'

'Fuck me.'

Bithun snorted. 'This is what you want. Right?'

She shuddered. This would work. This *had* to work. A real chance at finding her family and, for once, a clear path to her goal. It was in her hands now. And with what she could do with her maayin, surviving the Siphon was no longer just a dream.

She rubbed a palm over her chest, trying to ease the tightness out of it, and failed. It was inside her. It had come from *inside* her. Nilasi's blue tentacles had crawled under her skin, ripped their way out of her pores. How? Did they have claws of some sort? Were they part of a larger organism that had slithered into her from the nothingness? Maybe it had set up shop in her stomach, or on top of her lungs. Yes, her lungs, that would explain why she was struggling to breathe, it had wrapped itself around—

Stop it. She forced air into her lungs. And again. Another deep breath. *See? Nothing. All in your head. Just stop.* Whatever this was, whether it was malevolent or demonic or was riding her lungs like a rickshaw, was irrelevant. For once, she had something that gave her an advantage, and she would use it. Besides, what kind of mage was afraid of their own ability?

Embrace it. This is who you are now.

Kavi got to her feet, scanning the bookshelves until she found the book she was looking for. 'There might be a way to speed things up,' she said as she gently extracted a mid-size leather-bound book from the shelf.

'What do you mean?'

She placed the book in Bithun's hands and took a step back. 'Chapter three, there is a passage right at the beginning, on muscle hypertrophy.'

Bithun wrinkled his nose and flipped the pages. 'Muscular hypertrophy.' He pinched his chin. '*When a muscle is pushed beyond the threshold of its capacity and sustains damage, the body repairs the torn fibres by fusing them together and adding more fibres, thus increasing the size, mass, and strength of*— Yes, I already know this, what are you . . .' His jaw dropped.

'I need rats.' Lots of rats.

'Rats?'

'Yes, to use as a countervail.'

'I think I can manage that,' Bithun said with a hesitant nod. 'You – will this really work?'

'I have a feeling it will.' More than a feeling, she knew it would work. Her arm was proof.

'Very well.' He set the book aside and reclined with his hands clasped over his stomach. 'I have some business to attend to today, but tomorrow, if you haven't changed your mind by then, meet me in the courtyard after breakfast, and we can get started.'

Chapter 22

The next morning, she found Bithun waiting for her in his square of Kraelish sand. He wore a white baniyan that exposed a pair of stringy, muscular arms and a pair of loose-fitting trousers that flapped around in the gentle breeze. 'Breakfast?' he said.

'Had already.' One masala dosa with sambhar and the cook's special tomato chutney.

'Warm up?'

'Done.' A jog around the perimeter, stretches, lunges, sit-ups, push-ups, and squats.

'Good.' He extended a hand, and Tanool, who was hovering around the sahib like a mosquito, dropped a discoloured roll of cloth into it.

Bithun bandaged her hands; wrapped long strips of rag around her wrists, her knuckles, the base of her palms, the grooves between her fingers, and back around again.

While Kavi stood, flexing her fingers and clenching her fists, Bithun slipped on a thick padded mitten that looked like it'd been stolen from the kitchen, and slapped it with his empty hand.

'Come, slug it as hard as you can.' He shook it in front of her face.

She hesitated. He was an old man, a surprisingly sprightly

one, but still an old man. Was she really going to *slug it as hard as she could?* She took a tentative step in his direction.

He stood his ground and gave her an encouraging nod.

Another step.

She could do this. She wasn't trying to hurt him. She was merely hitting a kitchen implement attached to his hand.

Bithun smacked the mitten impatiently.

Fine. Don't cry if I break something. She wound up, like she was throwing a suitcase onto a moving train, and threw her fist forward.

A heartbeat before it made contact with the mitten, Bithun flicked his wrist, and deflected her punch.

Her feet scuffed the sand as she lost her balance and stumbled.

'That's all?' Bithun said with a grin. 'Did you see that, Tanool? Was she trying to tickle me?'

'It appears so, sahib,' Tanool said, shovelling rice into an empty punching bag.

Bithun thumped the mitten. 'Again, Kavithri.'

She chased that mitten till the sun was directly overhead, biffing and boffing but never landing a clean, satisfying hit, and when she was too tired and hungry to move, the mitten started hitting her back. Gentle taps turned into slaps and soon *thad-thaddaup-dham*, she was seeing stars as he clouted her in the side of her head with a series of rapid combinations.

'You have speed.' Bithun circled her, grinning like a five-year-old taking apart a toy train. 'Your people were famous for it. My grandfather once told me that *his* grandfather had seen a Taemu swordmaster fight. Like lightning, he said. Faster than the wind. I think you have that. But' – he swatted her across the face – 'you must learn to take the hits. You can't run forever in the ring; sooner or later, you will be cornered, or your legs will fail you.' He thumped her in the kidneys. '*Then* what are you going to do?'

Kavi ground her teeth. Was this some sort of test of her determination? Did he expect her to throw up her hands in frustration and storm off because things weren't going her way? She threw another weary punch, which he easily swatted aside. *Don't worry, old man, I'm just out of fuel.* Her stomach growled, and she swayed on her feet. *Wait till I have my lunch, then you'll see. You keep that mitten raised, and I will aim for it.*

'Tanool, some water, please,' Bithun said, slipping off the mitten.

Kavi dropped onto her haunches and rested her head on the bridge of her forearms. Her shoulders heaved with each loud, hungry breath.

'This is the only good thing the Kraelish left behind,' Bithun said with a satisfied sigh. 'Combat for the civilised man.'

'Trains,' Kavi said in a hoarse whisper.

'What?'

'Trains.'

'Trains?'

'Yes, you know, *choo-choo*, big metal boxes on wheels attached to—'

'Ah yes, I suppose you're right,' he conceded. 'Ringcraft and trains, then.'

Tanool returned with water – *iced water*, bless him – and she happily gulped it down.

'Remember, Kavithri,' Bithun said, sipping from a steel mug. 'You need to be able to think while your body reacts. You need to be planning ahead, setting up not for *your* next move, but your opponent's.'

'Yes, sahib,' she said and turned to Tanool with her most winning smile. 'Tanool-saab, some more water, please.'

'And another thing.' Bithun slipped his mitten back on and pounded it with a fist. 'You *cannot* be a fighter without anger. You must not forget *why* you're fighting. You understand?'

She paused with a fresh jug halfway to her mouth.

It was hard to forget *why* she was fighting. Everything she did was a distraction from her impending death. Every breath she took was a reminder of how little time she had left. She had a father to find, brothers to protect, naysayers to silence, respect to earn, faces to rub in the mud, and a dozen other boxes she needed to check before her maayin killed her. And her anger? No. It was best left where it was. Chained up and secure. She could do this without tapping into it. 'Yes, sahib, I understand.'

'Good, now watch carefully, I will show you what a jab looks like. Burn the image into your head. This is the only punch you will throw from now on.'

Bithun tucked his elbows in, lifted both hands to eye level, and with a whip-like motion, fired his shoulder forward. His left hand, the one without the mitten, snapped out; his wrist rotated, from vertical to horizontal as the arm went from bent-at-the-elbow to fully extended, and before she could blink, he was back in his starting stance.

'It is the quickest punch to land. A good jab will interrupt your opponent's rhythm. It will help you learn your range and maintain your distance. The jab isn't about power, it needs speed, accuracy, and most importantly, timing.'

'There are dozens of variations, but I will give you mine.' He did it again, adding a soft hiss – which somehow accentuated the speed of the punch – the moment his arm shot out.

'In most of my fights, I was smaller than my opponents, so I used my jab defensively. But if you step in as you throw it, you can close the gap, land a punch and be back out of range before your opponent knows what hit him.' He showed her the jab again, this time with the step in and out. 'Try it.'

She did.

'Wrong. Go again.'

Kavi tried again. Visualised poking a belligerent railway passenger in the eye, with her fist.

'Wrong. Again.'

She added the hiss.

'Wrong. Wrong. Wrong.' He raised his mitten. 'Here, try aiming at it.'

Kavi aimed and jabbed. Over and over and over again until he was satisfied that she'd learned the motion and the extension. Then he started moving around with the target and calling out the number of strikes.

'One.'

Aim. Jab.

'Two.'

Aim. Jab-jab.

He closed the gap. 'One.'

Aim, and jab.

He hopped away. 'Exhale when you punch, don't hold your breath. Two.'

So that's what it was for. Step in. *Aim. Hiss-hiss.* Step out.

The mitten and the old man's commands became her world. Time lost its weight. The heat was forgotten. Her hunger was an itch she could scratch later. She tasted the salt on her lips, inhaled the scent of the sweat-soaked leather Bithun wore on his hand, and lost herself to the rhythm.

She stopped needing to *Aim.* She knew her reach, she knew the timing, and when he called out a number, there was no thinking, just *jab-jab/hiss-hiss,* a roll of the shoulders and she was back in the stance, waiting for the next command.

Every now and then, he let a punch land flat on his mitten, no deflections or sleight of hand. Pure contact. The courtyard rang with the *smack!* and her arm sang with the response from the connection.

More.

She wanted to feel that again. She needed to soak in it.

One more.

By the time Bithun called an end to the session and suggested she grab a bite to eat, Tanool had hung up the rice-filled punching bag and arranged a row of weights like the ones used by the pehalwans.

'After lunch,' the sahib said, gesturing to the equipment, 'we work on building your strength. Remember, we want to build muscle, but not so much that it compromises your speed. We'll start with your most important weapon.'

Kavi flexed her biceps.

'Your legs.'

Eh?

'Squats with the number five weights till you tear a ligament. I will keep count while you do them.'

'How will I know that I've torn a ligament?' Kavi said, distracted by, *What's for lunch? Fried pomfret?* She'd spotted a basket of the fish when she visited the kitchen for breakfast.

Bithun snorted. 'Besides the pain? You'll hear it. A pop, or a snap, usually.'

That was an unusual sound to associate with a tear. If she had to choose, she'd say *pop* was the more likely of the two.

But would she be able to push herself till that happened? She'd lost faith in what she could and couldn't make her body do. She was, after all, just a slave to its needs. If it said, Eat, she said, *Yes, sir-ji.* Sleep! *Yes, sir-ji, closing my eyes now.* Shit! *Okay, but no need to shout.* Fuck! *Oh, come on, I can only do so much by myself.* Run away! *On it.* Hide if you can't run! *So wise, sir-ji, so wise.*

She was right about the fried pomfret.

She was late because of an impromptu afternoon nap.

She was wrong about it being a *pop*. It was very clearly a *snap*.

Kavi hurled the weights away with a yelp, collapsed, clutched her thigh, and hissed at it while she rolled around.

Bithun patted her on the shoulder. 'One hundred and six. Well done, Kavithri.'

An unfamiliar warmth – at complete odds with the shooting, toe-curling pain – radiated through her core. This was a wall she could break through. Sometimes it was a two-way street. Sometimes, her body obeyed the commands she gave it, even if it was hurting or falling apart. In this, it would not fail her. She clenched her teeth and said, 'Rats. When?'

'Tonight,' Bithun said, 'Rest until then.' He snapped his fingers. 'Tanool, help me with her.'

The rats arrived later that night in half a dozen crates transported via bullock cart. The driver gave Sebapetti a list of care instructions and helped him unload.

Cook Dibbo, who was rubbernecking, tsked and warned them about contamination. 'Why you need rats anyway, ah?'

'The sahib,' Kavi said, hobbling around the curious stray dog – who'd been returned hale and healthy – to get a better look at the crates. 'Some sort of artistic experiment, he said.' She reassured the man that they would all be dead and disposed of by the end of the week. Dibbo paled and left them alone after that.

Sebapetti, who was privy to the real reason vermin were being delivered to his gate, crowbarred a crate open, and they found the rats unharmed and cosy in little wooden compartments. Compartments which, according to the care instructions, were to be returned to the rat dealer for reuse, or purchased for the very low amount of ten rayals a piece. The crate contained exactly twenty-five of these boxes.

She used six.

Chapter 23

The next three months passed in a blur. Time warped into a disjointed panorama of pain, movement, and fear. Kavi lived with a heart-pounding restlessness, a constant reminder that she was running out of time, and it drove her to turn minutes into hours, hours into days, days into years.

She learned what Bithun called the power punches: the straight, the uppercut, and the hook. She threw them in combinations, mixed in head slips and rolls. He taught her strategy, sharpened her defence, beat positional sense into her.

Each session was a new lesson in pain. Squats until she tore her hamstrings or her abdominals or her calf muscles. Push-ups until she ripped her deltoids or pectorals. Shrugs and crunches and bridges until she shredded her triceps or rent the muscles in her neck.

Then she'd kill some rats, heal herself, and start all over again.

Push. Break. Heal. Repeat.

When she slept, her dreams were a kaleidoscope of dead rats and wraith-like cephalopods that chased her across viscous oceans and crumbling plains. She was running out of time.

Push. Break. Heal. Repeat.

When she wasn't training with Bithun or building muscle or killing rats, she was with her sword. She drilled and practised and experimented against imaginary Mojans while a suspicious Tsubu – she'd named the dog after her favourite author, Tsubumani – watched her from behind a mango tree.

Bithun stopped grinning during their spars. His mitten was no longer as elusive. Her punches were no longer a joke. She was faster. Stronger. Her body an instrument, which she tuned to hum with violence and controlled savagery.

Push.

Break.

Heal.

Repeat.

A week before her scheduled departure on the *Chimabali Express* to Azraaya, while she was whaling away on the punching bag like it was personally responsible for all her suffering, Bithun strolled up to her and cleared his throat.

'Sahib?' Kavi said, shuffling around to throw an uppercut.

He studied the battered punching bag and sighed. 'Take the rest of the day off.'

She paused mid-punch. 'Sahib?'

'I've found your opponent. We fight tonight.'

Chapter 24

Tamakhu, sweat, belches, and farts; men pissing on walls, men scratching their balls, men puffing out their chests and shoving each other in the face; cries of *Dai! I'll kill you*, or *You talk about my mummy? You're dead*, or *Bhai, don't be so greedy with your beedis, just one more – grab him!*

The air singed her nostrils on the way in, and for a heartbeat, she was back at the railway station, choking on fumes and jostling with the other porters to catch a passenger's attention.

Bithun nudged her with his bag. 'This way.'

Kavi followed him through a haze of beedi smoke and shrouded lamplight.

Regulars saluted him.

Older regulars shook his hand.

Kavi kept her eyes lowered and on his heels.

Inside the arena, men sat hunched over carrom boards, powdered fingers twitching as they waited their turn. An arrack kiosk kept punters juiced while another dished out skewers of charred and spiced meat. In the middle, with four corners, ropes, and an off-white mat stained with blood from countless fights, was the ring. Above it, dangling from a rope, was a single artificed globe that lit the ring in a blaze of yellow.

They squeezed through the crowd and forced their way to the bookies' desk.

'Sahib!' A man sitting at the end of the heavy wooden desk waved and beckoned him over. 'This is your fighter?'

Bithun nodded. 'When are we scheduled?'

'After next fight,' the bookie said, scribbling on a long piece of paper. 'Name?'

'Kavithri,' Bithun answered for her.

The bookie glanced at the sahib, then at her.

Kavi clenched her jaw. Which response was it going to be?

Woman fighter, ah? Okay-okay, nice joke, I laugh, now fuck off.

Or:

'A Taemu?' The bookie cringed. 'He'll kill her.'

'Just write it down,' Bithun said.

The man shrugged. 'She wants to die? Not my business,' he muttered. Then louder. 'You know where to wait?'

Bithun nodded.

'Good luck.' The bookie handed Bithun a token with the number eleven on it.

Where to wait, was a cordoned-off section beside the ring where fighters and their patrons waited on long wooden benches and discussed strategy, technique, the odds, politics, and the latest news on what the Kraelish were up to in the northern Deadlands:

Bhai, my uncle said they will invade, for sure—

Oh? And how're they going to cross the Deadlands? Your uncle will bring them or what?

But Bhai—

Shaddup!

The pair sitting directly in front of Kavi and Bithun, however, had no such concerns. They gushed, at great length, about the prostitute they'd shared last night.

'A bonding exercise,' Bithun explained, followed by, 'Don't look at me like that,' and 'We will be doing no such thing.'

A bell pealed through the arena, and the cacophony slowly subsided. A voice screamed, 'Ten. Number ten! Puchumani and Dhonda!'

Puchumani and Dhonda's fight was short and brutal.

Both fighters were evenly matched. Until Puchumani broke the stalemate by committing to a full-body right hook, which, as it turned out, was exactly what his opponent was waiting for.

Dhonda's eyes lit up, his muscles contracted, and he threw an immaculately timed counter that slammed into Puchumani's surprised face. A *one-two* follow-up broke Puchumani's nose and splattered the lungi-clad referee with blood. A lazy jab added insult to injury.

KO.

The bell rang. The referee made a face at the blood on his clothes and waved his hands in the air. The punters erupted with joy. Most of them, anyway. A collection of disgruntled gamblers hurled abuse and betting chits and chunks of grilled meat at the unconscious fighter.

Kavi pointed at a bespectacled man being ushered into the ring by the referee. 'Who?'

'House healer,' Bithun shouted over the racket.

A pair of scruffy-looking teenagers followed in the healer's wake. They carried a basket between them, filled to the brim with drowsy rabbits.

'Must be expensive,' Kavi said, 'to use rabbits.'

'Compliments of the house,' Bithun yelled back and leaned in. 'Did you see what happened there?'

'Counter-puncher.'

Bithun grunted. 'Sure. But that bleddy fool' – he cocked his head at the dazed Puchumani – 'walked into it. Threw his entire weight behind the hook. He knocked himself out.'

Brave, though. Kavi's stomach fluttered, and the empty pit in it gaped and called to her.

Relax. Remember your training. Last hurdle, then you're off to the capital. She bumped her bandaged fists together. Five rounds. Three minutes each. Fights couldn't be stopped. KO to win. No scoring like in Kraelin. If both fighters were standing at the end of all five rounds, it would be called a draw, and the punters who bet on it could rejoice.

A woman in a plaid sari flung a mop into the ring and followed it in with a bucket of water.

'Okay, here's the plan,' Bithun said. 'Use the first round to get a feel for the ring. Keep your guard up and feet moving. If you see an opening, test it with a jab.' He squeezed her shoulder. 'Breathe, Kavithri. Breathe.'

When had she stopped? She sucked in a sharp breath and nodded.

The referee, who'd changed into a fresh lungi during the break, sauntered over to the sahib. 'Eleven?'

Bithun showed him the token.

'Water, towel, equipment – you need?' the referee said.

The sahib gestured to the bag at his feet.

The referee bobbled his head. 'Rules?'

'Julo …'

'Yes-yes sahib, I know you know.' Julo raised a placating arm. 'Just doing my job.'

Bithun sighed. 'We know the rules.'

'Okay,' Julo said, satisfied. 'Be ready. Five minutes.'

She'd barely blinked before the bell was struck again and a disembodied voice called out, 'Eleven! Kavithri and Shezaan!'

Goosebumps rippled across Kavi's skin and she burst into a

cold sweat. Her feet – what was wrong with them? They seemed so far away. Trapped in the soft, sticky ground which spiralled deeper and deeper into— *Breathe.*

Move.

A hush fell over the arena as she ducked between the ropes and backed into a corner post.

Breathe. She puffed out her cheeks. *Breathe.* She counted her breaths just like Bithun had taught her.

One. 'A Taemu? This? Nah, madarchod.'

Two. 'Look at her. Open your bleddy eyes.'

Three. 'Shut up your face. How can she know how to fight? No, I don't believe it.'

Four. 'Fuck this. I want to change my bet.'

Five. A scuffle somewhere behind her. More swearing. A choked-off scream.

Six. 'No changes to the bets,' the bookie yelled. 'Sit down or we will make you.'

Seven. Quiet resignation and muttered curses.

Eight. She kept her eyes on her opponent's corner and waited for this Shezaan.

Nine.

Her breath caught in her chest.

No.

Walking through the crowd, with his huge fists bandaged and his hairy chest exposed, with his hair slicked back and his muscles oiled, with a half-smoked beedi clenched between his tamakhu-stained teeth and a triumphant smile fixed on his face, was hawaldar Bhagu. He climbed into the ring, slowly looked her up and down, and licked his lips.

She jammed herself into the corner and latched onto the ropes on both sides. She had to get out. Now.

The crowd closed in. The exit shrank away into the distance. Her bladder throbbed as she started to lose control of it.

'Sahib,' she rasped. 'I can't.'

'What?'

'I cannot fight that man.'

Bithun stuck his head into the ring. 'Why not?'

Why not? Because it was Bhagu. Because the first time she'd met him, he'd backhanded her across the face, shoved her to the ground, and kicked her while she cowered and whimpered and begged. The time after that, he locked her in a jail cell for two days and fed her scraps and mouldy cat food while he taunted her with, *This is what you like to eat, right? Eat it. I said, eat it.* He'd dragged his lathi across the bars. *Clang. Clang. Clang.* She ate it.

Her lips trembled. It was too hard to explain. 'He's a hawaldar.'

'And?'

'And? He's police, sahib. I can't—'

'Listen,' Bithun said, 'no one was willing to fight you. He was the only one.' He undid the straps on the bag and pulled out her mouthguard. 'You know him?'

She squeezed her eyes shut. 'He's police, sahib.'

'You see that man? Look, Kavithri.' He pointed to the mezzanine. 'Up there.'

She followed the line of his finger to a red diwan and the immaculately dressed man who sat on it. A pair of punkah-wallahs stood on either side and fanned him while he watched the ruckus below with boredom plastered on his face.

'He's a judge,' Bithun said, 'not just for Bochan, but the entire district.'

Kavi frowned. *And?*

'He owns this place.'

The judge glanced at Bithun, and the two men exchanged nods.

'You understand?' Bithun said. 'Nothing will happen to you, even if you kill your opponent.'

Or if my opponent kills me.

'Also, he bet on you.'

She jerked her head back to stare at the sahib. 'Why?'

Bithun shrugged. 'I told him I trained you.'

'But—'

'Mouthguard.'

She let him stuff the soft gumshield into her mouth and clenched her teeth to hold it in place.

'Think of this as the final exam,' Bithun said. 'Walk out of here in one piece, and you can consider yourself a graduate of the Jarayas Bithun school of ringcraft.'

'I'fe nefer been to schul,' Kavi said through the mouthguard.

'Well' – he slapped her on the back and stepped away – 'now you have.'

She clamped down on the mouthpiece as hard as she could and shuffled over to the middle of the ring.

Referee Julo checked the wrapping on her knuckles. Squeezed his fingers into it till he was satisfied they were sufficiently cushioned. Then he did the same with Bhagu. 'Mouthguards?' he said.

Kavi bared her teeth and showed him hers.

Bhagu removed his and held it out for Julo to inspect. He ran his eyes over the sinewy muscles on Kavi's arms and shoulders while he waited. 'The old man feeding you well?'

Shut the fuck up. She ground her teeth.

Bhagu spat at her feet. 'What I meant to say was.' He leaned in and reached for her crotch. 'The old man fucking you well?'

Kavi's muscles tensed. She drew a slow, steady breath and glanced at the referee.

'Dai,' Julo made a face and slapped Bhagu's hand away, 'put the bleddy mouthguard back in your mouth.'

Bhagu snorted. 'You know she's not leaving here alive, right?'

'Don't care.' Julo nodded to someone outside the ring and the bell *ding-ding-dinged*. 'The boss wants fights with mouthguards, so shut up and put it in your face.'

Kavi flexed her fingers and crouched into her stance: her fists made a bridge under her eyes, her arms covered everything vital beneath them; just like Bithun had taught her.

Hawaldar Bhagu took his time. He rolled his shoulders and cracked his neck. Threw a couple of practice jabs and nodded at friends in the audience.

The sahib wanted her to get a feel for the ring. She looked around. All that wide empty space around Bhagu. All that was hers to use. She gritted her teeth and bounced on her toes. *Come on.*

One moment he was oblivious to her presence, the next, he was frothing at the mouth and flying at her.

She kicked the mat and skipped away.

He chased her with wide, heavy swings.

She dodged and kept her distance.

He growled and threw a series of wild punches.

She danced through them, slipped under them, wove between them.

Slow. Too slow.

He had no finesse. No strategy. She could *see* his punches. The craft that Bithun loved so much was absent. Bhagu was here to brawl, to beat up on someone smaller than him. She had *nothing* to be afraid of.

The arena went silent. Bhagu roared in frustration and

charged her again, head first this time, like an enraged bull, or a spoiled brat throwing a tantrum because he couldn't have what he wanted.

It would be so easy to land a jab. The idea that a Taemu could hit him, much less hurt him, was so far out of his bounds of perception that he wasn't even *trying* to defend. Right there, into his temple. Bithun's flicker jab. She couldn't miss.

The bell dinged, and Julo threw himself at Bhagu. 'Round!' He shoved the man away from Kavi. 'Go to your corner.'

She blinked. *Three minutes already?* But they'd just started.

'Nicely, done,' Bithun said as she walked back to him. 'Water?'

She nodded.

'Same plan for round two.' He filled a steel mug to the brim and passed it to her. 'But one change.'

She spat the mouthguard out, took a sip from the mug, and emptied the rest over her head.

Bithun swapped the empty mug for a towel. 'He's wide open when he throws his hook.'

He's wide open when he throws anything. She nodded and wiped her face and head.

'*That's* your chance.' Bithun eyeballed the other corner. 'Combinations. Just like we practised. Okay?'

Bhagu shoved his second away and gestured for Julo to start the round.

Julo patted his lungi down, twirled his moustache, and just to make a point, leaned over and made small talk with a surprised punter. When he was done with his one-sided conversation, he smirked at Bhagu, and flicked a finger at the unseen bell-man.

Ding.

Bhagu left his corner with a snarl.

'Remember,' Bithun said, slapping her on the back, 'just like we practised.'

She'd practised to fight with rhythm, to look for that *one-two ba-bump bob-bob ba-bump shuffle-shuffle* sequence that matched the metronome of her heartbeat. She found it before Bhagu could even throw a punch.

He was a child trying to catch the wind.

She slipped through his fingers. Danced circles around him. He was in a different world from hers, one in which every movement was a struggle and the air itself was sluggish. She slowed down and let an uppercut whizz past her nose. *Easy.* What was she so worried about? Now all she needed to do was hit him.

Kavi faltered, lost her rhythm and scrambled to get out of the way of a vicious body blow.

Bhagu paused.

A chill ran up her spine. He knew something was off.

He grinned, slammed his fists together, and lunged at her.

She slipped under a hook aimed at her jaw, parried a jab, and scampered into a corner.

What was wrong with her? Was she really afraid of hurting this man? *Fuck, no.* She wanted him to bleed. Was she so used to running away that she couldn't bring herself to fight back? Maybe. But if she was, then what was she doing trapped with him in the ring?

She gritted her teeth. *Open your eyes.* This whole endeavour was doomed from the start.

She wasn't afraid of hurting him. She was scared of what would happen if she *did.* She was scared that it would unchain the ball of rage that lived inside her. That she would lose control, give in, and become exactly what they said she was: a mindless beast. A counterfeit human. Berserker.

And that could never be allowed to happen. She was flesh and blood. She was human. She would die before she allowed them to see otherwise.

Bhagu spread his arms, blocked her escape routes, trapped her in the corner.

Kavi flared her nostrils. That was one Hel of a stench wafting over from his armpits. She fought down a gag and narrowed her focus—

babump

until only his fists mattered—

Ba-bump

and his movements decelerated.

Ba - Bump

She was not trapped.

She was the wind.

She twisted her torso around body blows. Parried punches before they were fully extended. Rolled her head to let them whizz past unspent. The more frantic he got, the sharper and faster she became, and eventually, a way out of the corner flashed in front of her eyes.

She snapped her guard up and dashed—

A weight, as sudden as it was heavy, crashed down and locked her in place.

She stared at the large foot planted over hers. At the triumph on Bhagu's face. At the referee whose line of sight was blocked. She should have known. This was a man who only followed rules when they were convenient for him. There was no dodging now. She had to block. She had to take the hits and hope this round was close to ending.

Which one was it going to be? A body blow? *No.* The head? *No.* When did he get so fast?

She had her arms clamped around her head when his fist connected with her side. Ribs cracked. Agony lanced up into her chest and forced the air out of her lungs. Her face twisted and she ground her teeth into the mouthpiece as a thin stream of saliva dribbled down her chin.

He wound up for another one.

He was going for her body again. But if it was feint, and if he hit her in the head instead …

She'd be knocked out, or worse, killed. *No.* He was going for the head. It's what she would do. She kept her guard up, and was rocked off her feet by a liver blow.

She gasped and doubled over. *Have to get out. Have to leave the corner.*

She took a step. *So slow.* Her legs, it was like she was moving underwater. She'd lost them.

Bhagu shoved her back into the corner and hit her again. More ribs cracked. She struggled for air. *Stop. Please. I can't—*

He hit her again, in her stomach, and she couldn't help it, her arms dropped to her midriff.

Whumpf-thunk. It was as if a train had slammed into her temple. There was a spike of blinding pain, a sharp ringing in her ears, and she was back in the room with the adobe walls. This time, she was not alone.

A naked eyeball lay on the ground. Its optic nerve flapped behind it like a fish out of water as it swivelled up to gaze at her with a dilating pupil and irises the colour of blood.

A scream found its roots in the base of her throat, and the train rammed into the side of her head again.

The world was a yellow globe attached to a dark ceiling. *Where am I?*

A bell dinged. Once. Twice. Thrice. *The railway station? Which train?* She needed to get to the platform. Stationmaster Muthu would not be happy.

Warm hands circled her shoulders. Urged her forward. Forced her to sit. *Who? Appa? Khagan? Kamith? Haibo?*

No, they were all gone. But then who? There was no one else.

'Kavithri,' a familiar voice said. 'Let go of your mouthguard.'

She obeyed.

'Good. Now gargle and spit.'

She spat out something pink and viscous that reminded her of the dead jellyfish that washed up on the beaches.

'Drink.'

It burned her throat and set off little fires in her mouth, but she drank.

'Do you know what happened?'

Colours and sounds and pain came crashing down on her. She swayed. The hands held her upright.

'You were out cold on your feet.'

She glanced at the sahib. *Strange.* She could only see half of him.

'Don't touch it,' he hissed. 'Your right eye is swollen shut.'

She nodded, slowly, through a fresh wave of nausea and a sudden awareness of the headache trying to throb its way out of her skull.

'The bell was just in time, but …' He wrung his hands and studied her with concern in his eyes. Or was that fear? Either way, it was new. No one had ever looked at her with a face like that.

Don't worry about me, sahib, you've done enough, she wanted to say, but her swollen tongue was jammed into the roof of her mouth, so all she managed was, 'Bone wowwy.'

'You'll have to turtle,' Bithun said. 'Just – if you could just *fight back* …' His voice shook. 'Come back. Come back and we'll figure out how to deal with the next round.'

You know as well as I do that if I walk out there, I may not come back. But she gave him a tired nod and gestured for him to return her mouthpiece.

He forced it into her mouth and helped her to her feet.

Her arms were still functional. She could block, maybe parry. Her legs, however, were like sacks of rice. Heavy. So heavy.

She couldn't bring herself to look at Bithun. *You're a good man, sahib. I'm sorry I dragged you into this.*

But Appa would be so proud of her, walking to her death on her own two feet, clinging to his ideals of Taemu martial determination so stubbornly. She sniffed. There were so many things she wanted to do. So many things she wanted to experience. Her life had just started.

Ding. Ding. Ding.

Chapter 25

A sledgehammer fist slipped under Kavi's guard and crunched into her sternum.

She doubled over, slammed her teeth down on the mouthpiece to stop herself from spitting it out, and reeled into the corner.

Bhagu followed her in with a barrage of kidney blows.

Her insides turned into one big mass of agony that screamed and begged for the punishment to stop. But she gritted her teeth, ignored the dark spots dancing in front of her eyes, and kept her guard up.

Bhagu grunted in frustration and bludgeoned her arms and shoulders instead.

She could sense it in each punch, his demand for her to drop her guard so he could finish her off. What did he think she was? A nail to be hammered into the ground? *Ease up, arsehole, everyone knows you're winning*. Maybe she could pretend to get hit and go down. Buy herself some time.

Time for what? This wasn't Kraelin, there was no ten count here. If she was conscious, she would be forced to keep fighting.

Maybe she could let him knock her out.

Too dangerous. Besides, this dumb-fuck pride she'd inherited from her father wouldn't allow it. She had no choice but to soak up the damage, survive the round, and make it back to Bithun. He'd have thought of a plan by then.

Bhagu upped his tempo.

Kavi wrapped her arms over her head and slumped with the force of his punches. Something was wrong in her chest. Each breath – each *wheeze* – was accompanied by a sharp stabbing pain in her lungs, and there was a metallic fluid slowly filling her mouth.

Maybe she wouldn't return to Bithun after all.

It was unnerving. One moment she was a living-breathing bundle of emotion, and the next, she would just cease to exist. As if a God somewhere snapped his fingers and decided, *That's enough living for you, bleddy bhaenchod, next!*

Which is why we fight it so desperately, *no, sahib?* Through the crook of her arm, through a window of bruised flesh and sore muscle, Bithun stood with hands clenched and a face bereft of blood. *Why the long face? This was my choice. I'm nothing. You'll forget me in a couple of months.* Like a pet who died. Like a pet …

Who was going to feed Tsubu when she was gone? The chubby little shit was a picky eater. He liked a raw egg in his congee, hated anchovies, and loved to gnaw on discarded chicken bones. Someone had to feed him.

She clenched her jaw as Bhagu forced her deeper and deeper into the corner until the wooden post curved and dug, painfully, into her back.

Will you feed him, sahib?

Bithun's face scrunched up. Tears filled his bloodshot eyes and slowly trickled down into the wrinkles and folds of his cheeks.

Dai, enough. You've done enough. You let me dream. You—

Bhagu's fist slipped over her guard, and his knuckles smacked into her ear.

She wobbled.

Blinked.

Where am I?

Punches rained down on her arms and shoulders, and a low moan fought its way out of her throat. Her ear was on fire, someone was hitting her, and a loud keening in her head was making it hard to think.

She smothered her ears with her forearms and searched for the sahib's face. He'd know. Bithun would know what was happening. He'd help her. *There.*

The old man was staring at something with horror in his rheumy eyes. His lips moved but she couldn't make out – no, wait, *what have I done?* He was repeating it over and over again.

There was so much pain on his face.

Why?

For me?

No. Then who? Who was making him look like that? *Who is hurting you, sahib?*

She followed the line of his eyes. Peeked through her guard at the source of his anguish.

You.

I know you.

Bhagu's face was contorted with disgust: beedi-burned lips upturned, large ears red from exertion, fevered eyes filled with unfathomable hate. A thick layer of sweat coated his head and clung to the purple veins in his neck and the bulging muscles on his arms.

You're responsible. For everything. For the ringing in her ears. For the ache in her arms and shoulders. The daggers in her chest. The fire in her legs. For all the beatings. The humiliation. For year after year of failure and sorrow and loneliness.

For the agony on Bithun's face.

Stop.

She lurched upright.

That's enough.

She edged her left foot out.

You will not hurt my friend.

And *aim-hiss* threw a flicker jab.

It crunched into Bhagu's jaw. Tore his lips open. Rocked him back on his heels.

A hush fell over the arena.

Kavi's one good eye went wide. She waited. Waited for the berserker to tear its way out and consume her.

Bhagu flexed his jaw and stared at her.

Kavi cocked her head and stared back. She was still *her*. She was angry, yes, but the all-consuming rage that she was afraid of was still chained.

Bhagu slammed his fists together and came at her.

She tucked her arms in, bent her knees, and with the smallest movement – just like Bithun had taught her – pumped her shoulder out and *hiss* fired another jab.

Her knuckles crashed into his mouth. He staggered. Gaped at her in disbelief.

Appa was wrong. As long as she had someone to protect, as long as she was not hurting someone out of spite or hate, she could fight back. She stepped out of the corner.

Bhagu snarled.

She shut him up with another jab. Harder than the last one. Faster. More compact.

His nose exploded in a fountain of blood, snot, and shattered cartilage.

Strip away everything and they were just two bags of meat hitting each other for the amusement of more decaying meatbags.

She shuffled closer. And they called *her* people savages. These fucking hypocrites.

The hawaldar peered at her through bleary eyes and slowly raised his fists to protect his bloody face.

That won't work, boss. *You showed me how to get around that, remember?*

Kavi stepped in, a powerful stride that closed the gap, and with her weight on her front foot, spun her body around. She ignored the explosion of pain in her ribs and threw every ounce of strength into her blistered and calloused big toe; stretched the calves and hamstrings that she'd wrecked and rebuilt; twisted her hips and granite abdominals, rotated her bruised and battered shoulders, and forced her will into the fist aimed at his gut. *Speak for me.*

Her right hook screamed into his belly, *whumped* into it, and blew him off his feet.

Bhagu bounced back off the ropes. Stumbled and spat out the mouthpiece as he gasped for air.

Kavi stepped in again. Spun her body around.

Bhagu's eyes went wide and his arms dropped to his solar plexus.

This is it. This *is* what Mojan must have seen that day on the beach when she tried to block his strike. He'd changed his trajectory mid-movement to get around it. *How did he do it again?*

She sucked in a sharp, painful breath. Dropped her shoulder. Bent her backfoot. Tucked her elbow in. And her body-hook veered into an uppercut aimed at his chin.

Their eyes met.

His, wide and filled with panic.

Hers, clear and with a message in them: *you can threaten me, beat me, humiliate me, but bhaenchod, you will not be what kills me.*

Her fist slammed his jaw shut with a brittle *thunk* and sweat exploded off his head in glittering crescent. Bhagu's feet left the ground. His head disappeared into the globe of light that hung over the ring, and for a heartbeat, he was headless. A decapitated body hovering in the air. Then he fell.

Kavi cocked her shoulder. Primed another flicker jab to finish him off, and stopped.

Bhagu dropped to his knees. The empty whites of his eyes stared back at her. Blood climbed the cracks in his teeth and oozed down his swollen and fractured jaw.

All her life they'd told her she was nothing. That she was no one.

She let her shoulder relax. Turned her back on him and walked away.

She was done believing their lies.

I am not no one.

Bhagu hit the mat with a dull thud.

A heartbeat of stunned silence.

The arena erupted.

Chaos drowned out the bell and Julo's arm-waving was an afterthought. Men roared and screamed and stomped their feet. The punters crazy enough to bet on her celebrated. The ones who bet against her cried foul play and flung their chits at the ring.

The aches and pains and daggers in her lungs returned. Kavi hunched over and nursed the pain in her side as she limped to her second. *That's better. That's a much better expression.*

Bithun's hands were still clenched, but there was a gleam in his eye and a grin on his lips. He muttered something under his breath, shook his head in disbelief, and started packing their bag.

Kavi turned at a tap on her shoulder.

Julo took a cautious step back, and shouted over the din, 'You don't want a healer?'

She shook her head.

He frowned. 'But—'

'Julo,' Bithun yelled at him from the corner, 'we have our own healer.'

Julo shrugged a *suit yourself* and walked away.

'Hurry, Kavithri,' Bithun said.

She groaned and grimaced and crawled out of the ring while they pelted her with balls of paper and chunks of grilled meat.

'Quick.' Bithun tucked a shoulder into her armpit and wrapped her arm around the back of his neck. He swung his bag around to clear a path and glared at the punters who got too close as they inched their way toward the exit.

Just as they passed the carrom boards a voice boomed over the din and stopped them in their tracks. 'Come fight again, Taemu!'

Kavi craned her neck, along with everyone else around her, to find the source. Up on the mezzanine, the judge was on his feet, applauding with a smile on his face. He nodded at her.

Did you hear that, Appa? Soft, warm tendrils of pride wrapped themselves around her heart and squeezed. *He wants me to fight again.* Kavi opened her mouth to respond, but found that her throat had clogged up. She bit her trembling lips, stood straighter, taller, and nodded back.

Chapter 26

Kavi helped out in the kitchen. In the garden. She went on long meandering jogs where time lost its weight and her mind found a peaceful little verandah it could perch on and watch the scenery whizz past. She washed and brushed a squirming Tsubu. Put him on a leash and took him on long walks. He kept his distance from her, but once they got on the main road, he'd forget about her and scurry around sniffing vegetable refuse and lamp posts and parked rickshaws and lounging buffaloes and literally anything he could get his nose on.

There were two things she *wanted* to do, and one thing she *needed* to do, and she left them all until the evening before her train arrived.

*

Clouds gathered and split into clumps and gaggles. They blocked out the sun, peered down at an indecisive Kavi, and *hwak-thoo,* spat rain down on the sahib's compound.

She sighed and shook a coconut next to her ear till she could hear the swishing of the water inside. *This will do.* Into the satchel it went, alongside a candle, a roll of jasmine incense, and a matchbox.

Tsubu was lounging just out of reach. He lay flat on his belly with his head resting on his forelegs as he watched the spattering of rain kick up dust in the yard. She slung the satchel over her shoulder, shuffled closer, and patted him on the back (everyone knew his head was off limits). He responded with a low growl.

'See you when I'm back, you grumpy bastard,' she said, and left him to it.

Outside, she hailed down a rickshaw and gave the toothpick-munching driver her first destination.

Four months was a long time in the slums. People move in. People move out. People move on.

She strolled through her old neighbourhood with the satchel held over her head to protect her from the persistent drizzle. The place was exactly the same. Nothing had changed. Except for her hut. The bleddy bastards had burned it down and replaced it with a public toilet. There was someone in there right now, coughing and farting and stinking up the place.

Why did they even *need* a public toilet in the slums? The whole place was one big ... She sighed. This was probably some hare-brained politico's scheme to garner votes before the next election. *There,* she was right. The chootia had even put a sign over the door that said: *Municipal toilet most generously donated by Sree Jalan Lal Mintoe.*

Kavi sighed and picked her way up to Zofan's hut.

The man was away, so she plonked herself down on the porch and waited.

People stared as they walked past. Leaned in and whispered in each other's ears, but no one questioned her presence outside his hut. Zofan eventually trudged up with a sack of lentils over one shoulder. His beard hid the smile his eyes could not.

'I heard about the fight,' he said.

'Oh, ya? What are they saying?' Kavi said, trying to keep a straight face and failing.

He dropped the sack outside the door and joined Kavi on the porch. 'One punch knockout.'

She snorted. 'It wasn't just one punch.'

'It's what they're saying.' Zofan shrugged and reached for his hookah.

'Well, I guess there's no harm,' Kavi said, grinning from ear to ear. 'It was a knockout.'

She let him light up and take a couple of puffs before clearing her throat. 'Zofan-ji, I'm leaving for Azraaya tomorrow, to fight in the Siphon.'

He paused. Wiped the mouthpiece of the hookah on a sleeve. 'You think you have a chance?'

'I don't know.'

'But you have to try.'

'Yes.'

Zofan nodded. Nothing else needed to be said. No explanation required. He understood that there was no going back for her – not to what she once was. Death would be better.

'What about the artifact? The Venator?' he said after a long drag.

'The sahib has a contact who can get me access if I survive the Siphon and join the Vagola.'

He grunted. 'And have you thought about what you would do if your father and brothers are no longer …'

'Alive?'

Zofan's chin dipped, ever so slightly.

'No,' Kavi said, holding the thought underwater until it suffocated and died. 'One thing at a time.'

'Is there anything I can help with?'

Her eyes softened. 'No – yes.'

Zofan cocked his head at her. 'What?'

'Keep an eye on the sahib for me, please,' she said. 'Warn him if you hear anything … suspicious.'

'You think he's in some sort of danger?'

'No, not really, but—' She scratched the back of her head. 'Just in case.'

Zofan chuckled. 'I'll see what I can do.'

They spent a good hour reminiscing about her time in the slums – how she'd arrived, exhausted and half-dead. Her job at the seaside brothel and all the anecdotes she brought back. They swapped stories about Haibo, complained about the politicos, and by the time she said her goodbyes and made her way down to Raeth's temple, the artificed lamps were already burning, and shadows danced on the ominous black marble of the temple walls.

'I'd like to see the head priest,' she said to the duty swami at the top of the stairs.

The man gestured to the donation box.

She dropped a single worn and faded rayal into it.

He gave her an approving nod. 'Are you seeking Raeth's blessings?'

'Gods no.' She cleared her throat at his raised eyebrow. 'I would like to make an offering.'

He inclined his head and pointed to an enormous man tending to a tulsi plant in the middle of the stone courtyard.

The head priest, to her surprise, recognised her. He tapped his forehead. 'Sticky-girl. You are back for more blessings. Good!'

'Swami-ji, please.' She bowed. 'An offering for a soul.'

His mirth evaporated, and he gave her a grim nod. 'Come.'

Inside, at the foot of the altar, she got on her knees, aimed, mimed a practice hit, and hammered her coconut into the black stone. It split in two, splattered her arms and drenched the altar with its water. She slipped one half into her satchel and presented the other to the priest.

He accepted the offering with both hands, touched it to his forehead, and placed it with the other coconuts, ladoos, and bananas stacked under the protruding eyeball in the ceiling. 'When did the soul return to Hel?' the head priest asked.

'Four months ago.' Kavi pulled out a stick of incense, and while the priest held it in his large fingers, she struck a match and lit it, instantly infusing the air with the too-sweet scent of jasmine.

The priest took the stick of incense and stuck it into the soft white flesh of her coconut. 'Did their body have a name?'

'Haibo.'

'Was Haibo's return peaceful?'

The pain. The shock. Utterly powerless as uncaring strangers took his body apart. Alone and scared as his life dribbled down the sides of a cold gurney. 'No,' she said. 'It was not.' *Compound fractures*, the surgeon had told her, *infected with urine. We tried to amputate, but it was too late.*

'Then Haibo is blessed,' the priest said, dropping his voice to a whisper. 'Raeth will keep Haibo's soul close, closer than the others, so he can wash away their pain and suffering, so they may find a better home in the next life.'

Kavi put her hands together and closed her eyes. 'May they find a better home in the next life.'

The priest rang the bell. It echoed through the chamber and lingered in her ears as she walked out.

Both she and Haibo had been equally shocked the day they bumped into each other. Another Taemu in the same neighbourhood? The same age? They *had* to talk, but it had to be after dark. No one could know that two Taemu were speaking to each other.

After each payday, Haibo would show up at Kavi's hut with a flask of rum. They would drink and laugh and complain, share their dreams and plans, and one way or another, always end up discussing love. Haibo rambled on for hours about this woman across the bridge; a woman who could see past history and colour and skin, who laughed without reservation; who made his heart pound with a touch and his stomach somersault with a whisper.

When it was her turn, she'd talk about her brothers – Khagan, only a baby but already stoic and standoffish; and Kamith, curious, unafraid, and foolishly protective of her. She told him about her father, so proud, so strong, a man unaffected by his place in the world because he lived by an iron set of principles that acted as both shield and armour. And when she shared her plans for tracking them down, he was incredulous at first, but slowly came around, and wound up being even more enthusiastic than her.

Kavi glanced at the moon. Almost low tide. Time for her last stop. She adjusted her satchel and walked down to the beach.

Cool sea breeze ruffled her hair and forced her to blow it back out of her eyes. She stopped. It was supposed to be here. She'd followed his directions. Come at the right time. It was—

A pillar of moonlight slipped through the clouds and lit up a sheer face of rock the size of a three-storey building.

This is it. She clenched her toes.

You can see her name, Haibo had said.

Tell me.

No, you must see for yourself. It's beautiful.

Kavi's heartbeat raced. *Her name.* A being that was just for them. Just for the Taemu. Their very own Goddess.

Her initial reaction had been, *Fuck her.* This Goddess had abandoned the Taemu. She obviously didn't care about her people.

Maybe age had brought about a change of heart, maybe it was an awareness of her impending death, maybe it was the comfort she now found in ritual, or maybe it was just her way of saying goodbye to Bochan; either way, she wanted to know.

Kavi walked with one hand on the damp, cold rock, tracing the grooves and indentations that time and the sea had marked it with. Wet sand slipped into her chappals and filled the grooves between her toes as she snaked around the curve in the beach. *There is a shrine,* Haibo said, *a place that is ours. You can only find it if you are looking for it.*

She took off her chappals, slapped the sand away from them and tucked them into her back pocket. *Walk barefoot. When you feel stone, look right.*

It wasn't long before the mushy sand under her feet gave way to smooth, wet stone. She stopped. Searched and groped along the surface until she found it. The night made it appear like it was just one long, uninterrupted wall of rock. But there was a woman-sized length that lacked substance. A slab of darkness. And she stepped into it.

She fumbled in her bag for the candle. Used her body to block the funnelled breeze and lit it.

Shadows and stalactites hung from the ceiling. Some were low enough to turn into nascent pillars. A section of the floor was hewn into pockmarked stairs that climbed into a rent at the top of the grotto. Kavi smothered the fluttering in her stomach and followed them up.

Shadows danced on the walls. The candle's flame flickered, but held steady. Kavi extended her hand into the rent and flooded the shrine with light.

She froze. The hair on the back of her neck stood on end.

A single word was scrawled and scratched into the walls. Over and over again, like the scrawlers were afraid they would forget. It had no meaning. Not in Kraelish. Or old Raayan. But if she had to guess, she'd say that this was a word from *her* language.

DRISANA.

And tucked into the corner, with the word inscribed around its head like a halo, was a tiny humanoid idol. Faded blue with bulky arms, legs, and with swords in both hands. The face was a smudge, but someone had drawn a pair of angry red eyes on it. At its base was the paraphernalia used to write on the walls: a sharp piece of stone and another thicker, heavier block. Off to the side were rotting flowers and a stiff, black banana with the root of an incense stick in its carcass.

Kavi swallowed the lump in her throat, unslung her satchel, and sat cross-legged in front of her Goddess.

'Well, Drisana,' Kavi said in a quivering whisper, 'here we are.'

The red eyes stared back at her in silence.

'Do you know what they've done to our people?'

Wind howled through the narrow entrance to the grotto.

Kavi arranged her half-coconut in front of the idol. Used her candle to light an incense stick and jammed it into the coconut. 'Maybe one day' – she put her hands together and bowed her head – 'when you're done with your nap, you could come see.'

A sliver of the sun peeked out over the horizon when she finally left the grotto. She'd barely slept, but that was fine. There would be plenty of time to sleep on the train. This was her last morning in Bochan, and she wanted to soak it in.

The city was borderline pleasant when everyone was asleep. Populated only by buildings, rickshaws, and trees, which seemed to grow in whatever nook and cranny they could find. Coconut trees, guava and mango trees, massive, ancient banyans with long, dangling beards. Some of them were here long before the Kraelish arrived. Long before they uprooted her people and sailed them to the subcontinent.

Like most cities in Raaya, Bochan was given a new name – under the guise of patriotism – when the Kraelish had left. Bochalapatnam. No one used it except the officials. Bochan was just easier to say. Kavi stopped and stared at a poster for Sree Jalan Lal Mintoe's election campaign. What these wealthy politico types struggled to understand was that Raaya was a country of multiple allegiances. First, to the place you were born; second, to the deity you followed; and third, to the Republic.

Her new home, Azraaya, was Meshira's city. Goddess of fertility and copulation and wealth. Said to live in the seed of man and the eggs of women. *Yes, bhaenchod, she lives in your testicles and ovaries, but no, you can't get into her temples without a hundred rayal donation.*

Kavi was a no-place, no-God woman. Had always been. She didn't know where she was born. She had no love for the Republic. And as for faith, sure, she visited Raeth's temples when she needed to, but that was because it was the only place of worship that would allow her in.

But she was no longer that person. No longer this *nothing* they told her she was. She was a Taemu, and she had an allegiance.

An idea, scrubbed from the collective memory, that she'd now pledged her loyalty to. An idea, however abstract and unlikely, that no one could take from her, that gave her a connection, and a closeness, to her people.

She licked her lips, and said the name under her breath.

Drisana.

Chapter 27

'The man you will need to see about accommodation is called Massa Zanzane.' Bithun passed her a piece of paper. 'The address.'

The Imperial Rickshaw Company, 161 Gulab Chamcha Road, opposite Reddy's Dead Body Disposals. Kavi tugged on an ear. What the Hel kind of place was this? she asked Bithun.

'His business,' Bithun said, 'which also doubles as his residence.'

She narrowed her eyes. 'He manages a rickshaw fleet?'

Bithun sneezed and reached for his handkerchief. 'No, nothing like that, he inherited the company. Too lazy to change the name.'

'So, what does he do?'

'Oh, art, antiques, you know.' He glanced at her sideways. 'This and that.'

Right.

'You can trust him, Kavithri.' He patted her on the shoulder. 'He was friends with my daughter.'

She sighed and tucked her hands in her pockets. 'And your contact at the Vagola? The artificer?'

'They too were friends with—' He caught himself. 'Nice try.'

Kavi tsked and reached out to pet Tsubu – who the sahib had

on a leash – but the dog shrank away. 'Sahib, why not just tell me who they are.'

'Relax,' Bithun said. 'They will find you once you've made it into the Vagola.' He chewed his lip. 'Kavithri ...'

She cocked her head. 'Sahib?'

'You don't have to – there is no shame in changing your mind, you know.' He lowered his voice. 'If you fight in the Siphon, and if they learn what you really are – or if the Kraelish find out ...'

'I'll be fine, sahib,' Kavi said. 'No one will know.' Besides, it was a risk she was willing to take.

A bell pealed out from the stationmaster's office and Kavi's muscles locked up. She fought the impulse to wrap a cloth around her head and sprint, like the porters who now streamed past her, to the edge of the platform.

The incoming train whistled. Distant and faint at first, but with each booming heartbeat it got louder and closer and soared to a high-pitched crescendo of anticipation that was abruptly cut off when the dull-red *Chimabali Express* clamoured around the bend and chugged its way into the station.

Kavi wiped her sweaty palms on her salwar and lifted her trunk. 'Thank you, sahib.'

Bithun waved it off. 'Ticket?'

She reached into her pockets. 'Got it.'

'Money?'

The rolled-up wad of reddish-white banknotes were ensconced safely in her blouse. 'With me.'

Passengers disembarked. Porters jostled for their attention and haggled and hefted trunks onto cloth-wrapped heads. Kavi swallowed through the sudden thickness in her throat. That was once her, there, pleading with a passenger to allow her to carry his suitcase. And there, slumped over with the weight of the luggage on her head.

Her eyes prickled, but she ruthlessly shut it down. No tears. She'd promised herself. No tears.

'Remember your training,' Bithun said.

She turned and nodded to the sahib.

'And if you ever feel afraid, or alone in Azraaya, look for your people.'

She blinked. 'Sahib?'

'Now go' – Bithun ushered her along – 'or it will leave without you.'

According to the ticket, she was in *3-C*. First class with all meals paid for the duration of the journey. Two nights with an entire cabin to herself.

Bithun and Tsubu followed her up the platform until she found her compartment. Young couples, honeymooners she guessed (it was wedding season in Bochan), chatted excitedly while they waited their turn to board.

She was at a loss for words. There was so much she wanted to say to Bithun, so much she wanted to ask him, but all she did was stand there with her trunk in both hands and stare at the giggling young men and women in front of her.

When it was finally her turn, she climbed the steps with a pounding heart and was ushered in by the conductor before she had a chance to turn around and wave goodbye.

Breathless, she elbowed the door to her cabin open and hurled her trunk under the upholstered seats. She yanked the retractable glass partition over the windows open and peered through the bars. They were still there, waiting.

Bithun smiled and waved at her.

She grinned and stuck an arm out to wave back.

The engine, which couldn't have been more than three or

four compartments in front of hers, hissed and sent a rumble through the entire train.

Tsubu stopped sniffing a discarded ladoo wrapper and locked eyes with her. The cabin juddered, shook from side to side, and, with an ear-shredding whistle from the engine, lurched into motion.

Kavi's lips tightened. Her vision blurred. Bithun and Tsubu were not alone. Standing on the platform with them were the shades of friends and acquaintances she'd met in Bochan: Haibo, with his legs intact and his infectious smile on his face; a beautiful woman in an unusually sweaty sari, who looked familiar but who she just couldn't place; Zofan, watching her with those unreadable eyes of his; Dremanth and the girls from the seaside brothel; stationmaster Muthu who was glowering – wait, no, that was actually him. She smiled and waved. He scowled and spat.

Tsubu strained at his leash, and the sahib released him. He chased Kavi's compartment. Ran between porters and passengers. Barked at her until he ran out of platform and then stood, stock-still, with his tail tucked between his legs as he watched Kavi roll away.

Now you come around. She smiled and blew him a kiss as he shrank into the distance.

When Tsubu was nothing more than a tiny dot of fur, she pulled the window shut, tipped her head back, and closed her eyes. The tension in her muscles eased with each measured breath. There was nothing to do now but wait. And rest. She was one step closer. She was on her way.

The next morning, when the train stopped at the Hecca cantonment to stock up on food, Kavi bought a newspamphlet and spread it out on the table while she ate her breakfast dosa.

The front page was packed with news of the Imperial advance.

The Kraelish, like Bithun said, had continued to trade with Raaya post-independence; but the Council had recently signed a new agreement with the Hamakans and Fumeshis, who would provide base materials for Raaya's engines and steam-tech at half the price of what the Kraelish were charging. The Empire was not happy. But no one had expected mobilisation, and until now, the increased Kraelish presence in the north was only considered posturing. This news changed everything.

Apparently, they'd torn up their treaty with the insular northern kingdoms and launched a full-on invasion. A new weapon called – she mouthed the word – *makra*, had decimated entire armies in the space of day. An artist had drawn a charcoal impression of this weapon. She twisted the paper around to get a better look.

A sharp-edged, humanoid *thing* towered over the skyline of a walled city. She dipped a piece of dosa in some sambhar and shoved it in her mouth. Was that to scale? It couldn't be. Nothing was that big.

It said the makra were over five-hundred metres in height, and six of these weapons had been spotted so far. Speculation was that Kraelish artificers had built them out of material salvaged from the Deadlands. A chill ran up her spine and she flipped the page.

More news on Azraayan politics and the various factions debating over how the Council should respond to this threat. Some even said there was nothing to worry about.

She flipped the page.

Rickshaw accident injures family of four. Agoma task force announced by the Raayan Investigative Department. Arsonist sets fire to another brothel in the Lantern district.

Next.

Artificers create new water-heating device – on display at the

Artificed Hydraulics Centre (see artist's impression). Council announces unscheduled meeting at the Hive today. This month's Jishutra calendar.

She stopped. Ran her finger over the dates and the auspicious activities recommended for each day – safely travel, open a business, divorce a spouse, adopt a pet – until she arrived at today's date. *Ideal day for conceiving. Editor's note: Utilise the lounging buffalo position during climax for maximum benefit.*

She scratched her head. What the Hel was the *lounging buffalo position?* Did they want people to lay on their stomachs on the side of the road, munch on some hay, and act disinterested while their partner ploughed them? She snorted and went back to read the story on the water-heating artifice.

Once she'd exhausted her interest in the newspamphlet, she spent the rest of the day at the window, peering out at barren plateaus and mountain ranges which – as the sun reached its peak and dipped back down – became foaming rivers and palm trees and rice fields where people stood knee-deep in opaque water.

The wind ruffled her hair as she watched the lengthening shadows of the compartments chase after the train. Her eyes glazed over, her thoughts drifted back to the night of the fight – the smells, the sounds, the moment Bhagu had knocked her out on her feet and she'd gone back to the room with the adobe walls and woven mats. Just like when Mojan had broken her arm. What was that place? Another memory from a past life? There was no other explanation for it.

She'd been afraid to mention it to Bithun. Afraid that he'd say she was still recovering from the long-term effects of the concussion or something, and that she needed more time to rest. She wrinkled her nose. For a while it had really seemed like it had stopped.

Then she'd gone and got punched in the head.

She sighed.

Maybe that was it. Maybe she just needed to stop getting hit in the head.

*

The night was one long blur of darkness whizzing past; interrupted, occasionally, by a sleepy station where a handful of passengers exchanged places on the train.

But finally, at dawn, a rattle, a sputter, the cabin crested the horizon, and Azraaya leaped up to meet her.

Kavi caught a glimpse of an immense sprawl of blocky buildings punctuated by domes and minarets and spires, before it all disappeared as the train picked up speed and shot down a sharp incline. She clutched the windowsill, squirmed as her stomach dropped, and stared, mouth agape and light-headed, at the monstrous wall encircling the city.

Its shadow had transformed the lush, green countryside into dark, ubiquitous moss that spread like a carpet across the last kilometre to the tunnel. The *Chimabali Express* shot into it, and plunged the cabin into darkness.

One. Two. Three. Four. And she burst back into the light.

Kavi gawked as they breezed past a glittering peacock-blue lake that sat at the foot of a white marble temple. Meshira's priests, a gaggle of white and gold dhoti-wearing swamis, were skipping down its stairs for their ritual early morning plunge. She'd heard that once a year the entire city came to a standstill to celebrate the Goddess's famous festival.

The train whistled and slowed as it entered a residential area. Colourful two-storeyed houses sat wall-to-wall. Yellows, pinks, and blues blurred with the laundry that hung out of windows, while early risers on the terraces watched the train with bleary eyes.

Textile looms loomed and factory towers towered over dhobi ghats where men and women walloped smooth chunks of stone with wet clothes. The train chugged past botanical gardens and hawker centres and massive warehouses where rickshaw mechanics were already at work. It skirted the edges of the Azraayan slums, an enormous crescent of tightly packed huts and tents that hugged the far wall and covered over a quarter of the city's surface area, and if she guessed correctly, housed over half its population. Either way, if this was a city, then Bochan was a village.

Chapter 28

'Where to boss?'

Kavi gave the rickshaw driver the address.

He looked her up and down, lingered on her eyes, and finally bobbled his head. 'Can, seventy rayals.'

'Thirty,' Kavi countered, out of habit.

The driver sucked in his cheeks and spat. 'Fifty-five. I have a small baby to feed.'

Small baby? Really? 'Fine.'

Kavi shoved her trunk onto the backseat and was halfway in herself when she spotted the Taemu on the other side of the street. She slowly stepped back out of the rickshaw.

The woman slouched from the weight of a large burlap sack over her shoulder. Her eyes roved the narrow drains that lined the street, brows furrowed in concentration. She stopped. Bent. Picked up an empty idli wrapper and tossed it over her shoulder into the sack. They had the same hair, same complexion, same physique – the last few months had added muscle to Kavi's, but the woman even had the same wide shoulders and stocky build as her.

Was this place like Bochan? Would they get into trouble if they were seen talking? Maybe she could—

Loud, obnoxious laughter dragged Kavi's attention away. A

trio of men, dressed in Kraelish shirts and the garish blue lungis of the Dolmonda gang, exchanged jibes and chortled as they walked in the garbage-picker's direction. The woman was so absorbed in her work that she was oblivious to their presence.

The man in the middle spotted the woman at the last moment, stuck his chest out, and knocked her off her feet.

She stumbled, held on to her sack with both hands, and instantly fell into a series of bows, repeating with each one, 'Sorry, saab-ji. Sorry, saab-ji. Sorry, saab-ji.'

Kavi winced. She'd been there. That was the right thing to do. Exude subservience, make yourself small, and hope they lose interest. She glanced at the rickshaw driver. The man was tightening a screw on the lever at the base of his seat with a screwdriver. She narrowed her eyes. No wonder there were so many rickshaw accidents in this city.

She turned back to find the Taemu still hunched over, clinging to her sack of rubbish with her eyes firmly on the ground. The men berated her for her clumsiness and forced her to scurry out of their way as they stomped down the footpath.

'Okay,' the driver said as he pumped the lever, 'ready.'

The meekness in the woman's posture evaporated the instant the trio disappeared around the corner. She cracked her neck, spat in their footsteps, looked up and locked eyes with Kavi. A flicker of recognition passed through them, and she nodded.

Kavi nodded back an *I know what that feels like* acknowledgement.

The woman returned to her work. Hunched over with the weight of the sack as she moved down the street like a wraith.

The driver waited for Kavi to hop on. He screamed at a passing horse-drawn carriage, *Dai! You want to die or what? No respect for anyone else, these carriage chootia, I tell you,* and accelerated into traffic.

Where Bochan was sluggish, filthy, and seedy, Azraaya was fast, dazzling, and dizzy. Even the capital's run-down or derelict parts had a smouldering mystique to them – a promise of something more sinister behind the colourful facades and shopfronts.

They drove past bars that already had their shutters open, where goondas sat outside on wooden stools and stared at pedestrians with open suspicion. Past tall buildings whose streets were perpetually murky and mucky. Through squalid alleys where agoma addicts recovered from the night. And, finally, they screeched to a halt at the entrance to Gulab Chamcha Road.

'Cannot go down there, road is bad.' The driver shook his head and gestured for her to pay up.

Kavi hauled her trunk down the narrow, damp street until she found a sign with a poorly painted image of a cadaver and the words *Reddy's Dead Body Disposals* in front of a single-storey building.

A man – severely hung-over, judging from his dishevelled appearance and bloodshot eyes – peered at her over his shoulder as he urinated on the shutters.

On the other side of the street, *opposite,* like it said on the paper, was a long warehouse-like structure with two floors and half-finished pillars on the roof to give the builders the option to add a third.

There were no walls or gates, just a large hoarding facing away from her, a massive chained double door on the ground floor, and stairs leading up to a long verandah on the top floor where another door hung open. *The Imperial Rickshaw Company. Est. 2267* was emblazoned in faded Kraelish letters over the upper door's panel.

This is it. Kavi crossed the street, lugged her trunk up the stairs onto the verandah, and stopped. She stared, mouth open and brows furrowed, at the image on the hoarding.

A painting of a Raayan woman caressing her bleached face smiled back at her. Text underneath it screamed at Kavi to purchase and slather Homandu's Ointment all over her face so she could lighten her skin, because, of course, lighter skin would make her more attractive and confident.

Kavi ran a hand over the dark-brown skin on her face, over the layer of sweat that had crystallised into fine, white powder, and scowled. Another unwanted legacy of the Kraelish occupation that the Raayans just refused to cast aside.

She set the trunk down at her feet and peeked into the office.

A man sat behind a desk, puffing away on a beedi while he drew on a large piece of paper. He took a deep drag, balanced his beedi on the rim of an ashtray, and absent-mindedly stuck a finger up his nose. Kavi watched as he explored his cavernous nostrils, clawed out a piece of hardened snot, and gracefully flicked it into the ashtray. Then he moved onto the other nostril.

The man was a sahib, or at the least a member of the upper classes. There was no doubt about it – the Kraelish clothes, the immaculately oiled and parted hair, the clean-shaven face, the pale, unhealthy complexion, the finger up the nostril … well, except that. But she figured even the rich needed to pick their noses from time to time.

Kavi slipped out of her chappals, prepared a greeting, and stepped in.

The stench of burned tamakhu rammed its way up her nostrils, down her throat, and shut her up before she could speak. She struggled and failed to smother a gag.

The man froze. Carefully extricated his finger from his nose and stubbed out his beedi in the ashtray filled to the brim with old stubs.

'Welcome,' he said, turning to Kavi with a face-splitting

smile and a hint of surprise quickly suppressed. 'Please, come in, have a seat.'

'Good afternoon, sahib,' Kavi said, breathing through her mouth. 'My name is Kavithri. I was sent—'

'Kavithri? Yes. A powerful name for a powerful woman!' He cocked an eyebrow. 'So … is it your mother? Your father?'

She blinked. 'Sahib?'

'The possession: which one of your parents has the demon occupied? Or is it your sister?' The man stood, clasped his hands behind his back, and walked to the windows.

Kavi stared at the back of the man's head. *Demon?* 'What?'

'Highly unlikely that you're married' – he lifted a booted foot and planted it on the windowsill – 'which would be because you are having trouble choosing from all the men throwing themselves at your feet, of course.'

Men? Feet? 'Who?'

'Are *you* the victim? Fear not!' He levelled a finger at Kavi from across the room. 'You have come to the right place, Kavithri. These foul spawn of Raeth's droppings are no match for me.'

Kavi grimaced. 'Sahib, please—'

'Are you slow to wake in the mornings? Do you struggle with attention? Do you eat *way* too much?'

Wait, that does sound like me. Kavi started to nod but caught herself just in time. *Oh, this man is good,* really *good.* 'Sahib, wait—'

'Kavithri!' He turned from the window and stomped over. Placed a hand on her shoulder.

Kavi's eyes went wide. She tried to slip away, but the man's claw-like grip kept her in place.

'I'm here to help, Kavithri,' he said, blinking big sympathetic eyes. 'Talk to me.'

'Okay.'

The man nodded encouragingly.

'Sahib Jarayas Bithun told me to find you. I'm from—'

He started. 'You? You're the person from Bithun's letters?'

Kavi nodded. 'You're Massa Zanzane?'

He withdrew his arm from her shoulder. 'I wasn't expecting a …'

'Taemu?' Kavi said with a sigh.

Massa Zanzane shook his head. 'A woman.'

Oh.

'You know how the Siphon works, right?' He leaned in to peer at her. 'Half the applicants end up dead. Only twenty-five make it through. That's how it works. That's why it's called the Siphon.' He made a shoving-something-big-through-something-small gesture with his hands. 'You know what I mean?'

'I—'

'Well, if that's what you want.' He plonked himself down on a bright red divan. 'I've made all the arrangements, but' – he gestured for her to take a seat –'circumstances have forced a few changes.'

'Changes?'

'First,' Massa said, 'let me apologise. Jarayas mentioned your name but—' He coughed, a deep wheezing hack that made his eyes water, and pounded his chest with a fist.

Kavi winced. The man was what, four – maybe five years older than her? And he already looked like he was on his deathbed.

'Listen,' Massa said, catching his breath, 'you know what's been going on with the Kraelish?'

She nodded.

'Good. Now, before I get started—' He slipped a case of beedis out of his pocket. 'I have some bad news.'

Her mouth went dry. 'Bad news?'

'Yes,' he said, with a beedi stuck in between his lips. 'Very bad.' He used an artificed matchstick, a long, thin stick of steel, to light his beedi. 'My assistant, the bloody bhaenchod, recently quit. So, in exchange for lodging and feeding and arming you, I will need you to work for me.'

She sighed. 'As—'

'Only in the evenings, of course,' he said with a mouthful of smoke. 'I wouldn't dream of keeping you from all the punching and stabbing. You just need to man – *woman* the desk and deal with clients while I sit over there and pretend to look busy. You know, so it looks professional.'

'As you wish,' she said, then cleared her throat. 'What is it that you do? Sahib.'

'I acquire and sell art and antiques—' He took a drag. 'And conduct exorcisms and assist with any supernatural dilemmas my clients may have.'

She stared at him.

He stared back, unblinking.

'Exorcisms,' she repeated.

'Yes,' he said. 'Not many people know this, but sometimes a soul latches onto people – humans it bonded with during its sojourn among the living – and refuses to return to Hel. Over time, this soul, without the nourishment of Hel, morphs into what we in the business like to call a demon.'

'I see,' she said, trying to keep a straight face.

'Yes, when that happens, you have a possession.'

Kavi coughed into a fist and nodded. *What have you got me into, Bithun?*

'For instance' – the capillaries in his eyes flashed silver – 'the soul that is attached to you . . .' He paled. Swallowed. And took a long drag from a trembling beedi.

She frowned. What was that? His eyes had – no, she must've imagined it. 'Sahib?'

'Hmm?'

'You were saying.'

Massa frowned. Squinted at her. 'Oh, yes, the Siphon.'

'No, you were—'

'You wouldn't have heard about this down in Bochan, but' – he glanced at the ashtray that was just out of reach, sighed, and flicked ash onto the floor instead – 'the dates for the Vagola have been adjusted.'

Kavi cocked her head.

'The Siphon runs on Vagola time,' Massa said, 'and the Vagola brought the term forward because of pressure from the Council. The Council is pissing themselves because of the Kraelish. The Kraelish—' He made a face. 'Who knows what those chootia are thinking. Either way, the Council wants a new batch of Blades and somewhat-trained mages at the ready in case, you know, they need to send reinforcements to the border.'

'What does this mean for me?' Kavi said.

'Orientation is this evening. The Siphon starts tomorrow morning. I have submitted your enrolment papers and paid the donation. I didn't remember your name, so I used my neighbour's.'

Kavi's eyes bulged. 'Tomorrow?'

'Oh, yes,' he said, massaging his chest. 'And if you want to hear the head of the Vagola spout her nonsense *and* enjoy a free dinner, orientation is this evening.'

Kavi moaned and squeezed the base of her palms into her eye sockets. It was supposed to be a week away. They'd planned for her to have a week to find her feet and get used to the city. She took a deep, controlled breath. *It is what it is.* 'You said you used a different name for me?'

Massa, who'd been smoking and studying her in silence, chuckled. 'Subbal Reddy.'

'Reddy?' She jerked a thumb over her shoulder. 'From the dead body disposal?'

'The one and only. Don't worry.' He raised a placating arm at the consternation on her face. 'I asked him if I could. He said it was okay.'

'Not him, the Siphon. What if they learn I'm not this Subbal Reddy?'

'Oh, them.' He waved it off. 'They don't care. As long as you have the receipt for the donation, you could call yourself Emperor Luthar the Ninth and they wouldn't bat an eye.' He smiled. 'Entering the Siphon isn't exactly a competition, you know. The only people who do so are either batshit insane, or mad as cowdung.'

She stared at him, speechless, as her insides churned.

'Oh, also—' Massa tipped his head back and stared at the ceiling. 'Bithun mentioned you would need rats.'

'Yes, sahib.' How much did he know?

Massa glanced at her. 'Relax, Bithun filled me in. I will ensure you have a crate available at the end of each day.'

Kavi ground her teeth and looked away. Bithun should have told her first. 'Thank you, sahib.'

'Don't call me sahib.' Massa took an expansive breath, coughed, and stood. 'You can call me boss.'

'As you wish, sah— boss.'

'Good. Now, I was informed that I was to equip you with a sword. I happen to have a few that were scavenged from the ruins of Ethuran.' He gave her a meaningful glance. 'Weapons once wielded by the swordmasters, or so I was told.'

Her jaw dropped. 'Taemu swordmasters?'

'Oh, yes.'

Kavi sucked in a sharp breath. A real swordmaster's weapon. A Taemu sword. In *her* hands. Her heart threatened to thump its way out her chest.

'Oh, don't worry.' Massa left his beedi hanging between his lips and pulled out a set of keys. 'It's fully paid for, and they're all in tip-top condition. Sharp as they were three centuries ago. Now, would you like to see your room first? Or …'

Chapter 29

Two dozen ancient, rusted rickshaws sat squeezed into one corner of the warehouse. In the other, shelves were stacked with tamakhu, beedis, newspamphlets, and marble busts of dead sultans and kings. The rest of the ground floor of the Imperial Rickshaw Company was filled with hundreds of paintings: rolled up, propped up, covered, uncovered, framed, folded, and occasionally discarded under layers and layers of dust.

One particularly large piece of art – an oil painting of a bustling tea room – hung on the far wall and demanded Kavi's attention. Inside its gilded frame, waiters stood hunched over tables, patrons sipped on beverages, women laughed, and men read the dailies. And in the midst of all this everyday activity, a man lay on his back on a table, naked, ignored, and covered with bruises and cuts. His eyes were sewn shut. His mouth hung open in a soundless scream. His ribcage, or what was left of it, was splayed open as a bouquet of red tentacles erupted from his chest. He was drawn with such excruciating detail that it forced the rest of the painting into a blur.

'You like it?' Massa said, hovering over her shoulder.

It made her skin crawl. But maybe Massa liked the painting, or worse, was the artist. 'I don't understand it.'

Massa chuckled. 'I'd be concerned if you did.' He pointed

to the initials in the corner. *T.K.* 'This was painted by the Necromancer, Thaynush Kolari,' he said with a wistful fondness in his voice, 'a month before he took his own life.'

Kavi's lips tightened. 'How long ago?'

'Not long after we gained independence. A hundred and fifty years, give or take,' Massa said, and gestured for her to follow. He led her to a dusty bookshelf packed tight with ancient-looking tomes and stacks of paper tied with string. She recognised a dusty copy of *The Diary of an Unknown Mage*, but the rest …

'What's this?' She said, reaching for an enormous book titled *The Great Exodus.*

'Histories by Raayan academics.' Massa stood on his toes and groped through a top shelf. 'Recorded before the Kraelish rewrote our past – here we are, swords.'

Kavi yanked her hand away as he pulled down a bundle of scabbarded swords.

'Let's see,' he said, tapping the hilts. 'Cutlass, Kraelish rapier, Tulwar – aha!' He picked three swords out from the bundle and hurled the rest back on the shelf.

'Now …' He laid them out on the ground, hilts facing Kavi. 'Choose.'

Kavi got down on her haunches. Pursed her lips. 'How did you get these?'

'Pilfered from Kraelish infantry after Ethuran—' He wheezed, coughed, and pounded his chest. 'After the siege, I mean.'

Kavi frowned. *Well, of course, after the siege. When else?*

'Anyway,' Massa said, catching his breath, 'they were sold to collectors in Kraelin, who then sold them to visiting sahibs, who then went bankrupt, and' – he snapped his fingers – 'three centuries later, here they are.'

Kavi grunted, checked to ensure Massa was safely out of range, and drew the first sword.

It was perfect. The blade was double-edged, long, sharp. The guard was wide and thick. The round pommel was weighted to give the weapon immaculate balance and the grip fit in her hands like it was made for her. Perfect.

She reluctantly put it away, turned to the second sword, and scratched her head. She'd never seen anything like it. Instead of a guard, or a hilt, the blade ended in a bronze hand.

Massa squatted next to her with a series of groans and cracks. 'I suspect this one was purely decorative,' he said. 'Something a leader or a general would have carried.'

Goosebumps rippled across the back of Kavi's neck. She gently put the sword back down. If what he said was true, then this was more than a weapon. It was a symbol. It was sacred.

Still on her haunches, she shuffled over and reached for the final weapon.

The scabbard was black, scarred, and heavy. The hilt was as long as her forearm and wrapped in overlapping red and black thread. She held it with a high grip, fingers squished into an almost non-existent guard, as she unsheathed the blade.

Unlike sword number one, this one's blade was flat, narrow, and single-edged. It curved at the tip, like the top half of a crescent moon. Its steel was notched, chipped, and had lost its lustre. But there was no rust. Not a speck. She held it at arm's length. Tested its weight like Mojan had taught her. It was top-heavy, due to the strong tip. That skewed balance meant the sword encouraged forward movement. It wanted you to fight. To go all in.

'My supplier called this one a light sword,' Massa said, his eyes flicking between her and the weapon. 'Lethal, if used correctly.'

Light sword? It was as heavy as the others. Just more compact. Sure, it could be *lethal*, but that went both ways. If she made even a single mistake with it during a fight, she could have her fingers sliced off, or worse, end up dead.

On the other hand, if she somehow mastered it, the sword would fight with her. Not just a simple extension of her arm. It would guide her, tell her where to go.

This, out of all three, was a swordmaster's weapon.

Kavi bit the inside of her lip. Tempting. But the sensible and practical choice was sword number one. She didn't have the time to—

The air rushed out of her lungs and her body locked itself in place. The warehouse faded. Stars exploded on the edges of her vision. She hung, suspended, suffocating, in a dark abyss.

She was nothing. She didn't deserve air. She was a mote of dust. A speck in the eye of a Jinn. Her Jinn.

Raktha's dark orb contracted. A shudder ran through its core. And it dilated.

Maayin surged from its curvature. The crimson streams grew wider and larger. They merged and subsumed each other until they hung over Kavi like a colossal tidal wave of blood.

She was afraid. She was in awe. She wanted to *know.* Kavi lowered her head. Raktha. Mysterious, reticent, Raktha had something to say, and she would listen.

Raktha's maayin crashed down on her.

Obliterated her awareness.

Pieced
  it
    back
      together.
      And
    added
  something
new.

An idea as alien as it was familiar. Kavi's lips parted. And she gave the Jinn a voice:

Daughter.

'What was that?'

Kavi gasped for air. She was back in the warehouse. She could breathe.

'Did you say something?' Massa said from somewhere far away.

She was a daughter of the Jinn?

Kavi swallowed air in huge gulps. Impossible. It didn't make any sense. Could they even have children? Could they—

It started as a trickle. A hint of raw emotion, a curiosity that slipped into her chest and probed and tested, and in the space of a heartbeat, turned into an avalanche. Kavi rocked back on her heels. Shook with an anger that dwarfed her own. Mourned for a loss so vast and deep that it brought tears to her eyes. Drowned in a loneliness so overwhelming and tangible that she once again struggled to breathe.

'Maybe you should go with this one,' Massa said, poking the first sword, oblivious to her discomfort.

'No,' Kavi said in a hoarse whisper. She took a shuddering breath and slid the blade back into its scabbard. A tingle ran up her fingers. 'This one.'

She was not the daughter.

The sword was.

'You sure?' Massa said, peering at her.

She stood on shaky feet, sword held tight with both hands. 'Yes.'

'Great.' He clapped his hands and gathered up the rejected swords. 'Now, let me show you where you'll be sleeping.'

He took her to a room on the second floor, which – to her astonishment – had actual running tap water. There was also a mattress, a pillow, an old almirah, and a desk without a chair.

'I'll come get you for lunch,' Massa said, and left.

Kavi propped the sword up against the only window in the room, took a couple of steps back, and sat cross-legged, with her chin resting on her knuckles.

She stared at it.

She waited.

She pouted.

'You going to do something or what?' she said, after a good half-hour had passed.

Maybe she was wrong. Maybe she'd read too many Tsubumani novels. Maybe sentient swords were just a myth.

But what she'd felt was real. It had come from the sword. It was alive. Or something in it was alive and capable of human emotion. She just had to wait. Maybe Raktha would speak to her again and explain exactly what it meant by *daughter*.

All her attempts to strike up a conversation with the ancient wedge of steel were in vain. And Raktha, it seemed, had returned to its cone of silence.

Massa, as promised, knocked on her door when it was time for lunch. Which was a triple-decker tiffin-box delivered by a bespectacled man in a Kraelish flat cap. He finger-saluted Massa and left without saying a word.

Box one was packed with spicy chana-masala; box two contained five folded rotis smothered in ghee; box three was a drumstick of tandooried chicken. Massa Zanzane ate well, and she was glad for it.

He talked while she ate, and continued long after she was done. He ranted about politics, complained about the city's plumbing, bemoaned the state of the art world, lowered his voice and shared gossip: Reddy's wife was having an affair, scandalous.

Through it all, Kavi nodded with a pasted-on smile and eyed the clock in the corner. With each passing hour, the fluttering in her stomach got wilder. The pounding in her chest got louder. And her grip on her sword got tighter. Soon she would be walking into the Vagola. Not the way she wanted. But still, it was finally happening.

Massa was listing the various places in the city where one could purchase contraband, *if one were so inclined (wink),* when the stern man who'd dropped off their lunch knocked on the door frame.

'It's time,' Massa announced. 'We can continue our discussion later, but if you want to make it to the Vagola on time, you must leave now.' He motioned to the man standing in the door. 'Ratan will drive you there and back.'

Kavi bobbed her head and stood.

'Here,' Massa said, holding out a folded sheet of paper. 'Your enrolment papers.'

'Thanks, boss.'

Massa cleared his throat.

'Yes?'

'You can leave the sword here,' he said with a bemused smile. 'You won't need it today.'

Chapter 30

Ratan, it turned out, was a rickshaw driver Massa kept on permanent retainer. And Ratan, she learned, sitting in the backseat with both hands white-knuckled on the rusted handrail, had no sense of self-preservation.

He accelerated through the city like a Raeth-damned maniac; stopped only at intersections to glare at the red-helmeted men who directed traffic, and then he was off again, skidding through intersections and screeching past shocked pedestrians.

The vehicle eventually came to a sputtering halt outside a crowd of hawkers, and Kavi hopped off the rickshaw with a relieved sigh. She stood on unsteady feet, with one hand still latched to the rail, and cursed the inventors of the infernal machine.

'Vagola,' Ratan said, pointing to a shiny black dome that sat behind a long stretch of wall. Men and women were already milling around its gates, waiting impatiently for the stewards to check their papers.

Kavi swallowed a lump in her throat. It wasn't so long ago that she'd stood, just like she was now, outside the Yoma-Murthy Public School in Bochan – with trembling lips and clenched fists – and watched the throng of students on opening day. She'd yearned to be one of them. Dreamed of carrying a heavy, book-laden bag half her size. Longed to wear the white-blue chequered uniform and braid her hair and tie a white ribbon in it like all the other girls.

And here she was now. At the entrance to the greatest institution of learning in Raaya. No uniforms. No bags full of books. No ribbons. She wouldn't *really* be a student. But neither would she be a spectator.

'I'll be training at the Vagola,' she said out loud, just so she could hear it.

'No,' Ratan said.

'What?'

He flicked a thumb over his shoulder, at a fenced field with patchy grass where a herd of buffaloes grazed and watched the humans with utter disinterest. 'There,' he said. 'Training for the Siphon is always there. Sometimes in the Picchadi stadium. But mostly there.'

Kavi stared at a buffalo.

'But you can still *see* the Vagola, so …' Ratan shrugged.

Kavi opened her mouth to explain that it was not the same thing, that *seeing* was not the same as *being*, when she spotted the self-congratulatory I-just-said-something-hilarious smirk on his face. *Well, aren't you a funny son-of-a-bitch?*

'I'll find a place to park,' Ratan said, 'down by the canal. Find me when you're done.'

Kavi gawked as she followed the throng into the campus. She touched things to remind herself that this was really happening: the bricks in the wall, the cast-iron of the gas lamps, the damp leaves on perfectly manicured trees and plants, the rough stone of the pavement, the smooth marble of the building, the cool water in the fountains. She almost reached out to touch a passing warlock, but decided, wisely, that doing so would not end well.

All the signage and chatter indicated that today's orientation was solely for the college of warlocks and the cadets for the Siphon. Artificers and healers would have their own orientation on another day in a different part of the massive campus.

The building with the black marble dome turned out to be at the heart of a series of interconnected structures that spread out from it like spider's legs. *Lamira's halls. Lecture theatres A to H,* said the sign at the entrance. The orientation was in *Theatre C:* an arm that ended in an open-air auditorium with tiered seating and a wide space under the stage.

A Vagola stooge checked Kavi's papers and directed her to the area without seats, which was already half-full with thugs and ruffians. Artificed lamps painted them in lurid yellow light and lent them an aura of subdued menace. No one paid her any attention. At least overtly. She was sure they'd sized her up and dismissed her.

'Are you sure about this, Yella?' the man in front of Kavi was saying.

'Yes, yes,' Yella replied with a reassuring pat on his twitchy friend's shoulder. 'Once we make it into the Vagola, we're set. Think about it, bhai … a stipend, a pension when we retire—'

'Retire? What about the Kraelish, aren't they—'

'Listen, Blades are just for show these days. Okay? We won't be involved in any fighting. Besides, how're the Kraelish going to cross the Deadlands? Hah? No. We're safe. It's just the bleddy Council making a fuss about nothing. And you know what?' Yella leaned in. 'I don't think any of the others here have as much experience as us. We'll be in the twenty-five. Easy.'

Must be nice to be that confident. There were at least a hundred cadets in the auditorium. Twenty-five out of a hundred were not the worst odds. But the chances of being killed were a lot higher than that. *A lot higher.*

Not that it discouraged those like her from entering.

When the Vagola was first created, there were a bunch of people grumbling about the tests, about how it was unfair that they couldn't be mages even though they wanted to, and how they couldn't be Blades either since the candidates were all being chosen from the military. They grumbled and moaned and more people joined them and then election year comes around and some genius politico decides:

Hey, why don't we kill two rats with one broom?

How, bhai? Tell me more. (Some sycophant, probably.)

We allow, say, twenty-five members of the public to join the Vagola to train as Blades.

Bhai, what a great number. Too good. More, please. (Same sycophant.)

We allow twenty-five into the Vagola … but only if they pass a test.

Wah! A test!

Yes, a test… which culminates in an event held in an arena where everyone in the city can attend. They can get drunk, gamble, watch people die, and blow off some steam. What say ye?

They said: *Oh, ye, what a genius, you have my vote*, and so the Siphon was born and some arsehole got elected to the Council. The event turned out to be immensely popular with the public, and the body count continued to soar with each passing year. It was possible, hypothetically, to have a Siphon where no one died. But hey, that was not a good look for the people in charge.

Kavi sighed and craned her neck to get a better look at the warlocks, who, unlike her ilk, had the privilege of parking their buttocks on the cold brick that served as seats. They came in all shapes and sizes, but *something* was slightly off about them. Their gait was just a fraction too heavy. Their eyes would be alert one moment and glazed over the next. And their facial expressions often seemed at odds with their words and gestures.

Warlocks and cadets continued to trickle in and soon Kavi was standing shoulder-to-shoulder between a tall, scarred woman and stocky man who stank of arrack. A gong, loud enough to make her wince, finally rang through the auditorium and forced the gathering into a hushed silence.

'Vice-Chancellor, Archmage Farrah Duggal!' a man's voice announced from everywhere and nowhere at the same time.

The Vice-Chancellor's black robes of office swished and her boot-heels click-clacked as she strode onto the hardwood stage. She stopped in the middle and on the outermost edge – where Kavi could almost see up her nose – and held out a single, extra-large grain of rice.

'Do you know what this is?' she said in an artificially amplified voice.

The Vice-Chancellor waited. No one said a word. A dog barked somewhere in the distance. She levelled a finger at a warlock. 'You. Can you *create* this?'

The man gaped at the grain of rice Farrah Duggal held aloft.

'Can you? With your Jinn? With Harith's maayin?'

He flinched. 'No, ma'am.'

The Vice-Chancellor smiled, nodded, and pocketed the grain of rice.

'Maayin can heal. It can destroy, it can modify, it can enhance. But it cannot *create.*' She paused and surveyed the warlocks. 'I don't care what preconceived notions you have come here with. Forget them all. From this day forth, you will spend the rest of your lives in service to those without access to a Jinn.'

There was a disgruntled shuffle-and-grumble somewhere in the back row.

'We serve' – she raised her voice till it boomed through the auditorium – 'because without the farmer, we would starve. Without the soldier, we would still be under Imperial rule. And without the people . . .' She paused, glared at the warlocks. 'We would not have a Raaya.'

Someone in the corner began applauding and soon the rest of the theatre joined in. Kavi added an obligatory *clap-clap*.

'The Vagola has been the backbone of Raaya for over two hundred years,' the stone-faced Vice-Chancellor said when the applause died down. 'Our healers save countless lives every single day. Our artificers are the pride of the country and the envy of the subcontinent.' She lowered her voice. 'But after centuries of peace, the enemy is once again at the border, and our warlocks *must* be ready.'

More applause, louder this time.

'There are exactly one hundred and eighty-three novice warlocks here today, many of you with the potential to one day be an archmage.' The Vice-Chancellor dropped her gaze to the men and women standing at her feet. 'And we have ninety-six brave cadets who will fight in the Siphon.'

Kavi's mouth went dry. She fought a sudden, mad impulse to run. To elbow the foul-smelling man on her left in the gut and sprint for the exit.

'The warlock is unique among mages,' Farrah Duggal said. 'The only class that can manifest and manipulate tangible maayin. But the price they pay is extraordinary. Complete immobility – their bodies, for the duration of their cast, are home to a sliver of Harith. A splinter of a Jinn. Can you imagine, cadets? The crushing weight on their bodies, the fire that scorches through their veins. But in the era of the First Mages, warlocks were able to negate the effect of their countervail by bonding with a warrior who could share the countervail. The bond gave the warlock the gift of manoeuvrability, because their Blade paid a portion of the price.'

The Vice-Chancellor adjusted her robes. 'The tradition of the

Blade is sacred. The role may have changed – the knowledge, and hence the ability to create the bond, is lost – but you are still the last defence a warlock has. A mediocre warlock in sync with their Blade is far, *far* superior to one who works by themselves. You will all learn this in the coming months.'

She took a deep, expansive breath. 'In light of the threat on our borders, the Council has decided that this year, the number of cadets chosen directly from the military academies and pulled from active duty will be increased.'

Kavi went completely still.

'This year – especially this year – we will only need the best of the best,' Farrah Duggal continued. 'Which means that the number of cadets chosen through the Siphon will be reduced.'

There was a moment of stunned silence as the statement hung in the air, then came crashing down in a susurrus of whispers.

'Madarchod . . .' the woman on Kavi's left muttered.

The drunkard on her right simply shook his head in disbelief.

The nervous man in front of Kavi tried to make a run for it but was held in place by his friend.

Farrah Duggal raised an arm for silence. 'If any of you wish to withdraw from the Siphon, we will provide a full refund.' She waited.

A man by the entrance threw his hands up in the air, swore, and stormed out.

'But if you choose to remain,' she said, 'know this. At the end of the Siphon, regardless of how many remain standing, we will only choose *five*.'

Chapter 31

Kavi clutched her enrolment papers behind her back and squeezed them so hard that they became permanently creased.

This was just another obstacle. Nothing more. This just meant she had to fight harder.

The Vice-Chancellor gave the remaining cadets a grave nod. 'Azraaya *needs* the Siphon. It is important, in times like these, that the city has something to look forward to. The Republic thanks you for your bravery, and wishes you the best of luck.'

Farrah Duggal then addressed the warlocks and spoke about the history of the college and the footsteps they'd be walking in, and how she expected them to achieve great things. Kavi used her little finger to clear out the wax in her ears while the other cadets grumbled and shuffled around impatiently.

'We have organised a welcoming banquet for you in Theatre D,' the Vice-Chancellor finally announced after what felt like an hour. 'Mingle; get to know each other. Faculty will also be present, so don't be afraid to come up and talk to us.'

Mingling, Kavi immediately suspected, was out of the question.

Her fellow cadets were a distant and wary bunch. They piled food on their plates, glanced around with open suspicion, and drifted away to devour their meals. The novice warlocks, on the other hand, were a bunch of gossiping aunties and uncles.

They stared. They whispered. They sniggered. *Taemu … look at her … let one in … compulsion to steal … Mummy said all are stupid … don't get too close … can catch something … she really thinks she can … the eyes.*

She did, however, encounter another Taemu, a street-sweeper outside the Vagola, who stared at her with a mixture of awe and pride. She waved at him with a bemused smile and he ducked his head and scurried away.

That night, after she organised the recently arrived rat crates in a spare room, Kavi locked her door, opened her trunk, and pulled out a dark, round pebble from in between her clothes.

Everyone had their myths. Their legends and their ideals to live up to. The Kraelish had their knights and their code. The Raayans had their demigods and epics. The Taemu? All gone. Well, almost all gone.

'They're going to try to kill me,' she whispered as she ran a finger over its smooth surface. She'd stolen – borrowed it from Drisana's shrine in Bochan. As a token. A reminder. A link to a past she was blind to.

She left the pebble on the desk, extinguished the oil lamp, and let the barking dogs and honking rickshaws lull her to sleep.

Kavi spent a restless night dreaming of Raeth's rotund priest. The man chased her through the city, dual wielding tentacles, howling with laughter, and screaming: *Hel awaits, Kavithri. Hel awaits. You cannot run forever!*

The next morning, after a quick breakfast and another harrowing ride in Ratan's rickshaw, she stepped through the gates of the city's Picchadi stadium, tired but hopeful, and was promptly yelled at to get in line.

'Dai! Can't you read?' A woman stormed over with a clipboard and a pencil. She stopped and squinted at Kavi's eyes. 'Oh, okay, listen, what's your name?'

'Kav— Subbal Reddy,' Kavi said, gripping her sword tight.

'If you say so.' The woman shrugged and ran her eyes over the clipboard. 'Squad Nine. Junior Artificer Salora Juali for armour and weapons.'

'Thank you.' Kavi hesitated. 'Uhm …'

'Yes, problem?'

'No,' Kavi shook her head. 'No problem. Just – one question, memsaab.'

'Go on.'

'Will Blade Captain Greema be training us?'

The woman snorted. 'Not for the Siphon. The Captains only work with cadets at the Vagola.'

Kavi had hoped to meet the woman again. Maybe ask her for some tips and advice. Show her how much progress she'd made. But that would have to wait.

Junior Artificer Salora Juali was waiting for her in one of the stadium's myriad locker rooms. She stood, sized Kavi up, and said, 'Strip.'

Kavi shut the door, turned her back on the woman, and obeyed.

'You will see me before and after each training session,' Salora said. 'I will use my maayin to reset your armour and reload your weapon.' She flung a balled-up blouse and a pair of trousers at Kavi's feet.

'Hand me your sword,' the artificer said when Kavi was done.

Kavi hesitated.

Salora clicked her tongue. 'Sword. Now.'

Kavi handed it over.

'For the duration of each session, your weapon will be sealed.' Salora pressed a tiny metal square into the base of the scabbard. Four silver threads slithered out from the edges of the square and wrapped themselves around the sword's hilt. 'The device will also nullify the weight of the scabbard and reinforce it to withstand impact.'

Salora returned the sword to Kavi and keyed a locker open. She passed Kavi a helmet, a cuirass with magnetised hooks at its back, vambraces that latched over her forearm, gauntlets that protected the back of her hand and wrist but allowed full use of her fingers, a pair of cuisses – with a single pistol holster – that fit snug on her thighs, greaves that she tightened over her boots, and a thick convex shield with rolled-back edges that was dented in several places.

Salora's hands lingered on each piece of armour she handed to Kavi. 'This entire set is connected,' she said. 'It is artificed to absorb a percentage of the Harithian maayin it comes into contact with.'

She reached out and raised Kavi's wrist to her face. 'Do you see that?'

The inside of the gauntlet was embedded with a flat, glassy, orb-like device, and underneath it, were a pair of small discs.

'Always keep track of the gauge during a fight.' She tapped the orb with a finger. 'It will fill to indicate how much maayin has been absorbed. When it is full, it means the armour and the shield are both saturated, and they will stop negating maayin attacks. When that happens, you must push one of these buttons' – she tapped the discs – 'to release the stored maayin.'

'The button on the left, the one with a X on it, releases the maayin in a targeted blast from the surface of the shield. The range is up to fifteen metres. The one on the right discharges the stored maayin across the surface of the entire armour' – she pointed to the ceiling and made a circle with her finger – 'in a five-metre radius. Both, if used correctly, are powerful weapons. Does that make sense?'

Kavi swallowed. Nodded.

'You will not be exposed to enough maayin to saturate the armour today, but to ensure there are no accidents, the release buttons will remain inactive for the session. At the end of the day, I will drain the stored maayin and reset the armour for use.' She handed Kavi a flintlock pistol. 'Three shots. Never fire them all. Save one. Again, I will need to reload it for you.'

'Save one?' Kavi said, brows furrowed. Was this some sort of artificer quirk?

The artificer sniffed. 'Military tradition. Always save one in case of capture. For yourself.'

'I see,' Kavi said, trying to mirror the woman's nonchalance.

Salora tapped the pistol. 'Check the charges.'

The side of the long barrel was lined with three tiny glass orbs; miniature versions of the one at the back of her gauntlet. They glowed a bright orange.

'Need me to explain?' Salora said, taking a step back to assess a fully kitted Kavi.

Three charges. Three shots. 'No.'

'Try moving around.'

Kavi slipped the pistol into the holster on her thigh. Hooked the shield and sword on her back. Twisted. Stretched. Ventured a little hop. The armour was light and barely hindered her movement.

'Questions?' The artificer said.

'No – yes.' Kavi studied the gauge on her gauntlet. 'What if I get hit *between* the armour?' Like in her armpits or her knees or her neck.

Salora smiled and shrugged.

Kavi nodded. *That's what I thought.*

'Anything else?'

There were so many questions: *What have you seen? What have you studied? What does your Jinn feel like? Do you know an artificer called Suman? If you do, can you tell her she's a wretch?* 'How much did you lose?' Kavi tapped her chestplate. 'To do this?'

Salora raised a brow. 'You want to know how my countervail works?'

Kavi hesitated. 'I—'

'It's hard to explain to someone who's not a mage …' Salora sighed. 'But imagine – try to imagine your last meal. The moment you sat down to eat. Take that moment, freeze it, and look at it. Really look. You will find a hundred things you didn't even know you remembered … for us, those are a hundred things to forget.' She drew a long, slow breath. 'Come back in one piece. Next!'

Chapter 32

Sawdust and the musk of dried sweat clung to Kavi's nostrils. She sneezed and wiped her nose and mouth on the inside of a sleeve. Around her, carpenters and labourers scurried around half-finished buildings while supervisors stood, arms on hips, and screamed instructions.

The sky above was clear, cloudless, and even the wind seemed to hold its breath. Walls rose on all sides, row upon row of seating loomed behind them and Kavi swayed with a burst of vertigo. She was an armour-clad grain of rice at the bottom of a spinning bowl.

The instructors, men and women in khaki military uniform, ushered new arrivals into a sunny corner of the field, away from the construction, and ordered them to stand at arm's length from each other.

Kavi took her spot. Squinted under the glare of the sun and stuck a finger under her cuirass to let some air in.

By the time the last cadet was armoured up and slotted in, Kavi's helmet had soaked up and collected enough sweat to fill a small bucket. She slipped it off, emptied it at her feet, and held it in the crook of her elbow.

An instructor stepped forward – a clean-shaven man with a nose broken in at least three places and a chin you could ram a rickshaw into. He waited until the last dregs of chatter withered away, then gestured to one of his colleagues.

A woman who seemed to suffer from a permanent case of heartburn tucked a horsewhip under an arm and unfolded a long piece of paper.

'Repeat after me,' she shouted. 'I am volunteering, of my own free will and without coercion, to participate in the Siphon.'

Kavi joined the chorus and mumbled along.

'I understand the dangers, and acknowledge that the Vagola will take no responsibility in the event of my death.'

More mumbling until they got to the last three words, which were uttered in a sombre whisper.

'I agree to obey and follow all orders from my superiors.'

Kavi agreed to obey and follow orders. To arrange for her own healer or physician and not rely on the Vagola to provide such services. She promised to bear arms responsibly, to fight with honour, to defend her brothers and sisters, and a dozen other statements that went through one ear and came out the other, intact and untouched, until the woman folded the paper and lapsed into silence.

The man with the mangled nose nodded at her and cleared his throat. 'My name is Walia Grofar,' he said. 'I will be your lead instructor.'

He motioned to the other instructors standing one step behind him. 'You will address us as sir, or ma'am, no need for all that saab-memsaab dogshit over here.'

'My number one advice to you – do not get friendly with your colleagues. Half will die, some will drop out, most of you will just be rejects.' He paused. 'The reason we are doing this *training*, instead of sending you straight into the Siphon, is not because we want to give you a chance. It's because we want to give the people, the spectators, a spicy show.' He cracked his neck. 'Understand one more thing: you are extras. *Egg-es-tras.* A fund-raising scheme. A sideshow. If each and every one of you was killed at the end of the Siphon, we would just pick more soldiers from the military.'

He raised his voice. 'For the Siphon, and for the rest of your training, you will work in squads of twelve. Eleven of you idiots, and one warlock.' He jerked his head at the cadet in front of him. 'You. You're wondering what you're doing *here*, aren't you?'

The cadet shook his head.

'You're *here*, because this is where the Siphon will be held.' Walia dusted his uniform down. 'Three months from now we will cover the ground with structures that match the eastern quadrant of the city, and you will fight in a simulation of a siege.'

A sharp intake of breath. Kavi's lips tightened.

'The walls have fallen. The enemy is inside. Your objective is to hold them off until a flare is fired.' He held up three fingers. 'The grounds will be divided into three sections. You may retreat into sections one and two, but you *must* hold at section three. The enemy will consist of deserters from the army, debtors from the debtors' jail, and an assortment of criminals all armed to the teeth and fighting for a pardon.'

He strolled down the row of cadets. 'If the enemy breaches section three, they will receive their pardon. If you are alive at the time of the flare, and are standing on or outside section three's line of combat, you will be in consideration for the five.'

'If you are thinking of hiding, think again. If you are considering foul play, I urge you to reconsider. There will be observers stationed throughout the arena. There will be no roofs and the buildings will be adjusted so the spectators can enjoy your suffering.'

'Now, before you split up into squads and begin your training, how about a getting-to-know-you session?' Walia said with a smile. 'How many of you have come from mercenary groups?'

Two dozen-odd raised their hands.

Walia hawked and spat. 'Fuck-ing hate mercenaries. Walking around, thinking you know everything about weapons and war. You don't know shit! Any caravan guards?'

Hands fell. Hands rose.

Walia made sympathetic tsking sounds. 'You sad, sad bastards, where do I even start? Fighting untrained thieves and bandits and calling yourself warriors – shut the Hel up,' he hissed at a cadet who opened his mouth.

He went on and on:

Hawaldars? 'Arseholes on a power-trip. Cowards. The first to drop their weapons and run.'

Bodyguards? 'Whose body have you been guarding? Hah? Look at this face. You want to be Blade? Chootias, all of you.'

Bouncers? 'Fuck off back to your bars and rum dens. Bleddy brawlers.'

Walia had a problem with every single cadet in the stadium. Eventually, he stood right in front of Kavi and shouted. 'I heard one of you is a fuck-ing Taemu.'

Kavi blinked. Looked around for this fucking Taemu – *oh.* 'Sir, I am,' she said.

'You.'

'Yes, sir.'

'What the fuck.'

'Sir, I—'

'Did I ask you a question?'

'No, sir.'

'You don't belong here,' Walia said. He glared at her till she wilted, then nodded to himself and returned to his spot at the head of the assembly.

He stood with hands clasped behind his back and watched as the other instructors split the cadets into squads and put them through their paces.

Kavi ran in her armour. Jumped in it. Crawled and rolled and climbed in it.

Then she shot her pistol.

She followed instructions and stood side-on. Brought the pistol up to eye level. Bent her elbow a fraction, aimed, and pulled the trigger. An artificed slug erupted from the barrel with a loud *dhoom* – sent reverberations up Kavi's arm – and buried itself deep in the pile of hay. An orb on the barrel went dark. She stared at the weapon with bulging eyes as the hair on the nape of her neck stood. She was supposed to save one for herself?

The cadets were dismissed for lunch after everyone had fired their pistol. Kavi's ears rang from the concussive *dhooms* as she descended into the stadium's canteen to eat a quick lunch – a paltry two idlis with diluted sambhar – before returning to find the training area covered with a series of chalk circles.

Gomathi, the heartburn-suffering instructor in charge of Kavi's eclectic squad of eleven, ambled up and jabbed a finger at her.

'Reddy. You're with Yella.' She jerked a thumb at a tall lanky cadet Kavi recognised from last evening's orientation – the man who'd stood in front of her and whispered sweet nothings to his twitchy friend.

Gomathi motioned to a chalk circle. 'Armour check. Shields up. No time limits. Spar till one of you is down or the circle is broken.'

Kavi burped. Wiped sweaty hands on the back of her trousers. She puffed out her cheeks. *Here we go.* One step closer to

Appa and her brothers; another stride away from who she once was.

She checked her armour. Hefted her shield up to her chin. Thumped it with her sword. And stepped into the circle.

Watch me, Drisana.

Chapter 33

Yella scratched the stubble on his neck, his chin, his cheeks; and stepped into the circle with an exasperated sigh.

'You know what you're doing?' he muttered.

Kavi glanced at Gomathi, who was still arranging the rest of the squad into pairs. Behind the instructor, in the seating overlooking the training, a group of bored-looking men in Council uniforms shooed away a lone samosa-vendor.

'I've never fought with a shield,' Kavi said.

'Good, this will be easy then.' His sword-arm flashed up and over, like a whip, and *thonked* into the top of her helmet.

Kavi stumbled. Her ears rang. She flexed her jaw and fought for balance.

Yella attacked again with a hooking motion that went under Kavi's shield and connected with her ankles. While she hopped around in pain, he snapped back into his original stance – shield under his nose, sword at eye level, elbow just slightly above – and lunged at her.

Kavi twisted her head out of the way. Yella's sword brushed past her neck. And when he yanked it back, the coarse wood of his scabbard caught, scraped, and peeled her skin off. She hissed. Bared her teeth in a silent snarl. *Enough.*

She waited for him to attack again. Dug her toes into the

sand. Rotated her hips. And slammed her shield into his.

Shock ran up her arms, and the *clang* of the collision echoed in her ears. She held her ground and braced herself for a reaction … which never came. Yella was on his back, several feet outside the circle, with a look of utter confusion on his face.

'Whatthefuck – what the Hel are they feeding Taemu these days?'

Kavi checked the bruise on her neck and grimaced as her fingers came away with spots of blood. She glared at him. 'Show me how to' – she tried to mimic the overhead and underhand strikes he'd used on her – 'do that, and I'll tell you.'

Yella stumbled to his feet. Dusted himself off.

'Fuck you,' he spat, and stepped back into the circle.

Despite his reluctance to *teach* her, she did end up learning. She learned that since the shield covered a fighter's entire midsection, the only realistic targets were the head or the legs, so she needed to go over, under, or around it. She learned that holding the sword over the shield, instead of the side, placed less strain on her arm and wrist, especially since she was wielding such a top-heavy weapon. She also learned that if she'd been using a naked blade, that she would have hacked her own toes off by now.

An ear-shredding whistle brought the spars to a halt. Walia, who'd stood in the same spot the entire afternoon, beckoned them over.

'It looks awkward,' Yella mumbled as they walked over with the other cadets.

Kavi frowned. 'What does?'

'Your shield.'

She stared at it. 'Am I holding it wrong?'

'The *strength* of a warlock can be measured by three things.' Walia's speech put an end to their conversation. 'The size of their pool of maayin – which we call krasna – their control over it, and the time it takes to replenish it. An archmage can replenish their krasna in less than fifteen minutes, a novice may take up to two hours.'

Out of the corner of her eye, Kavi spotted a gaggle of men and women entering the arena. At their head was a man with a long, curled-and-oiled moustache that glistened in the late afternoon sun. He pointed at the cadets.

Too well dressed to be construction workers. Not enough armour to be cadets. Warlocks. These had to be their warlocks.

'They are trained to aim for an enemy's heart or their head,' Walia said. 'If you take a hit to the chest, depending on the warlock, you could either end up with a crater, or a large hole. If they nail you in the head, the projectile *will* penetrate your skull, and, depending on the warlock, turn your face into blood-and-bone chutney. If you are really unlucky, and you get hit in the abdomen or limbs, it could take you a few hours to bleed out. An extremely painful death. I would not recommend it.

'Why am I telling you this? Because I want you to know what your armour is protecting you from. Even when it's maxed out, it can still save your life.' He paused and let that sink in.

'If you wish to be a Blade, you *must* understand what a warlock can do. You must learn what *your* warlock can do. You must familiarise yourself with their range, their krasna, and their piercing power.' He scanned the row of cadets. 'To do this, you must *feel* the full force of their maayin. For the rest of the day, you will work with the warlock assigned to your squad. You will act as their practice dummy. Don't panic' – he raised a hand to forestall a protest only he could hear – 'they will only use blunted projectiles.'

Walia dismissed them to their squads where they waited while the warlocks were given their instructions.

Kavi nudged Yella with her elbow. 'What were you saying about my shield?'

'Hah?' he said, distracted by something his friend, who was on squad three, was signing to him.

'My shield.'

He waved it off. 'You're no good with it.'

Kavi tsked. That wasn't helpful at all.

'Line up!' Gomathi stomped up to them with a warlock in her wake. 'This is novice Ze'aan Salasari.'

'I look forward to working with you,' Ze'aan said, giving Yella a stiff handshake. Her voice was deep, almost hollow, and when she spoke, she had the calm assurance that Kavi always associated with people who'd grown up being admired and respected. She was obviously Kraelo-Raayan, a descendant of Kraelish officers who were encouraged to take local women for wives. Tall, light-skinned, and blessed with a patrician nose and a powerful jaw that most Raayans would kill for. Ze'aan moved slowly, deliberately, as she walked down the line and introduced herself to the squad.

Kavi straightened, extended her hand to the woman, who, after a moment's hesitation, shook it.

'Surprising,' Ze'aan drawled.

Kavi glanced at Gomathi. How was she supposed to address the warlock?

'Ma'am?' Kavi said, tentatively.

'Surprising,' Ze'aan said again, with a hint of disappointment in her voice, 'that you would choose to fight for the Republic after what they did to your people at Ethuran.'

Kavi blinked. What the Hel was she talking about? 'The Republic had nothing to do with the siege at Ethuran. That was the Kraelish, and it happened centuries ago.'

'Centuries ago?' Ze'aan frowned. 'Are you dull, girl? I'm not talking about the siege, I'm talking about what the Raayans did thirteen years ago.'

Kavi opened her mouth to tell the pompous wretch that the Raayans hadn't done—

Pilfered from Kraelish infantry after Ethuran – after the siege, I mean, Massa had said.

Why would he need to clarify that it was after the siege? And that number, thirteen …

The blood drained from her face.

Thirteen.

There was something … *something important* that had happened thirteen years ago.

A fist closed around Kavi's lungs and slowly, painfully, squeezed the air out. A memory, fluid and ancient, lost its camouflage and slithered up to her. She reached out to it. It thrashed, slipped through her fingers, and sank into a writhing mass of images and emotions.

But it left something behind. A pitch-dark sludge that clung to her and coated her insides with sights and sounds and smells – scalding flames and burned flesh; swollen tongues sticking out of dead mouths; bloated men and women floating down an ochre river; the smell of mushrooms, of faeces, of blood; a room with adobe walls, a peephole, and through it, mocking laughter, pleas, screams, moans, *wheezing.*

Kavi dropped to her hands and knees and vomited.

The men on either side swore and jumped away. Ze'aan spared her a puzzled glance and moved on to the next cadet.

Kavi stayed where she was – panting, eyes watering – and stared at the half-digested idli-sambhar on the ground.

'Cadet,' Gomathi said, towering over Kavi. 'Clean yourself up. You have five minutes.'

Kavi stumbled down to the canteen. To the row of taps and

the long metal sink that hung under them. She turned one on, let the water run, and stuck her head under it.

Those were not her memories. She'd never seen corpses floating in a river. The only dead bodies she'd ever come across were at the crematorium in Bochan, where she'd snuck in to steal their hair before they were burned to ash.

Maybe her initial inclination that these dream-memories were after-images from a previous life was correct after all. It was the only explanation that made sense. The alternative, that some external force was manipulating her memory, or that she had tapped into a collective memory of some sort, was far more terrifying and she refused to consider it.

There is nothing wrong with me.

A voice, her voice, cackled back at her, *Bhaenchod, there is so much wrong with you.*

'I'm not crazy,' she whispered.

The cackle got louder.

She clenched her fists. *I'm not.* She was a little desperate. A little angry. But her mind was still hers. She pulled her head away and cupped her hands under the stream of water. She gargled, spat, and drank.

What the Raayans did thirteen years ago, the warlock had said. She'd assumed Kavi – that everyone – would know about whatever it was that happened thirteen years ago. If it was such common knowledge, then maybe she could just ask. Massa would be happy to tell her. He seemed to enjoy the sound of his own voice.

The handle of the tap squealed as she turned it off.

When she returned to her squad, she found Ze'aan standing with her back to the wall, hands tucked into her pockets while she waited for Gomathi to finish talking.

'You will not need your sword,' Gomathi was saying to a

cadet. 'Use your shield. Take the hits. The release is disabled, but monitor the gauge and yell out when it's full. Got it?'

'Yes, ma'am.' The cadet linked his sword to the magnetised hooks on his back and walked up to Ze'aan. He left a distance equivalent to an entire train compartment between them and raised his shield.

Gomathi nodded to Ze'aan. The warlock nodded back, tied her hair into a ponytail, and froze.

The air around her shimmered. A droplet of iridescent green materialised a hand's width from her chest. It grew into a pebble. The pebble ballooned to the size of a medallion. The medallion gained in mass, as if it was being pumped from inside, until it settled into an orb the size of a rickshaw tyre.

The cadets murmured. Kavi stared. An average warlock's krasna was half of what Ze'aan had just summoned.

'Begin,' Gomathi said.

Chapter 34

The cadet with the shield stepped forward. A splinter of maayin separated from Ze'aan's krasna, elongated into a bolt, and hovered at her side.

The cadet took another step, and the bolt flickered out of existence.

There was a crack, like glass hitting a marble floor, and the cadet hurtled back to his starting position. The bolt, which was now where the man had stood seconds ago, fizzed and crackled and spat.

Kavi's jaw dropped. That was fast. Too fast.

The cadet stood, tightened his grip on his shield as the bolt of maayin drifted back to Ze'aan, and took a cautious step in her direction.

A shudder ran through the bolt.

The cadet flinched. Relaxed when the bolt remained exactly where it was.

Twin coins of maayin erupted from the larger, stationary orb hovering in front of Ze'aan's chest, and in a stunning display of control, they flew in opposite directions – criss-crossing, never touching – before slamming into the cadet's sides.

He gasped and dropped to his knees.

The bolt, which had been faithfully hanging by Ze'aan's

expressionless face, twisted, warped, and split itself into half a dozen slimmer bolts that sailed over to the dazed cadet and surrounded him.

He waved his shield in the air. Tried to fend the maayin off.

The bolts fizzed, retreated, rearranged themselves – along with the twin coins of maayin – into a crown that hung over the man's head. They pulsed in mid-air. Waiting for instructions from their mage.

Ze'aan eyes flashed.

Crack-crack-crack. Into his back, his legs, his shoulders. The maayin fizzed, regrouped, and prepared for another assault.

'Full!' The cadet cowering under his shield screamed. 'It's full!'

The bolts lengthened, spun, surrounded the cadet, and just when Kavi thought they were going to launch themselves again, Ze'aan withdrew her maayin.

Gomathi stepped up to the cadet, drew a line in the dirt at his feet, and turned to the squad. 'Try to do better than this.'

They tried.

Some managed.

Most were sent flying or were pulverised into submission by Ze'aan's maayin.

By the time it was Kavi's turn, the rickshaw-tyre-sized krasna had shrunk to half its size. Ze'aan was still frozen in place. The only parts of her body that moved were her cold, impassive eyes; and they followed Kavi closely as she tightened the straps on her vambrace and stood behind the smudged line in the ground.

The first impact – the collision between Ze'aan's maayin and the reinforced metal of Kavi's shield – almost knocked Kavi off her feet. She checked the gauge. A tenth was filled with orange light. If *this* was supposed to be mitigated damage … she swallowed and stepped forward.

A green blur whizzed at her. She ducked her head and winced as the maayin glanced off the side of her helmet.

She took another step. Ze'aan launched another bolt.

It looked so fast on the sidelines. But now, with it right in front of her, Kavi could *see* it. She timed her head slip to miss the bolt of maayin by a fraction of a heartbeat, and stepped forward again.

This was as close as Ze'aan had let anyone get. This was where she started attacking with increased intensity. Kavi drew a measured breath and let her mind drift.

The maayin came from all angles.

And she *saw* it coming.

She twisted. Spun. Swerved between the maayin. Her pulse raced. Blood pounded in her temples. The cadets faded away. The warlock and the stadium behind her dissolved into colourless murk. The maayin twinkled as it tore through the air.

Like emeralds.

Kavi reached out, and using the back of her gauntlet, batted one away.

There was a collective gasp from somewhere behind her. She ignored it. Swayed away from another bolt of maayin. Stopped mid-movement. Waited for the bolts and the coins to change trajectory. Then shifted her weight and surged in the opposite direction. To where Ze'aan stood locked in her cast.

The whites of the warlock's eyes filled Kavi's vision. The scent of the coconut oil in her hair wiped away the residual tang of vomit in Kavi's nostrils. Another step and she'd be able to reach out and touch the warlock.

Ze'aan's krasna, the orb that hovered inches from her chest, shot out and slammed into Kavi's chest.

Kavi scuffed her feet as she struggled to regain her balance. She'd forgotten about the krasna itself. Stupid. She checked her gauge. Only a third full. No need to panic yet. She glanced over her shoulder for maayin. Nothing. Ze'aan had recalled it. Ze'aan …

Kavi's mouth went dry. While she'd been regrouping, the orb, the krasna, had disintegrated into a hundred pellet-sized projectiles that now swirled around Ze'aan like a swarm of green locusts.

Kavi locked her shield in place. There was no dodging this. She'd just have to take the hits.

The swarm dived at Kavi. It bypassed her shield. Drummed down on her. Drove her to her knees. Rattled her teeth. Slipped between the gaps in her armour and tore into her flesh. She screamed. Bared her teeth and tried to lift her head. A pellet tore through her cheek, shattered her molars, ripped her tongue open and exited through a gash on the other side of her mouth.

Blood gushed onto Kavi's tongue. She swallowed the debris of her ruined teeth. She choked. Spat. Dark spots filled her vision as she searched for her gauge. It was full. *Stop.*

She punched the release buttons. They hissed and bounced back up. Nothing happened.

And with nothing to mitigate the damage, without its reinforcement, the armour bent and broke from the force of the maayin. Shards of metal sliced through her skin and lodged themselves in her thighs, her forearms, her back. *Stop.*

She tried to shout. But found that she couldn't move her mouth. Amid all the pain, she'd not noticed that her jaw had dislocated. She huddled under her shield. *Why won't she stop?*

Why won't anyone make it stop?

She was on the brink of losing consciousness when Gomathi shouted, 'Enough.'

The onslaught withered away.

Kavi stayed where she was, shaking, bruised, bleeding,

'Cadet,' Gomathi said, 'find yourself a healer. You're dismissed.'

Everyone around her had stopped what they were doing. They watched as she used her shield as a crutch and pushed herself back to her feet.

Her mouth hung open, and blood dribbled down her chin. She wiped it away. More came spilling out.

She had nothing to be ashamed of. The warlock had tried to humiliate her. Maybe in their eyes she'd succeeded. But as Zofan had once said to her, you couldn't feel humiliation until you chose to suffer. And as much as the latticework of wounds and cuts and bruises hurt, she was *not* suffering. She refused to.

Ze'aan had dismissed her maayin and now studied Kavi with curious eyes.

And it was those eyes that pushed Kavi over the brink.

There was no hate in them. No anger. No disdain or pity. To the warlock, Kavi was just an object. A trinket to play with. She'd *known* that Kavi's armour had maxed out.

The rage in Kavi's core called to her, and for once, she allowed a whisper to slip through: *Make her bleed.*

She flung her shield at the warlock's feet. Limped up to her and grabbed her by the collar. *Why?* She wanted to roar, but her jaw, dangling off its hinges, wouldn't obey. So all she managed was a garbled, 'Aaahhy?'

'Cadet!'

She heard Gomathi shout. She heard the sound of hurried footsteps. But she didn't care.

'Aaaahy?' Kavi tried forming the word again, but blood and saliva gushed into her mouth and she spat it into the warlock's face instead.

Ze'aan barely flinched. She wrapped her fingers around Kavi's wrists and squeezed till they released her collar. She leaned in to Kavi, almost till their faces touched, and whispered. 'Know your place, girl.'

Kavi blinked. *My place? You want me to—* She growled, yanked her head back and was halfway to breaking the warlock's nose when she was dragged away by a stringy pair of arms.

'What the fuck are you doing, Taemu?' Yella hissed in her ear.

Let me go. She struggled to no avail. She had no strength left. *Fully empty,* like they said in Bochan.

'They will disqualify you,' Yella growled. 'Is that what you want?'

'Aaahy?' *Why do you care?*

He hurled her to the ground.

Kavi looked up to find Gomathi bearing down on her.

'Kneel,' the instructor said.

Kavi kneeled on her bruised and lacerated knees.

Gomathi lifted her horsewhip and brought it down over Kavi's back.

Kavi hissed. Gritted her teeth and snarled. But stayed on her knees.

This was her punishment, then, for baring her fangs. So be it. She would come back stronger, faster. In three months, this would be a distant memory. She would learn how to fight with a shield, learn how to push the armour to its limits, and – she clenched her fists – at the end of the Siphon, when she was still standing, they would learn to respect her.

Gomathi whipped her. Over and over again. Kavi refused to flinch. Refused to let any emotion show on her face. Until Walia strode up to her, lifted a booted foot, and *whumph*, kicked her in the face.

She went down. Muscle memory took over. Hands wrapped themselves over her head. Feet curled up into her chest.

Walia kicked and stomped and spat.

The cadets around her stopped moving. The other instructors gathered around. Even the construction workers stopped to witness the beating.

Kavi withdrew into her shell and let Walia tire himself out. She may have changed, but – how could she forget? – the world around her was still the same.

'That's enough.'

Walia stopped. 'Novice?'

'I said that's enough.'

Kavi peeked through her fingers. Ze'aan had turned her unnerving, dispassionate gaze on Walia, and was staring him down.

Walia inclined his head and stepped away from Kavi.

'Will that be all for today?' Ze'aan said.

'Yes, Novice Salasari,' Walia nodded. 'And rest assured, we will remove the cadet from contention for the Siphon.'

Kavi's eyes went wide.

'That won't be necessary,' Ze'aan said.

'Very well, we will ensure that she is suitably punished.'

Kavi coughed and spat and got back on her knees. Wasn't this the punishment? What more could they do to her?

Walia and Gomathi saluted the warlock. Ze'aan nodded, spared Kavi a glance, and walked away from the squad.

'Cadet Subbal Reddy.' Walia spat Kavi's false name. 'You are forthwith suspended for three weeks.'

No.

'You will not be allowed to attend training. You will not be permitted to attend the tactical theory sessions. You will not have use of the armour to train privately.'

Kavi's shoulders slumped, and she bowed her head.

'If you ever lay your hands on a warlock again,' Walia said, 'I will personally slit your throat. Cadet, you are dismissed.'

Chapter 35

Lights and colours whizzed past. Reds, yellows, and blues lingered and stretched until they too withered away into nothing.

The rickshaw *bu-bumped* into and out of a pothole.

'Sorry,' Ratan said, and cast a worried glance at the backseat.

Kavi barely felt it. Barely felt anything at all. Not when they dragged and dumped her outside the locker rooms where her artificer sat waiting. Not when Salora had cut the pieces of her armour away and used a pair of tweezers to pull out the bits stuck in her flesh. Nothing. She was numb.

The rickshaw stopped at an intersection where a white-gloved hawaldar stood on a raised platform and directed traffic. On the side of the road, in a gutter with rubbish and vegetable refuse, was a dead beggar. Kavi stared at his tattered clothes and weathered, drooping skin; his dented, empty begging bowl still in his hands; his eyes, wide open and swarmed with flies.

Even in death, his indignity continued. The body would be left to rot until someone from the lower classes – a Taemu, a tribeswoman – could come and carry him away to be cremated. It was below the rest to touch someone of his stature. Even in death.

Even in death.

'Almost there,' Ratan said.

What had come over her? There was no rational reason for her to confront the warlock. Had she really believed Ze'aan would own up to her sadism, bow her head, and apologise?

No. But she was not wrong to try.

She'd earned Bithun's respect. Won her fight in Bochan. Held her own in the duelling circle today. She was not wrong.

They were.

The rickshaw screeched to a halt outside the warehouse. Ratan jumped out, bounded up the stairs, and returned with Massa.

'Meshira's balls,' Massa said as he slung one of her arms over his shoulder and helped her out. 'What did they do to you?'

He took her up to the room with the crates. Set her down on the floor. Passed her a rat box. 'How many do you need?'

Nilasi's maayin tore its way out of her skin, slipped through the cracks and crevices in the box, and drained the animal of its life.

'Keep them coming,' she rasped.

Massa passed her another box.

She touched her forehead to it, whispered, 'I'm sorry,' and killed another rat. Then another. And another. She took and took and took. The animals scurried and squeaked and chattered. Their backs snapped, the air hissed out of their mouths, and their bones *crack-crack-cracked.* Just like the sound Ze'aan's maayin had made when it connected with her armour. While she lay helpless on her knees. Trembling. Wondering if it would stop.

The lump in Kavi's throat got bigger. Her hands shook. And all at once, the *feeling* returned. She shrank away from the rats until her back hit a wall. Wrapped her arms around her knees. Buried her head between them.

She heard Massa's footsteps patter to the door, heard it shut behind him as he left, and she gasped. Great, shuddering sobs wracked her chest. She sniffled. Sucked in air. And cried the way she would when she was a young girl.

She missed her father. Her brothers. She missed Bochan. She'd never thought she would. She hated the place. But she missed the comfort of knowing its streets and understanding its people. She missed the luxury of having a friend. She'd only known Bithun for a few months, but she'd not realised how much it had affected her, how confident and assured it had made her to know that she had someone to rely on.

Kavi wiped her face on her sleeve. *I'll write to him.* When this was over, if she was still able, she'd go back to Bochan and thank him again for his help.

The tension eased out of her. Her chest got lighter. She got on her knees, and as the last sobs withered away, said a quiet prayer for the rats.

When she was done, she washed up, changed into a clean salwar-kameez, and went looking for Massa.

The proprietor of the Imperial Rickshaw Company was at his desk, chewing on a beedi stub and scribbling on a piece of paper. He spared her an awkward glance and nodded. 'How did the uh … recovery go?'

'Fine, boss.'

'Great, have a seat. I'll be with you in a moment.'

Kavi was halfway to the divan when he cleared his throat.

'The divan is for clients.' He jerked his head at the desk-chair combo by the door.

She bobbed her head. 'Sorry, boss.'

He waved it off.

Kavi sat and explored the new gaps in her mouth created by her missing molars. The gums were firm and sealed, like she'd never had teeth there to begin with, and it made a weird *srruuk* noise when she sucked on her cheek. She'd have to get used to eating on one side of her mouth.

Massa put his pen away with a flourish and blew on the piece of paper. 'When a client enters,' he said, 'there are five questions you must ask them.'

She blinked. 'Boss?'

'Since you're suspended for three weeks ... or was it two?'

'How did you—'

He raised an eyebrow.

'Three,' she said.

'Excellent.' He clapped his hands. 'More time for you in the office. So, your job as my assistant is to attend to any potential client who walks through that door. You must ask them five very simple questions.'

'I—'

'Name. Address. Appointment time. Job. Payment.' He lit up a beedi with his artificed matchstick. 'You can practice on the next client – and remember to try to make them feel *wanted.*'

She stifled a sigh. 'Can I write that down, boss?'

There was paper and pencil in the drawer, and with Massa's blessing, she made a list. She'd just finished memorising it when Massa *pssst-ed* at her and waggled his eyebrows at the door.

A man stood in the doorway. Perfectly still. Silent.

'Welcome,' Kavi said, eyes darting between Massa and the man, 'to the Imperial Rickshaw Company. How may we be of assistance?'

The man stepped into the office, wrinkled his nose, and frowned. 'Who're you?'

'New assistant,' she said.

The man hesitated. He glanced at Massa who was scribbling away with renewed intensity.

'Sahib,' Kavi said, deciding to err on the side of caution with the honorific. 'Can I have your name, please?'

He clenched his jaw and glared at her. 'I have a job for your boss.'

Kavi gestured to the chair facing the desk. 'Please, have a seat.'

'My name is Gahrul Dilo,' he said, still eyeing Massa in bewilderment as he sat.

'Thank you. Address?'

The man paused, considered. 'Number 57. Fultari Street.'

Kavi wrote the address down and turned to the man. 'Appointment time?'

'As soon as possible.'

'And the job?' she said, impressed with how well she was handling this.

'Exorcism.'

Kavi paused, pursed her lips. 'I'm sorry, sahib, did you say exorcism?'

A muscle in his jaw twitched. He leaned closer. Rested his elbows on the desk and fixed Kavi in place with the intensity of his gaze. 'Yes.'

She swallowed and wrote the word down. 'Payment?'

'Two hundred rayals.'

Kavi suppressed the urge to whistle. That was a month's worth of meals in Bochan. She quickly scribbled the number.

'When will he come?' Dilo said.

'He um …' She squinted at Massa, who was still studiously ignoring them. But his free hand, the one without the pen, was wiggling its index finger. 'In one … day?'

Dilo shuffled in his seat, clearly unhappy.

Massa made a fist and extended just the index finger.

'So sorry, sahib, I meant in one hour.' She glanced at Massa. He flashed her a thumbs-up.

Gahrul Dilo sighed. 'I will be waiting.' And with that, he stood and walked out.

Kavi studied the empty door frame. *Two hundred rayals.* He must really believe in it to pay so much. But demons? Living inside humans? It had to be a scam. *Had to.* She swallowed.

Or was it?

The silence in the office was suddenly ominous and sinister. Shadows collected in the corners and seemed to move with a life of their own. Even the air grew thick and heavy—

The clock in the office *dinged.*

'Bhaenchod,' Kavi exclaimed, starting.

Massa chuckled, reclined, and put his feet up on the desk.

'The Empire, in their pursuit of homogeneity,' he said, apropos of nothing, 'once issued a ban, punishable by a public stripping and beating, on all eight Raayan languages and their multitude of regional dialects.'

Has he lost his mind?

'Only Kraelish could be taught and spoken by the citizens of the Empire. Punishment was viciously enforced, and our local languages faded away until the only things left were their imprecations, whose usage, in a *perverse* gesture of goodwill, was permitted. Over time, a few choice phrases joined the bhaenchods and chootias, and thus, a new hybrid language was born.' He grinned. 'Cusses from Raaya, words and letters from Kraelin, and cadence from whichever part of the Republic you grew up in.'

Kavi scratched her chin. 'I didn't know that.'

Massa shrugged. 'People forget.'

'Boss,' she said – now was as good a time as any – 'may I ask you a question?'

He gestured for her to continue.

'Thirteen years ago …' She took a deep breath. 'Did something happen at Ethuran?'

His feet stopped shaking. 'Ethuran?'

'Yes. Thirteen years ago.'

'You don't know?'

Kavi shook her head.

'You really don't know?' Massa gave her a puzzled glance and reached for his case of beedis. 'Thirteen years ago,' he said with a sigh, 'the Council decided, for once, to do something truly altruistic.' He lit up a beedi with his artificed matchstick. 'They passed legislation that gave Ethuran back to the Taemu.'

Kavi frowned and tongued the empty spots in her mouth.

'It was an attempt to reintegrate the Taemu back into Raayan society. Everyone with an education knows about Kraelish propaganda and the misrepresentation of Taemu in the public consciousness. So, there was a movement in the cities to embrace the Republic's secularism, its pluralism. But sadly this sentiment, as we came to learn, did not extend to rural Raaya.' His eyes glazed over. 'That morning, thirteen years ago, more than four thousand Taemu were killed in Ethuran by a mob of men and women – Raayans – from the surrounding villages, who objected to the reintegration.'

Everything slowed down. The words that left Massa's lips slurred and dragged. The smoke from his beedi hovered in front of his face in sensual undulations.

'Most of the Taemu who died that day were children and the elderly.'

'Why?' she whispered. What about the men? The women?

'They couldn't run fast enough to escape.' Massa looked away. 'I'm sorry.'

Kavi couldn't bring herself to respond. Her feet had turned

into bricks. Her arms felt like they were stuck to her sides. Her breath turned shallow and her airway constricted.

How could she not have known this?

Massa bent and rifled around under his desk. He pulled out a heavy leather sack and a stick-broom.

'Here,' he said, passing her the broom, 'leave the sword and carry this. We have a job to do.'

Chapter 36

They rode the rickshaw to the supposed exorcism in silence. Massa smoked, Ratan drove, and Kavi imagined the lead-up to the massacre at Ethuran.

First, someone would've convinced the villagers that they needed to be saved from their unhappy fate, that there was no future if the present reintegration proceeded unchecked. This leader would then have told the villagers that the city-dwellers – who'd organised the Taemu reintegration in the first place – mocked and called them uncouth and dull-witted, even though it was *they* who didn't understand how life outside the cities really worked.

Then, they would have drummed up fear: Look, see how they allow the animals to return to Ethuran; the Taemu will bleed our land dry, rape our women, pollute our waters, and so on and so forth until the Taemu were utterly and completely dehumanised.

And finally, this leader would have offered the villagers a path to salvation: We must take matters into our own hands. We must kill them all.

Kavi clenched her fists.

Massa shimmied closer. 'It's not too late to drop out, get a full refund.'

'What?'

He took a drag. 'You understand the risk you're taking by fighting in the Siphon?'

She'd gone over this with Bithun. 'I'm—'

'Not talking about death,' he said, and flicked his beedi. The wind caught the ash and carried it away. 'Half the city will be in the stadium, and the other half, the ones who can't afford tickets, will be following the event in other ways. If you survive, everyone will know who you are, and if you're not careful, they might learn *what* you are, too.'

'I'm aware of the risks, boss,' she said with an exhausted sigh.

'Are you? Because if, Raeth forbid, the Kraelish find out that you're an Azir . . .' He pressed his thumb into his chin and pursed his lips. 'A fate—'

'Far worse than death awaits,' she finished for him. 'Yes, I know. And I will ensure that my *ability* is kept a secret.'

'Just checking,' he mumbled and glanced at her sideways. The rickshaw slowed to a crawl as they drove through a crowded street and Ratan poked his head out to yell at a group of men to get out of the way.

'Political rally,' Massa said, by way of explanation, and pointed to a white-saried woman standing atop a stage with a child on either side. He made a face. 'People with children should be disqualified from positions of power.'

'Why's that?' Kavi said, peering at the chubby politico and her offspring.

'It makes you selfish,' Massa said. 'You can't help but think more and more of your own children, and less and less about everyone else's.' He glanced at her. 'Which is the sole purpose of the job, you know.'

'Whatever you say, boss.'

The steam-rickshaw eventually stopped outside a row of

two-storey brick houses and Kavi hopped off with her broom.

'Listen up,' Massa said as he lugged the bag out behind him. 'When we – can I call you Kavi? Or do you prefer Kavithri?'

'Kavi, boss.'

'Good. So, during the exorcism, when I say, *Be at peace*, you must throw a handful of rice at the possessed. And when I shout, *Vacate this vessel!*, you must hit them on the head with the broom.'

'You want me to beat the client with this … broom?' Kavi held up the stick-broom.

'On the head,' Massa confirmed.

Kavi stared at the collection of thin sticks tied up with a hemp cord.

'I'll explain after the exorcism,' Massa said. 'Trust me.'

And so she did. Between bouts of gibberish, Massa would yell, *Vacate this vessel!*, and Kavi would step forward and thwack the terrified boy – Gahrul Dilo's teenage son – on the head with her broom like it was a mace. After more prancing around and chanting, Massa would then whisper, *Be at peace*, and Kavi would hurl uncooked rice at the boy's face.

This went on for almost half an hour before Massa announced – to the relief of everyone in the room – that the demon had been exorcised. Surprisingly, the client (*the victim, poor fool)* seemed to have regained some colour and was in a much better mood.

'Thank you so much,' Gahrul Dilo said as he escorted the exorcist and his assistant out the door. 'You have saved my son.'

'Just doing our job, sir. The payment …'

'Ah, yes, of course.' He gestured to one of his maids, and she returned with a blue envelope.

'Thank you.' Massa accepted the envelope and immediately

peeked into it. 'Please let us know if you require any other services.'

Gahrul Dilo inclined his head and extended his arm in the direction of the front door.

'All there? Boss?' Kavi asked once they were outside.

'Looks like it,' Massa said, thumbing the sheaf of red rayals and looking over his shoulder as if Dilo was going to burst out the door and ask for the money back.

'Where to now?' she asked.

'Back to the office.' Massa tucked the envelope into a pocket. 'After a quick stop.'

The quick stop, it turned out, was a detour to the Azraayan slum-city.

Ratan's rickshaw rattled past half-erected walls and ramshackle houses where monkeys screamed and hopped from roof to roof.

'The exorcism itself,' Massa said when he stopped at a traffic intersection, 'is easy. We simply remind the soul of its true purpose. Reconnect a thread, so to speak. The rest, I suppose, is an act, but a necessary one.' He noted the dubious look on Kavi's face. 'It works. You saw the boy.'

'Sure, boss.'

They left Ratan and his rickshaw outside a gully that was too narrow to drive through and set out on foot. Massa in front, Kavi at his heels.

The Azraayan slums were nothing like Bochan's. For one, they seemed to have risen out of the ruins of an older city, which itself was rumoured to have been built over the remains of an enormous artifact from a time before the Retreat. The streets of this older city, now tunnels, apparently ran through subterranean Azraaya like veins.

Another difference that stood out to her were the buildings

in between the huts and tents: remnants of multi-storeyed mansions that must have dated back to the Imperial era; tall, crumbling towers where crows sat and shat. And then there were the people: men and women with elephantiasis who sat with swollen limbs riddled with flies and boils. Cripples with dead eyes who were being ferried around in wheelbarrows by children. More children with distended bellies, naked and covered with dirt and sores, who chased each other through the human wreckage.

The city had shut its eyes to these slums. No politicos building water pumps to curry favour and earn votes here. No Zofan, no rules, no code. These were truly invisibles.

'What are we doing here, boss?' she said over Massa's shoulder.

'There's someone who wants to meet you.'

She slowed. 'Meet *me*?'

'Oh, yes,' he said, motioning for her to catch up.

They finally came to a halt outside a hut at the intersection of two streets. An elderly woman squatted at its entrance. She fanned a pile of burning coconut husks that sat between two bricks over which a blackened metal pot bubbled with congee.

'Hessal,' Massa said in greeting.

The woman glanced up at him, tired eyes and wrinkled skin lit by the flames she tended.

Kavi's muscles went stiff, and she had to force herself to relax. The woman was Taemu.

'Massa,' Hessal said. 'How's business?'

'You really want to know?'

Hessal peered at Kavi. 'No. This is her?'

Kavi didn't hear Massa's response. Behind the woman, inside the hut, a single dia-lamp burned at the feet of a tiny blue statue. She knew that statue. There were no names scrawled into the walls around it. But she knew it.

'Go ahead, child,' Hessal said. 'Go inside and ask for her blessing.'

Kavi hesitated. 'I don't have an offering.'

Hessal smiled. 'It's fine. Go.'

Kavi left her chappals at the entrance and walked into the hut. With the exception of the shrine and a pair of charpai-beds, the place was bare. She sat cross-legged in front of the statue and stared at it.

So, we meet again.

The statue of Drisana glared at her with its furious eyes.

She sighed and lowered her head.

'Done already?' Hessal said when Kavi re-emerged.

Kavi nodded. 'Thank you.'

'That was quick.' Hessal stirred her pot of congee. 'Where is it you're from?'

'Bochan.'

The old woman raised both her eyebrows. 'What have you been doing so far south?'

'I . . . I'm not sure.'

'Not sure?' Hessal turned to Massa. 'She says she's not sure.'

Massa shrugged. 'She only found out about the massacre at Ethuran today.'

Kavi winced. Now why did he have to go and say that? 'I'm sorry—'

'You must've been eight? Nine years old when it happened?' Hessal asked with both brows raised.

'Eight, I think,' Kavi said, softly.

The older woman tsked. 'You should've known. The Raayans have done their best to erase it from their memory. Most in the south have already forgotten or pretend that it never happened. But you should've known, child.' She grunted and raised her voice. 'You can come meet her now.'

Kavi frowned. 'What—'

They slipped out of the cracks. They came out of huts. From in between huts. Over walls or through gaps in them. They stopped what they were doing and turned and walked in her direction. Men with soot-smeared faces and bloody fingernails. Women with scars and bent backs. Children clutching their father's hands. Mothers carrying their babies. Some limped. Some crawled. Some walked with heads held high. But they all had one thing in common. They were Taemu.

Kavi's mouth went dry. She recognised one of the Taemu. The woman from the railway station. The garbage-picker.

Hessal followed her gaze. 'You've met Elisai?'

'I – not really.'

'She was at Ethuran too,' Hessal said. 'Lost her husband, her parents, her sisters.'

Kavi's temples throbbed with a sudden surge of anger.

'Most of us don't talk about Ethuran,' Hessal said. 'It fills us with shame. We left children to die to save our own skin. We told ourselves that we didn't have a choice, that we must live so we may have *more* children. It never occurred to us to fight back. We didn't know how. We'd forgotten.'

'And now here you are.' She threw a mug of water at the flames and extinguished them. 'A Taemu who wants to be a Blade. Who takes up a sword and fights like our ancestors. None of us care who you end up fighting for – Kraelish, Raayan, what's the difference? But every Taemu in this city knows who you are. We – look at me, child.'

Kavi's lips trembled, but she obeyed.

'We know what happened today,' Hessal said, softly. 'Some of us were working at the construction site.'

'I'm sorry,' Kavi said, voice cracking. She'd let them all down. She was weak. Selfish. Arrogant. She hung her head in shame.

Hessal reached out and clasped Kavi's quaking chin with her calloused fingers. 'When you walked into the Vagola last night, you made us feel something new.' Her eyes gleamed like twin embers and she slapped her chest. 'You gave us pride.'

She wiped away the tears on Kavi's cheeks and pulled her closer. 'Kavithri, child, you are not alone.'

Chapter 37

The time that she should've spent training, learning to use the armour, learning to fight with a shield and in a group, was instead wasted in Massa Zanzane's office.

What did you do this morning? he'd asked.

I ran, boss, practised with the sword on the terrace, did some exercises.

Oh? And now? What's your plan?

She scratched her head. *No plan, boss.* There was only so much she could do by herself.

Massa clapped his hands together. *Great! You are now promoted from part-time to full-time assistant.* And just like that, he gestured to Ratan, who was lounging on the divan, and the two men left on some half-arsed errand and left her in charge of the office.

She swept the floors, organized the contents of the drawers, dusted off the furniture, paced the office, searched the cabinets for snacks, and finally groaned and rested her head on the desk. Three more weeks of this while the other cadets got stronger – she glanced at the clock. Barely two hours had passed since Massa had left. There had to be something she could do. Spy on the training sessions? Wear a disguise and sneak into battle theory lectures? But what if she was caught and her suspension increased?

She banged her forehead against the desk. It was no use. She was well and truly—

'Kavi!'

She shot to her feet. 'Welcome to the Imperial Ricksha—Boss?'

'Let's go, Hessal has asked for you,' Massa said, waving for her to hurry.

Hessal wanted to see her again? So soon? She fumbled with the keys as she locked the office and jogged to catch up with Massa.

'What's this about?' she said, slotting in beside him in the rickshaw's backseat.

'You'll see,' he said, and gave her a cryptic grin. 'Oh, watch your feet.'

Kavi lifted both feet onto the seat as Ratan, huffing from the effort, shoved a heavy-looking sack, which clattered and clanged, onto the footrest.

'To the slums, Ratan,' Massa said, latching onto the handrail.

'Boss.' Ratan tipped his flat cap, slid into the driver's seat, and pumped the ignition lever.

*

'There are stories from the war,' Hessal said, kneading a ball of dough then flattening it with a heavy wooden pin. 'From what the Raayans and the Kraelish call the Methun Revolt.'

Kavi, who sat cross-legged at Hessal's side and kneaded another ball of dough, nodded.

'The Kraelish knew we were the biggest threat. We'd fought for them, once, and they *knew* what we were capable of.' Hessal slapped the dough with the flat of her palm and flung a handful of flour at it. 'The Raayans captured were treated as prisoners of war, given three meals a day and shelter from the heat. The Taemu, the rare few they managed to take alive, were taken to a hidden location and tortured.'

Kavi extended a hand and Hessal slapped the rolling pin into it.

'We found them, eventually,' Hessal said, 'we'd never abandon one of our own. But when we flung the gates open and urged the captive Taemu to run, they refused. So we dragged them out, and they pissed and shat themselves with fear, gibbered and begged to be returned to their cells. Do you know why, Kavithri?'

Kavi, jaw tight and chest heavy, shook her head.

'The Kraelish tortured them with a singular, bloody-minded purpose. They wanted to teach the Taemu, the most feared warriors on the continent, to be helpless.' Hessal turned and spat. 'And they succeeded.'

'You can see it even now. We can't run from this life, we can't fight, so just like the captured Taemu, we stay where we are. Trapped, afraid. We wouldn't know an opportunity if it walked up to us and slapped us in the face.' Hessal's eyes gleamed as she nudged the heavy sack Ratan had left by her feet. 'The Kraelish might be returning, Kavithri. Teach us.'

Kavi frowned. 'Hessal?'

The older woman leaned over and undid the string around the sack.

Kavi craned her neck to peer inside and started. Staring back at her were the pommels of at least two dozen practice swords.

'Hessal,' Kavi hissed, 'we'll get in trouble if—'

Hessal raised a hand to cut her off. 'Let me worry about that.'

'But what about—'

'Not everyone wants to learn, but there are some,' Hessal said, and waved at no one in particular. 'And there is no need to worry about one of us berserking – just like you, that part of us died long ago.'

Kavi blinked. She opened her mouth to say, *Oh, it's not dead. It's very much alive, in fact, it's sitting right next to you,* but decided against it.

'Will you teach them, Kavithri?' Hessal said, eyes weighing, measuring.

And Kavi found she didn't have it in her to disappoint the woman. 'I will,' she said, with a grim nod.

'Good.' Hessal nodded back. 'Now give them their weapons.'

A group of Taemu had converged on the hut. Massa, who stood off to the side, smoking, crushed his beedi underfoot and crouched at Hessal's shoulder. 'You sure about this?'

Hessal nodded without looking at him.

'You have a lookout?' Massa said.

Hessal cocked her head toward a scrawny-looking boy who stood with the help of a crutch. One of his legs was missing beneath the knee.

Kavi stared at the boy, who immediately averted his eyes.

'We're starting,' Hessal said, louder.

The boy nodded. His eyes flickered to Kavi and away again.

'Who is that?' Kavi said. There was so much of Haibo in this boy. The slant of his shoulders, the timidity in his gaze that transformed into awe when he looked at her.

'Chotu,' Hessal said with a smile, 'it means *little one* in old Raayan. We don't know his name and he doesn't really speak, so I gave him the name myself.'

Chotu hesitated, then bobbed his head and limped away.

Kavi took a measured breath and turned to the Taemu waiting. She'd never taught anyone *anything* before. Where would she start? When Mojan had trained her he'd forced her to build a base before he even let her touch a practice sword.

She studied the powerful shoulders and arms of the men and women who'd gathered – labourers, construction workers, gravediggers. That wouldn't be necessary here. She reached into the sack and started handing out the practice swords.

They bowed and thanked her like she'd just given them a gift, ran their hands across the wood. Tapped it. Hefted it. Burst into enthusiastic chatter.

Elisai accepted hers with mute curiosity. Then stopped. Nodded at Kavi, and said, 'Thanks, Akka.'

Kavi flinched. 'I'm not—' *your older sister*. But the woman was already walking away.

A Taemu, an entire head taller than Kavi, jabbed a thumb at his massive chest. 'Sravan.'

Kavi offered Sravan a sword.

He accepted it and pointed at the stack behind her.

'You want a different one?'

Sravan shook his head. Gestured to the practice sword he held in a hand that covered almost the entire grip. 'Two.'

'You want two swords?'

He grinned.

Kavi handed him another practice sword with a shrug. 'It will be easier to learn with just one.'

The big man shook his head. 'Two is good, Akka.'

She tsked. 'Stop calling me—'

'Line up!' Hessal yelled.

Kavi sighed and chose a practice sword for herself. She went over the order in which Mojan had taught her the basics. Grip. Stance. Strikes. It had worked for her so it should work for them. And if they were like her, once they were familiar with the basics, they would make adjustments, experiment, and find their own style.

And if they didn't?

It's fine.

Not like they'd ever be in an actual fight.

So she showed them how to hold a sword. Walked around and checked and adjusted until she felt everyone was doing it right. Then she ground her heels into the dirt and showed them how to stand while they held a sword. They were clumsy, off-balance, unsure, but every single one of them, without exception, was determined.

About thirty minutes in, an ear-shredding whistle interrupted her while she was trying to explain to the big Taemu, Sravan, that if he was going to fight with two swords, it might be worthwhile to use one defensively. 'No. Attack only,' he said.

'Swords away,' Massa hissed and shook the empty sack at the group.

Once the swords were stashed in the sack and inside the hut, Massa reached into a pocket with a flourish, pulled out a deck of playing cards, and started dealing to the Taemu who were now gathered in a circle.

'This is risky, Hessal,' he said under his breath.

'Just deal, no one will care,' she muttered.

And she was right. A group of slum-dwellers trudged past, barely glanced at them (*Ah, your hand is a real stinker!* Massa yelled and was promptly poked, painfully, in the ribs, by Hessal), and once they were out of sight, the training resumed.

By the time they were done, and Kavi had made reassurances she would return tomorrow, there was a visible difference in the bearing of the Taemu. They stood straighter. Their eyes were brighter. And much to Kavi's annoyance, each and every one of them had taken to calling her Akka.

'Kavithri,' Hessal said, grabbing her arm as she left to follow Massa back to the steam-rickshaw. 'Thank you.'

'I—' The genuine affection in the woman's eyes threw Kavi off balance. She pressed her lips together and bobbed her head.

'Tomorrow, then,' Hessal said.

Kavi didn't trust herself to speak, so she just smiled, and nodded.

True to her word, she returned the next day, and the day after, and the day after that; every single day until it was time for her to return to the Siphon. She would train in the mornings, assist Massa with his exorcisms or sit in the office and wait for clients in the afternoon, and in the evening, she would be in the slums, teaching her group of novices – who took to the sword like they were born to it.

On the last evening before her return to the Siphon, she paired up her nineteen Taemu, and asked them to spar. Elisai, the odd one out, ended up as Kavi's sparring partner.

'Don't hurt each other,' she said, but there was no point, they were already circling each other, grinning and calling out where their opponents were about to be hit.

'Here—' Sravan tapped his partner, Jiboo, on the hips. 'Also here.' He pointed to Jiboo's thigh with his other sword.

'Shaddup, you,' Jiboo said, clearly not impressed.

Kavi frowned at the pair. Maybe she should have paired up with Sravan.

'Akka?' Elisai said, waiting in her stance.

'Sorry,' Kavi said, distracted. If Sravan injured Jiboo, she would smack the bull-headed bastard on the head until—

One moment Elisai was standing still, the next, she was gone, her practice sword a blur as it cut through the air.

Kavi caught the strike on the outside of her sword, stepped in for a shoulder-barge, and slammed into what felt like a brick wall.

'I wasn't ready,' Kavi mumbled, throwing her full weight into what had now turned into a shoving contest.

'Sorry,' Elisai said, grunting with the effort, 'Akka.'

Kavi bent her knees, put her back into it, but still couldn't force Elisai to budge. The other woman was stronger. Kavi snarled. So what? She was faster.

She waited for another several heartbeats, until she was sure Elisai had thrown her entire weight into it, then disengaged.

Elisai stumbled.

Kavi lunged. Brought her sword down in an arc that would've connected with the other Taemu's shoulder. But to her surprise, instead of fighting for balance, Elisai had rolled onto her knees and was ready to receive the strike with the flat of her blade.

Kavi pulled her strike. Stepped back. Acknowledged Elisai with a nod. That was good. She would have to take this seriously.

They circled. Kavi sucked in a lungful of air. And attacked.

The next few seconds were a whirlwind of cracking swords as Kavi slowly pushed Elisai back.

They separated, sized each other up, breathed deep, and dived in again.

Kavi couldn't help the grin that slowly spread across her face. There was no doubt in her mind that Elisai would some day be the superior sword-fighter. She was powerful. Fearless. Smart. And ruthless.

Kavi probed at how this made her feel, and warmth radiated through her chest when instead of shame, envy, or anger, she only found pride.

They disengaged, circled. The only sounds: her heartbeat, the scuffing of bare feet on the ground, Elisai's laboured breaths.

Kavi frowned. Raised a hand, lowered her sword, and stepped back.

None of the others were sparring. They all stood, swords at their sides, watching.

Kavi glanced from the others to Elisai, who still stood with both hands on her sword, eyes unblinking, focused solely on Kavi.

'Enough,' Kavi said. If they continued to spar, she would have eventually found an opening and beaten Elisai. It was better this way. Let the other think they were evenly matched. Which, to be honest, was not far from the truth.

Elisai blinked. Looked around her like she'd just come out of daze.

'You did well,' Kavi said. 'Switch partners, Sravan, you're with me.'

By the time they were done, Kavi's arms were shaking from the powerful blows they'd had to fend off, and Sravan was nursing a sore hip and shoulder from where she'd connected.

The swords were collected, tucked away in Massa's sack, and after she promised she would return to train with them on her days off, they said their goodbyes, and Kavi and Massa picked their way out of the slums in silence.

Halfway through, as they passed one of the derelict towers packed with crows and covered with their droppings, Kavi heard the soft echo of an 'Akka' and turned around.

Hurrying toward them, arm waving in the air, was Elisai.

'Boss, wait,' Kavi said and tracked back.

'Akka.' Elisai stopped, caught her breath, 'I wanted to ask if you …' She puffed out her cheeks and straightened. 'Do you drink tea?'

'Tea?'

'Yes.' Elisai nodded.

'Uhm—'

'What's the hold-up?' Massa shouted, struggling with the

heavy sack of practice swords she'd manipulated him into carrying because *Boss, can you, please? My arms hurt, that bleddy Sravan, I tell you.*

'One minute!' Kavi said over her shoulder. 'Yes, I like tea.'

'If you have some time, I can make some for you, at my hut.' Elisai gestured in the vague direction of where Kavi assumed her hut was.

'Boss! Go on ahead.' Kavi waved him on.

Massa grumbled something she couldn't hear but waved and continued on.

She smiled at Elisai. 'Lead the way.'

Elisai's hut was a five-minute walk from where the rest of the Taemu lived. It sat at the end of a winding gully and consisted of a thatched roof and four crumbling walls that Kavi figured had once belonged to a room in a larger building.

What made it special, however, was the window Elisai had carved into the back wall, which offered a spectacular view of the sunset and the Azraayan skyline.

Kavi sat cross-legged facing the window while Elisai passed her a mug. They watched the sunset and drank in silence. The tea, heated in a heavy iron kettle on a pile of smouldering charcoal, was weak and bitter. Kavi finished the mug and asked for more.

Elisai's face lit up. She downed her tea and topped them both up.

'Thank you,' Kavi said, accepting the mug with both hands.

Elisai bobbed her head and sipped her tea. After several minutes had passed with just the sound of the occasional slurp, she cleared her throat, and said, 'It's a good thing, what you've done for us.'

'The training?'

'Yes, we've had something to look forward to every day. But now that it's over . . .'

'I'll still be—'

'It's not the same,' Elisai said.

Kavi lowered her head. She knew it was important to them, and it hurt her to stop, but she had no choice.

'Hessal says you didn't know about Ethuran.'

Kavi flinched. 'I don't – I should've known, I'm sorry.'

'It's okay, Akka, no one thinks any less of you,' Elisai said, a melancholic smile on her lips. 'I was there, you know.'

Kavi nodded. 'Hessal said.'

'Did she tell you what happened?'

'Yes, she . . .' Kavi glanced at Elisai, at the faraway look in her eyes. 'Not exactly, no.'

Elisai set her mug down. Placed a hand on each knee and gazed straight ahead.

'They came in the morning,' she said, after a lengthy pause, 'while we were preparing breakfast. First, they took my husband. He was a brave man. Tried to protect us. They dragged him away. Hacked his limbs off. Set him on fire.'

Kavi stared at the dregs in her mug. Mouth dry. Heart slowly breaking.

'My mother and father, they shielded me while I ran. I could hear them being beaten. I held my baby, my son, to my chest, tightly, like this' – she raised her arms and squeezed them to her chest – 'but they took him. Pulled him from me. Threw him into a fire. And then, they . . .'

Kavi reached out, took Elisai's hand in both of hers. Squeezed it. 'You don't have to tell me.'

Elisai shook her head. 'The next thing I remember, I was running in a field, naked, covered in blood.'

Just like Haibo. Alone. Scared. Surrounded by men and

women whose hate she could not reason with. Kavi's hands shook, and she said, through a pounding in her ears, 'I'm sorry—'

'But it wasn't my blood, Akka,' Elisai said.

Then again, softer, as she tightened her grip on Kavi's hands. 'It wasn't *my* blood.'

Chapter 38

'Each squad will consist of a warlock and three cadets,' Walia said, staring down at the cadets from a makeshift podium. He gestured to a board with a long piece of paper nailed to it. 'Find your squad. Remember your allocated date. Prepare yourself, this is the closest you will get to the real thing. Healers will be on hand, but make no mistake, if you are not alert – if you are careless – you will die.'

Kavi waited until the crowd in front of the board had cleared before walking up to it. On the left: a column with dates. On the right: names that matched up with a date.

She started at the top, searched for her name – there. *Kavithri Taemu.* She'd told Salora about the unfortunate mix-up and the Siphon administrators had cleared it up right away. She'd also apologised to Subbal Reddy for borrowing his name. The man had grunted and asked for money: five rayals for each day she'd gone by his name. She'd agreed that it was a fair price, and that Massa would pay.

According to this list, her visit to the Vagola to duel a third-year warlock and their Blade was two weeks away. Her squad included Yella, a man called Nijesh, whom she'd never met, and their warlock – Kavi groaned, of course it had to be her – Ze'aan.

A week had passed since Kavi's return from suspension and she'd only encountered the warlock twice. Both training sessions where she had to stand still, grit her teeth, and let her armour absorb the fizzing missiles Ze'aan sent her way. Only this time, once the gauge was full, she was allowed to push the button on her forearm that released a portion of the stored maayin in a targeted blast. She'd never felt more powerful in her life.

Ze'aan had barely acknowledged her. Which was not saying much; the woman only spoke to the trainers, and even then, only if they approached her. But Kavi had expected something. An, *oh look, the Taemu is back with her tail-between-her-legs* reaction. Or a knowing, *I put her in her place* glance. She got nothing.

Over the next two weeks, cadets would leave each day for the Vagola, return ashen-faced, hollow-eyed, and would refuse to answer any questions the others asked them. Sometimes, a cadet wouldn't come back at all, and when that happened, there would be no questions; Gomathi would walk up to the board and scratch their name off the list.

*

The duelling arena was a large hole deep inside the bowels of the Vagola. Like the stadium, tiered seating rose to surround it, but it only held room for a hundred spectators at the most.

A row of artificed globes hung from the ceiling and lit up the oval and its white sand with simulated sunlight.

Kavi checked to ensure her armour was secure, her shield strapped in, the gauge that measured the absorbed maayin was empty, and the twin buttons underneath it were functional.

'How many times are you going to check?' Yella said.

Kavi shrugged. 'Can never be too safe.'

Nijesh, the third member of their squad, stood perfectly still, staring at the wall of the tunnel they were waiting in.

'Bhai.' Yella shook him by the shoulder. 'Nijesh?' And when the man didn't respond, he turned to Kavi and spat. 'We're fucked.'

Ze'aan, who stood all the way in the back, snorted.

Kavi peered at the catatonic man. 'Maybe it's a ritual or something.'

Yella slapped the wall and shook Nijesh again. 'What the fuck are you looking at?'

'Cadets.' Gomathi cleared her throat and walked into the tunnel. 'Novice Salasari.'

Ze'aan acknowledged her with a nod, and Kavi and Yella snapped to attention.

'What's wrong with him?' Gomathi frowned at Nijesh.

'Concentration ritual, ma'am,' Kavi said.

Gomathi made a face and muttered something under her breath, then checked the clipboard tucked under her arm.

'You will fight without restrictions today – your swords will be waiting for you in the arena. The format follows traditional Blade-lock rules, similar to what we use in the tournaments, except you will have an advantage over your opponents: *your* warlock will have three Blades.' She gave them a meaningful glance. 'There will be third-year warlocks and Blades among the invaders during the Siphon, so this is the only opportunity you'll have to experience their power. Learn as much as you can.

'Now, the rules: at each end of the arena, you will find a pedestal with an artificed crystal affixed to it.' She spread her hands apart till they were as wide as her hips. 'Approximately the size of an adult chicken.'

What the Hel kind of comparison is that?

'Each Blade-lock will be allocated a crystal. Your objective is to destroy the enemy crystal before the five-minute round is complete.' She flashed all five fingers at them. 'If both crystals are still intact at the end, the match is ruled a tie. Official matches last ten minutes, but five is all you will need.' She flicked a thumb at Ze'aan. 'The warlock must remain behind the crystal at all times and can only be attacked if they are casting. Understood?'

Kavi pursed her lips. Nodded with the others.

'Now, Novice Salasari,' Gomathi said, 'please advise your Blades on how long it would take for you to replenish your krasna.'

'Between an hour and ninety minutes,' Ze'aan said.

Gomathi nodded. 'So, if a warlock's cast is interrupted, they are essentially useless for the rest of the match.'

Ze'aan's eyebrow twitched. But she remained silent.

'Any specific abilities your Blades should know about?' Gomathi prompted.

'I can use a tracer,' Ze'aan said.

'That won't be useful here—'

'What's a tracer?' Kavi said, and to her surprise, Ze'aan answered.

'A concentration of my maayin that can trace an alternate source of Harithian maayin to its mage.'

'It can find an enemy warlock,' Gomathi said. 'Very useful in actual combat, not so much for Blade-lock matches. Now, you will be called soon. If you wish to strategise or plan, now is the time – and, oh, one last thing. Your opponents have instructions not to hold back.' And with that, she strode out into the arena, waving at someone Kavi couldn't see.

Kavi and Yella glanced at each other, then at Ze'aan.

Nijesh, who'd just emerged from his stupor, muttered, 'Limua watch over me,' and stumbled out into the arena.

'Taemu,' Yella said as he followed Nijesh out. 'Stay with the warlock.'

The warlock, it turned out, had no intention of waiting in the tunnel either. She strode past, head held high, eyes fixed on nothing and everything.

Kavi ran one last check on her equipment, cracked her neck to work the stiffness out of it, and followed Ze'aan out into the arena.

She emerged midway through the sandy oval. A white line divided the arena in half, and another ran under the waist-high marble pedestals at each end.

Nijesh and Yella were waiting by the pedestal on the left, both staring at the chicken-sized crystal that hovered over it. They held their swords now, the naked and polished blades shimmering in the artificed light.

Kavi's sword was waiting for her, propped up against the pedestal. She spat on her sword-hand as she trudged over, kneeled and rubbed it into the sand at her feet, and wrapped her fingers around the hilt. She sighed with satisfaction as its weight tugged on the muscles in her arm and shoulder.

Ze'aan took up a spot a metre or so behind the crystal, well behind the white line that she was presumably required not to cross.

Kavi glanced from her to the crystal. Who was she supposed to protect? If the crystal was destroyed, the match was over. But if the warlock was nullified, they lost any chance of winning.

'Kavithri? The list said your name is Kavithri, right?' Ze'aan said.

Kavi lifted both eyebrows and nodded at Ze'aan.

The warlock gestured for her to come closer.

Kavi set her jaw, but obliged. She shuffled closer until she was a hand's-length away from the taller woman.

'I know the warlock we'll be facing today,' Ze'aan said, and paused.

Kavi waited. Studied Ze'aan's profile.

'He has range,' Ze'aan eventually said, 'and will not hesitate to kill.'

'I know.' Kavi nodded. 'They've been telling us that all wee—'

'No, not you. He will not hesitate with me.'

'Did you go and insult him too?' Kavi said, and ducked her head. Gods-dammit, she didn't mean to say that out loud.

Ze'aan arched one perfectly groomed eyebrow, and the tips of her lips curved in a half-smile. 'Something like that.'

Bhaenchod, that's what you get. 'So, what's the plan?' Kavi said.

'Don't worry about the crystal,' Ze'aan said, 'watch my back. Do that, and I will make sure you survive this.'

Kavi narrowed her eyes. 'Are you asking for my help? After what you—'

'I've watched you, these last two weeks,' Ze'aan said. 'You have good eyes.'

Flattery will get you nowhere, but, Kavi sighed, the woman was being sincere, and she found that despite the grudge she still nurtured, she couldn't turn her down. 'What do you need me to do?'

Ze'aan bobbed her head in thanks, a gesture that Kavi decided did not suit her at all, and pointed to a spot several paces behind her. 'I will try to deflect as much as I can, but when I fail . . .'

'I'll take care of it,' Kavi said, then frowned. 'Isn't it against the rules to attack you when you're not casting?'

Ze'aan smiled like she knew what Kavi was hinting at.

'So why don't you just stop?' Kavi asked.

'There are mages watching, powerful men and women,' Ze'aan said. 'I cannot appear weak in front of them.'

Kavi gazed out at the spectators, most of them gathered as a group and seated at the midway point. She paused. Then leaned closer to peer at a woman sitting on one of the higher tiers – cropped hair, massive arms folded over her chest, and even from where Kavi stood she could make out the dark tattooed fangs on the woman's chin that marked her as a Gashani warrior.

Greema.

She wanted to wave. To shout. But Greema's eyes were firmly fixed on the tunnel, out of which a burly Blade and his equally bulky warlock were striding.

Kavi puffed her cheeks out and slapped the top of her helmet. Maybe it was better not to be recognised here. It would be so much more meaningful if she survived the Siphon and showed up at the Vagola as a first-year Blade.

The atmosphere in the arena shifted as their opponents made their way to their crystal. The Blade took a position in front of the pedestal, and the warlock shuffled backwards until his shoulders touched the wall.

Kavi's pulse quickened. The anticipation, the contained violence – just like the fighting rings in Bochan, only less rowdy.

In the audience, Gomathi stood, raised a metal baton into the air, and brought it down.

The crystals hummed, a faint orange light emanated from each core, and they began, ever so slowly, to rotate on their axes.

Ze'aan gathered her hair up, twisted and tied it into a high ponytail – her arms were halfway down to her sides when she froze.

From where Kavi stood – shield raised and sword resting on it – she could make out the edges of Ze'aan's krasna, the rickshaw-tyre-sized orb of emerald-green maayin she was so familiar with.

On the other end of the oval the enemy warlock summoned his own krasna, which rose to sit over his head. It was denser, flatter. It bent, almost like a slingshot, and with a hiss, fired a sequence of missiles into the back of the Blade who was already sprinting at Yella and Nijesh.

The maayin connected with the Blade's armour with a series of loud *thunk-thunk-thunks.* The Blade barely flinched. It pushed him to run even faster. Straight at Nijesh, who stepped out to meet him.

Kavi gritted her teeth and raised her shield as more long-range missiles grazed the roof of the arena and came plunging down at them.

Ze'aan responded. Her krasna tore itself into pieces. A ball of maayin flattened to shield the crystal. Another section burst into an array of discs that negated the barrage raining down on them. And a fizzing cluster of pellets hammered into Nijesh's back.

He stumbled.

Kavi's shoulders tightened as she locked her knees and fought the urge to run to his aid. The man should've known it was coming. He should've braced himself. They hurt, yes, but it was a weapon too.

Run. Get out of the way.

But Nijesh, once he'd regained his footing, just stood there as the enemy Blade closed the gap.

Run.

Kavi watched in horror as the enemy Blade closed in, flung his sword into the ground and wrapped two massive arms around Nijesh in a bear-hug. There was a soft hiss, and the Blade's armour released the maayin it had stored in a concussive blast that made Kavi flinch.

The Blade let go of Nijesh, and he fell, like a rag doll, every bone in his body shattered. Blood streamed from his eyes and nose and mouth. He convulsed. And went still.

Kavi's breath came in short bursts. She tasted bile at the back of her throat and swallowed. There had been no need to go that far. No need.

A green blur whizzed past Kavi and she swivelled as it scraped the wall, changed direction, and came screaming at Ze'aan.

Kavi kicked the dirt as she put herself between the maayin and her warlock, and braced herself behind her shield.

The maayin hit with a bone-rattling thunk. Kavi glanced at her gauge: a tenth full. She could do this. Protect the warlock. Stay alive.

More missiles blurred as they broke past Ze'aan's defence and circled around to target her back. But Kavi was there. Her shield absorbed and deflected, while her eyes roved the space on both sides of Ze'aan. She was vaguely aware that Yella had engaged the Blade, but she had no time to pay any attention to the duel, or to what Ze'aan was doing.

She understood the point of the matches now. How it could train a warlock to defend, to attack, to support their Blade, and to look for openings, all at the same time. The situational awareness that it demanded was astonishing. And as for the Blades? They could learn the power and weight of their warlock's maayin, learn their quirks and limits, and master the armour.

Kavi's pulse raced and her muscles quivered as she batted another missile away. She had the timing. Nothing would get past her now. Nothing ...

She glanced at a cloud of green dust that flickered in Ze'aan's blindspot, and a chill ran down her spine as it fizzed and coalesced into an arm-length spike.

She flung her sword at it. Missed. Scuffed her feet as she took a step back, wound up, and leaped into the air – into Ze'aan's blindspot and into the path of the spike. She ducked her head under her shield and curled herself into a ball.

The spike shattered against the shield. Pain flared up her shield-arm. She'd stopped it, she'd saved the warlock. But the force with which the spike hit sent her barrelling into Ze'aan.

They collided and went down in a tangle of limbs.

Ze'aan, knocked out of her cast and useless for the rest of the match, shoved Kavi away, got to her feet, opened her mouth, shut it, and stared at the dent in Kavi's shield.

It was over. There was nothing protecting the crystal now and the other warlock couldn't attack Ze'aan without bringing down the collective wrath of the Vagola on his head.

But there was no signal to stop. No bell like in the ring fights. The enemy warlock was now sending his maayin at Yella, who struggled to keep the enemy Blade at bay.

Yella blocked a vicious slash with his shield, crouched, and punched a button on his shield-arm.

The enemy Blade had read his mind. He mirrored Yella. Lowered his shield and triggered the release. A dull *boom!* echoed through the arena as the blasts from the shields negated each other.

The enemy warlock pulled his missiles back. He was going to let the cadet and the Blade fight it out.

Well, fuck that.

Kavi sprinted to her sword. Without breaking stride, she bent, let her fingers graze the sand until they snapped around the hilt. She shifted her weight, and running in a curve, hurtled toward Yella and the Blade.

Her eyes flickered to Nijesh's crumpled-up body, and she pulled her lips back to bare her teeth. They'd used him like a toy. Wanted to use her like a toy. Just another practice dummy. Just—

Maayin crackled, fizzed and thunked into her arms and torso.

Sent her stumbling and off course. But she brushed it off with a growl, kept her eyes locked on the Blade, and sped up.

More missiles came hurtling down at her, but missed. The wind whistled through the gaps in her helmet as she brought her shield-arm up to her mouth and ripped the straps open with her teeth. She caught the shield before it fell, and shouted, 'Yella!'

The man cast a sharp glance at her and immediately disengaged. The Blade followed.

Kavi twisted her body. Launched her shield at the man. It spun through the air and crashed into his side. Halting him in his tracks.

Her calves and hamstrings screamed as she took two powerful strides and flung herself at the Blade – sword raised over her head, free hand rushing to wrap around the hilt. And holding it two-handed, she slammed it down on the man.

Their swords met with a deafening *clang!*

The Blade couldn't get his shield around in time and was forced to use his sword to defend. He grunted as he tried to shove her away.

But Kavi had the momentum, the power, and she muscled her sword down. Pushed the Blade to his knees.

The tip of her sword caught on his shoulder, and to her astonishment, sliced right through his armour.

The Blade rammed his shield into the side of her head.

She shook it off. The veins on her neck stood out. Her hands clutching the sword trembled.

He hit her again.

And the rage in her core tested its chains and shrieked.

Kavi roared back: at the berserker inside her, at the man on his knees in front of her, at the warlock on the other end of the arena. She took one hand off the hilt, raised it above her head, and brought it back down like a hammer.

Her forearm crashed into the hilt of her sword. Forced its edge deeper into the Blade's armour.

He hissed and hit her in the head again. Harder this time.

You think you can punch? Fucking Bhagu hits harder than you.

She raised her hand, made a fist, and slammed it back down on the hilt.

The sword sliced into flesh. Caught bone.

The Blade gasped and hit her again.

But his power was gone. She barely flinched. The vision in her left eye was hazy, like she was looking through a film of red, but she could tell he was scared.

Good.

Good.

She bent her knees. Breathed in the stench of the man's sweat, and ground the sword deeper into his shoulder. Blood spurted from the slice in the armour, and he cried out in pain.

He was trapped. He couldn't reach the button on his shield-arm, so the armour was worthless. His warlock wouldn't dare attack her because *her* armour was not, she could still trigger a release, but she didn't need it. She made a fist and raised her hand.

There was a crack, and a loud keening cut through the arena. Kavi blinked. Looked for the source.

Back in their half of the field, Ze'aan stood beside a shattered crystal that was slowly reassembling itself.

'It's over,' Gomathi shouted.

Kavi stared at the man clawing at her sword. He had shown Nijesh no mercy. Did he really expect her to—

'It's over, cadet!' Gomathi said again.

Kavi sighed. Yanked the sword out. And stumbled.

An arm wrapped itself around her shoulder and held her up.

'Enough,' Yella said, grunting as he struggled with her weight and his own injuries.

Kavi wheezed as she caught her breath. 'You okay?'

He snorted. 'I'll survive.'

Silence hung over the arena and amplified the sound of her heavy, ragged breaths, and the wounded Blade's grunts of pain. She gazed over at the spectators, half of whom were standing as they watched her. Greema was among the ones who remained seated.

Kavi felt more than saw the almost imperceptible nod the woman gave her.

She nodded back. Glanced at Ze'aan as they began limping toward the tunnel.

The warlock stared back at her, unblinking, her mouth set in a thin line.

'You did good, Taemu,' Yella said, patting her shoulder. 'They won't forget you now. You did good.'

Interlude – II

Drisana

I was paralysed from the neck down.

My nostrils were clogged with blood and vomit, but my jaw, twisted and dislocated, hung open and allowed me to breathe through my mouth.

I remember the warmth of the tears that trailed down my cheeks. The shudder that ran through the pilot's pod. The shriek of the saw as it got closer. I remember slamming the back of my head against the pod to knock myself out because I knew that if I lost consciousness I would never wake again. The Harithians were coming for me, sister, and I was scared.

A slim column of light tore its way into the pod as the screeching got even louder and the sounds I made as I sobbed and gibbered were, to be truthful, more animal than human. I called for my mother. Begged her for forgiveness. Pleaded with her to save me.

But my mother was dead, taken captive by the Harithians when I was just a girl, never to be seen again. I was alone.

The saw withdrew and a metal appendage ripped the pilot's pod open.

A man – sharp-featured with stern, unyielding eyes – peeked in, and flinched at the sight and the smell of my broken body.

'Get her out,' he said to an invisible colleague, and my heart raced at the sight of his uniform.

The soldiers who gently extracted me from the pod and laid me down on the battered surface of my makra wore the same grey uniforms and orange shoulder badges.

They were soldiers of Kolacin. They were on our side.

The man with the cold eyes, who also wore Kolacin's uniform, kneeled by my side, almost reverently, and said, 'Pilot Drisana, can you hear me?'

Our eyes met. I nodded.

'The Harithians have withdrawn, Pilot, they have sent all their forces to the Zubhran front for a final assault.' He placed a warm hand on my shoulder. 'They will be too late.'

My eyes widened.

'The last transports for Nilasi will leave soon. The Chain will be broken, and the Gates closed forever. We've won.'

My chin trembled as I took in the destruction around *Gayathri*. The hordes of broken destroyer units and shattered pieces of Harithian makra that littered the ground from horizon to horizon. I turned back to the man, and I couldn't stop my torn lips from curling into a grin.

His eyes softened. 'They were not prepared for a berserker makra to single-handedly hold them off for so long.' He swallowed, and I could hear the awe in his voice. 'We watched you fight, Pilot Drisana, some are already calling you a God.'

I coughed as I tried to chuckle.

He squeezed my shoulder. 'Kolacin wants to offer you the Transplant.'

I went completely still. Tears welled up in my eyes.

I'd heard of the Transplants. Heard they were being offered to select mages on their deathbeds; mages who were supposed to be the best of us.

The Harithians had learned to capture the spark that gave flesh and bone life, the soul, and drag it back from the afterlife; the engineers on Kolacin had discovered a way to block it from ever leaving our reality. A soul that spent time in the afterlife lost its identity, but the souls in Transplants never completed the transfer. They retained their consciousness, locked forever into an artifice and unable to ever affect the physical world again.

'When the Chain is broken, the engineers believe it will also lock the survivors on Nilasi away from maayin, from the Jinn,' he said. 'They intend to leave a set of Transplants. If the Jinn and maayin are discovered again, they will need guidance.'

If? What if it never happens?

He read the question in my eyes. 'If the Jinn are never found, you will remain dormant. Unaware. In a painless sleep. Only a surge of maayin can activate your consciousness.'

Pain, sharp and sudden, lanced through my chest, and I arched my back as I bit down on the moan that left my throat.

'You're going into haemorrhagic shock, Pilot. Make your choice.'

Breathe, daughter, Raktha whispered in my ear. A warmth spread through my body, and just like that, I could breathe again.

I thought you'd left.

I've never left.

But your voice, it's … faint.

It has already begun. The Chain is disintegrating.

What will happen to you?

We will be silenced. Maybe forever. Even if we are found again, we will never be able to speak to our children, not like this, and our gifts to them will be stunted.

Why— Is there no other way?

My children are dying, Drisana. And they are being brought back. I can feel their torment. Their confusion. Raeth's touch has spread through Harith, contaminated her maayin, but her people continue to draw from her. She wants it to end.

What will happen to me, if I accept?

If you accept the Transplant, you will be silenced. Trapped. Like us. Time will contract. And you will wait.

For how long?

Until we find each other. Until you find my maayin, and bond with one of my children.

How will I know the right one? How – what if I fail?

You will know. You are a daughter of Raktha. You will not fail.

My breaths came in shallow gasps. The thought of being trapped, alone, with no escape, and no release .... the hair stood on the back of my neck.

Do this for my children, Drisana. For our people.

'Pilot Drisana,' the man said. 'Do you accept?'

I swallowed, and nodded.

'Remember something – think of something peaceful,' he said, extracting an artifice that resembled a sword's hilt from a bag. 'Ready?'

I closed my eyes, ignored the pain, and searched for the sound of my bells: tinkling and jangling as I glided across a soft wooden floor on bare feet. Louder when I stomped my heels into the ground, softer when I swayed to the sound of my teacher's rhythmic chanting.

I opened my eyes with the bells in my ears, kept my eyes locked on Kolacin's burning sky, and nodded.

The man slammed the artifice over the implant in my forehead.

I gasped.

The air evaporated from my lungs.

And I died.

*

The silence, something I'd so desperately yearned for, was a relief.

But it did not last long.

Soon I could hear – words spoken in a language I couldn't understand.

Then I could see – vast oceans and deserts and snow-capped mountains.

And always a beach.

And on its sand, footprints. A child's footprints. Whether they dragged me along or whether I willingly went, I do not know, but time lost its meaning.

I followed the footsteps, tracked this child across worlds, always on the same stretch of beach, and then, with no warning, a scream. In it, pain. Grief. Rage. Maayin unlike any I had ever encountered. And at its core, you.

It is too late for you, sister. The corruption has already set in. I cannot save you.

But, if you can understand me, if any of this reaches you, know this: I accept you.

You may not be the child Raktha is waiting for, but this choice is mine, and mine alone to make.

I will answer only to you.

Speak only to you.

And for as long as there is breath in your chest and the fury of our people in your heart, I will fight with you.

Part Three

Chapter 39

Dear Sahib,

I hope this letter finds you in good health.

The suspension, as you predicted, was merely a setback. I have caught up to the other cadets and may even have surpassed some of them. Also, since our last exchange, another twenty-one cadets have dropped out. My odds have improved.

Relations between the warlock and me are also better. She now appears to have a grudging respect for my person and my abilities, as do most of the squad, which has made training much more bearable. She has never apologised for the incident on the first day, but she has, to my surprise, made an effort to discuss with me (unprompted) such topics as the weather, the food, the plumbing issues plaguing the city, and whether or not Azraaya's Picchadi team will take this year's trophy. I sense she may regret her actions, but then again, the woman is as inscrutable as she is opaque, and I can only guess at what she is thinking.

The instructors, on the other hand, remain aloof and outright hostile. Hel awaits.

Massa Zanzane sends his regards. ~~He continues to con hardworking citizens~~. I am honoured to be assisting him with the many services he provides the community. Truly, a great man.

You asked if I had managed to meet and connect with the Taemu in Azraaya; I am pleased to say that they have accepted me with open arms. Some of them have even taken to calling me Akka. While it is flattering to hear it from the young, it is deeply discomfiting when someone older refers to me as their big sister. Also, I have been spending evenings showing some of the Taemu the basics of the sword (the hawaldars here don't enter the slums, so the risk is minimal). They have taken to it much faster than I ever did.

Now, to answer your other questions:

No, I have not forgotten your training. It continues to serve me well.

Yes, I am still reading. Although it's mostly the newspamphlets these days (you may have heard that all the northern kingdoms have now fallen to the Kraelish – the city is nervous).

Yes, I am sleeping well.

No, I do not require money. Massa Zanzane is as generous as he is wise. He has lent me ink and paper, and out of the kindness of his heart is critiquing my grammar, punctuation, and penmanship. Truly, a great man.

Once again, sahib, I cannot thank you enough. It is heartening to hear that Tsubu has been adopted by the staff at your estate. I hope I will have the opportunity to visit Bochan at some point in the future to see you and him again.

By the time you receive this letter, the Siphon will have concluded. I will write to you again, if I am still able to; if not, Massa Zanzane will write on my behalf.

Your friend, always,

Kavithri

*

'—Taemu and Squad five,' Gomathi bellowed into the locker room, 'you're assigned to the north-eastern quadrant. Remember that the battlefield has been divided in three equal sections. You will begin in section one – where you will engage the invaders. Your objective is to prevent the enemy, at all costs, from breaching the line of combat in section three. The battle will end when the flare is released.' She paused. Tsked at the twitchy cadets. 'Listen, it's okay to be afraid down here, but out there, you *must* set it aside. If you don't, it will cripple you and ruin your judgement.' She gave herself a satisfied nod and slammed the door shut.

Kavi exchanged a glance with Yella, who rolled his eyes.

'Must've spent hours in front of the mirror rehearsing that,' he said.

'Didn't seem rehearsed,' Kavi muttered. She dug a finger under the collar of her cuirass and pulled at it. Maybe it was the nerves, maybe she'd put on weight, but the armour was tighter today. Uncomfortably so. She'd mentioned it to Salora, but the artificer had shrugged it off and told her she was imagining things.

'Stop squirming, damnit,' Yella said.

'It's my armour, bleddy thing . . .' She tsked and scratched her armpit.

The furnace that was the locker room – the nine other sweaty men and women who sat stewing in their armour and puffing away on beedis – was not helping. Besides a few pointless exchanges, most of the squad observed an intense, almost religious silence; interrupted every few minutes by a dull roar followed by muffled applause that rumbled through the walls.

The Council needed to give their speeches. Artificers needed to show off their latest inventions. Warlocks needed to put on a display. Healers would be given medals for service. The winner of the yearly lottery would be announced. Bets would be placed. Booze would be consumed. Patriotic songs would be sung. Fisticuffs would ensue because a punter didn't join in during the national anthem. Guards would be dispatched to deal with the ruckus. Bribes would be exchanged. Everyone would laugh, *Misunderstanding, bhai, just joking, this bhaenchod is my brother-in-law – Damn good, yaar, so he's actually a bhaenchod? – I'll kill you.* And when the stadium was nice and warmed up, the Siphon would commence.

Kavi cast a furtive glance at Yella. The man was busy reading scripture from Limua's *Diary of the Lost Year*. The child Goddess was forever stuck in the form of a six-year-old girl; cursed by uncle Raeth for an afternoon of mischief-making in Hel to sleep for all eternity; believed to be snoozing under the fertile soil of the Tholar delta with her holy bolster between her knees and her thumb stuck in her mouth. The Goddess of the harvest was fanatically worshipped in western Raaya, where Yella and his friend Baanchu hailed from.

When she was sure that he was not paying any attention to her, she twisted, tested the lock on her locker – still secure, like it was the last seventeen times she tested it – and blew the air out of her cheeks. Massa had insisted that she keep a few rats with her. *Just in case,* he'd said. *You never know.*

The door to the locker room squealed open and Ze'aan, decked out in shiny warlock's armour, strolled in. Her armour was a more powerful version of the protection the cadets wore; not that she really needed it. The only way she'd get injured was by accident. And even that was unlikely given the number of observers – most of whom were fully fledged warlocks themselves – on the ground during the battle.

The *only* way to defeat a warlock today was to overcome their Blade. Do that, and they would surrender. No one was permitted to attack the warlocks directly, not even the warlocks themselves. If that rule was broken, the observers could step in and take action: disqualification if the rule-breaker was a warlock themselves, death or dismemberment if they were not.

Ze'aan arranged herself in the empty spot next to Kavi.

'Apparently,' she said, sotto voce, 'the invaders will have recently graduated warlocks and Blades among their ranks.'

Invaders was the blanket term the instructors and cadets used to refer to the enemy they would face today; much easier than *desperate convicts fighting for a second chance.*

Kavi made a face. 'Where did you hear that?'

'Briefing with Archmage Jefore.'

Kavi chewed the inside of her cheek and picked at her armour.

Ze'aan watched her squirm and wriggle. 'Afraid of the killing?'

'I'm more worried about the dying.'

'You shouldn't be.' Ze'aan tucked a loose strand of hair behind an ear and gazed, unblinking, into Kavi's eyes. 'When you hit your stride, when you go to that ... *place* you go to. You're fast. Faster than all of them.'

Kavi stopped fidgeting. Was that a compliment? That was a compliment. The nerves must be getting to the warlock too. 'That's – what if I was *afraid* of the killing?'

Ze'aan cocked her head. 'Are you?'

'Yes.' She was.

'Don't be,' Ze'aan said. 'Think about it. If we're all going to Hel, if we're all stuck in this cycle of death and reincarnation' – she shrugged – 'what harm is there in taking a life?'

'Even if they're *your* people?' Kavi said, studying the warlock's unreadable eyes.

'My people?' Ze'aan frowned. 'You mean the Raayans?'

Kavi blinked. 'Who else?'

Ze'aan went perfectly still. Her face twitched and something dark seemed to pass over it. 'They are not *my people*. My people – *my people* wouldn't torture, rape, and kill because our beliefs didn't align. They wouldn't steal land and displace families who've lived on it for thousands of years. *My people* would never praise a criminal, a man who instigated genocide, and allow him into a position of power.'

Kavi winced. She'd touched a nerve.

'That's what we're fighting for,' Ze'aan said, voice dripping with disdain. 'A country where the man who instigated the massacre at Ethuran, whose actions led to the death of thousands of innocents – thousands of *your people* – can rise to a position on the Council itself.'

The muscles in Kavi's stomach clenched and hardened. She'd guessed that there was a leader, a chief instigator, but had never imagined that the person responsible for her people's pain would be part of the elite running the Republic. She fought to keep a still face while Ze'aan continued.

'No one talks about it,' Ze'aan said. 'There is this ... this cultural defensiveness. Outsiders walking on eggshells and insiders closing ranks and refusing to see or say anything bad about themselves. I see it all the time. The Republic is great. Our food is the best. It's such a colourful place. So vibrant. So secular. So exotic. Come visit. Did you know they tried to build walls around the slums so that royals and politicos visiting the area didn't have to see them?'

Kavi nodded. She'd seen the half-erected walls herself.

Ze'aan clenched her jaw. 'I've watched, an outsider in the country of my birth, as this rot has grown and spread. I've watched brave men and women, driven by their belief in humanity, utterly selfless, try to stop it, and instead get swallowed whole and spat out in pieces.' She straightened. 'The Kraelish may have snuffed out civilisations, exterminated races, plundered nations, and kicked the subcontinent to the ground, but make no mistake, it was the Raayans who slit its throat and left it to bleed out.'

Kavi stared at the warlock. The anger in her voice was palpable. Relatable. 'So why … What do you want?'

'Want?' Ze'aan's lips curled into a smile. 'I want change. I want people to respect *strength*, not power. But to do that, I first need power.' She dropped her voice but maintained its intensity. 'Anyone – *anyone*, who stands between you and your dream is an enemy. And if they refuse to move, you do not hesitate to move them. You understand?'

Kavi bit her tongue. 'Sure.'

'Good. I want you on my flank.'

'What?'

'On my left,' Ze'aan said.

'Gather!' Squad leader Barun, a former hawaldar and part-time pehalwan, spread a map of the battleground on the floor. It was divided into three clean sections, each marked with a number. He waited until the squad huddled around him, then jabbed a finger at the map's north-east corner, in the section marked 1.

'That's us.' He traced a route through the artificial streets and buildings, through section two in the middle of the battlefield, and all the way down to the line of combat in section three where the cadets were instructed to hold the enemy, and beyond which lay the invader's goal. 'We fight, building-to-building, room-to-room. We chip away at the enemy, and' – he slapped an open space that looked like a yard – 'we make our stand here.'

Kavi grimaced. 'Why don't we funnel them, let them take section one, wait in two, bait them. Here.' She pointed to a long corridor between two structures. 'There's no need to face them head-on in every section. We hit them and move. Funnel them in and let our warlock take them out.'

Barun spat. 'Our instructions are to defend. To hold the invaders and only fall back to the next section if there is no other choice. We will fight, not run and hide like cowards."

Kavi glanced at Yella. He would know she was right. But all he did was sigh and give her a what-to-do shrug.

'Any other objections?' Barun said, glaring at Kavi.

He got a chorus of *No, boss; Room-by-room; Meshira protect us; One last beedi,* which seemed to satisfy him.

'Line up,' he said. 'Armour check. Pistols. Shields. Swords.'

Kavi fiddled with the straps on her armour until Gomathi popped her head into the room and bellowed, 'Squad five. Move!'

They moved – single file – through dim, narrow corridors; past uniformed attendants and tray-bearing waiters; up urine-soaked stairs littered with oil-soaked newspamphlets the samosa vendors used as makeshift plates. Kavi's heart drummed to the beat of the squad's footsteps. Her clammy hands opened and closed. Opened and closed. A circle of light grew larger and larger. The clamour and the cacophony got closer and closer. She stepped over a threshold, walked through a wall of sound, and burst out into the sunlight.

A bowl of humanity surrounded her. Hawkers screamed as they navigated the aisles. Men and women laughed and pointed. Children caterwauled and cried. Soldiers stood to attention. And lost somewhere in the tumult, maybe up in the grey mass that was the nosebleeds, maybe tucked away underneath the stadium, her people waited. The Taemu had been hired to clear away the dead.

Barun led them to the north-eastern quadrant. They jogged past other squads already in position, over wonky bridges and empty canals, past buildings and walls where observers sat crouched and waiting.

Once they'd settled into an alleyway behind a two-storey building, Barun sidled up to Ze'aan. 'Ma'am,' he said, 'I will ask that you retain the majority of your krasna till we are in section three.'

The warlock inclined her head. 'As you wish, squad leader.'

He turned to Kavi. 'Taemu, you're up front—'

'She will remain at my side,' Ze'aan said.

Barun's eyes darted between the two of them. A vein on his forehead throbbed, but he quietly acquiesced.

The stadium erupted in a roar that shook the structure to its foundation.

Kavi swallowed. The *invaders* were here. Convicts fighting for a pardon, and based on Ze'aan's intel, a group of recently graduated warlocks and Blades.

Their weapons: unknown. Their numbers: unknown. But it was a safe bet that the cadets were outnumbered.

Barun walked among the squad, checking equipment, giving each cadet instructions and a pep talk. He was midway through a sentence when something big and green connected with his neck and produced a loud *splat.*

His headless body toppled to the ground. Twin geysers erupted from his neck and sprayed the cadet he was speaking to with bright-red blood.

Kavi screamed. Stared at Barun's corpse – still pumping blood – with her mouth hanging open.

Run.

That should not have happened. The armour should have negated the damage.

Run.

Tight. Itchy. Uncomfortable …They'd changed the armour. *They fucking changed the armour.*

Run.

Men and women screaming at the top of their lungs and wielding spears and axes and swords came hurtling down the street. Over their heads whizzed more emerald projectiles.

An ululating battle cry pierced through the roar of the crowd and jolted Kavi out of her trance.

She grabbed Ze'aan by the wrist and ran. The warlock was their only hope, and she was useless in roving combat. They had to get to the yard.

Kavi dragged Ze'aan through dust clouds and debris as maayin punched into walls and buildings. They ducked under spears flung blindly into the air. They ran past cadets crushed under brick and wood. Past men and women laughing and sobbing. Crying and gurgling. And behind it all the screams of the spectators. Urging them on. Herding them in.

They crossed into section two. Kept running. And found the yard Barun had chosen for their stand.

Ze'aan stopped and turned. Her hands blurred. She tied her hair and as she dropped her arms to her sides, they slowed, stalled, and froze halfway to her hips. The air in front of her chest shimmered and her krasna forced its way into existence.

The squad fell into formation around her. Kavi drew her sword, unhooked her shield, and stayed at the warlock's side. Her last defence.

They waited. Ze'aan split her maayin into a row of sharp bolts that hovered in the air. Kavi tightened her grip on her sword and shield. Crouched into her stance. Her heart thrashed and pounded. Sweat dripped down her face and chin. Seconds turned into minutes. An observer hopped onto a windowsill and watched. The crowd continued to scream and holler. A cadet carefully inched forward.

Three successive projectiles took his head off. *Crack-thunk-splat.* The first grazed the top of his helmet, the next hit it square-on, and the last sent him flying, trailing a crescent of blood and brains.

More green maayin came careering at them. Ze'aan deflected half. The rest—

A scream and a cadet was writhing on the ground, holding the stump of his arm that kept pumping blood through his fingers.

Kavi crawled to his side. Dragged him back.

'Can you move?' she shouted at him.

He nodded.

He shook his head.

He burst into tears.

All their training. For what? Just to be sent into a massacre?

Something bumped into her shoulder, and she looked up. A ball of maayin pulsed at her side. It nudged her again. She searched for Ze'aan and their eyes met.

The tracer.

The ball started to move forward in the direction they'd just come from.

Kavi gritted her teeth. Nodded. 'Send it,' she growled.

Ze'aan's eyes flashed green. The ball spun and raced away.

Kavi tucked herself behind her shield. And sprinted after it.

Chapter 40

Every few metres, the tracer would *pop-fizz* and lose some of its substance. If Kavi was too far behind, it would wait, pulsing impatiently in mid-air until she caught up, panting, straining against the weight of the counterfeit armour, fighting the stitch in her side. She chased the ball of maayin through gullies and streets and intersections all the way back into section two, where she ran face first into a skirmish.

Squad two had engaged the enemy. Their frontline was chaos: a tangle of limbs and sharp ends. Their warlock stood at the back with his arms raised while a long slab of maayin hung over his head. Bulbs sprouted on his krasna and propelled themselves into the enemy backline, where they exploded into screams and pinpricks of iridescent green. Overhead, maayin continued to whizz past to where Kavi's squad waited with Ze'aan.

The tracer rose above the melee and zoomed out of sight.

Kavi cursed and ran, parallel to the skirmish line, until she found an empty building. She barged through the front door and into a trio of haggard-looking, terrified men in invader armour.

They froze.

Kavi hesitated. 'We don't need to—'

The man in front screamed and lunged at her.

She bashed him on the head with the butt of her sword, and he collapsed in a heap.

The others exchanged glances.

'We don't need to fight,' Kavi said. Yet.

They nodded.

She shuffled around them. Once she was clear, she burst into a sprint again. The tracer zoomed out in front of her, left tiny green particles in its wake. It was substantially smaller than when it had started.

Kavi sped up. Jumped over barricades. Burst into and out of buildings. And found the long-range warlock.

The tracer accelerated toward a Blade and warlock standing on top of a fake water tank. The larger man spotted her, drew his longsword, and hopped down. His warlock, the long-ranger picking off Kavi's squad, remained frozen in place and continued to send projectiles arcing into the heat of the battle.

The tracer evaporated. Its job was done. It was Kavi's turn now.

Her people were watching her. The squad was waiting for her. Ze'aan had trusted her.

Without breaking stride, she leaped onto an empty cart and, with a roar, flung herself at the Blade.

Their swords met, the *clang* drowned out by the clamour of the crowd. They separated. They re-engaged. Their swords blurred. Their shields slammed together. She screamed in his face and forced him back. He hacked at her feet and she skipped away.

There was no time. No time to play these games. She undid the strap holding her shield to her arm and let it fall.

The Blade stopped. Raised an eyebrow.

Kavi took a deep breath, released it, and in one quick movement, drew her pistol and pulled the trigger.

Dhoom.

The slug lodged itself in the man's foot. He dropped his weapon, hopped, fell, and clutched his foot. He stared up at her with open-mouthed astonishment.

What? Feeling betrayed? She shrugged. 'Better than being dead.'

She looked up at the water tank. The warlock was still in his cast. 'Surrender,' she shouted, 'your Blade is down.'

He ignored her.

'Hey!' She climbed up on the tank. 'Hey—'

A projectile knocked the sword out of her hand and sent it spinning away.

Kavi flicked her hand back and forth and glared at the warlock. He sent more missiles into the distance, like she wasn't even there. Kavi searched for an observer and found one: a short-haired woman perched on a wall, watching them without expression.

So that's how it is. Fine. She punched the warlock in the face.

His krasna disintegrated. He stumbled, fell flat on his arse.

Kavi glanced at the observer, waiting to see if she'd interject. She stayed where she was.

'You,' the warlock said, outrage in his eyes, 'you—'

'Shut the fuck up.'

He would be worthless for at least another hour now. Not even Ze'aan could replenish her krasna that quickly.

Kavi hopped off the tank, picked up her shield, fastened the straps, bobbed an apology to the wounded Blade, and broke into a run. Somehow she was aware of exactly where her sword had fallen, and when she passed it, she stomped on its hilt, sent it whirling up, and snatched it out of the air.

Kavi sprinted back, past the skirmish that was steadily being pushed deeper into section two, and into the yard where seven cadets were left standing with Ze'aan. The enemy had not reached them yet. She'd made it on time.

Ze'aan's eyes flashed with triumph when she spotted Kavi.

'What's happening?' Yella said as she took her place on Ze'aan's flank.

'Squad two are retreating. They'll be here soon.'

Yella gave her a grim nod. 'May Limua be with you.'

'Hel awaits,' Kavi muttered.

She'd expected – *hoped* – some of squad two would join them. But when heads and bodies began entering the yard, she couldn't spot a single one in cadet's armour. Observers, at least half a dozen, hung out of windows or crouched on pillars around the yard. The crowd that could view the area grew quiet.

The men and women in mismatched armour kept coming. Twenty. Thirty. Fifty. Seventy.

Kavi stopped counting.

They filled up one half of the yard and slowly moved to surround the eight cadets and their warlock.

'Retreat?' Yella said, casting an anxious glance at the alleyway behind them. An alleyway that would take them into section three, and beyond the line of combat they were instructed not to cross if they wanted to pass the Siphon.

'We won't be able to fight our way back if we do,' Kavi said. Which would mean the last three months would've been for nothing.

Yella spat and yelled up at an observer. 'How long till the flare?'

The woman shouted back, 'At least an hour.'

Yella's face dropped. 'Fuck this, I'm—' The spear caught him mid-sentence and pierced the roof of his mouth. He stared at Kavi as he tried and failed to grip the butt of the shaft. His eyes rolled back into his head, and he fell to his knees.

The spear-thrower screamed a garbled battle cry, and the invaders charged.

The squad closed ranks around Ze'aan and the warlock let her maayin fly.

Arm-length bolts of maayin rammed into the delirious men and women and they dropped in waves. Their comrades stepped on them, over them, and continued their charge.

Kavi locked her shield in place with the cadets on either side, just like they'd trained, and as the first convict – woman or man, she couldn't tell – ran into range, her sword lashed out, and plunged into soft flesh. Her eyes went wide.

The woman – *it was a woman* – batted, helplessly, at the sword sticking out of her neck. Her chance at freedom dying as blood gurgled out through the wound.

Kavi's muscles stiffened. She stared at the scared, desperate face and the blood she'd drawn. *I had no choice. I'm sorry. I had no choice.*

Lies, a voice cackled in her ear.

Her lips trembled, but she refused to look away. She burned the dying woman's face into her memory. The short, hacked-off hair, the glazed, watery eyes, the missing teeth, the burned lips, the pustules on her cheeks and forehead.

She yanked her sword out. Another face instantly replaced the one that'd fallen. And her sword flashed out again.

Cries of pain filled her ears. She blocked it out. She moved on.

The stench of their breath, their sweat, their piss, and their shit. Which was hers? Which was theirs? She couldn't tell. She didn't care. She fought on.

The convicts were untrained. Scared. But they had the numbers. One by one, Kavi's squad fell and were dragged away. Kavi fought on.

Her arms burned from hundreds of cuts. Her legs ached with the weight of the armour and blows they withstood. Her throat, dry and hoarse from all the screaming, turned each precious breath into searing agony. She fought on.

Soon it was just her and Ze'aan. Kavi's breath came in short, ragged gasps. Spots danced at the edge of her vision. Her sword-arm dropped to her side, her wrist a swollen and bruised mess.

And as if the enemy sensed this, they stopped and gave her a moment's respite.

She had nothing left to give. It was over. She couldn't hold them off alone. Where was this fucking flare?

The yard was crammed with bodies, seething with both living and dead. But the living, for some bizarre reason, were carefully backing away with fear on their faces, their eyes glued to a spot over Kavi's head.

Kavi turned. Her jaw dropped.

Ze'aan's krasna, which for the last three months had been a single rickshaw-tyre-sized orb of maayin, had grown to twice that size. It now hung over her head, and on either side pulsed twins of the orb in the middle.

Kavi's eyes bulged. Her mouth worked, but words failed her. This was an archmage's krasna. Maybe even more. A first-year warlock was not capable of something like this. A low moan left Kavi's lips. Was Ze'aan even a first-year warlock? What was she doing in the Siphon?

The roar of the crowd crescendoed. Ze'aan's halo of emerald suns disintegrated.

Kavi refused to look. She knew what came next. She dropped to her knees and stared at the ruined bodies of the cadets who'd died protecting the warlock.

Thousands of pellets ripped through the yard. Through flesh and bone. Steel and brick and wood. It was over in an instant.

The unlucky, who'd not taken a direct hit to a vital, were left maimed and bleeding out. Their screams of pain drowned out by the exhilaration of the spectators.

'You could've saved them,' Kavi heard herself say.

There was a *boom,* and a red flare shot into the sky.

Ze'aan undid her ponytail. '*Them?* They wouldn't have thought twice about saving you.'

Kavi hung her head. *That's not the point.* 'Why, Ze'aan?'

The warlock stepped closer, and Kavi shrunk away. 'War is deception,' Ze'aan said. 'You hide when they think you will fight. You attack when they think you are unable. You know this.'

'Why – you could've saved them,' she said again.

Ze'aan extended a hand. 'You survived the Siphon, and will no doubt join the Vagola. Isn't that what you wanted?'

Kavi studied Ze'aan's long, delicate fingers. The soft skin on the back of the warlock's hand that was not stained by a single drop of blood.

Ze'aan withdrew her arm. 'We all have our dreams, Kavithri. Remember what I said. These people happened to be in the way of mine.'

Kavi kneeled among the dead, under the eyes of satisfied spectators and icy observers, and relived, over and over again, the deaths of her squad, of all the men and women she'd killed. Fathers, daughters, brothers, sisters – she'd killed them all just to pass a test. In the hope that it would bring her closer to her father and brothers. What gave her the right? What made her hopes, her motivations, and desires purer than theirs?

Her face twisted. But she'd had no choice. This was inevitable. Ze'aan was right.

Kavi clenched her jaw until it hurt.

No, nothing was worth so much death. Not even her family. Her father would be ashamed of her.

An observer tapped her on the shoulder.

'You must heal and assemble for commendation,' he said.

She nodded mutely.

'Do you require a healer?'

She shook her head.

'As you wish.' He pointed to a path out of the grounds. 'It will take you to the locker rooms.'

Chapter 41

The locker room was empty. The air still held the tang of stale sweat and smoked beedis, the walls still carried the scars of daggers and knives and the initials they carved into it, but it was quiet. No screaming. Crying. Shouting. Pleading.

Kavi collapsed onto the bench, slipped a boot off one foot, and shook it till a small, flat key fell clinking to the ground. She unlocked her locker, pulled out her rat boxes, and let Nilasi heal her wounds.

When it was done, when Nilasi's maayin had fed and slithered back into her, when her cuts had scabbed over and the swelling in her wrist had subsided, she returned the boxes to the locker, and rested her head on the door. It was done. She would pay for her crimes in Hel. But now, she could move forward. Bithun's artificer would be in touch soon. She'd be able to use the Venator. She would find out where her family was.

Kavi shut the locker door and froze.

There was someone standing perfectly still, off to the side, at the entrance to the bathrooms. Kavi's skin crawled as she swallowed and glanced at – her mouth went dry –*Ze'aan.*

'I've heard you will receive a commendation for bravery,' the warlock said, stepping out.

Sweat beaded Kavi's lips and forehead. 'Did you?'

Ze'aan strolled to the door. 'The novices at the Vagola are already fighting over you.'

Kavi kept her face still while her mind cartwheeled. How long had Ze'aan been standing there? Did she see? How much did she see? What if she told someone? Who would she tell?

The warlock stopped at the door. Drummed her fingers on the frame. And glanced at Kavi. 'I will see you at the Vagola.'

Ze'aan slammed the door behind her, and Kavi sank onto the bench. Her hands shook. How could she have been so stupid? She should've checked to make sure she was alone. Should she run after Ze'aan? Beg and plead and ask her to keep her secret?

But what if Ze'aan hadn't seen anything?

In the end, Kavi's indecision won, and she chose not to act.

She washed, changed into a new set of training muslin, and allowed an observer to usher her to a makeshift stage packed with dignitaries and politicos.

They gave her a medal. Paraded her with four other numb cadets. Said she was a symbol for Taemu rehabilitation. Said they couldn't wait to follow her progress in the Vagola. She shook hands. Bowed when it was appropriate. Smiled when they smiled.

The audience, the few left in the stadium, applauded, patted themselves on their backs. *Look, see how modern we are, a Taemu in the Vagola? Only in Raaya, bhai, long live the Republic!*

No mention was made of the dead. Her people had already carried the bodies away to be cremated.

When it was all over and done with, when the sun had dipped out and the moon had taken its place, Kavi walked out of the empty stadium with her bag of dead rats, her sword, her medal, and searched for Massa and Ratan. They had agreed to meet – if she was still alive – at the stadium's southern entrance.

Besides a few pedestrians and a slow horse-drawn carriage, the street was empty.

'Kaveethree Tay-mu?'

'Yes,' she said, turning with a frown. She'd never heard that accent before.

A man, pale and gaunt with short dark hair and uneven eyes, smiled at her. 'Pleased to make your acquaintance.' He reached out with a long slender finger and tapped her on the forehead.

Kavi jerked away. The rage in her core spat and hissed and screamed at her to grab his finger and break it in ten different places. How dare he lay hands on her? After what she'd been through that day, she had no time for this. She opened her mouth to ask him what the fuck he thought he was doing, when a cloudy white film slithered in from all corners of her vision. Her head spun. She stumbled. Someone caught her.

'Don't panic,' a voice said. 'Stop fighting. Sleep … sleep.'

Sleep. That's right. She was exhausted. She didn't want to fight anymore. She could do with some sleep. What a kind stranger. Yes, she would sleep.

She let go. And she faded out.

Chapter 42

She faded in.

It was dark. It stank. She was in a space so small that she couldn't even move.

Her head was pounding. Her chest was tight and constricted. She wanted to vomit, but there was no space for that either.

Muffled voices. The rattle of a rickshaw. Her stomach dropped.

She struggled to breathe.

She faded out.

Chapter 43

Kavi opened her eyes in the dark. The reek of old vomit filled her nostrils as she sucked in huge gasps of air. She tried to move, but her arms and legs wouldn't budge. She was in a chair. Her bare skin, covered in sweat, was stuck to its coarse wood. She strained against her restraints. *I'm dreaming. This isn't real.*

She opened her mouth, and the '*Help*' she whispered echoed and shuttled between her ears. She shook, uncontrollably, and her bladder emptied itself. *It's real.*

A spark, followed by the dazzling orange-yellow of a flame, burst into life.

Kavi squeezed her eyes shut. When she slowly opened them, she found a man – pale, gaunt, and with an oil lamp dangling from one hand – standing in the corner of a windowless cell.

'Imagine our surprise,' he said in that strange accent, 'when we heard that you could self-heal.'

Kavi's questions – *whoareyou whyareyou whatdoyou* – all died on her tongue. Her blood went cold. He was Kraelish.

'A real-life *Nineteen*,' the man said, with awe in his voice. 'A myth. A legend. Gifted and cursed at the same time. A healer who can *only* heal themselves. How long do you have left?'

She licked her dry lips. *Fuck you.*

He nodded, as if he'd heard her thoughts, and smiled.

Kavi's head swam, and she stared at the cobbled stone at his feet. Events from the last three months toppled over each other as she sifted them and searched for some explanation. Had Ratan betrayed her? Had Massa? No one else in the city knew. No one except *her*. Ze'aan had given her up to the Kraelish.

'If you obey, follow instructions, and let us do our job,' he said, 'when we're done, we will release you.'

Kavi squinted at him over the glare of the oil lamp. A tremor ran through her body. He was lying.

'So, for the sake of transparency, and for your own peace of mind, here is what will happen: we will collect your blood. You will regenerate. We will take more until all our vessels are filled. Then' – his eye twitched – 'the empiricists at the college require data. They have sent us a list of experiments. Once they are complete' – he gestured at the door to the cell – 'you will be free to go.'

She wanted to beg, to plead, to say she didn't understand any of this, she was just a stupid Taemu who'd forgotten her place, *please, let me go, I promise, I won't tell anyone about this, about you*; instead, she clenched her jaw, and said, 'Where are we?'

His brows shot up. 'Where do you think?'

How long had she been unconscious? Could he have moved her outside of Raaya? 'Kraelin. Imperial territory.'

A smile crept up the corners of his mouth. 'Why would we waste resources taking you to the Empire when the Empire can come to you?'

A chill ran up her spine. 'What—'

'Hush,' he said and stepped behind her.

Something heavy and metallic was dragged across the floor. Kavi's shoulders tightened, and she held her breath as a long, bluish-gold cylinder wobbled into sight and thunked down beside her. Once he was satisfied that it was stable, he kicked a lever at the base of her chair. With a groan and a sharp jerk, her backrest fell away, and a plank popped out from under her feet and forced them straight, leaving her supine and utterly exposed.

'Why—' Kavi tried to school the shrillness out of her voice. 'What are you doing?'

'I told her,' he said, 'we need her blood.'

Kavi blinked. *Her?*

He drew a slim knife from his pocket, tested its edge, and made a delicate cut high on her forearm.

Kavi winced as he pressed the end of a cold, thick wire into the cut. There was a pop, and the artificed wire sealed itself to her skin and began to pull.

She tried again. 'Why?'

He ignored her and wiped his knife on a handkerchief.

'Why do you need my blood?'

'Shhh, save your strength,' he said, walking to the door. 'We will return with your countervail.'

The corridor he exited into was dark and offered no clues as to where she was. Kavi strained at her restraints until the strength oozed out of her arms and legs. Surely someone would come for her. The Vagola knew who she was now. Ratan and Massa would know she was missing. The Taemu in the city would know; would be looking for her. She was still in Azraaya. It was only a matter of time before someone found her. She just needed to hang on.

It was hard to keep track of the time in the dark.

She tried counting the seconds. It calmed her, initially, but when she lost count, her mind started to drift and it just added to the frustration. The blood loss was making her light-headed, her thoughts had turned foggy, and eventually, she gave in to the entropy and lay there while the artifice sucked her dry.

He returned, after what felt like a lifetime, with a wheelchair. A woman sat in it, head lolling, eyes shut, while the oil lamp burned in her lap. He left the wheelchair by Kavi's feet and checked on the cylinder.

Kavi stared at the sedated woman. The cheap, all-blue sari she wore marked her as a maid of some sort. She was young. Maybe from the south.

'Okay,' the man said, and yanked the wire out of Kavi's arm. 'This one's full. Now she will need to—' His eyes lost focus and he peered at Kavi. 'Go on,' he said, 'use her.'

Kavi's eyes darted between the man and the woman in the wheelchair. 'What?'

He blinked. Peered at her like she was stupid. 'Use her as your countervail.'

Kavi swallowed. 'That's not how it works.'

'We are not asking you to heal,' he said with a smile. 'We want you to regenerate.'

Kavi's mouth went dry. 'That's not how it works.'

The man ground his teeth and nodded to himself.

'We had a cat once,' he said, pulling out his knife. 'Nussie, we used to call her. One day, something got into Nussie's eye, and she started scratching at it. She scratched and scratched and scratched and dug the eye out of its socket. Do you know what she did then?' He squeezed the tip of the knife under Kavi's eye.

Kavi flinched. The blade sliced through her skin, and warm blood dribbled down the side of her face.

'Nussie ate the eyeball, nerves and all. Do you understand?'

Kavi's lips trembled. She knew what he was asking her to do; had known *how* to do it since the first time she'd healed, when the Jinn had shown her a truth that violated everything she understood about maayin and the Jinn. It was the reason her people had once locked up hybrids like her. And it was something she'd decided that no matter what, no matter how bad things got, she would never use.

She glanced at the woman in the wheelchair and whispered, 'No.'

Fingers dug into her temples. Squeezed down on her forehead. The knife flashed. And plunged into her eye.

She screamed. Needles of blinding, searing agony sank into the back of her skull. Her body twitched. Convulsed. Half her vision went red. The other half blurred and clouded over.

He cut. He pushed. There was a pop. Red turned into black.

He squeezed the sides of her jaw till her mouth opened. He shoved the eyeball in. Forced her mouth closed. It caught between her teeth and exploded. Warm, gooey fluid gushed down her throat. She gagged, retched, and spat. Any hope she'd had that someone would find her, that she would walk out of this cell, that she would somehow escape, evaporated.

'Oh, come on,' he said with a chuckle, 'you can grow it back. Just take it from her.'

Kavi ignored him. Burrowed deep into the recesses of her mind where she'd be safe. Where he couldn't hurt her.

He sighed.

There was a sudden sharp pain in her abdomen, and her body locked up. Her eye bulged as she felt him make a long incision just above her belly button, and slowly, inch by inch, pushed his fingers inside her. Her chest expanded, her skin stretched taut as his hands crawled up her chest wall. She tried to smother herself into the table. Her head arched back and her mouth opened in a soundless scream. His fingers wrapped themselves around her heart.

'There will be another like you, if not in this age, then the next, it is inevitable,' he whispered. 'Your defiance is well meant, but meaningless. The countervail will die, either at your hand, or, more painfully, at ours. You either obey, or I make a fist, and you die. Choose.'

A voice from deep within screamed, *Live.* It drowned everything else out. She had to live. Even if it was for a few more hours. Even if it was selfish. Even if she was being used. She had to live. She strangled a sob and called her maayin.

The threads of Nilasi that tore their way out of her were darker, thicker, and hungrier.

Him, she commanded, *take it from him.* They lunged at the man. And recoiled.

She took a sharp, painful breath. *Mage.* He was a mage.

'Okay,' she said with a gasp. 'Okay.'

He nodded, and slowly, carefully extracted his hand.

She moaned as the pressure inside her ebbed. The maayin slithered out to the woman in the wheelchair. *Take.*

Threads sank into the unconscious woman's eye. Her jaw. Her stomach. Her chest.

Kavi winced as teeth sprouted in the empty spaces in her mouth. The vision in her left eye returned. The slit in her belly sealed itself. Her light-headedness evaporated. She was once again alert.

'See,' he said, 'isn't this more effective than animals?'

The woman in the wheelchair had gone deathly pale. Blood was slowly spreading, like an inkblot, on the sari over her abdomen. More blood trickled out of the corners of an eyelid, and although she couldn't see it, Kavi knew the woman would be missing a few teeth. Nilasi took material, broke it down, transferred it, and reshaped it for its mage. For Kavi. That was how the other half of her ability worked. The half that allowed her to regenerate using humans as a countervail.

The woman began to convulse and froth at the mouth, and Kavi's captor, without an instant's hesitation, slit her throat.

'You took too much.' He cleaned his knife on the dead woman's sari and walked around the table to study the skin over Kavi's abdomen.

An uncontrollable shudder swept through Kavi's body.

She'd killed in the Siphon. She was already a murderer. But this – this ruthless *taking* – was so much worse. Her life would never be the same again. There was a Kavi before she'd used her maayin on another human, and a Kavi after. The two were irreconcilable. Mutually incompatible. The bile rose in Kavi's throat and she forced it out with great heaving retches.

She was a monster. Her people were right to keep others like her imprisoned. It was what she deserved.

He forced her new eye open and gazed into it. 'Did you try it on us?'

What was the point in lying? 'Yes.'

He nodded. Returned the oil lamp to the dead woman's lap. Rolled her out. Shut, latched, bolted the door, and left Kavi in the dark.

Chapter 44

He drained her. Cylinder after cylinder of blood. And when he was satisfied that he'd met what he called his *quota*, he brought his clipboard.

He started small, with cuts and bruises that Kavi had to fix using a human countervail while he jotted down notes in a slim journal. Once that was accomplished, he measured her earlobes, sliced them off, and measured them again when they regrew.

Fingers and toes were scissored off; hands and feet were cut off; attempts were made at sawing her arms and legs off, but the larger amputations were abandoned when she kept passing out from the pain.

He then moved on to crushing her organs.

She tried to let herself bleed out. He noted this on his clipboard, left the cell, and returned with a pouch of chilli powder, which he fastidiously coated her wounds with.

The pain was astounding. Kavi never tried it again.

Occasionally, she would be blindfolded and gagged. The sound of footsteps would filter in from the corridor, and he would go to work on her. These sessions were by far the worst. The gag forced her to swallow her own vomit, and the blindfold amplified her fear and panic. She tried to search for these spectators with her maayin, to try to use them as her countervail, but he'd tested her range, and they were always just out of reach.

When the catatonic men or women in the wheelchair died, he would roll them out, and return with a new countervail. She convinced herself to stop seeing them as people. She lied and told herself that their blood was on *his* hands. She emulated her captor: dehumanised them the way he'd dehumanised her. They were countervails. Nothing more. Nothing less.

There was a stretch of time – it may have been a week, or a month, or even a year, she wasn't sure – when he ceased his experiments, and just left her in the dark.

The heat intensified the stench of her filth. Spiders, cockroaches, and rice-bugs crawled up her stomach and her neck and head. Even the rats came for payback and peeled her skin away.

Her ears leaked thick, warm fluid. Her eyes burned and itched. Her bowels, she was sure, evacuated blood. Her pelvis and abdomen burned. Fevers came and went.

She dreamed of metal behemoths falling from an orange sky. Of waves crashing on a dark, empty beach. Of delicate feet with bells around ankles that danced on a soft, wooden floor.

When the light came, when he finally returned to her, she was exultant. She was vaguely aware of the animal noises she was making as he covered his nose and washed her and her prison. He was her only connection with the outside world, and after that, in a perverse sort of way, she looked forward to his visits.

Chapter 45

Sometimes, he would talk to himself and refer to 'Jarard': *Jarard will send the missive, Jarard didn't pick up the rice for the week, Jarard shouldn't have talked back to the Major;* and it took her addled brain several such utterances to realise that *he* was Jarard, and he was not alone in his head.

She knew what was happening to him. The books called it the mind-sink, and there was only one class of mage that suffered this way: a type of Azir called the Mylothurgist: Zubhra-Kolacin hybrids who could navigate the mind. Their countervail, the price they paid, was that they permanently retained the memories of those they tapped into. This caused all sorts of issues, the least of which was the erasure of their sense of self. It was why he referred to himself as *us,* or *we*. Kavi guessed from his deteriorating appearance that he was nearing the end of his seven years.

Jarard was muttering to himself and running through a checklist on his clipboard when she asked him about it.

He stopped and blinked at her. 'What?'

'You're a hybrid,' she said. 'How long do you have left?'

A flicker of annoyance flashed through his eyes. 'Have you heard of the Taemu blood banks?'

'I – yes.'

'Do you know what they are?'

'Taemu blood for the Venator,' she said.

'Initially, yes. But the term is a euphemism – the blood banks are where we keep our Taemu.'

She frowned. *Our Taemu?*

'We sedate them with agoma and keep them alive until their blood is no longer fit for use.'

Kavi recoiled. She stared at him with bulging eyes as bile coated the back of her throat.

'There are more Taemu in our blood banks than there are in the whole of Raaya,' he said, puffing his chest out. 'You'll see, it's where you will end up once we take the city.'

Monsters. They were all monsters. 'Why?'

'Why? Because we left something behind,' he said, studying his clipboard. 'Material from the Deadlands whose value we didn't fully understand back then. There are stockpiles buried all across Raaya – the biggest right here in Azraaya – and now that we know how to use them, we want them back.' He paused. 'We could ask for it, of course, but then the greedy Raayans would find out and just keep it for themselves—' He nodded when she opened her mouth to interrupt. 'The trade agreement? A farce. We couldn't care less. Just an excuse.'

'I didn't mean—' She swallowed. 'Why do you need *our* blood?'

'Today will be different,' he said. 'Today—'

'Jarard,' she said, '*what* do you need our blood for?'

'For our mages to gain access to Raktha.'

'Why?'

'You wouldn't—' He clenched his jaw. 'Jarard will not answer that question. Now, we are going to look inside.'

She reeled in alarm. 'Inside?'

'Yes, we have been instructed to look for patterns, signs, anomalies …'

No. Her mind was the only place she had left to hide.

'They're using you, Jarard,' Kavi said. 'How much of you is even left? How long do you have?'

Jarard slipped a translucent disc the size of a coin out of pocket. 'We need you to relax,' he said, then pressed the disc into the skin between her breasts and watched it dissolve.

The agoma surged through Kavi's bloodstream. Eased the tension in her limbs, slowed her breathing, emptied her mind, silenced her feelings.

The walls crumbled and fell away.

Synapses sparked.

Disparate, detached memories linked.

Faces and voices metamorphosed.

Lies melted and trickled away and left her exposed to cold, jagged-edged truth.

A scream found its roots deep in her belly, travelled up her chest, into her throat, and she was back in the room with the adobe walls and woven mats, hands clamped over her mouth, whimpering as they set foot inside her home.

There were four. Three men and a woman.

One: bare-chested and hairy.

Two: lower lip protruding and twitching.

Three: large red bindi and a copper nose-ring.

Four: wheezing with each heavy breath.

They clapped. They jeered. The wheezing man's eyes gleamed.

Kavi told herself it was a bad dream. That it would stop at any moment. That she would wake up and they would all go away.

A woman stood facing the intruders. Her shoulders taut with tension. Her spine straight and proud. And even though she was facing away, Kavi knew that the woman's eyes would be a perfect reflection of her own.

Kavi's mother pleaded with the intruders.

They pulled her hair.

She tried to fight them off.

The wheezing man hit her.

Kavi had wedged herself into this tiny space, a crack in the wall at the back of their allocated home. It was so tight that she could barely move. She'd bruised her elbows and knees when Amma had forced her inside, and now they burned and itched.

They kicked Amma to the ground. Grabbed her ankles and dragged her and mocked her screams of pain. They spat in her face and ripped the hair off her scalp. Gouged her eyes out and there was blood and blood and wheezing and blood.

Kavi sobbed in silence and prayed, over and over again: *Drisana, save Amma. Please, help her. Drisana, please. Please.*

The bare-chested man had a knife, and he cut Amma's neck open. Her blood sprayed everywhere, and this annoyed the wheezing man. He punched her in the stomach. In the chest. In the head. He picked up a rock. Brought it down. Again and again and again, while the nose-ringed woman egged him on.

Amma's body spasmed. And she was still.

Kavi bit the insides of her cheeks till blood filled her mouth and spilled down the sides of her lips. *Amma? Amma, please.*

They left.

Kavi stayed.

The sun went down.

She stayed in the crack in the wall.

The sun came up. The shouts and cries outside died away. Kavi slipped out. Stumbled. And crawled to her mother.

Amma had no head. They'd hit her until it had turned into mush. The only thing left intact was an eye.

Kavi traced the lines and curves of henna on Amma's hands. Wiped the blood away and picked out the broken nails. Round and round the henna curled and twisted. Amma had told her she could get her own when she turned eight.

Kavi squeezed her hands over her ears. The sound of her mother dying would not go away. She dug her fingers in and scratched and scratched until her ears bled and it finally stopped. The air rushed out of Kavi's lungs and then she too died.

When she woke, Amma was laying there on her back, smiling up at her.

Kavi smiled back and held her hand. She would stay with Amma. She would not leave her side. She would not move unless Amma moved. Would not eat until she ate. Would not sleep until she slept. She would never leave her.

But her mother squeezed her hand and said, 'Kavi, you have to go.'

Kavi shook her head. She was not leaving.

'You must get to the tunnels,' Amma said.

No.

'Walk straight to the tunnels. Don't look at what's around you. Just walk.'

Is this what you really want?

'Yes.'

Kavi released her mother's hand and stood.

'Go,' Amma said. 'Find Appa. Protect your brothers.'

Kavi nodded. I will, Amma, I promise.

'I love you, Kavi.'

I love you, Amma.

She walked through the ruins of Ethuran. She kept her eyes on the path and away from the bodies. Some were stripped of their skin; some were missing fingers and toes; some had severed genitals in their mouths.

She started to cry when she walked past the body of a tortured woman whose unborn baby had been cut out and stomped to death – the empty womb was filled with black, burned rags. Kavi dropped to her knees and vomited when she had to step around the corpse of elder Gurugan, whose eyes were burned out and had irons shoved down his throat.

Kavi picked her way to the river. Waded through bloated bodies with blue-black faces whose swollen tongues stuck out like they were mocking her. And just like Amma had asked her to, she found the tunnels.

A scavenger crew found her wandering the edges of the Deadlands a few days later. Lost. Confused. Frightened and fevered. She'd exited the tunnels at the wrong place and had just kept walking.

They fed her and brought her to the refugee camp the Raayan military had set up for the survivors. The military general-man said *sorry for your loss*, gave her a blanket and fifty rayal, and sent her on her way.

There weren't many survivors, and eventually, she found Appa and her brothers. Kamith hugged her and cried. Khagan, who was just a baby, cried because his brother was crying, and Appa took the money the general-man gave her, and spat.

Why?

Yes, why?

More memories came bursting through. Her parents arguing. Her father shouting, cursing, saying he should have drowned Kavi the day she was born. He wanted a son. It was safer. Better. With a daughter, one day, he would have to pay a dowry. He didn't have much, but he'd have to part with *something*. And that ate away at him.

He'd been with the boys in the fields when the mob descended on Ethuran. He'd abandoned her and Amma and run.

She'd buried it all. Filled the emptiness that her mother had left with her father. Her words became his. Her actions were his. The more he hated Kavi, the more she loved him. And then, a few months after the massacre, he sold her to the Chutti-Mohan beggar crew, and she never saw him or her brothers again.

It started as a wail and ended as a sound more animal than human.

But it was not coming from her.

It came from Jarard.

He lay curled up in a ball at her feet. Sobbing. Shaking.

She wanted to reach out and console her tormentor. To tell him it would be okay. That it had never happened to him. That those were her memories and experiences. Not his.

He wept and wept.

Kavi didn't shed a single tear.

A fog had lifted. She was whole again. She would mourn her mother, but for now, all she wanted was to relive the memories in which her mother had been alive. Her smell. Her voice. The way she laughed. Her warmth. Her face when she was angry with Kavi. When she was surprised. When she was disappointed. She'd found her mother and she would never lose her again.

Jarard staggered to his feet, stumbled out of the cell, and left her in the dark.

But this time, she was not alone.

It began the moment he locked the door. A heartbeat of warmth. Not from inside her, but from behind the wall on her left. It pulsed and throbbed and turned into a wave that enveloped her and eased her grief.

'Thank you,' she whispered, distracted, not fully aware that she'd spoken. And the pulse, in what she assumed was the adjacent cell, responded with another wave of emotion. It sent her *determination.* It told her, without words, to not give up hope.

Kavi stared wide-eyed into the dark, and said, 'I won't.'

Every time she cried, every time she cycled around to the memory of Amma's death, a warmth – palpable and real – would emanate from the wall and wrap itself around her. If she was reliving a joyful memory, the presence would hum with pleasure. If the memory was painful, they would send her the warmth. If the memory evoked anger, they would sing – it was wordless, but Kavi could make out a tune: a violent, percussive ululation that made her heart race.

Or, maybe, she'd finally lost her mind.

When she wasn't reliving fragments of Amma's life, she pretended that she would one day leave this place, and imagined all the things she would do when that happened.

First, was food. She made a list of all the things she wanted to eat: biryanis, samosas, dosas, peratals, rotis and spicy curries, naans and tandooried meat, rasam-rice-fried pomfret.

Then, the people she wanted to see again: Bithun, Tsubu, Zofan, Massa, Ratan, Hessal, Elisai, Yella – Yella was dead – and Ze'aan … Ze'aan had betrayed her. Kavi was sure the warlock was responsible for the Kraelish finding out about her. Why? She couldn't say why …

She set the thought aside and moved on. Places she wanted to visit: Ethuran. If she got out, she would go back to Ethuran and find the home her family had lived in. Would it still be standing? She would find out. It would be a pilgrimage.

And what about love? She'd learned early on that the rules were different for her and so had never entertained thoughts of love or romance. If she had a need, she fulfilled it herself. She was Taemu. Such things were not for her. She only had to look in the mirror. A wretched child of a wretched people. Ugly. Repulsive. Her own country told her she didn't deserve love.

But if she lived, if she somehow left this miserable cell, maybe she would find someone. Someone with warm eyes and a kind heart. Someone who'd understand her sense of humour and laugh at all her terrible jokes. Maybe they could leave Raaya; stowaway on a ship and sail to the Hamakan Isles; build a hut on a beach and live off the sea. And when her time was up, when her seven years were done, Kavi, satisfied that she'd known love, would die a painless, peaceful death.

Death.

The rage inside her hissed and spluttered, and the prisoner in the adjacent cell sang.

They could all burn. The Raayans. The Kraelish. Every man and woman who'd hurt her people. Every single one who believed that her people were subhuman, who took pride in their made-up superiority, who profited off Taemu misery and suffering. They could all burn.

Yes, she wouldn't be there to see it, but she found solace in the knowledge that, eventually, whether by fire or sword or disease or age, they would die. Their hate, the poison they pumped into their children's brains, would cripple another generation, and then they too would die.

But if she lived, if she left this place knowing that some people were truly monsters, she would – what? Kill them all? Get on her knees and pray that all the *bad* people died off? And what if they did? Then what? Kavi cackled.

Then we'd just find more.

Chapter 46

Jarard eventually returned, pushing a wheelchair with another woman in it and acting as if nothing had happened.

Kavi's heart sank. *No. Not her. Please, not her.*

'We will try the larger amputations again today,' he said, 'and study the effects of using an older countervail, one that is' – he lifted the countervail's drooping chin – 'like you.'

'Please,' Kavi said, voice cracking.

'Relax,' Jarard said. 'We're almost done.' He kicked the lever at the bottom of Kavi's chair and forced her to lie flat.

'We will return with the equipment.' Jarard paused, cocked his head. 'Do you know her? Would you like us to wake her?'

Kavi turned away and fixed her eyes on the wall. For once the presence in the other cell brought her no comfort; instead, it reflected her horror twofold.

'You may have the light as well,' Jarard said, and left the oil lamp at her feet.

Kavi waited until the door was shut and latched before she turned back around to gaze at the old woman whose eyes were slowly fluttering open.

'Hessal,' Kavi said, voice trembling.

The Taemu elder flexed her jaw. Her eyes roved the dark walls of the cell until they settled on Kavi.

Hessal's lips curled into a smile. 'Kavithri,' she said, slurring her words, 'we've been looking for you.'

A jolt ran through Kavi's body. 'They know you're here?'

'Where ...' Hessal blinked and squeezed her eyes shut. 'I was outside the mushroom farms, it was busy, people rushing to get ready for Meshira's festival. We searched the city for you, but ...'

'How long? How long have I been here?'

Hessal looked around the cell with fresh eyes. 'Looks like I was close.'

'Hessal—'

'A month.'

That's it? Just a month?

'What are they doing to you?' Hessal ran her eyes over Kavi's body and the straps that tied it to the table.

Kavi took a deep breath and told her everything. About what she was. What she remembered. What was going to happen when Jarard returned.

When she was done, Hessal grunted, and said, 'So I won't be awake when you ...'

Kavi bit her lip. 'He puts them to sleep because he doesn't like the screams.'

Hessal nodded, distracted, lost in thought.

'I—' Kavi didn't know how to say it. Didn't know how to explain away the fact that she had killed people whose faces she could no longer remember. She was ashamed. She didn't want the older woman to think less of her. 'I'm sorry.'

'For what?'

'For killing all those people.'

Hessal's eyes flashed. 'You did what you had to. Do you think they would've hesitated if they had to kill a Taemu to survive?'

No. There would have been no hesitation. 'Hessal, do they know where you are?'

'The Taemu?' Hessal shook her head. 'No one is coming for me.'

Kavi moaned and banged the back of her head against the table. She would refuse. Let him kill her. She was never getting out. Better to die knowing that she'd not killed another Taemu.

'Shh, child.' Hessal reached out and stroked Kavi's head, pushed the grime-filled hair away from her eyes. 'You will do what he asks you to.'

'I will not—'

'Listen to me, Kavithri.' She pressed down on Kavi's forehead until she was still. 'They don't know anything about us, or about you. Our people did not keep Taemu like you captive. We would never do that to one of our own. If you were born three centuries ago, you would have been removed from society, yes, but not to be kept in a cage. You would have fought for us in the shadows.'

Kavi tucked her lower lip in and stared.

'We have forgotten the words, but you would not have been called a Nineteen. That is a Kraelish invention. You are not a monster.'

'I'm a killer. So many – I've lost count of how *many* I've killed.'

Hessal lifted her hand off Kavi's head and reclined.

'My grandmother used to tell me stories, impossible tales of how the Taemu once held the gates while humanity fled to this world. Without us, without Drisana, none of us would be here. When I was older, she told me about the ones like you, who fought for us in the dark. Who did not need to carry a sword into battle, whose bodies were weapon enough.' She lowered her head. 'I didn't believe her. Dismissed them as senile fantasies.

But you're real, Kavithri, which means everything else she told me could also be true.'

Hessal squeezed Kavi's hand. 'Our people are meant for something *more.* Use me. Find a way out. Go to them.'

The sound of the door being unlatched silenced her.

Neither of them paid any attention to the man who walked in with a bag of saws and knives. They didn't break eye contact when he dropped it on the ground. Or when he walked up behind Hessal and tapped her on the forehead. Even when her eyelids grew heavy; even when she slumped into the wheelchair, her red irises stayed locked with Kavi's until they rolled up into her head, and she passed out.

'Open your mouth,' Jarard said.

Kavi obeyed.

'Try to stay awake this time,' he said as he gagged her. He paused. 'Would you like a blindfold? Maybe it would help?'

She shook her head.

He shrugged, returned to his bag of equipment, picked out an artificed saw, and started sawing off her leg below the knee.

She bit into the gag as the jagged blade dug into her flesh. She strained against her restraints when it scraped against bone. By the time the metal of the saw met the scarred wood of the table, Kavi had retreated into that familiar corner of her head, as far from the pain as she could get, and numbed herself.

'Begin.' Jarard jerked his head at Hessal.

Kavi took a shuddering breath and allowed the writhing mass of Nilasian maayin to chew its way out of her. The threads, always hungry, knew exactly what they needed to do. They wormed their way around Hessal's right leg and began dismantling it.

At the same time, bone and nerves and muscle grew out of the base of Kavi's knee. She watched, panting, as the bone grew, as tendons and tissue wrapped themselves around it, as skin began to grow on the flesh, and a pool of blood gathered under Hessal's wheelchair.

'Good,' Jarard said, nodding to himself. He slipped a measuring tape out of his pocket and wrapped it around her ankle. 'Good. She is getting better.'

Then he moved on to the other leg.

Their bodies were enough, Hessal had said. Their bodies were enough.

He undid the restraint on her arm and sawed it off just below the shoulder.

Didn't need a weapon, Hessal had said. Kavi stared at the blood pumping out of her shoulder.

'Begin.' Jarard picked up the severed arm and dumped it in a box in the corner.

It had never occurred to her before. But … would the maayin obey?

She sent the threads the command. They froze. Quivered. And instead of circling Hessal's arm, picked at it like a horde of angry vipers. The arm slowly disintegrated, and Kavi's took shape.

Kavi clenched her jaw, willed only parts of it to grow, and forced it into a shape.

Jarard returned from his box of horrors and started at the sight of Kavi's arm. His brows furrowed, and he leaned over to peer at it.

He was so secure in his safety, so absorbed with the curious fashion in which her arm was regrowing, that she'd lifted it and rammed the end of sharpened bone into the side of his neck before he reacted.

His jaw dropped. His mouth opened and closed like a

suffocating fish. He tried to push her arm away, but she forced it deeper and pulled him closer.

Blood clogged his windpipe. Rushed up into his mouth. His nose. Dribbled down onto Kavi and she tasted copper on her lips.

He struggled. She twisted her arm and held him in place. Locked eyes with him and watched as his life slowly slipped away. She had nothing to say to him. She felt no anger. No elation. Only pity.

With one final choke and splutter, he collapsed over her shoulder.

She pulled her arm out of his neck and shoved him away. He dropped to the ground with a wet *smack*.

Kavi caught her breath. Stared at the sharpened bone at the end of her arm. And used it to saw at her restraints, until they fell away and she was free.

Hessal was a bleeding, limbless torso, but she was still breathing. A low moan left her lips and Kavi crawled to her side.

Hessal's eyes fluttered.

Kavi used the armrest to drag herself upright. 'Hessal,' she whispered.

Bleary eyes took in Kavi's face, the blood around her neck, the sharp end of her arm. They searched the cell and found the dead mage. Then scanned the length of her own body. Tears came trickling out, and she moaned again.

'I'm sorry,' Kavi said with a whimper. 'I'm sorry.'

'Take it,' Hessal rasped and motioned with her head to the half-eaten arm.

'I'm sorry,' Kavi said again, and let her maayin finish its work.

Hessal gasped as the rest of her arm crumbled away and reformed on Kavi's body.

'Kavithri,' she gasped.

Kavi reached out and held Hessal's head with both hands. 'Promise to protect them.'

Kavi strangled a sob. 'I promise.'

There was a soft hiss as the last dregs of air left the woman's body, and she was still.

The presence in the other cell howled with grief.

'I'm sorry,' Kavi said, and lowered herself to the floor.

She stayed at Hessal's side until her feet regained their strength and balance, then she frisked Jarard. Found keys, money, and a note with a date scribbled on it. She picked up the oil lamp, took a deep breath, and pushed the door open.

The corridor outside was dark and empty. Kavi searched for and found the door to the adjacent cell. She didn't know what the person was or how they could project their emotions the way they did, but she would not leave them here. She tried the keys with trembling hands until one finally fit, and she pushed the door open.

The light from the lamp washed over boxes and sacks and trunks.

'Hello?'

There was no answer. There was no one there. But she could still sense the presence. It hummed quietly in a corner, waiting. Kavi swallowed and stepped inside. Followed the humming until she stood in front of a rusted old trunk. She set the lamp down and opened it.

Lying on top of a stack of clothes was a sword with a notched black scabbard and hilt wrapped in red and black thread.

A part of her had refused to believe it, but she'd always known. Kavi reached into the trunk and wrapped her fingers around the hilt.

The next thing she knew she was on her knees, trembling from head to toe, chest on fire, gasping for air as she wept.

Fragments of memories from a time she could not imagine, of a war on a scale she could not fathom, hammered their way into her head.

Hessal was right. She was right.

And at the core of the violence, the heart of these visions: an awareness. A will. A name.

'Drisana,' Kavi whispered, and gently, almost reverently, touched the pommel to her forehead. Not a Goddess, then. Only a warrior, *like the rest of us.* 'I hear you, sister.'

The sword hummed with pleasure.

What made you decide to start talking to me?

The hum dropped to a deeper, more resonant throb that could only mean sorrow.

You felt Amma die?

The throb intensified.

I miss her too.

Kavi rifled through the trunk and picked out a pair of men's trousers and a khaki shirt. Once she was dressed, she picked up her sword and the oil lamp, and continued down the corridor.

She'd barely taken a few steps before the noise reached her. The incoherent muffle of people cheering and shouting and chanting. *The festival.* She quickened her pace and arrived at another large door at the end of the corridor. She tried the keys. Edged the door open. And inhaled the earthy scent of fresh rain.

Outside, boxes wrapped in canvas lay piled in a corner of a courtyard. A pair of tall, pale, muscled, and armed Kraelishmen watched over them; while at the other end, by the gate, a podgy Gashani sat on a stool, sipped on a cup of tea, and watched the procession pass.

Kavi snuffed out the oil lamp and left it on the floor. She drew her sword. Waited for her eyes to get used to the light.

She was a killer now. No hesitation. No unnecessary movement.

She tiptoed behind the Kraelish guards, flicked her wrist, and in two quick movements she sliced through their spinal cords. They were dead before they hit the ground.

And when they fell, she felt nothing. Her mind didn't spiral into *what about their family, their children, their friends, their dreams,* or how horrifying it was to snuff out an entire lifetime of experience and memories and emotions. There was nothing. She sensed the approval of her sword.

The guard by the gate was oblivious. She slipped up behind him with her sword raised and stopped. He wasn't Kraelish. He was just a tribesman. He probably had no idea what was going on inside the building. She gently rested her sword at the back of his neck.

'Stand,' she said in a hoarse whisper.

Kavi walked him, at sword-point, to the corridor, and locked him inside. She left the keys in a potted plant and drank the rest of his tea. Gods, she was hungry.

She wiped her mouth, left the teacup on the stool, and walked out into the rain and the procession.

Chapter 47

Musicians pounded their tablas and mridangams. Gaudy papier-mâché idols of the Goddess Meshira bobbed along on shoulders until they were ceremoniously dumped in the canals. Hundreds of worshippers and revellers thronged the streets of Azraaya. They sang, danced, and flung powdered reds, blues, pinks, yellows into the air.

Kavi slipped into a damp alley and slithered away from the procession. There would be hundreds of these mobile celebrations crawling through the city today. The festivities would drag on until sundown. Then the booze would start flowing. Brothels would be visited. Fights would break out. And the city would moan and groan and return to work the next morning.

She searched for landmarks and street signs and, bit by bit, clawed back her bearings. Her prison had been inside a bungalow, smack-bang in the middle of an upper-class neighbourhood. Massa had visited the area for a job several weeks ago: a man claiming his wife was possessed because she had a tendency to sleep-talk about penises: *she is innocent lady only, sir, how can she talk about cock-gobbling, chi-chi, please, help.* Massa told Kavi there'd been no possession. After they'd conducted the exorcism.

The memory of the rickshaw ride back to the warehouse was still fresh, and she used it to find her way home.

Reddy's Dead Body Disposals had their shutters open. A sign hung over the door that said: *Two-for-one festival special.* Kavi kept her head lowered and walked past. The last thing she needed now was to run into Subbal Reddy.

'Akka?'

Kavi froze.

'Akka, is that you?'

Elisai stood under the hoarding outside the Imperial Rickshaw Company, eyes wide and worry etched into her face.

'Elisai—'

The woman rushed up and wrapped her in a bear hug.

Kavi grimaced. Tried to wriggle out.

'We've been looking everywhere for you.' Elisai released Kavi from her embrace and wrinkled her nose. 'What happened to you?'

Kavi, suddenly conscious of how badly she reeked, brushed past and took the stairs up to the office while Elisai clambered up behind her. The office door was open and she could hear voices – one was unmistakably Massa's, the other, more feminine, she couldn't place until she peered through the door frame.

She tensed.

Seated on the divan with Massa, and chatting to him like he was an old friend, was Junior Artificer Salora.

'Did you know?' Kavi said, bearing down on Salora. 'Did you know the armour was switched?'

Massa blinked. Raised both bushy eyebrows, shot to his feet, and put himself between them. 'Kavi, wait—'

'Boss.' She gently nudged him aside. 'Stay out of this.'

'Yes,' Salora said, crossing her legs. 'I didn't have a choice. But—'

Kavi's arm was a blur as she reached for her sword.

But when she tried to draw, she found her wrist locked in place by a powerful grip.

'Akka,' Elisai said, 'listen to the artificer. She is a good person.'

Kavi turned her gaze on the woman. 'You saw what happened, right?'

Elisai loosened her grip. 'Do you trust me, Akka?'

Kavi clenched her jaw. But nodded.

'Then you must not hurt her,' Elisai said. 'Let her speak.'

Salora sighed and stood. 'The instructions came directly from the Council. None of the artificers had a choice. We either obeyed, or risked disbarment. But, Kavithri—' She took a deep, pained breath. 'For what it's worth, I truly am sorry for those you have lost.'

Kavi's stomach growled. She was too tired to deal with this now. *Later, later* she would … what? Kill the artificer as revenge? Beat her to a pulp as punishment? How would that make her any different from them? She scowled and turned to Massa. 'Do we have anything to eat?'

Massa shook his head. 'No, but I can arrange – where *were you?*'

'Please, boss,' Kavi said. 'I—' She stared at the dried blood coating her feet. 'Can I wash and eat first?'

He exchanged a glance with Salora and nodded.

Elisai followed her back to her room, and when Kavi firmly, but kindly, told the woman that she wanted some privacy, Elisai grudgingly acquiesced, and stood guard outside the door instead.

Kavi sat cross-legged on the bathroom floor, turned the tap on, and watched the water crash into the bucket. When it was halfway full, she picked up the mug and scooped the cool water onto her head. She gasped.

She was really here.

She emptied another mug over her head.

This was real.

And another.

Jarard was dead. Hessal was dead. Her sword … it had lapsed into silence after she'd killed the guards. But she knew that if she needed it, it would answer.

She reached for the bar of soap, started scrubbing, and found an unfamiliar body under her hands. Her core had shrunk, her arms and legs were reduced to bone with what felt like the barest string of muscle around them.

She hung her head. It was all Hessal had had to give.

Kavi lost track of how many buckets of water she went through. She washed until all the blood, dirt, and grime she'd brought with her was scrubbed off. And then she scrubbed some more.

When she was done, she cracked open the box of talcum powder she'd bought before the Siphon. She'd planned to use it if she got into the Vagola, which she now had, and although she wasn't really going anywhere, she wanted to smell nice. So to Hel with it. She slapped it under her arms, around her neck, and coughed as it puffed in a cloud around her. She changed into a loose, soft salwar-kameez, sighed as the soft material glided over her skin, and slipped into her rubber chappals. She attached an old baldric to the scabbard and slung her sword over her shoulder. If they came for her again, she would be ready.

Ratan was in the office, waiting with several triple-decker tiffins.

'All for you,' he said, arranging them on the desk.

She tried not to cry as she opened them up. But when the scent of roti and dal and cumin and mutton hit her nostrils, she couldn't help it, the tears came spilling out of her eyes.

'Thank you,' she said, and dug in.

She started talking after she licked the first tiffin-box clean.

Massa and Ratan knew what she was, but the other two didn't. She told them about her healing but left out the regeneration and the bit about human countervails.

Salora remained stone-faced. Elisai looked like her eyes could pop out of her skull.

Kavi said nothing about Ethuran, her mother, or about Jarard's mylothurgy, and when she got to Hessal and the escape, she lied.

'He got sloppy,' Kavi said, 'forgot a scalpel. I found Hessal in another cell.'

Elisai's breath caught.

'They—' Kavi stifled a sharp pang of guilt. 'She got too close. They killed her.'

'No,' Elisai whispered with both hands over her mouth.

Massa paled.

Kavi clenched her fists behind her back. They could never know the truth. It would die with her.

'The Kraelish are in the city,' Salora said with a sigh. 'We need to inform—'

'Sal, wait.' Massa searched his pockets for his beedi case. 'You really think they could get into the city without someone on the Council knowing?'

Salora pressed her lips into a thin slash. 'I don't—'

A shudder travelled up from the floor and into the walls and ceiling. Windows and furniture rattled. Empty tiffin boxes toppled. Kavi rushed to catch them before they fell off the desk.

'Earthquake?' Rattan said, peering outside the office.

The rumble tapered off and everything was still once again.

Kavi stood on unsteady feet with an armful of tiffin boxes. She'd never been in an earthquake before. Shouldn't they be running out of the building? Or hiding? Or doing something?

There was an ear-splitting *boom* and the entire building seemed to leap up and fall back down – as if a giant hand had just slapped the ground.

Ratan staggered out onto the balcony, and froze. 'Sweet Meshira . . .'

They rushed outside, just in time for another wave of thunder to roll up from the ground. Kavi grabbed the balcony ledge and, along with the others, stared at the apparition looming over the city.

A dark, bulbous, metallic head the size of a small hill towered over the wall. Its jagged edges glinted in the sun and she could make out what was supposed to be its face: a long protuberance for a nose, sunken empty eyes, a chin that jutted out like a spade.

A chill ran down Kavi's spine. She had seen this thing before.

It appeared to take a step back, and another *boom* forced them to their knees.

'WhattheHel?' Massa said, staring not at the colossal head, but at the artificer, Salora, whose face had lost all its colour.

'Makra,' Salora whispered, fidgeting with the pendant around her neck. 'How did they get so close without us knowing?'

Kavi remembered the drawings in the newspamphlets. This was the weapon, the monster the Kraelish had used to conquer the northern kingdoms. But also – she tightened her grip on the ledge – it was the behemoth from Drisana's war.

There was another thunderclap, but this time, it was followed by a series of sharp cracks, and a monstrous metal fist powered through the wall.

Elisai gasped and latched onto Kavi's arm. 'Akka, what is happening?'

Kavi, struggling to stand, knees weak, head spinning, wanted to turn around and bark, *How the fuck should I know?*

She did turn around, but when she saw the look of utter terror on Elisai's face, the only thing that she could think of was her promise to Hessal. *Protect them.*

How? How did you fight something like that?

Blow after concussive blow. Detonations shook the city to its foundations. The wall crumbled. The makra stepped into the city, and Kavi's sword shrieked with horror.

It quivered with revulsion. Wrong. This thing was wrong. It wasn't the same.

The makra took another thunderous step through a cloud of dust and stopped. Went limp.

The city mimicked it. All movement ceased. People down on the street stood frozen in place. Massa struck his artificed match on the balcony ledge and lit a beedi. Ratan muttered a prayer to Meshira. Kavi held her breath. Had it run out of steam? Out of fuel?

There was a loud, discordant shriek, and the torso of the makra sank to its feet. Hatches popped open on its chest, its legs, its feet; and from them poured dots of silver and gold – the colours of the Kraelish military. More troops, Kavi noticed, were streaming through the gap in the wall. Flashes of green leaped into the sky. The percussion of artificed weapons being discharged filled the air.

They were never planning a siege. This was a smash and grab.

'Inside, now!' Massa screamed.

They dived into the office, got on their hands and knees, and ducked under tables.

Kavi wrapped an arm around a trembling Elisai. 'It'll be okay,' she lied. 'It'll be fine.'

Chapter 48

When they finally emerged from the office during a lull in the chaos, they found the city covered with pillars of dark smoke. The makra remained where it was, frozen with its torso between its feet.

Kavi's first visceral reaction was *Good. Let them kill each other.* Then Elisai tugged on her shirt, and said, 'The others, they will not know what to do without Hessal.'

Kavi gritted her teeth. If the past was anything to go by, it would not end well for the Taemu if they got caught up in another fight between the Raayans and the Kraelish. 'Let's go,' she said, and started down the stairs.

'Where're you going?' Massa called after her.

She stopped. 'The slums.'

'And then?'

'We – I'm not sure.'

Massa nodded. 'Ratan, get the rickshaw. Sal, coming or not?'

'Will we fit?' Salora said.

'Easy.' Massa locked the door to the office, and they bounded down the stairs.

Kavi stopped outside the doors to the ground floor warehouse. 'Boss.'

'What?'

'Swords.' Kavi glanced at Elisai. 'For the Taemu.'

He chewed the inside of his cheek, nodded, and slipped the keys out of his pockets.

Kavi pulled down every single sword she could find on the shelves. Two dozen and then some more. She passed half to Elisai, and with steel-laden arms they waited outside for Ratan and his rickshaw.

Massa found a pair of ancient-looking flintlocks and a bag of slugs. He handed one of the weapons to Salora. 'Will they still work?'

The artificer pulled the hammer back, dropped two slugs into the weapon, and ran a finger over the barrel. The twin orbs on either side lit up in bright orange. She passed it to Massa and charged the other weapon.

Massa, Salora, and Elisai squeezed into the backseat of the rickshaw and held the swords in their laps. Kavi shared the driver's seat with Ratan, who'd shimmied over to give her room. She hung onto the rail over her head with a white-knuckled grip as they barrelled down the street. Everywhere: screams, the clang of weapons, the crack of Harithian maayin, crying, people running, standing in shock, administering first aid.

This was not her fight. She had to get to her people. Had to find a way to keep them safe.

They found the Taemu gathered around Hessal's hut.

Shouts of 'Elisai' and 'Akka' greeted them as they approached.

'Hessal has not come back,' one of the men said.

Elisai glanced at Kavi. 'The Kraelish killed her.'

Cries of despair erupted from the men and women. Some started weeping. Others, still in shock from what was happening to the city, stared dumbly at Elisai.

Kavi dropped the stack of swords at her feet and motioned

for Elisai to do the same. 'Listen,' she said, 'we need to move. We cannot stay here.'

'There is nowhere to go,' said an older Taemu who she'd never spoken to.

'There is. The tunnels that the trains use to enter the city, through the western wall, we can use them to escape.' Kavi bent and handed Elisai a sword. 'If we are lucky, we may not need to fight, but—'

'We know nothing of fighting,' the old man said, accompanied by nods from some of the Taemu.

Kavi turned to Sravan, who was waiting with arms extended. She dropped a pair of swords into his massive hands, and he bobbed his head in thanks.

'We can choose to stay here, be captured and tortured by the Kraelish,' she said, handing another sword to one of the Taemu she'd trained. 'Or we can run, live, and fight if we have to. The choice is yours.' She couldn't help the ones who didn't want her protection.

She tried passing a sword to their lookout, Chotu. He shook his head. Gestured to his wooden crutch and the stump under his knee.

'Keep it, just in case,' she urged.

He tightened his lips and shook his head again.

'Stay close to me,' Kavi said, and moved on to the next person.

Many turned down the offer of weapons – the older Taemu were especially reluctant to take up arms – but she managed to find a home for every single sword, even the decorative piece that ended in a hand.

'I cannot promise safety,' she said with all eyes on her and with her own doubts and reservations amplifying with every *boom* that echoed through the city. What else was there to say?

All she could do was put herself between them and the Kraelish. 'But I will do my best to protect you.'

She drew a deep breath and studied the group of sixty-odd Taemu, a quarter of whom held swords. If they did wind up facing the Kraelish, they wouldn't stand a chance. She smothered the thought. 'Will you follow me?'

She saw nods and blank faces.

Kavi turned her back on them and caught Massa's eye. She could only do so much.

He nodded.

In the end, no one stayed behind. A few grumbled, but when she organised them into a spearhead, they obeyed. She put the elderly, the children, Massa, Salora, and Ratan in the middle, and the Taemu with swords around them. She took point.

As they crept through the city, they started picking up people. Terrified Raayans noticed her group of Taemu, moving with a clear sense of purpose and direction, and slowly began filtering in, adding to the mass of the spearhead.

Kavi ignored them. They meant nothing to her. If they got too close, she snarled and shoved them aside. If they carried a weapon, she commanded them to the perimeter. They were not her problem. The monsters were free to kill each other. Only her people mattered.

So why couldn't she turn them away?

She gritted her teeth and smothered the ache in her chest. The train station loomed in the distance. Its clock tower, another remnant of the Imperial era, still stood …

Kavi froze. Raised a hand and brought the group to a halt. She sensed her sword's renewed horror, its revulsion – visions from Drisana's war flickered and flashed in front of Kavi's eyes. She was a cockroach under a monstrous foot. A speck in a metallic eye. She was naked, defenceless, and a slave to an ancient instinct that tore at all her senses and compelled her to, 'Run. Now!'

The Raayans in the group ignored her and hurried into the railway station. The Taemu turned on their heels and ran.

A deafening *whuummp* rocked them off their feet. Cries of shock. Fingers pointed up.

The head of another makra, this one more insectoid than human, bulged over the wall.

Boom.

Kavi shoved Elisai and screamed at the Taemu to run faster.

Boom. Crack. A rumble, a thunderclap, and the wall collapsed. Showered Kavi and the Taemu with dust and debris. Crushed the tunnel and killed or trapped the fool Raayans who'd gone ahead despite her warning.

Kavi gritted her teeth, squinted to keep the dirt out, and dragged Chotu – one arm around his waist, the other carrying his crutch – away from the demolished railway station.

The torso of the makra shrieked as it sank to the floor. Kavi could hear the *clack-whump* of the hatches popping open; the *thud-thud-thud* of infantry marching out; the *hiss* of swords being unsheathed, and then the cries and the screams.

She stopped and turned. The dust from the collapsed wall was starting to settle, and the silhouettes gained substance. The silver and gold armour of the Kraelish: hacking, stabbing, chopping. The dirt and blood-smeared Raayans: dying, dying, dying.

Kavi passed Chotu his crutch. He gaped at her, eyes darting between her face and the incoming massacre.

One day, in this life or the next, the ends will meet, and the circle will complete. Her mother had once said that to her.

It's happening, Amma.

But where was the satisfaction? This was what the Republic deserved, right? *Right?*

Then why was she so angry?

She drew her sword. Everyone was just flesh, bone, and blood. They were all the same. All meaningless. But some people, like the ones in silver and gold, were bullies, and Kavi fucking hated bullies.

She sucked in a lungful of air, and from deep in her stomach, all the way up to her throat, with veins standing on her neck and muscles straining, she took years of submission, a lifetime of silence, and screamed, louder than she ever had in her life, the two words that would have once been a death sentence to her people:

Aadhier Taemu.

Chapter 49

The forbidden battle cry echoed through the ruins of the railway station and it was as if time itself had come to a standstill: the shouts and cries and panicked voices died away, dust particles seemed to hover and slow their descent, the Kraelish stopped slaughtering the Raayans, and stared.

They assessed. Wiped bloody weapons on bloody sleeves, exchanged nods, and as a unit, switched targets and stalked in Kavi's direction. Calm. Fearless. Assured.

Kavi tightened her grip on her sword – which buzzed with exultation – and gently pushed Chotu away.

A green blur whizzed at her, and without thinking, without blinking, she flicked her wrist and deflected it with her blade.

It thunked into a Kraelish soldier's chestplate. He stumbled and fell.

Kavi stared at her sword. No cracks. Not even a notch.

You're immune to Harithian maayin?

It purred with disdain.

Well then. She evened out her breath. Let her mind drift and sink into that place where she became the rhythm. Where the only sound was her own heartbeat. And somewhere, far within the recesses of her mind, a bell *dinged.*

She exploded into motion.

One moment the Kraelish were carefully advancing on her, the next, they were gurgling on blood and dying at the sharp edge of the whirlwind that was her sword.

The muscles she'd spent months building, the stamina she'd developed, all of it was gone, so she had to rely on speed. She needed to be precise. Economic. No wide movements. No flourishes. If a flick of the wrist got the job done, that was what she would use.

Plan for their next move, not yours, Bithun yelled in her ear.

Yes, sahib.

Each strike was a deathblow. She hit her target, over and over and over again. Her sword was built to cut and slash, and its heavy tip guided her, unerringly, to the jugular and the femoral.

They underestimated her. Came at her in twos and threes instead of burying her in a dogpile. By the time they realised what they were dealing with, it was too late.

She broke their confidence. Stole their composure. And gave them fear.

Kavi fought without armour or shield, with stolen bone and muscle forged in a lifetime of backbreaking labour, and with a hold on her reality that was absolute. She was vaguely aware of the men and women who joined her and fought on her flanks; who hacked and stabbed at the Kraelish when they tried to go around her; who always seemed to move and adjust and keep her at the tip of the spearhead.

They cut down another wave of silver and gold, stepped forward, and the Kraelish retreated.

She heard no cheering, no cries of triumph; no one chased after the Kraelish or swore or cursed.

Kavi drew a long, deep breath, tasted the metallic tang of blood at the back of her throat, and exhaled with a sigh. She wiped her sword – ran the flat of the blade down the inside of her elbow – and sheathed it.

She turned around, half afraid of what she'd find, and blinked at Chotu's blood-splattered face. He stood with his crutch under one arm and a Kraelish spear held aloft in the other. A bloody cloth tied around the sharp end of the spear fluttered in the breeze like a flag. Or a standard.

Goosebumps slid along the back of Kavi's neck. He'd made sure that the Taemu had known where she was. He'd given the Kraelish, at the cost of his own safety, a target to aim at. He'd not struck a single blow in the fight, but had single-handedly kept most of them alive.

Chotu gave her a grim nod and lowered the blood-soaked standard.

Behind him, standing bruised and bloodied, were the Taemu from the slums and the Raayans who joined them along the way. Elisai had fought on her left, and Sravan on her right. Both were covered in bloody cuts and bruises. Both, to Kavi's utter discomfort, saluted when their eyes met.

'Stop it,' she said, searching for Massa and Ratan. 'Boss?'

A hand with a beedi between its fingers waved at her and she sighed in relief. The Raeth-damned conman was still alive.

She glanced at Elisai, who'd thankfully dropped the ridiculous salute. 'How many dead?'

'I'll find out, Akka,' she said, and trudged away.

They lost twelve Taemu, killed at least a hundred Kraelish, and emerged battle-hardened, resolute, and bonded to Kavi in a way that both reassured and scared her. The Raayans tended to the wounded. The Taemu piled their dead into a corner and muttered promises to return when it was safe.

Salora insisted that the Raayan army would set up their base of operations at the Vagola and that the campus was their best chance of survival. Kavi agreed. The only problem, besides the Kraelish, was that the Vagola was on the other side of the city.

*

More people joined them as they fought their way through: mothers searching for their children, children searching for their parents, soldiers who'd lost their units, men full of anger who'd lost everything and wanted to make the Kraelish hurt.

Kavi took the scraps of battle theory she'd learned, and applied them:

She ran when she judged the numbers against them were too great and attacked when she was certain her people would prevail. She fought the Kraelish head-on in gullies and alleyways and hit them on the flanks on the roads and intersections. She baited them into buildings and split them up and picked them off. She attacked when they expected defence. She held her ground when they thought she would retreat. She gave them no respite. No rest. If a warlock stood among them, she had Elisai take point, and she hunted the mage down. They couldn't run from her. The closer she got to them, the more violent the song from her sword became. It hated them. And some of that hate seeped into Kavi.

She was aware of every muscle, every tendon in her body, and she pushed them all to their limit. She was calm. She was implacable. She threw herself into the skirmishes with a single, bloody-minded resolve. And for their part, the Taemu rallied behind her. Even the Raayans started calling her Akka. They saluted her. Whispered in awe when they thought she couldn't hear them and did not hesitate when she issued an order.

With each skirmish, the spearhead sharpened. Her Taemu took to the sword like they were born to it. Her band of misfits and irregulars fought like veterans. And through it all, the bloody standard stayed up. Its bearer got more bruised and battered. But the banner never wavered. Chotu never complained. Never said a word. And his eyes never left her back.

By nightfall they'd covered over a third of the distance to the Vagola and Kavi brought the spearhead to a halt. They were tiring; she was tiring, and it would be a disaster if they ran into the Kraelish now.

She found the group an abandoned bungalow to occupy. The Raayan military and their sepoys had created a barricade in the business district and had stalled the Kraelish in the north. In the west, where the railway station once stood, Raayan mages, Blades, and the city-guard were fighting a defensive, retreating action. The Taemu would be safe here for the next few hours.

Kavi set up a watch, sent out scouts, and finally sat, exhausted, with Massa, Salora, and Ratan around a pot of simmering congee. The previous occupants had left behind enough rice in their kitchen to ensure everyone would rest on a full stomach.

They ate in silence; and when Kavi put her bowl away, Massa shuffled closer and said, 'You should heal, we can find you something to use as a counter vail.'

Kavi shook her head. She was covered in cuts and bruises, but the thought of using Nilasi again made her nauseous. Instead, she set her jaw, and studied the artificer sitting across from her.

Her easy familiarity with Ratan and Massa, her presence in the offices of the rickshaw company… 'Salora,' Kavi said, not bothering with an honorific, 'when this is over,' *if this is over*, 'will you still help me?'

The artificer cocked her head. 'With what?'

'You're Jarayas Bithun's contact in the Vagola,' Kavi said, 'aren't you?'

She exchanged a glance with Massa, who shrugged.

'If we make it out of this,' Salora said, 'and if the device is still intact, I will help.'

Kavi still needed to find her brothers, and despite the truth, despite the knowledge of what her father had done, she still wanted to find him. She accepted a cup of tea from Ratan and turned to Massa. 'How do you two know the sahib?'

'Freya,' Massa said. 'We knew Freya.'

Kavi frowned. 'Who?'

'His daughter,' Salora said.

Ah. The woman from the paintings.

'We met at the Vagola,' Salora said, sipping her tea. 'I introduced her to Massa, and Massa introduced her to Aadhi.'

'Who's Aadhi?'

Salora blew over the rim of her teacup. 'Bithun didn't tell you anything?'

'*Ask me in a year's time and I'll tell you,*' Kavi said in her best impression of the sahib.

Massa snorted. 'You don't want to wait?'

Kavi gestured to the bungalow and its scrappy inhabitants.

Salora nodded. 'Aadhi was her lover. He was a Taemu.'

Kavi's eyebrows shot up.

'Jarayas disapproved of the relationship,' Salora said. 'Freya and Aadhi planned to elope. To marry and leave for the Hamakan Isles. Jarayas got word of her plans, travelled all the way up here, and took her back to Bochan. Long story short: Aadhi followed her down south, Jarayas hired some men to rough him up, they went too far, he died. Freya found out, took five discs of agoma, and overdosed.'

Five? She would've been dead within seconds.

'It's not that simple,' Massa said, glaring at Salora.

'What else is there to say?' Salora glared back.

Massa scratched his two-day stubble. 'Well . . .'

Salora tsked and turned back to Kavi. 'Jarayas rightfully blamed himself for their deaths. His wife, too, blamed him. The family fell apart.' She took another sip. 'You ever wonder why he looks so old? He's barely sixty. Time has not been kind to him.'

Kavi studied the dregs of tea floating in her cup. The Bithun she knew would never hurt a Taemu. He was her friend. His past was his past, and she found that she couldn't bring herself to hate him for it.

Massa cleared his throat. 'Jarayas returned a month later. Threw himself at the feet of Aadhi's family and begged for forgiveness. They wouldn't give it. He offered them money, a home, a new life. They refused him and left the city. Then he came to us. Asked for our forgiveness. Asked for our help.'

Salora sighed. 'You should've seen him. Truly, a broken man. None of his power or authority. Grief-stricken. Still mourning … we couldn't turn him down.'

'He began sending us money to use for the Taemu in the city. He said he couldn't find any in Bochan' – Massa glanced at Kavi – 'at the time.'

'We couldn't be too obvious,' Salora said, 'nothing ostentatious. So we used it on clothes, food, and accommodation. Hessal told us who needed what, and we'd arrange for it.' She paused. 'He asked us to let the Taemu in Azraaya know you were coming, that you would change things for them.'

Kavi pressed her lips together. He'd believed in her, right from the start.

'You look a lot like him, you know,' Massa said. 'Like Aadhi.'

'I know,' she said. Bithun had almost been run over by a rickshaw because of the resemblance. And Massa, when he first saw her, had been shocked, not because she was a woman, but because of who she reminded him of.

They sat in silence after that, lost in their own memories and thoughts, until Salora tapped Kavi on the shoulder. 'You should walk around,' she said. 'Make sure everyone sees you.'

'Memsaab,' Ratan said before Kavi could respond, 'let the girl rest.'

Kavi studied the artificer with tired eyes. She sighed and forced herself upright, groaning as her exhausted muscles were pushed into more activity, and searched for Elisai.

The woman was sitting with a group of Taemu, polishing her sword while the others ate.

Kavi walked up behind the older woman and tapped her on the shoulder. 'Elisai.'

All the eyes in the group turned up to Kavi.

'Akka?' Elisai said.

'I want to walk around, check on everyone,' Kavi said. 'Will you come?'

Elisai sheathed her sword and stood. The others in her group had stopped eating and seemed to be waiting for something.

Kavi cleared her throat. Made eye contact with each of them. 'You fought well today.'

They burst into grins. 'Thank you, Akka.' 'All because of you.' 'Did you eat?' 'Please, have some.'

She declined their offer of food, patted her stomach and told them she'd had her fill.

'I'm sorry,' Kavi said when they walked away from the group. 'I know you're tired.'

Elisai shook her head. 'No, I – it's strange, I feel … alive. You know what I mean?'

'I think I do.'

They went from group to group, checked whether wounds had been treated, whether they had enough to eat; and wherever Kavi went, she was greeted with brave smiles and awed faces, even from the Raayans and assorted riff-raff, who now outnumbered her Taemu two to one.

Halfway through, she began noticing the armbands: strips of blood-soaked cloth that almost everyone had tied around their upper arms. She glanced at Elisai, who was also wearing one. 'Why?' she asked, pointing at it.

'You don't have one?' Elisai frowned. 'I thought he would've come to you first.'

He? 'Who?'

'Come with me.'

They found him sitting under his banner, tearing scraps of bloodied cloth into armbands for the men and women gathered around him.

Kavi waited until he was alone, and with Elisai at her side, walked up to him. 'Chotu,' she said.

He looked up at her, saluted, lodged his crutch under his arm, and started to stand.

'Please, there's no need.' Kavi sat on her haunches. She picked up an armband, stiff from all the dry blood. 'This was your idea?'

He nodded, mouth upturned in defiance, as if he was expecting some sort of rebuke.

'Can I have one?'

His eyes lit up, and he motioned her closer. He took the cloth from her hand, set it aside, and picked another longer, darker, bloodier piece of cloth which he carefully tied around her arm. When he was done, he smoothed the creases out and patted it down with a satisfied nod.

'Did you eat?' Kavi said.

He gestured to the empty bowl at his side.

'Want more?'

He shook his head.

'Rest,' she said. 'Tomorrow will be a long day, and I will need you at my back.'

He puffed up. His lips parted, like he was finally going to say something, but he changed his mind and saluted her again.

Kavi sighed. She'd managed to get almost everyone to stop saluting her. Almost. This was the one command Chotu stubbornly refused to obey.

'Have you ever heard him speak?' she asked Elisai as they walked away.

'Not to me,' Elisai said, 'but I heard him speak to Hessal when he first joined us. Four – maybe five years ago? But we knew who he was long before that. The Dolmondas took his leg and put him to work, begging outside the temples. Hessal saved up enough money to buy his contract from them, and he came to live with us in the slums.'

Kavi's lips tightened. The men who'd killed Haibo had belonged to the Bochan chapter of the Dolmonda gang. 'They cause you a lot of trouble?'

'Who?'

'The gangs,' Kavi said.

Elisai made a face and spat. 'Sometimes.'

When they were done, when everyone had seen her face and been accounted for, Kavi and Elisai stole a couple of boxes from the kitchen, sat outside on the verandah, and watched the sporadic mushrooms of fire that ballooned in the distance. Kavi could just about make out the silhouettes of the makra: perfectly still, silent, waiting.

'Akka,' Elisai said after she stifled a burp. 'Why do you think we fought for the Kraelish?'

Kavi tugged on an earlobe. 'What do you mean? We aren't fighting for them.'

'No, not now,' she said, shooing a mosquito away, 'when they first brought us here, from our homeland.'

'I think we…' Kavi sighed. What was a good way to say this? 'The Kraelish, they took everything. Our land, our culture, our language, our history … they stole what made us, *us.* I think, maybe, we fought for them because they gave us a chance to regain some of our humanity.'

Elisai nodded. 'You're really smart, Akka.'

Kavi tsked. 'Shut up your face.'

Elisai chuckled, leaned forward, and rested her hands and chin on the top of the balustrade.

Unless the scouts returned with news, in another four hours, or as soon as the sun peeked over the horizon, they would move again. It was a pitiful amount of rest for what they'd been through, but based on the frequency with which the Kraelish were breaking through the Raayan line, it was all they had.

Kavi swallowed a lump in her throat, lodged her chin in a groove on the balustrade, and together with Elisai, watched the city burn.

Chapter 50

They walked through streets bathed in the blood-orange of the rising sun. The sound of violence – the clash of weapons, the cries of pain and anger – echoed through empty buildings and hollow gullies where even the sewage ran red. Every now and then, Kavi stepped over a severed hand, an ear, a clump of hair attached to its scalp, or some unidentifiable viscera that she did her best to ignore.

The black dome of Lamira's hall peeked over the rooftops when Kavi came across the first Raayan sentry. She brought the group to a halt.

The sentry tensed. His eyes flicked to the bloody banner flying over her head, and he relaxed. He gestured for them to proceed and Kavi led her band of Taemu, thugs, and Raayans into the Vagola.

Lawns, once immaculately manicured, were now overrun with refugees from the northern quadrants of the city. Soldiers and staff ran back and forth. Physicians and nurses consoled crying children and distraught families. Exhausted healers with buckets of dead animals tended to maimed men and women.

Movement ceased when Kavi and her band walked into the compound. Fingers pointed at the red banner. At the red armbands. At her. *Taemu battalion*, they whispered. *Have not lost a battle. Swordmaster captain. Mage-killer.*

Kavi made a face. *Mage-killer?* 'Elisai,' she said. 'Can you find us a spot?'

Elisai nodded and waved for the group to follow her.

'Boss.' Kavi grabbed Massa's arm as he sauntered past. 'Come with me, please.'

Massa glanced at Salora.

Kavi sighed. 'Fine, she can come too.'

The throng parted around her – from fear or awe, she wasn't sure – and Kavi led the duo deeper into the Vagola until they found a tent and a desk outside the entrance to the lecture theatres where a bespectacled man was furiously scribbling away.

'I need to speak to an officer,' Kavi said.

'Name?' he said, without looking up.

'Kavithri Taemu.'

'No, not yours, the name of who you want to …' His pen stopped, and he slowly looked up to gaze at her face.

'We need food, water, healers,' Kavi said, 'and I need to know what you have planned.'

His eyes shifted to Massa, to Salora, then back to Kavi, where they lingered on the sword hilt that jutted over her shoulder. He licked his lips, pocketed his pen, and stood. 'Wait here.'

Massa had just lit up another beedi, and Kavi had just asked him where the Hel he was getting them from, when a man in military uniform with epaulettes on his shoulders came rushing out of the building. He had a roll of paper tucked under his arm and a slightly frantic look on his face.

He spotted the trio and stomped over. 'I heard you want to be part of the plan.'

Kavi pursed her lips. 'That's—'

'Excellent.'

—not what I said.

He spread out his piece of paper on the table, which turned out to be a map of the city. 'Here.' He jabbed a finger at a pair of long black lines two-thirds of the way down. 'Your battalion can take the chokepoint.'

Kavi leaned in for a closer look.

'Hold this position until you see a flare in the sky,' the officer said. 'Then you run like Hel.'

She frowned. 'Like the Siphon?'

'Exactly like the Siphon.' He pointed to a large pink circle painted over the map, on whose southern edge this chokepoint sat. 'You will have five minutes after the flare is deployed to leave the weapon's radius.'

'Weapon?' Massa said before Kavi could get a word in. 'What weapon?'

'The details are classified.' The officer straightened. 'And who may you be?'

'Massa Zanzane, businessman and art collector.' He gave the officer a half-assed salute. 'And who may *you* be?'

The officer bristled. 'Brigadier Thordali. I am here to speak with the Captain of the Taemu Battalion only, so if you will please—'

'Don't talk to him like that,' Kavi said, studying the map. 'Where are the other troops positioned?'

The side of Brigadier Thardali's face twitched as he pointed to areas deeper inside the pink radius.

'We would only have to fight if the lines in front of us collapse,' Kavi said. Which, given the way things were going, was more than likely to happen.

'That's correct,' Thordali said. 'Despite your … prowess, you are still considered irregulars, so you will only be used as a last defence.'

It rankled to turn her people into another cog in the Raayan military. Especially now that she understood how badly they'd failed the Taemu in the past. She pulled at an ear. But if this plan failed, and the Kraelish took the city …

'Tell me about this weapon,' she said. 'Why haven't you used it yet?'

Thordali hesitated, sighed, and said, 'It charges in increments. Requires multiple artificers to maintain and reinforce the code. They have been working through the night.'

'And what does it do?' Kavi asked.

'The device creates a zone' – he gestured to the pink circle – 'and exposes it to conditions that are unsuitable for human survival. Once it goes past the meridian, no living thing inside will survive.'

Kavi wanted to ask the man *How? What conditions? What the Hel is a meridian?* but from the way his face closed up, Kavi knew that this was all the information she'd get from him. 'And what about the makra?'

'Non-issue, thank Meshira,' the Brigadier said. 'According to our intelligence, the makra are only used to breach enemy defences and to deploy troops. It's how the Kraelish have used them in the northern kingdoms.'

Massa flicked his beedi. Spilled crumbly grey ash on the map. 'Can you imagine if we had to, you know, fight the makra?'

Brigadier Thordali blew the ash off his map and glared at Massa. 'That day might not be too far away.'

'Thank fuck it's not today,' Massa said through a mouthful of smoke.

'Captain.' Thordali addressed Kavi with veins popping on his forehead. 'Will the Taemu battalion join us in the defence of the Vagola?'

Kavi knew what her answer was. But she couldn't speak for

the others. 'I will ask the battalion and let you know.'

The Brigadier gave her a sharp nod. 'You have an hour to decide. I will send over rations and healers.'

The battalion's decision was unanimous. Elderly, children, and the wounded would stay behind. Everyone else would head to the chokepoint.

'This is our city,' they said, slapping their chests, 'if *we* don't fight, who will?'

Kavi suggested, 'The army.'

They responded with unimpressed faces and bobbling heads.

She told them that most of them would die.

They gave her grim nods and said, 'We fight, Akka.'

She relayed the decision to the Brigadier, who gave her a firm handshake, and said, 'The city will not forget, and neither will the army.'

I wouldn't be so sure of that. But she bit her tongue. Besides, both the city and the army might be gone by the end of the day.

A haggard-looking healer was waiting for her when she returned to the battalion.

'They insisted that I heal you too,' he said, rolling up his sleeves. 'Where—'

'No need.'

He shrugged, muttered, 'Whatever you say,' and picked up his basket of mongooses.

'Wait.'

He cocked an eyebrow.

'We don't have a field healer,' Kavi said. Most military units included a warlock, an artificer, and a healer. They had the artificer, a warlock would be nice (her sword, she sensed, disagreed), but a healer was what she really needed.

The man hesitated. 'Isn't there—'

'You could really make a difference,' she said. 'If we fail, the city falls. You know that.'

He made a face. But after a lengthy, expressive, internal debate, he sighed in resignation, and said, 'Okay, fine.'

A bell, which on any other day would've signalled the end of one lecture and the start of another, pealed through the campus. Soldiers rose to their feet, checked their weapons, fastened the straps on their armour.

Salora brought Kavi a set of standard-issue armour and she grudgingly allowed the artificer to help her into it. She was the last to be kitted out, and the battalion waited and watched in silence. When Salora was done, Kavi gave her a meaningful glance and turned to the men and women gathered around her. They clearly wanted her to speak, to say something that would lift their spirits, maybe even promise them victory, but all Kavi had was the truth.

'This battle will be different,' she said. 'There will be no room to manoeuvre. No place to hide. We will live and die by our line. If it breaks, the enemy pours in, cohesion is lost, we get flanked, we break into smaller groups, we lose.'

The battalion listened with rapt attention. Whispered her words to those at the back who couldn't hear.

'Most of the battle will happen in the first rank, and the ones immediately after if they have longer weapons. Their warlocks and artificers will be stationed in the backline, behind the other soldiers waiting to reinforce the frontline, to fill the gaps.' *To fill in for the ones killed or wounded.* 'Do you understand?'

There were nods and a chorus of hushed, '*Yes, Akka.*'

'Good,' Kavi muttered. She'd done her best to prepare them. What happened now was out of her hands.

*

The chokepoint was a long, dried-out plot of land that had once served as a park. It had one entry and one exit – both through narrow gullies at either end. The park itself was surrounded by tightly packed multi-storey buildings that gave it the effect of a courtyard. An empty well stood in one corner and the rusted ruins of park benches littered the area.

The battalion filtered through and fell into the shape of the spearhead they'd become used to fighting in. No one said a word. The only sounds were the rustling of the standard and Massa's wheezing cough.

They waited. The minutes dragged on. Kavi allowed herself to hope.

Maybe they wouldn't need to fight. Maybe the Kraelish had scouted the area and decided that this derelict park favoured the defenders and that it was not worth attacking.

Then things changed. It started with a single Kraelish soldier. He stepped out of the gully facing the battalion and stared at the Taemu.

Kavi's muscles tensed. Her mouth went dry.

He made some sort of hand signal and the rest came pouring out behind him. Dozens at first. Then in their hundreds. A river of silver and gold.

Kavi drew her sword. Heard the *shiiing* echo through the park as her battalion mimicked her. She glanced at the sky. Clear and blue. No sign of a flare. Her heart pounded. Her hands trembled. But she raised her sword, parted her lips, and was almost blown off her feet by the roar that erupted from the battalion. It sent goosebumps screaming up the skin of her arms and legs, and when they roared again, she added her voice to it. Spittle flying: 'Aadhier Taemu!'

Neck muscles bunched and stretched: 'Aadhier Taemu!'

Throat raw and torn: 'Aadhier Taemu!'

The Kraelish charged.

The ground shook as Kavi ran to meet them. She trembled with a sudden masochistic need to hurt. To feel something. To shout at the Taemu flanking her, *I killed your beloved leader. I killed innocent men and women.* But she couldn't. And so they couldn't punish her. But the Kraelish could.

She flung herself at the silver and gold line – bodies-armour-weapons collided with the sound of thunder – and she welcomed the fist that connected with her temple; the sword that pierced her thigh; the hands that grabbed her hair and yanked; the spear that sliced her cheek open; the pressure from both sides that trapped her in place and threatened to crush her bones.

Why drag this out for seven years?

A Kraelishwoman panted in Kavi's face and slammed her pommel into the side of Kavi's head.

Kavi stared at the freckles on the woman's face. At the piercing blue eyes and copper eyebrows above them.

The hair at the back of her neck stood up. *You're too close. Get the fuck away from me.*

She cocked her head back and slammed it into the woman's face. The perfect eyes lost focus. The pale skin was now splattered with blood. And something inside Kavi trilled with glee; with a desire to destroy everything that was beautiful. To ruin everything she would never be.

She headbutted the woman till she dropped, elbowed a spear away and stabbed its wielder in the neck before the crush squeezed her into his body and forced them into a lover's embrace. She held the dying man close as his warm blood spilled down her face and neck and she slashed at the soldier behind him.

The battle found its pulse – frontlines met, engaged, withdrew.

Projectiles and insults were exchanged.

Injured were replaced.

And they engaged again.

All her speed, her finesse, was meaningless. Sweat dripped into her eyes and clouded her vision. Her bladder was full and with nowhere to go, she pissed herself. She struggled to breathe and every ounce of intelligence she possessed screamed at her to leave. But she was trapped between her own people and the enemy, and even if she wanted to run, there was nowhere to go.

For a while, it seemed like they were holding their ground; but the men and women they faced were professional soldiers, and while the Taemu battalion had bested them in the labyrinth of the city, here, where they were forced to fight head-on, the Kraelish had the advantage. Inch by inch, the battalion was pushed back, until finally, with a calamitous crash of metal and flesh, the Taemu line folded.

Chapter 51

Kavi punched her sword through the mouth of a Kraelishman, kneed another in the crotch, and backpedalled to avoid being flanked.

She stumbled over a corpse and fell. Hands grabbed her arms and pulled her up while bodies surged past her to reinforce the line. She stared up at Massa's bloody face as he dragged her away. Behind him, Salora reset the artificed shield Chotu carried over their heads like an umbrella while Harithian maayin *thunk-thunk-thunked* down on them.

'We won't last much longer,' Massa shouted over the racket.

She shook him off.

'Kavi!' Massa pulled her back. 'Listen, please, I can help.'

She tore her eyes away from the battle and frowned at the need in his voice.

'I've been waiting for this,' he said with wild intensity in his eyes and a grin on his face.

'Boss?'

The blood slowly drained from Massa's face. 'I won't be coming back. You will have to—'

'Boss?'

'Listen!' A film of silver slowly coalesced over Massa's eyes. 'Take care of the company.'

'What—' She grabbed his shoulders. *'What're you talking about?'*

Massa's face went slack. 'The threads are always there,' he mumbled. 'Waiting, waiting, waiting. All I need to do is ...'

The temperature plummeted. Kavi's breath fogged. And a chorus of low-pitched gurgles erupted from the ground.

She took a step back and froze. A dead Kraelish soldier had just blinked at her. She stared, wide-eyed and transfixed, as the skin around the corpse's mouth stretched and expanded until it tore with an ear-shredding *Rrrrip* that brought all movement in the park to a halt.

Everywhere she looked, corpses of fallen Raayans, Taemu, and Kraelish convulsed as the skin on their bodies ripped itself to shreds. Their eyeballs withered and dropped out. The empty sockets fused themselves shut. A thin slice appeared in the middle of their foreheads. White pus oozed out, and it widened and solidified into a single bloodshot eye.

Kavi glanced at Massa. He turned to her with a rictus grin as silver leaked from his nose and ears and eyes. 'Fight with them,' he whispered.

The bones of the dead shattered with a deafening crack. The bodies crumpled. Went still.

Kavi held her breath.

Tentacles erupted from chests and backs and shot the bodies upright. As one, they turned and faced the Kraelish line.

A shriek from the other end of the park broke the trance. 'Necromancer!'

Tentacles slithered, wound, tightened, and catapulted the undead at the Kraelish.

Kavi's voice trembled. 'You're an Azir? Why didn't you tell me?' How much longer did he have?

'It won't last long,' Massa rasped. 'Help them.'

She squeezed his shoulders. Adjusted her helmet, and without waiting to see if anyone was following, turned and charged into the chaos.

The unblinking eyes of the undead swivelled to stare at her as she ran at the Kraelish.

They knew her.

She bodyslammed a Kraelishman. A tentacle latched onto his leg and dragged him away.

No, not me. She'd made this mistake before. They knew her *sword.* They were afraid of her sword. Afraid of what lived in her sword.

Kavi ducked under a spear and slashed up at the hands that carried it. Her sword cut through a silver and gold gauntlet and severed the spearman's fingers.

The ground rumbled as the battalion charged past her and crashed into the disintegrating Kraelish line.

How could she have not known about Massa? He'd talked and talked about souls and possessions – he'd met Salora at the Vagola, why'd she not questioned that?

An undead sped past, latched onto a Kraelish soldier, wrapped its tentacles around him and tightened its grip until arms and legs popped, neck cracked, spine snapped, and his eyes rolled up into his head.

Kavi parried and sliced her sword up into a Kraelishwoman's armpit. She should have known. She could have asked him so many questions. He wasn't just a friend. He was like her. An Azir. And he was dying.

Her sword howled as she stomped down on a spear-thrust and slashed its wielder's neck open. Tears welled up and spilled out. Her vision blurred. And she screamed her grief into the tangled mass of the living and the undead.

*

'Hold!' Kavi yanked back an overeager Raayan. They'd forced the Kraelish to the edge of the park and crossed into the radius of the weapon. There was no need for them to go any further. The undead, as if they'd sensed her thoughts, stopped. Their eyes rolled up into their heads, and they fell, like a horde of puppets whose strings had been cut.

The Kraelish were in no shape to mount another assault. It was over. All Kavi's battalion needed to do was to wait for the flare and fall back once it was in the sky. 'Hold,' she shouted, and left the frontline to look for Massa.

He was lying on his back, head in Salora's lap, perfectly still, empty eye sockets staring out at nothing, while the mongoose healer checked his vitals.

Salora ran her fingers through Massa's thin hair and looked up at Kavi with a sad smile on her face. 'He got to choose how it ended.'

The sword throbbed with sorrow. Kavi kneeled, slack-faced and exhausted. 'What happened?'

'His countervail,' Salora said. 'Every cast, every time he looked past the veil, or' – she gazed out across the carnage – 'brought a soul back, he would see the other side, and leave a part of himself there.'

The other side? In Hel?

'The Necromancer's curse. The more they cast, the more they see …' Her lips trembled and tightened as tears crawled down her cheeks. 'Until Raeth himself comes to take their eyes.'

'How long have you known about him?' Kavi squeezed Massa's hand. Cold. So cold.

'Since the beginning.' Salora reached into Massa's shirt pocket and pulled out his beedi case and artificed matchstick. 'Almost seven years ago.'

Kavi nodded. He'd died on his own terms. And saved the city.

'Here.' Salora passed her the metal case. 'He wanted you to have this.'

'I don't smoke,' Kavi said, but accepted it anyway.

Salora shrugged. 'It's what he wanted.'

Kavi bit her lip and dabbed at a runny nose. 'Did Bithun know?'

'No, he—'

'Akka!' a voice screamed from the frontline.

Kavi exchanged a glance with Salora.

'Go,' the artificer said.

Kavi picked her way through the dead and their tentacles and was ushered up to Elisai who pointed at the Kraelish line.

The Kraelish had stepped aside to allow a woman, a warlock in Raayan colours, to walk out into the park. She had a white handkerchief tied to a wrist, which she raised as she strolled through the dead.

The blood rushed into Kavi's ears. *Ze'aan.*

'Are they surrendering?' Elisai said.

'Wait here,' Kavi said, stepping out to meet the warlock.

Elisai linked an arm under her elbow and yanked her back. 'It's too dangerous.'

'Release me,' Kavi growled, eyes not leaving the warlock who was casually studying the tentacled carcasses strewn across the park.

'Akka,' Elisai said, holding Kavi in place. 'You can't, let me go instead.'

Kavi's throat burned from the short, sharp breaths she was taking. It was all Ze'aan's fault. All that time trapped in the dark. The fear. The pain – Jarard's knives, his scissors, his saw.

Her jaw clenched, unclenched, and clenched again. Hessal would still be alive if it wasn't for her. 'Elisai …'

'Am I wrong, Akka?'

Kavi turned to face the woman. Curbed the tension from her voice. It was not Elisai's fault; she just didn't understand. 'You told me to trust you, when you asked me not to hurt Salora, right?'

Elisai blinked. Loosened her grip on Kavi's arm.

'I need you to trust me now, please,' Kavi said. 'I have to speak to her. I have to know if she was the one who sold me out.'

'I trust you, always, but this …'

'It'll be fine,' Kavi said. 'I have everyone watching my back. We're just going to talk.'

Elisai sighed, and with a reluctant nod, let Kavi go.

She walked until she was halfway to the Kraelish line, then stopped and waited for the warlock to come to her.

Ze'aan lowered her arm and kneeled to poke at a tentacle. She picked one up, raised it to the light and rotated it for a better look. When she was satisfied, she flung the appendage away, wiped her fingers on a dead soldier's sleeve and stood, expressionless. She stared at the battered and exhausted remnants of the Taemu battalion as she picked her way through to Kavi.

'Why'd you do it?' Kavi said, when Ze'aan was within earshot.

The warlock frowned and continued walking until she was an arm's length away.

'Why'd you give me up?' Kavi said again.

'I thought it might be you,' Ze'aan said in a measured tone. 'A living Taemu swordmaster leading a unit of untrained civilians. Who else?'

'Ze'aan…'

'It wasn't me,' Ze'aan said. 'A healer from Bochan sent

word several months ago that a Taemu Azir was on her way to Azraaya.'

Kavi started. 'Healer?' *The healer?* Bithun's healer from the hospital? *That fucking quack?*

The warlock glanced over Kavi's head, at the battalion watching them with weapons drawn, and took another step closer.

Kavi tensed. Tightened her grip on her sword. 'Why – when did you switch sides?'

Ze'aan gazed down at her. 'You remember what I told you about dreams?'

Anyone who stands between you and your dream is an enemy. And if they refuse to move, you do not hesitate to move them. Kavi pursed her lips.

'I've spent my whole life trying to escape this place,' Ze'aan said. 'I used to think there was something wrong with me. That I was the only one who could see its divisions, its obsessions, its rituals that kept everything in its place – the greed and rot at the top, the poverty and desperation at the bottom, the indifference in between.' Her eyes glazed over. 'I searched for others like me, people who didn't belong to either world. But the ones I found I had nothing in common with. They lived with an asphyxiating closedness. Intoxicated with wealth. Blind to—'

Ze'aan's face contorted in disgust. 'I couldn't stand to be around them. I packed my bags, bought tickets – but then, the week before I was meant to leave, I was forced to test.' The muscles in her jaw tightened. 'Once they learned I was a warlock … I was trapped. I was a mage, and I would serve the Republic. The Vagola would never let me leave. I'd spend the rest of my life in service to the people I hated.

'I had nowhere to go, no one to turn to, so I reached out to them, and they offered me a way out. A new life in Kraelin. But I would have to earn it.' Kavi could feel Ze'aan's breath on her face as the warlock leaned in and dropped her voice to a whisper. 'I don't belong here, Kavithri, and neither do you. Surrender, and they will let your people live. Fight, stand in my way, and I will not hesitate to *move you.*'

Kavi's mouth twisted, and she jerked away. 'Fuck you—' Her eyes went wide. Ze'aan had stopped moving. Over her head, like a halo, hung three shimmering emerald suns that were already disintegrating.

'Run!' Kavi screamed and aimed her sword at Ze'aan's chin.

It never connected.

One moment she was on her feet, the next, she was lying on her back with a hole the size of a watermelon in her stomach. Her spine was still intact, but her spleen, her liver … Kavi's cries of pain were drowned out by the screams of her battalion and the wet *thunks* of Ze'aan's maayin piercing their armour and flesh.

Just like the Siphon, just like the first time she'd faced Ze'aan, it was over in seconds. Kavi had no idea what was going on. She groaned as a spike of razor-edged agony shot up into her chest. She was dying. It was over. She should have killed Ze'aan the moment she stepped into range.

She searched for the warlock. The Kraelish were saluting her as she walked away from the massacre.

Come back. Kavi tried to force herself up, but gasped and twisted as the pain sucked the air from her lungs.

Behind her, the survivors dragged and carried the wounded away from the approaching Kraelish. Kavi turned to watch them, and staring right back at her, through lifeless eyes so much a mirror of her own, Kavi found Elisai.

She lay flat on her stomach, head propped up by a ruined chin, arm outstretched in Kavi's direction, as if she'd tried to rush to her aid. Dozens of holes had been punched through her armour, and a single fissure in her temple leaked dark, viscous blood down the side of her face.

She should have listened to Elisai. She should've – Kavi choked on a strangled sob.

She'd searched for heroes for as long as she could remember. She'd looked for them in books, in stories, in legends. But they'd been around her all along. Warriors who went into battle every day, knowing that what awaited them at the end was failure. They smiled, bowed, scraped. Never faltered. Never permitted the dignity of rage. *They* were her royalty. Her heroes. And now they were dying.

Kavi grabbed a Kraelish ankle as it stomped past. *Stop. Let them go.*

An armoured gauntlet backhanded her across the face. Dark spots swam across her vision, but she held on. He hit her again. The percussive, pulsating howl of her sword's fury filled her ears. She held on tighter. He hit her harder.

The ball of rage that lived inside her strained at the chains she'd built around it, and a link snapped. One by one, they all snapped. A dam burst. The unbearable pressure evaporated. An explosion of emotion – sadness and fear and loss and horror and foremost of all, anger, rocketed from chest into her limbs and someone or something took control of her throat and roared in a voice she'd never heard before.

Kavi retreated, shrank away, and the berserker took control.

Nilasian maayin ripped its way out of her body, latched on to the closest soldier, and *took*.

They fell, blood dripping from their torso.

The berserker stood, her armour and clothes a ruin, but her body whole and without a scratch on it.

The Kraelish soldier with the armoured gauntlet had a moment to register the grinning, red-eyed woman standing in front of him before the berserker backhanded his jaw off his face. In the same movement, she slipped under another soldier's sword, drew the dagger from their hip, and *smack-smack-smack:* armpit, neck, eye.

Spears flashed out. Swords descended. The berserker let them sink into her body. Let them hack off her limbs. And laughed. And took their own limbs in payment.

She fought with her sword in one hand and an enemy weapon in the other. She bludgeoned and clubbed and used her weapons like hammers. When both her hands were occupied, she used her teeth on necks and faces. She gouged out eyes and left soldiers dismembered and bleeding out. The berserker did not fight to kill. The berserker fought to hurt. To make them feel Kavi's pain.

The Kraelish swarmed her. She let them land their blows and trapped their weapons. She used Kavi's body like a shield. She screamed and laughed and moved faster than Kavi ever had. She hit with more power than Kavi ever could.

Bones cracked. Blood flowed. The Kraelish died. And through it all, the berserker took and regenerated.

When they tried to run from her, she chased them. Laughing. Mocking. *Are you running from me? Is the big Imperial soldier running from a poor Taemu?* She hurled her sword and giggled when it plunged into their backs.

And when she called the sword back to her. It came. Hurtling through the air and shattering bone and cartilage as it connected with her waiting palm. Nilasi gleefully fixed her hand. And the berserker roared.

She hacked and slashed and decimated the Kraelish line. Forward, always forward. The berserker had a goal. There was someone she was looking for, and she would not stop until she found—

There. Through the mask of blood and gore, the berserker grinned at the tall woman who stood frozen at the end of the gully.

The blood drained from Ze'aan's face.

The berserker, without taking her eyes off the warlock, swayed out of the way of a spear and punched the spearman in the trachea. Her smile widened as the man gagged and choked and fell to the ground.

I will make it slow. A thousand little cuts and slices. One for each Taemu you killed. The rest, for Kavi. She cackled. *You can't run from me. It doesn't matter where you go. I will find you.*

A cry, a single desperate word screamed in an unfamiliar voice, cut through the bloody haze and brought the berserker to a halt. She cocked her head. There it was again. A plea. A word that could mean so many different things. Friend. Mentor. Teacher. Leader. But when this voice said it, there was only one meaning.

Sister.

It blew the rage away. Kavi forced her way back out. Grappled the shrieking berserker into submission, and chained it in a deeper, darker prison.

'Akka!'

All around her were the broken, twisted bodies of the dead and dying. From the roots of her scalp to the grooves between her toes, blood clung to her skin. Her throat burned from the screaming. The laughing. Her arms, so light, so powerful, hung heavy and aching at her sides. Kavi wiped the blood out of her eyes. Blew it out of her nose. Retched and spat out the rest.

'Akka!'

Her legs trembled, but she locked her knees in place. With a shuddering breath, she added the slaughter – because that's what it was, they'd never stood a chance – to the ledger of unresolved horror and violence for which she was responsible, and searched for the voice.

'Akka!'

She found it at the other end of the park, past the carnage, where Chotu stood with Salora's arm slung over his shoulder. Their eyes met. He raised a hand and pointed a finger at the sky.

A red circle of light with a long foggy tail hung over the city.

Kavi wiped the blood off her face and spun around to face Ze'aan. The warlock was gone. She clenched her fists and stepped into the gully.

'Akka!' Chotu shouted again and pointed at an injured Taemu who was struggling to stand.

Kavi blinked. *What am I doing?* The flare. Five minutes.

She sheathed her sword, broke into a jog, and when she reached the injured Taemu, slipped a shoulder under his arm and took his weight. She dropped him outside the radius of the weapon and sprinted back to look for more survivors. There was still time.

She found Taemu and Raayans who'd been maimed, trapped under heavier bodies, or too weak to stand, and carried them to the edge of the park. Each time she returned, Chotu muttered a worried 'Akka' and gestured to the flare, and each time, she said, *One more,* and went back looking for more survivors.

Salora said nothing. She hung off Chotu's shoulder and watched Kavi with empty eyes.

Kavi had dropped off a Raayan woman and rushed back in when there was a sound like thunder, and everything went dark. Tiny flickering dots of light, like stars, filled the sky, and for a heartbeat, all five Jinn hung suspended over the city.

Her ears popped. The air turned sour. Pungent. It thinned and thinned until her hands went to her throat as she gasped for air. Sharp pain pierced the space between her eyebrows. Her eyes felt like they were being sucked out of their sockets. Her chest ballooned and her skin went numb. She scrambled on her hands and knees and froze.

It was faint, but she could hear it. *Akka.*

She dragged herself in the direction of Chotu's voice.

It got louder and louder. She got closer and closer. Until she stumbled over something soft and mushy, and her legs gave out. She collapsed. Gasped and thrashed around as she fought for air. She could sense Nilasi searching, probing, looking for someone or something to use. *They're all dead. Just go away. You've done enough.*

The threads withdrew and slithered back into her body. And as if that was a signal, she was moving again. Being dragged along as she kicked and flailed.

She burst out in the light, and air flooded her lungs.

Kavi swallowed giant gulps of air. Feeling returned to her toes and fingers. The pain in her head subsided. The same warm hands that had dragged her out brushed the hair out of her eyes, and she found a familiar face looking down on her.

'Akka?'

'Chotu,' she said in a hoarse whisper, 'help me up.'

He dragged her into a sitting position and she rested her back against the legs of a park bench. 'Thank you.'

He offered her a water canteen. 'Take.'

Kavi froze. Stared, eyes bulging, at the pitch-black walls of a colossal dome that covered half the city. No light entered it. Nothing escaped from it.

She glanced at Chotu. 'You went in there? For me?'

'Take,' he said, and shoved the canteen into her hands.

She twisted the cap open and drank. All around her, the leftovers of the Taemu battalion sat nursing their wounds and staring at the opaque dome of darkness.

Eventually, after what could've been an hour or a minute, the dome began to disintegrate. Anyone who had been alive when the weapon detonated was now dead. Their bodies bloated and ruined and mangled beyond recognition. The city, home to incessant noise and cacophony, was silent; and in the distance, beyond the broken walls, the shapes of the makra retreated.

Kavi breathed a sigh of relief. She returned the empty canteen to Chotu and studied his earnest, bruised, and bloodied face.

She pushed herself to her feet. 'Where's our fucking healer?'

Chapter 52

'A gift from Jarayas,' Salora said. 'He wanted us to give it to you after the Siphon.'

Inside a darkwood frame, on a long, white canvas, the dirt-smeared face of a woman with red irises gazed out at Kavi. Her mouth was swollen on one side. Her lips were torn and chapped. Her tattered clothes, far too big for her, hung off her slumped shoulders. Everything about the woman reeked of desperation and sorrow. Except for her eyes, which held the only colour in the painting, and were alive.

Kavi ran her fingers over the smooth frame. She'd come so close to giving up. Now, she was a first-year Blade at the Vagola and, in a roundabout way, the owner of an Azraayan business.

Salora was the official proprietor of the Imperial Rickshaw Company, but she wanted nothing to do with the place so had left it to Kavi. And Kavi had returned the company to its roots.

She offered the Taemu in the city employment as rickshaw drivers. Most accepted. Some didn't. But she had enough for an entire fleet. Ratan was promoted to chief assistant while she inherited the holier-than-thou title of Boss.

Some of the Raayans who'd fought with them had joined as well. The others, who had lives to go back to, swore to never mention what they'd seen her do – what they'd seen the berserker do. *We have a bond,* they said, flashing her the freshly tattooed red armbands. They trusted her, and she, in turn, found she had no qualms about trusting them.

Last week, they'd gathered in the park where they'd fought the Kraelish. Cleaned and dressed the dead. Arranged them on pyres and set them aflame.

Kavi had sat with the survivors and watched the black smoke billow into the sky. Less than a quarter had survived. There was grief. Mourning. And a palpable sense of pride. They came up to Kavi, 'Akka,' they said, and embraced her.

Kavi wept for Elisai. For Massa. For the mothers lost. The children orphaned. The fathers who'd sacrificed themselves for a city that had already forgotten them.

'I'm sorry,' she said, over and over again.

They shushed her. Said it was their choice, that they had died fighting. They had died with a sword in their hands and with a purpose.

'Are you ready?' Salora said, snapping her back to the present.

Kavi's lips tightened. She nodded.

Her sword, which was lying on the divan, pulsed a word at her. *Where?*

Family, Kavi answered.

It responded with a warm pulse of hope.

Kavi smiled to herself and followed Salora out of the office. Her sword was now capable of shaping words and concepts inside Kavi's head. It was unnerving, but she was getting used to it.

'Kavi. Memsaab.' Ratan tipped his flatcap to Salora. 'Where to?'

Salora shimmied into the backseat of the rickshaw. 'Artificed Hydraulics.'

*

The city was covered with scaffolding. Demand for construction workers was at an all-time high and labourers from all around Raaya were streaming into the city. The work on the walls was almost complete, but the official inquiry into how the Kraelish were allowed to get so close to them without warning was still underway. Salora didn't come out and say it, but she'd implied on several occasions that there was someone on the Council who had compromised the city's security.

The security at the monstrous monolith that was Artificed Hydraulics, however, was not so lax. They saluted Salora. Frisked her. Checked Kavi's Vagola badge that identified her as a first-year Blade. Stared at her face. Checked the badge again. Conferred. Frisked her too. And let them in.

Salora strode through the atrium with Kavi at her heels. Past the reception. Past another guard station where the guards saluted her, and through a door that led to a staircase that spiralled down into the bowels of the building.

'Why is it called Hydraulics?' Kavi said as they made their way down.

'The top two floors are the administrative offices for the city's water engineers.'

Kavi scratched her head. 'Okay.'

They'd made it to a floor labelled *7D* when Kavi felt it.

She froze. Peered down the long corridor that trailed away in darkness with wide eyes. 'What's down there?'

Salora cocked her head. 'Why?'

Her mouth went dry. There was *something*, something big, calling to her. She blinked, and a kaleidoscope of alien images and sensations fizzed through her.

She was suspended. Suffocating. Needles as long as her arm plunged into her sternum and the space between her eyebrows. She opened eyes that were not hers in a body the size of a mountain. Static. The crunch of metal colliding. Maayin coursing through her veins. A battlefield that stretched into the horizons. A chain. A gate. A name. *Gayathri.*

'Kavithri?'

'Nothing,' Kavi whispered, leaning against the railing. That was the first time she'd seen one of Drisana's visions with such clarity.

Salora continued to give her curious glances as they descended further and further into the structure, until finally they hopped off the staircase and entered a deserted corridor lit by a single, blue artificed lamp.

'Not many artificers come down here,' Salora said.

Kavi ran a finger along the wall and it came away thick with dust.

Salora stopped outside a handleless door midway down the corridor. She placed a hand on its surface. There was a click, and she pushed her way into the room.

Kavi drew a long, deep breath. Wiggled her tingling fingers and toes. And followed Salora inside.

A dark marble slab the size of a small boat sat in the middle of the room. In the corner, a pair of cables dangled like withered vines.

Salora motioned to the cables. 'One on the inside of each elbow. I will let you know when we have enough blood.'

Kavi jabbed the needles of each cable into her arms, suppressed a shudder, and waited. The translucent cables turned an opaque red as her blood was sucked out of her body.

'Almost there,' Salora mumbled.

A dozen heartbeats later, 'Done.'

Kavi blinked, light-headed and dizzy, and pulled the cables out of her arms.

Salora leaned out over the marble slab and pressed her hand

into it. The surface of the slab shimmered. Cracks appeared; indentations deepened; the marble rose and fell and reshaped itself into a topographic map of Raaya.

'It was last updated almost six decades ago by an artificer with too much free time,' Salora said as she took a step back.

Kavi had seen maps of the subcontinent in textbooks, but none with as much detail as this. The sea and the rugged, triangular coast in the south; the Deadlands in the far north; the mountain ranges in the east; the basins and deltas in the west; and smack-bang in the middle of it all, the massive plateau that made up the bulk of Raaya.

A pulsating red dot appeared over a walled city in the north that matched the location of the capital. Was that supposed to be her?

Salora chewed the inside of her cheek. 'How many in your family?'

'Three – four, including me.'

'I'm sorry,' Salora said with a sigh.

Kavi held her breath. 'For what?'

The artificer pointed at the red dot with one slender finger, and Kavi's stomach sank.

It was her. She was the last one left. 'How— What if my family have left Raaya?'

Salora jabbed her finger at the pulsing red dot. 'The Venator detects every Taemu that shares a blood-trait with the donor. If the rest of your family is alive, it will show you their location. If they were alive when they left the borders of Raaya, the device will show you their last known location within its radius. If they're dead …' She let her hand fall.

'Are you sure?' What a stupid question.

'Its accuracy has been proven.'

So that was it. They were gone. *I'm alone.* She massaged her chest. Why did it feel so heavy?

Salora cocked her head. 'You're not alone.'

Kavi blinked. Had she said that out loud?

Salora gestured to the red dot. 'Someone is still alive.'

'What?'

'Someone who shares your blood is alive.' Salora ran her fingers over the marble. It dissolved and reshaped itself into a bird's eye view of Azraaya with the pulsing red dot in the top-right corner. 'And they're in the city. Eastern quadrant, not too far from the slums, outside a temple.'

'That's not …' *me?* The weakness in her limbs turned into weightlessness. 'Can you tell who?'

Salora shook her head. 'Only that they share a bloodline with you.'

Warmth infused Kavi's entire body. She trembled with a sudden injection of energy. 'I have to go.'

The artificer nodded, a melancholy smile on her lips. 'I'll see you at the Vagola.'

Kavi memorised the location of the dot on the map. Sprinted out the door, up the stairs, through the atrium, past the surprised guards, and down onto the pavement.

She ran through pungent gullies where agoma addicts sat slouched over, through packed streets where street hawkers bayed and hollered at construction workers to *take-break have-snack!*

Legs pumping. Face flushed. Heart pounding. She dodged pedestrians and jumped over barriers and burst into the square that fronted Meshira's great temple.

Sweat dripped off her brow and trailed down her chin as she nudged her way through the thinning crowd. Afternoon prayers had ended. People were heading back to their lives. She craned her neck. Searched for Taemu who resembled her. Bumped into a group of musicians leaving the temple and bobbed a distracted apology as they cursed her and checked their tablas and sitars for damage.

There was a commotion outside the chappal stand. A group of lungi-wearing gangsters, Dolmondas, were harassing a crippled beggar while a cluster of bystanders gathered to watch the fracas.

Kavi stopped. Her breath caught, and she stared at the beggar.

He was just a boy. Early teens at most. Scruffy haired like her. Dark brown skin, like hers. Deep red irises, just like hers. But that was where the similarities stopped. The boy was missing half a leg. He sat with a wooden crutch at his side. And peeking out on the short-sleeve shirt was the rim of a solid red tattoo that circled his arm. Kavi had refused to get one of those. *Absolutely not,* she'd said when they'd suggested it.

One of the gangsters finally managed to yank the copper begging bowl from the boy's hands and the coins in it went flying.

A coin landed and wobbled flat at Kavi's feet. She bent, picked it up, and with a fluttering stomach, strolled over to the boy.

He sat with his head bowed while the gangster berated him. 'What madarchod? Did you ask permission to sit here? Hah?' The gangster winked at one of his cronies, who guffawed. 'This is our square. Dolmonda gang, remember that— Hey!'

Kavi shoved the gangster away. When was the last time she'd said his name out loud? Would it even sound the same? Her lips parted, the back of her tongue curved as she shaped the plosive first syllable, and she said, 'Khagan.'

The boy whose name no one knew, who went by Chotu,

who'd helped save the city from the Kraelish, who now sat humiliated outside a temple he was not allowed into, slowly raised his head.

His eyes bulged. His lips trembled. He blinked. And the tears came pouring out of his eyes.

'Akka,' he whispered. 'Kavithri Akka.'

Kavi dropped to her haunches and took his hands in hers. She could tell that he'd suspected, maybe hoped, but now he knew. 'Why didn't you tell me?'

Khagan sniffed. Lowered his eyes. 'Appa said you were dead.'

She wrapped her arms around him. Stroked the back of his head as he buried it in her shoulder and wept.

A foot nudged her in the back. 'What the fuck is this?'

Blood roared in Kavi's ears. Her jaw hurt from how hard she clenched it. An overwhelming urge to protect her brother, to pulverise and rip to shreds anyone who hurt him, anyone who made him cry, surged through every vein and artery. In the back of her mind, the berserker reared its head. *I could make them all go away.*

Kavi eased the tension out of her jaw. *I don't need you for this.* She squeezed Khagan's shoulders. 'We need to talk.'

He wiped his face with a dirty sleeve and nodded.

'Ai, is this pig his mother?' More cackles from the gangsters.

Kavi stood. Reached into her pockets and slipped out Massa's beedi case. The artificed match caught on the first strike and she fired up a long, grey beedi. Ratan had told her that to be the Boss, she had to smoke. She had no idea where this unspoken rule came from, but it was true. Every Boss in Azraaya smoked and once she'd accepted that the habit wouldn't have enough time to kill her, she'd started to enjoy the small buzz it gave her and the sting of the smoke travelling down into her lungs.

She blew a stream of it into the gangster's face.

He puffed up. Lifted his lungi and tied it so it hung over his knees. His goondas, all five of them, mimicked him.

The small crowd held their breath.

There was a time when she'd have begged and pleaded to avoid a confrontation. Bowed and scraped and smiled and done whatever was needed to get out of a sticky situation. That could work here. No doubt. But nothing would change. These men would continue to bully her brother. So:

Sometimes,

– she grabbed the gangster by the hair, twisted his head, pulled him close,

to deal with violent men,

– stubbed the beedi out on his forehead,

you need to speak in a language they understand.

– and said, in what was a roar to her, but a whisper to the square:

'Aadhier Taemu.'

Excerpt from the *DIARY OF AN UNKNOWN MAGE*

Pages 52–53

The Five Jinn and Their Mages:

Harith – the warlock's jinn
Countervail – paralysis
Status: active
The only class of mage that can tangibly manifest and manipulate a jinn's maayin. They think it makes them better than everyone else. (Yes, I know, I'm a warlock too, so trust me when I say.) Avoid interacting with these dead-eyed arseholes at all costs.

Kolacin – the artificer's jinn
Countervail – memory
Status: active
The first jinn ever discovered. Its maayin can be used to alter what the artificer's call an object's *code*. Incredible skill, but the price they pay is too steep in my opinion.

Nilasi – the healer's jinn
Countervail – non-human life-force
Status: active
The most useful class of mage (I wouldn't be alive if it wasn't for

them). But I do feel for the creatures they use as their countervails. Cruel, so cruel.

Zubhra – the illusionist's jinn
Countervail – vision
Status: inactive
Never met or seen one in my lifetime. They supposedly traded their sight for their ability. Sounds like a raw deal to me.

Raktha – the biomancer's jinn
Countervail – lifespan
Status: inactive
Dangerous, lethal, and batshit insane. Its mages could enhance, modify, and strengthen parts of their bodies. Be glad you don't have to deal with them.

Acknowledgements

A heartfelt thanks to:

My agent, Ernie Chiara. My editor, Brendan Durkin, and the wonderful team at Gollancz.

My father and brother. My wife. My mother, who once asked me, 'What's the point of reading so much if you don't write?' I'm sorry it took so long. I wish you were here to read it; you would've loved Kavi.

And you, dear reader, for picking up this book, investing your time in it, and sticking around inside Kavi's head for the entire journey. Thank you. I hope she's found a place in your heart like she has in mine.

Credits

Aman J. Bedi and Gollancz would like to thank everyone at Orion who worked on the publication of *Kavithri* in the UK.

Editor
Brendan Durkin
Áine Feeney

Copy editor
Abigail Page

Proof reader
Gabriella Nemeth

Audio
Paul Stark
Jake Alderson

Contracts
Dan Herron

Design
Nick Shah
Rachael Lancaster
Joanna Ridley

Editorial Management
Charlie Panayiotou
Jane Hughes

Finance
Nick Gibson
Jasdip Nandra
Sue Baker

Marketing
Javerya Iqbal

Production
Paul Hussey

Publicity
Jenna Petts

Sales
Jennifer Wilson
Esther Waters
Victoria Laws
Rachael Hum
Anna Egelstaff
Sinead White
Georgina Cutler

Operations
Jo Jacobs
Sharon Willis